For
ALEX ELIZABETH PAGE-WARBURTON
aka
Pud (short for Pudding)

Born 31 December 2008

Many people scoff at the idea of love at first sight, but I am living proof that it can happen. I fell for you hook, line and sinker the instant I set eyes on you. In fact, I was the first to see you as you arrived to join our family. I promise to love, cherish and nurture you, to do my utmost to be the best grandmother I can be and (don't tell your mother and father) to spoil you rotten.

Your devoted Gran

ACKNOWLEDGEMENTS

To Dr Aubrey Stewart and John Grenfell. Two wonderful gentlemen who dedicate their time to running the Leicester Royal Infirmary Museum and who both eagerly gave me their expert knowledge to furnish me with all the medical facts I required, and more besides, to write an accurate account of how the medical profession operated in the 1930s.

CHAPTER ONE

The man was so angry his jugular vein looked to be in danger of bursting.

Banging his fist hard on the table until it caused a battered tin cup to topple off, he yelled, 'Now you listen 'ere. That fuckin' wife of mine is n'ote but a lazy cow who'd do anything for a day in bed. It's just a bad cold she's got. I've got one, worse than she has, but do I take to my bed? No, I suffer in silence and get on with it. If anyone needs a bloody rest, it's me – from her constant whining, not to mention from *her* blasted kids always bickering. No one 'cept me had any business calling you in, least of all our nosy bleeder of a neighbour.'

He paused long enough to give a hacking cough, spitting out phlegm which fizzled in the dying embers in the grate. Turning back to the man he was verbally attacking, he continued, 'As yer can see, we don't exactly live like kings, so where the hell am I expected suddenly to find the money for someone to take care of us while the wife takes her *holiday*?'

Through eyes the turquoise green of glacial meltwater, the man to whom this furious tirade was being addressed flashed a quick glance over the speaker's shoulder. Seven ragged-looking children, ranging in age from ten months to eight years, who until their father had appeared on the scene minutes ago had been noisily making their presence known, were now all silently clinging together in one corner, looking fearfully back at him. In the fireplace a large, blackened cauldron-like pot was hanging over the dying flames. There were chunks of things swimming in an unappetising-looking mixture, cooling now as the coals beneath dwindled, not having been replenished since the woman of the house had collapsed earlier that day.

Fighting to quash the nausea that was creeping through him, he ignored the competing odours of stale cooking, soiled nappies, unwashed bodies and general decay, and stole a glance around the rest of the miserable room; at the few pieces of rickety furniture sitting on bare floorboards, large patches of mildew patterning the damp, dingy distempered brick walls, yellowing, holed net curtains wafting in the draught swirling through the rotting window frames. He thought too of the sick woman upstairs, lying desperately ill on a filthy, sheetless, bug-infested flock mattress, a threadbare Army greatcoat all there was to cover her.

Her chances of recovery were slim, though had the more affluent, charitable folks of Leicester not found it within themselves to fund a hospital for the free care of the very poorest in the city, even that slim chance would have been denied her. But if her brute of a husband wasn't going to sanction her admission to the General Hospital, for his own selfish reasons, then the doctor might as well not waste any more of his precious time and sign her death certificate now.

He brought his attention back to the emaciated, shabbily dressed figure before him, his pallor ingrained with dirt, what teeth he had left crooked and blackened with rot, like loose tombstones.

'You get the money to pay for help from the same place as you find it for your daily supply of drink and cigarettes, I presume,' he told the sick woman's husband impassively.

Face flaming with rage, and clenching one fist, Cedric Simmons bellowed back, 'You what? How I spend my brass is none of your business, you self-righteous ...'

Before he could say another word he was cut short by an even-toned: 'Mr Simmons, you may intimidate your family but you don't me, in anyway whatsoever. It's very apparent from just looking at your wife and children where the majority of the money that comes into this house goes, and it's not on their welfare, is it? If I'd been called in when it was first apparent your wife was suffering from much more than a cold, it's probable you wouldn't now be looking to pay someone to care for yourself and your children. If Mrs Simmons doesn't receive immediate hospital treatment, she'll definitely die in a matter of a day or so. Now, do I go back to my surgery and arrange for an ambulance to call, or leave it to you to arrange a funeral?'

Whatever Cedric's response had been going to be, it was halted by the arrival of a thick-set, middle-aged woman who appeared in the doorway to the stairs. She was dressed in a threadbare black skirt and faded ecru twill blouse which strained over her matronly bosom. She had a faded wrap-around apron over the top, and her greying hair was scraped into a tight bun at the back of her head.

She was looking very anxious as she blurted, 'That amb'lance is tekin' its time, in't it? Win's breathing's got worse since you came back down here, Doctor. I'm really worried she won't make it if we don't get her to the hospital soon.'

He responded matter-of-factly, 'And I am doing my best to arrange that, Madam.'

Fanny Cook eyed him strangely for a moment as he didn't appear to be doing anything that remotely resembled urgently summoning an ambulance. She then looked at Cedric and the truth of the situation registered. Face screwed up in angry disbelief, she challenged him, 'Am I to understand the amb'lance hasn't bin called yet 'cos *you* . . .' she wagged one fat fist at Cedric '. . . ain't happy about the fact yer might have ter bung someone a few shillings to tek care of you and the kids while Win's getting better?'

She spun round to face the children then and ordered them, 'Go next door and tell my Rosie to get you each a slice of bread and dripping, and some milk for the bab.'

They didn't need telling twice. The eldest scooped up the baby and fled. Once they were all out of earshot, Fanny shook her head in disgust at the children's father. 'What I have to say to you ain't for your kiddies' ears.'

Fixing him with her eyes, she blasted him. 'I've always kept me gob shut 'cos I knew Winnie would suffer at your hands if I spoke me thoughts aloud, but enough is enough. You've always put yourself before your family, Cedric Simmons. My old man insists on a pint on his way home of an evening, to wash the dust from his throat after his shift in that filthy factory, but he wouldn't put that, or his betting money for that matter, above food on his family's table. Unlike you.

'You might think yer clever 'cos you only thump

Winnie and the kiddies where it doesn't show, but don't think for a minute we neighbours ain't aware you're handy with your fists. Win and the kids live in terror of you! They'd have starved more times than I can remember if me and the other neighbours hadn't fed 'em with what we could spare, and helped clothe the kids with our lots' cast-offs. You're just a bloody bully, and selfish to the core! Words like that ain't strong enough to describe you, in my opinion, but what you're doing now amounts to murder and I won't stand by this time and say n'ote about that.

'And don't you look at me like that! Refusing to send Win for proper treatment at the hospital is as good as sticking a knife in her heart. Win's sick. Real sick. She ain't suffering from an ailment that can be eased by a couple of doses of one of the old woman's potions. And what she's got might not have turned so nasty in her if her stamina hadn't been so low . . . 'cos the housekeeping you give her each week would hardly keep a dog, let alone a growing family.'

Without pausing for breath she went on, 'Not that you deserve it, but I can't stand by and watch your kids suffer more than they do already. So me and the other neighbours will mek sure yer all seen right while Win's away, and we won't tek no payment for it neither.' She paused just long enough to eye him contemptuously before adding meaningfully, 'Now, if you don't give the doctor the go ahead to call the

6

ambulance, I'll personally sling Win over me shoulder and get her there meself. But be warned ... I'll let everyone around here know that you was prepared to let her die, sooner than go without yourself.'

Cedric stared back at her murderously for several long moments before he gave a grunt, spun on his heel and left the room. Seconds later the back door was heard to slam shut. Fanny knew that he'd gone to one of two places. Either to spend what money he'd got in his pocket in the local pub or else under the arches over on Great Western Road for an illegal game of cards.

She realised the doctor was still there and shot him a quizzical look, wondering why he hadn't rushed off to summon the ambulance. Then the reason struck her and she assured him, 'I'll personally see to it you get your fee, Doctor. I'll have it sent round to yer surgery. Now, I'd appreciate it if you'd get that am'blance here quick.'

Without a word, he picked up his black bag and left also.

Her face thoughtful, Fanny followed him out with her eyes. So that was the new doctor who had taken over James McHinney's practice after the old doctor had served the community tirelessly for forty or so years. Several months ago, the seventy-six-year-old Doctor Mac, as the locals had affectionately called him, who had originated from Donegal in Ireland

and whose thick Irish brogue at times had been very difficult for them to decipher, unexpectedly died in his sleep from natural causes. Until the end, though, he'd been lively and active, still agile enough to give chase and clip round the ear any cheeky kid and his brain as sharp as it had always been. He'd been a formidable character – woe betide you if you crossed him, whoever you were – but possessed of a kindly streak, would part with his last penny to help out anyone in dire need. He'd been well respected by everyone who knew him. All in all, a hard act to follow.

Until two weeks ago when this new chap arrived on the scene, the locals, including herself, had resigned themselves to the fact that they'd never get a replacement for Doctor Mac, and when in need would now have to go further afield for their medical help, else go without. Though to Fanny's mind it wasn't surprising that new doctors hadn't exactly been clamouring to fill Doctor Mac's place. A simple living, marginally better than the locals could scratch for themselves, could doubtless be had here, but a fortune was never going to be made ministering to the sick of these parts.

The majority of Doctor Mac's patients had paid his dues in kind: with goods, such as a bucket of coal or pile of wood, a meat pie, cake or casserole; or by tackling his sewing and mending, ironing, washing, and maintenance jobs around his house and garden. The arrangement had worked well for them all. The sick who wouldn't normally have been able to afford his professional services had been treated, and the bachelor doctor received a regular supply of home-cooked meals and didn't have to fork out to have jobs done around his house.

Fanny had a feeling that method of payment wasn't going to be acceptable to the new doctor. He hadn't seemed ready to budge until she had assured him he'd receive the fee for his attendance. Since it appeared extremely unlikely that Cedric would willingly hand over the money, it was apparent that it was she herself who was going to have to do so. It would have to come out of her pitifully few Christmas savings, but in the circumstances she didn't begrudge a penny. Neighbours in these parts came to each other's aid in dire times, and Win would have done the same for her if the circumstances had been reversed and she'd been in a position to help. Fanny had been friends with her long enough to know that.

To her, though, this new chap didn't look old enough to be a doctor, barely out of nappies, let alone have studied years for his medical qualification. It was difficult to tell what part of the country he hailed from as he'd no accent, but from his cultured tones and the quality of his clothes he came from a moneyed background. He was certainly good looking, fine featured and with thick corn-blond hair, and those eyes . . . she'd never seen such a mesmerising shade of pale turquoise-green before. He'd certainly have women's hearts around these parts fluttering, those single ones who could afford the price of paying regular trips to his surgery anyway. They'd be dead set on making themselves known to him, she was sure, since one thing they all knew about the new doctor was that he was single.

But he certainly hadn't displayed any of the qualities old Doctor Mac had possessed. *He* most definitely wouldn't have waited to be given the go ahead by the likes of Cedric. Doctor Mac would not have held back from blasting the miserable bully with a piece of his mind then gone ahead without his permission, taking Win to the hospital himself in his old jalopy and staying there long enough to make sure she was being attended to. And he would have given coppers to her kids, ordering them to the chip shop, since it would not have escaped his all-seeing eye that they hadn't been fed that day, due to their mother's incapacitation and their father's sheer selfishness.

The new doctor certainly seemed to know his stuff, though. Only seconds into examining Win, he'd announced she was suffering from severe pneumonia. Fanny herself had seen enough cases of that terrible illness during her time to agree with his diagnosis, though his manner had left a lot to be desired, to her mind. He seemed so detached, strangely matter-of-fact . . . could have been examining a side of beef rather than a human being. And he'd definitely been looking down his nose at them all, giving the strong impression he deeply begrudged having to mix with this sort of family.

Well, if that was the case, why on earth had he chosen to ply his trade in this area, instead of choosing to minister to people of his own class? Fanny's brow creased in thought. What had brought him to these parts when it was very apparent it was the last place he wanted to be?

Her curiosity, though, was going to have to remain unsatisfied for now. She had far more pressing matters on her mind. Spinning on her heel, she returned upstairs to offer what comfort she could to her gravely ill friend while they waited for the ambulance to arrive, both of them praying that it wouldn't be too late.

CHAPTER TWO

Ty Strathmore emitted a deep sigh as he sank down in an antiquated leather captain's chair behind the desk of his surgery.

A year ago he'd had everything he could ever have aspired to: an income that afforded him a high standard of living; a lovely home to which he'd have been proud to welcome the most affluent among society; a beautiful wife he adored who, like himself, possessed all the desirable social skills. She'd also been expecting their first and much longed-for child.

And now what did he have?

No lovely home, no loving wife or expected baby, and certainly no prospects ... definitely not in this hell-hole of a place he'd unwittingly landed up in.

In his mind's eye a vision of Anthea, the very last time he had seen her, rose to torment him. She stood framed in the doorway of the house they had lived in so happily together, seeing him off to work as she had done every morning, her red-gold hair cut into a fashionable bob framing a face that never failed to take his breath away each time he caught sight of it. Her tawny-green eyes were sparkling with good humour, her full lips curved into the smile she displayed only to him. Her 'Mona Lisa smile', he had termed it, because like Leonardo Da Vinci, he was the only man who knew what lay behind it: her unstinting love and devotion to him. Her arms were cradling her swollen belly, protecting the precious cargo she carried.

The vision vanished as quickly as it had arisen. Pain at his overwhelming loss, so great it could be likened to a hand being plunged inside him and ripping out his insides, consumed his being while simultaneously a surge of pure hatred flooded through him against the man who had single-handedly taken Anthea from him, along with everything else he had held dear. What that man had done was not out of any sense of vengeance against Ty, but through sheer unadulterated selfishness. Ty didn't believe that violence resolved anything, but in this case it had been fortunate the man in question had seen to it that he wasn't around to be punished for his crime, or Ty himself would have faced the gallows for murdering him.

Taking a deep breath and forcing away excruciating memories, he leaned back in his chair and took a slow, despondent look around him. The last surgery he had worked from had been spacious, light

and airy, owning the very latest in medical equipment and employing a highly qualified nurse to help
with the care of the patients. It had been housed in
its own late-Edwardian villa in a tree-lined street in
an affluent suburb. He would drive the short
distance to it from his home each morning in a
leather-seated black Daimler sedan, and on arrival
he'd be greeted with a tray of tea delivered by his
smartly attired receptionist. They'd had close asso-
ciations with the local hospital. A quick telephone
call was usually sufficient to secure a bed there and
the best medical attention for any of their moneyed
patients.

This surgery's finances couldn't support either a
receptionist or a nurse, and to obtain a hospital bed
and treatment for any of his patients, Ty had virtually to get down on bended knee and beg for them.

Another surge of anger erupted within him against
the person whose selfish actions had reduced him to
this level. At the time of the terrible catastrophe, the
pain of his loss was so unbearable that, by way of
protecting himself from ever suffering such emotional
devastation a second time, he had vowed never to
allow himself to become involved with another human
being on a personal level again. And if people thought
him rude and arrogant because of it, then so be it.
He'd ostracised himself from all his former friends
and turned his back on the medical profession,

wanting nothing more to do with it. By sheer frugality, for over two years he'd managed to exist on the paltry amount of money he'd been left with, but when that had virtually run dry, and with his landlady not the type to let him lodge with her free, he was left with no alternative but to get himself a job. Unfortunately for Ty, he wasn't a man who could turn his hand to anything. After being fired from several menial labouring jobs, he was left with no choice but to seek another position back in the profession he had made such an effort to disassociate himself from.

The thought of applying for a hospital position and having his past delved into was something he wanted to avoid at all costs. This practice had seemed like the answer to a prayer to him when he had spotted it advertised in a medical journal. Thriving practices changed hands for large sums of money, depending on their size and location. But this one was being *given* away. Ty had assumed that the deceased doctor had had no partner to take it over and was against his estate going to the Crown. He'd assumed that many other doctors would be after it, young men starting up or others rendered short of funds like himself, and didn't think his chances of being awarded it were high. He was most shocked to receive a letter back by return from the solicitor handling the estate of the late James McHinney, offering him the practice without even an interview.

He was later to come to the conclusion that no other doctor had even applied. If other interested parties had had the foresight to take the time and trouble to visit the area, unlike himself, they'd no doubt swiftly have decided against it. The astute James McHinney had without doubt known that upon his death, unless he lured a doctor here by giving his practice away, the local community of around five thousand patients would be left without a medical practitioner.

The three-bedroomed corner terrace house that housed the surgery stood in the middle of a rabbit warren of sooty streets. The rundown terrace houses had two or three bedrooms and tiny paved back-yards. Water was obtained from stand pumps in back alleys, and several families shared each outside toilet. Ty's was the only house to have its own water pump and toilet in the backyard. Arriving with all he possessed in one trunk, he'd accused the taxi driver of delivering him to the wrong address when the vehicle had stopped outside the grim-looking house in the middle of this deprived area, and had been mortified to find no mistake had been made.

The inside of the house was as bleak as the outside. Despite the heavy chenille curtains at the windows all being pulled back, hardly any light penetrated the rooms due to the closeness of the surrounding properties. The furniture was all of the plain, heavy dark oak sort, no ornaments or adornments to soften its harshness. The floorboards were dark stained. The only rug lay in the sitting room in front of the hearth, its original pattern long since faded away and its pile flattened by age. The previous occupant obviously hadn't felt the need for fripperies of any kind. Ty was, though, gratified to find the place spotlessly clean, the fires in all the rooms laid ready to be lit and his bed freshly made, albeit with aged linen, threadbare in parts. The pan of mutton stew that just needed heating had turned out to be delicious, and a few basic food essentials had been laid in. He'd assumed, in his ignorance, that the housekeeper had been busy . . . only to discover the next day that the surgery's finances didn't run to the extravagance of a housekeeper either. The food had been provided and the cleaning done by several well-meaning local women, by way of a welcome to their new doctor.

The room the surgery was housed in appeared to be far smaller than it actually was due to the amount of furniture in it. The large old oak desk he was sitting at had years of use evident on its surfaces. The huge bookcase to one side of him was crammed with ageing, musty-smelling medical journals, while a table behind him held five large wooden boxes, each divided into four drawers, and each drawer rammed to overflowing with patients' records dating back to God knew when. How many records were in respect of people still actually alive was debatable. He'd skimmed a look through them on first arriving and noted the ages of some of the patients and the date of the last entries. At some point they must be overhauled. He had besides an examination couch, a washstand and bowl, a cupboard full of medical supplies, and a table on which was displayed an ancient microscope and some gruesome-looking old medical instruments.

A thick, dark brown dado rail divided the walls into two, the bottom half painted brown, the top half cream, which had turned to dark yellow after decades of Doctor McHinney's dedicated smoking habit. He had obviously had a penchant for a drink, too, judging by the number of empty whisky bottles Ty had discovered in the dank, cobweb-filled cellar, along with a half-filled bottle in the desk drawer. Ty didn't smoke himself, but since arriving in his new post had taken to having a glass of malt before he retired to bed, in the hope it might help him gain a better sleep than the fitful and disturbed rest he'd experienced since his life-changing experience two years ago.

It became immediately apparent to Ty on his first surgery that James McHinney had been revered by his patients. He suspected that as long as he himself remained in this post – which as matters stood for him would be until he, too, was carried out in a box – he would never match up to Doctor Mac in the locals' eyes. Not that Ty cared what they thought of him. His only desire was to deal with their medical needs, which he would do his best to serve, and not to allow himself to become any further involved with them than that.

A faint murmur of voices filtered through to him, coming from the waiting room across the corridor. Ty heaved another despondent sigh. He had been called out twice on emergencies during the previous night, so what sleep he had managed to get had not proved beneficial. He had taken a twenty-minute break earlier during which he had gobbled down a hastily put-together sandwich. He had been out on house calls since, had just returned from the last one in fact, and was hoping that evening surgery would be a light one so he could catch up with sorting out the surgery, something that up to now the demands on his time hadn't allowed ... but the noise level coming from the waiting room was warning him otherwise.

From what he'd observed of the locals while dealing with their medical needs in the week he had been in this post, he'd come to the conclusion that they were an uneducated lot, obviously not averse to living in what seemed to be appalling conditions, some of the houses so dirty farmers would have considered them unfit for pigs, or they'd have done something about it. Some of the people whose houses he had visited didn't even practise the most basic hygiene. The majority of the women looked far older than their years, slovenly in both their appearance and housewifely duties, while their menfolk appeared interested only in the local pub and collaring the bookie's runner for their bets. And it was debatable if many of the undernourished, barefoot, raggedly dressed children he'd encountered to date would actually reach adulthood, considering the way their parents were raising them.

The way James McHinney had operated financially was of grave concern to Ty. If he carried on the way his predecessor had, then he was deeply worried he wouldn't be able to meet his bills each week. Thankfully a couple of local factories had paid him a retainer each year to care for their workers' medical needs, so at least Ty could count on that money still coming in, but he had been under the impression that the bartering system had died out in Britain in the Middle Ages. Out of all the patients he'd seen up to now, though, nearly three quarters had paid in kind with goods or promise of manual labour, turning a deaf ear to any requests for hard currency instead. Not to be thwarted, before he'd departed on his morning rounds today, Ty had penned a very clear notice and pinned it on the wall of the waiting room, advising them that in future only cash would be accepted in return for his services.

The din emanating from the waiting room rose

several decibels, heralding more arrivals. He visualised them all packed into the small room, squashed together on the unyielding wooden bench spanning three of the walls. The stench from their collective body smells would be nauseating. Ty sighed again as he took his pocket watch out of his waistcoat pocket and looked at it. Evening surgery started at six. It was eight minutes to. He could sit here for those eight minutes, keeping them all waiting as he savoured this little bit of time to himself. Or he could make an early start and get it over with. He decided to make the early start.

His first patient was a shrunken, dirty, toothless old woman whose visit was for him to lance a nasty-looking carbuncle on her chin. While he got his instruments and dressings together, he was forced to listen to her list all the remedies she had tried, including stabbing a sewing needle into it. He doubted she'd thought to sterilise it first and the result had been to worsen it, not cure it. The pus that oozed out of the carbuncle was a vile shade of green and yellow, the stench of it stomach-churning. Having dressed the residual gaping hole and scrubbed his hands with carbolic soap, using the jug and bowl on the marble-topped table, Ty sat back down in his chair and opened his mouth, preparing to tell the old crone the fee for his work, when she pre-empted him by pulling out a battered Peek Frean biscuit tin from her old shopping bag, putting it on his desk before him and saying, 'Thanks fer sorting me out, Doctor. The pain I was suffering was worse than I've ever experienced and, believe me, I've suffered more than me fair share of aches and pains in me life, 'specially when I trapped me hand in the mangle and broke four of me fingers.'

She sucked in her cheeks as she pulled a pained expression. 'That hurt like the blazes, let me tell yer, and at the time I had eight kids to feed and a bleddy wastrel of a husband who was out of work more times than he were in, so no money to spare for the likes of yerself. Had to strap it up meself.' She held up her hand, showing him her four misshapen fingers. She then pushed the tin towards Ty. 'Doctor Mac used to love my Welsh cakes.'

He eyed her sharply. 'Madam, I am not Doctor McHinney and . . .'

Before he could utter another word, eying him sardonically, she cut in, 'No, yer not, more's the pity. He actually made yer feel welcome when yer came in to see him, not like yer was intruding, and he chatted to yer about this and that while he was seeing to you. It's like being in a morgue, being seen to by you. Still, if that's how yer are, that's how yer are. We ain't a choice around here who we get to be our doctor, just mortally grateful we've got one to come to when we need to.' Getting up from her chair, she scuttled out with the agility of a woman half her age.

Ty stared blankly after her. He didn't care what she thought of him personally. He had successfully dealt with her ailment, but the old woman needed to consult an optician about her eyesight as she obviously hadn't seen the very clear notice in the waiting room, informing her that payment in kind was no longer acceptable. He knew where those Welsh cakes were going and it wasn't into his stomach, not if the dire state of the maker of them was anything to go by.

He picked up his pen in order to write notes on the old lady's record card. It had taken him precious time to find this. His predecessor might have been revered by his patients for his doctoring skills and his compassion towards them, but keeping records in alphabetical order seemed to have been beyond him. The door opened unexpectedly then and a thickset man dressed in work clothes came in, shutting it behind him, taking a seat on the chair to the side of the desk and looking at Ty expectantly.

Respectfully taking off his flat cap, he announced, 'Evening, Doctor. I've come to see you about me arm.'

Ty eyed him steadily. Had the people in these parts no manners? He'd been taught that it was polite to knock before entering an occupied room, and to wait for a response from the occupant before invading their privacy. He tersely announced, 'I'm not ready for you yet. I'll call you through when I am.'

The man pulled a bemused expression. 'Oh! Well, in Doctor Mac's day, when one came out of the surgery, the next went in. Anyway I'm here now. I don't mind waiting while yer finish what yer doing.'

Ty minded. Patients' records were private and he was not going to risk anyone peering over and possibly seeing what he was writing, then feeling at liberty to relay that person's medical problems to all and sundry. Fixing the man with his eyes, he reiterated slowly, 'I'll call you through when I'm ready to see you.'

The man stared at him, taken aback for a moment, before he slapped his cap back on his head and rose, saying, 'As you wish, Doctor.'

It took Ty less than thirty seconds to finish writing up the old lady's notes. He then put the record card on an ever-growing pile on top of the drawers, his intention being to go through all the records as soon as time allowed him and re-file them correctly. He got up from his desk, opened the door and crossed the corridor, taking a deep breath before he opened the door to the waiting room, preparing himself for the smell that would hit him. Those chatting inside immediately fell silent and everybody sat looking at him. He could tell by their faces that they thought him wrong for insisting the patient who had entered the surgery unbidden should return to the waiting room, but Ty didn't care what they thought. He ran his own surgery his way, and that was the end of it. Keeping their records secure was important to him. He announced in a clear voice, 'Next.'

The man he had sent back to await his summons rose, taking off his cap. 'Well, as you know, that'd be me, Doctor.'

Back in the surgery, Ty asked the man's name, which he gave as William Bates, and got out his records, which again took him precious minutes. He eventually found them tucked in a pile in the drawers labelled G,H or I. Taking a quick look at William Bates' past history, which was hard to decipher as James McHinney's handwriting had been very spidery, it appeared that the last time he had sought medical help was fifteen years previously, when he had fractured his leg after being clipped by a runaway cart while crossing a road. Either he'd a hardy constitution and had not been ill again or he'd resorted to home remedies for any ailment since then. Ty knew that many locals did so and this practice infuriated him. Did these people not have the intelligence to realise that resorting to quack cures, instead of trained professional advice, could prevent many initially minor ailments from becoming much worse, possibly life-threatening – and being allowed to become so purely in order to save the doctor's fee?

'What can I do for you, Mr Bates?' he asked.

'Well, it's as I told yer before, Doctor. It's me arm. I nicked meself at work this morning and I'm needing a stitch or two.'

William Bates didn't look the kind of man to come here if an ailment could be dealt with at home, so Ty suspected that the word 'nick' was being used wrongly in this case. Bates eased off his jacket to reveal an arm wrapped tightly from elbow to wrist in a grubby piece of cloth saturated with dried and fresh blood. Without seeing the actual wound, Ty could tell by the amount of blood visible that what lay beneath was definitely no minor injury needing a couple of sutures. What he discovered, though, when the cloth was removed, was far worse than he'd expected. The gaping gash was bone-deep and at least six inches long. Ty just hoped that no infection had gained hold between the time Bates had done it and his arrival here or there was a severe risk the man could end up losing his arm.

While deciding how best to proceed with treatment, Ty asked, 'How did you do this?'

Bates' face darkened thunderously and he spat, 'Through the bloody owner being too tight fisted to get a fault fixed on me machine. Months it's been broke. All he cares about is his profits, to keep his family living the grand style they live in. Doesn't care a jot that his workers are risking their lives, or can hardly keep themselves and their families on what he pays. Some workers are lucky as their bosses pay their doctors' fees for injuries at work. But the bastard I work for sees his employees as easily replaceable.'

Ty's previous life hadn't bought him into contact with the likes of lowly factory workers, but a close friend of his father's had been a factory owner and the man always seemed to be complaining of how lazy and incompetent his workers were, never satisfied with their pay and conditions, not at all grateful that if it weren't for the likes of himself, providing them with the means to earn a living, then they and their families would all be in the workhouse or on the streets. His father's friend had been justified in his complaints about his workers, it seemed to Ty, judging by this man's attitude. Then something he'd said struck home. 'You did say you did it "this morning"? Why didn't you go straight to the General to get it seen to or else come to me then?'

Bates looked at Ty as though he were stupid. 'And lose me pay for not finishing me shift?'

Ty was struck dumb. His injury must be excruciatingly painful yet this man had been prepared to endure the pain and face the consequences of delaying treatment, sooner than lose any pay. Obviously the loss of his beer and gambling money was far more important to him than the prospect of losing a limb!

After thoroughly cleaning the wound with boracic

acid, then a thick layer of sulphur ointment as an antiseptic, Ty set to work with his needle and cat gut to close it up. However neat he was in his stitching, William Bates was going to be left with a terrible scar. It took twenty sutures to complete the closure, and despite Ty's low opinion of the man, he did admire the fact that throughout the procedure he sat stiff backed and unflinching, when Ty knew he must be in agony.

William Bates was preparing to take his leave. Ty made to inform him of his fee when the man pre-empted him by announcing, 'As soon as me arm lets me, I'll be around to do whatever jobs yer need attending to around the house.'

Ty eyed him closely. 'You obviously haven't seen the notice I put up in the waiting room, Mr Bates, informing all patients that payment in such a way is no longer acceptable.'

He looked bemused. 'Well, it wa' good enough for Doctor Mac . . .'

'I'm not Doctor McHinney and . . .'

Narrowing his eyes and giving Ty a look of disdain, William Bates interjected, 'No, yer definitely not, are yer? Proper doctor he was, not some kid wet behind the ears who looks down his nose at his patients 'cos they obviously ain't good enough for the likes of *him*. Don't worry, Doctor, you'll get yer fee.'

With not a flicker of emotion crossing his face at

the insulting comparison to the late James McHinney, Ty hurriedly jotted down the amount payable on a piece of paper and held it out to Bates, saying matter-of-factly, 'I'd appreciate payment as soon as you can.'

Both men jumped in surprise then as the door unexpectedly burst open and a young woman dashed into the surgery. She was in her mid-twenties or thereabouts, her light brown hair cut fashionably to chin-length, her shapely figure dressed in a floral, belted work dress that would have looked dowdy on any other woman but, the way she wore it, was very fetching on her. She wasn't beautiful, but good looking enough to stand out in a crowd, and she had a confident air about her.

It wasn't her physical attributes that were making Ty take notice of her now, though. This woman could have been the most beautiful in the world and he still wouldn't have noticed; the emotional damage that had been done to him in the past had seen to that. Instead he was angered by the fact that she had had the audacity to barge rudely into his inner sanctum uninvited while he was actually in consultation with a patient.

He opened his mouth to make his feelings known to her, but she forestalled him by crying out, 'You've got to come quick, Doc, it's me mam!'

The fact that she was addressing him with what he saw as disrespect didn't go down well with Ty. He snapped back, 'It's *Doctor Strathmore*. As you can see, I'm busy with a patient. Now, please wait your turn like everyone else is in the waiting room. I'll attend to you as soon as I can.'

His reprimand about her informal way of addressing him was obviously lost on her. In a frenzied state, she cried, 'But this can't wait, Doc. Me mam's bad . . . real bad.'

William Bates took this chance to make his departure. Without a word, he skirted around the young woman and hurried out.

She demanded again, 'You've got to come *now*. Me mam's collapsed on the kitchen floor and her lips are all blue . . . I've tried all I can think of to get her to come round but nothing worked. She don't look good, Doc. She don't look good at all.'

The condition of this young woman's mother didn't sound good to Ty either. From what she had informed him, he was already fearing what he'd find. He made to grab his bag then thought he had better take a look at her notes first, to familiarise himself with her past medical history in case it affected the medication he prescribed for her now.

'Name?' he demanded.

The woman looked at him dumbstruck. 'There's no time for that. *Will you just come now?*'

She was indeed infuriating. 'Name?' he snapped again.

She shot back, 'Oh, for God's sake, if you must have it ... Aidy.'

While she waited impatiently, he twisted around in his seat and pulled out the drawers labelled A to C, praying that for once James McHinney had filed a patient's records in the correct location. He hurriedly flicked through all the As, then the Bs and Cs for good measure, but could find no sign of a Mrs Aidy at all. Swivelling back round he said to the young woman, 'Has your mother ever visited this surgery? Only I can't find a trace of a patient with the surname Aidy.'

The young woman gawped at him. 'Eh? Oh, me mam's not called Aidy – that's my name. Aidy Nelson. You should have made it clear whose name you wanted. Hers is Jessie ... Jessica Greenwood.'

Why on earth had she thought he'd be asking for *her* name when it was her mother that was in need of him? Ty refrained from telling the young woman how stupid he thought her for wasting precious time in this situation. Swivelling back in his chair to face the drawers again, he yanked open the one marked G to I and, lo and behold, found Jessica Greenwood's record card filed where he would have expected it to be. From quickly scanning the spidery writings, it appeared that Jessica Greenwood, like his previous patient, was only an infrequent visitor to the surgery. The last time she had sought the help of a doctor had been twelve years ago, in 1918, for glandular fever.

Jumping up from his seat, Ty grabbed his bag, saying to Aidy. 'I'll just inform those in the waiting room I have an emergency to attend, then you can take me to your mother.'

She ran him through several miserable terrace streets until she turned down an alleyway to enter the back yard of a dilapidated three-bedroomed house, set in a long row of equally decrepit two- and three-bedroomed abodes.

As he followed her into the kitchen, he couldn't fail to notice the pungent smell that hit him as soon as he stepped over the threshold. Something had been cooked earlier, but it wasn't food. What exactly it was he hadn't time to work out. Like other houses he had been inside since arriving in his new post, it was evident this was a lower-class dwelling. But unlike most of the others he'd visited, this one was spotlessly clean and tidy. He noticed it only fleetingly, though.

As soon as he clapped eyes on Jessica Greenwood, Ty knew she was dead. Regardless, he went through the process of checking thoroughly for any vital signs.

Finally he stood up and addressed Aidy. 'I'm sorry to tell you this but there is nothing more I can do for your mother.'

She blurted out, 'What do you mean, there's

nothing you can do for her? You're a doctor! If you can't then ... Oh, we need to get her to the hospital, is that it? They'll make her better, won't they? You'll be wanting to hurry back off to yer surgery to telephone for an ambulance, won't you? You will tell them to come quick ...'

She made to cross to her mother's side, fully expecting him to dash off and summon the ambulance, but he stopped her. 'I'm afraid you misunderstand. I'm sorry. There's nothing I or anyone else can do for your mother. She's dead.'

She stared at him, befuddled. Her mam, that vibrant women who had faced and dealt with more than her fair share of terrible traumas, couldn't just be dead. In an accusing tone she declared, 'You've made a mistake! My mam's not dead. You haven't even *tried* to do anything for her. Some bloody doctor you are!'

Incensed that she should dare question his medical skills, he responded coolly. 'I'm afraid there's no mistake. She was already dead when I got here.'

Aidy stared at him for several long moments before, bottom lip trembling, she uttered, 'But she can't be 'cos ... 'cos ... she's our mam. We can't do without her.' Then she beseeched him, 'Please, *please*, just try to do something for her? Please, Doc, please?'

The look he returned told her she was wasting her time. Jessica Greenwood was beyond help.

Aidy's whole body sagged and she stepped back to

slump against the wall as she tried to take this in. Then, with a look of horror filling her face, she wailed, 'How the hell am I going to tell my sisters and brother that our mam is dead? And my gran too ... This'll kill her, I know it will. She worshipped her daughter. How could Mam die just like that, Doc? She wasn't ill. Got the stamina of an ox, she used to tell us. We could all be down with colds and she'd never catch them off us.'

'So she hadn't been complaining of any pains in her chest or feeling more tired than usual recently?' he asked.

Aidy shook her head. 'Not to me. The only ailment I knew she suffered from was a bad back which used to give her gyp now and again, though Mam wasn't a complainer. But anyway, Gran would have noticed if she wasn't well and told me. She lives here with Mam, me brother and two sisters. Gran's the sort who's got eyes in the back of her head. She misses nothing.'

'Well, if your mother wasn't suffering from anything you and your grandmother were aware of, then it's my considered opinion that her heart just gave out. She died from natural causes.'

There was nothing more to be done here. Ty wanted to get back to the surgery or he risked still being there until midnight at this rate, but despite how annoyed he was at what he perceived to be this woman's disrespectful attitude towards him, he couldn't quite bring himself to leave her on her own.

'Your father ought to be informed,' he told her. 'Maybe a neighbour could go and fetch him for you, if you know where he'll be?' He thought to himself, Most likely in the pub. That's where the majority of the men around these streets seem to head straight from work.

There was a flash of anger in her eyes and a harshness to her voice when she responded, 'Knowing me dad, he'll be in the pub . . . but *which* pub is anyone's guess. We ain't seen hide nor hair of him since before our Marion was born and she's eight.'

Ty wasn't surprised by this information. There seemed to him to be quite a number of absent husbands locally, some admittedly having been forced to seek work further afield, the depression that had started in America now making its ill effects felt in England and jobs being less easy to find. But just as many men had selfishly abandoned their wives to struggle to raise their children alone, merely because they'd better things to go off to. 'Then your grandmother needs to be summoned back home then. A neighbour will maybe oblige?'

Aidy was fighting hard to comprehend and accept this terrible turn of events. She was hardly listening to Ty but aware that he had said something and automatically muttered, 'Yes . . . yes, Doc.'

'*It's Doctor Strathmore,*' he reminded her again. 'Look, I really need to be getting back to the surgery. If you'll call in the morning, I'll have the death certificate ready for you.' And of course there was the matter of his fee, but it would be very remiss of him to mention it or expect her to in these circumstances. He would bring up the subject when she called to collect the death certificate in the morning.

Picking up his bag, he made to depart but was stopped in his tracks by the back door opening and the arrival of a small elderly woman. She was dressed in a well-worn black coat that came down to just above her ankles, a black dress underneath, black woollen stockings, and sturdy black lace-up shoes on her size two feet. A black felt hat was pulled well down over her iron-grey hair which was cut pudding basin-style just below her ears, the sides gripped behind them. The new arrival's attention was fully fixed on searching through her capacious handbag for something.

'Bloody hell! That Vi Jones can't half talk, our Jessie. I've never known anyone with so many ailments, and it's my opinion all are the making of her own imagination. I ain't one to refuse a penny or two for me concoctions, as you well know, but this is the third time this week I've had to make up summat for her! I've other folks that need my services besides her, and I can't help out me other clients if Vi's hypocondriousity is taking up most of me time. If she sends her daughter around again this week, I want you to tell her I've gone off on one of me plant-collection jaunts and yer not sure when I'm due back.'

Having given up her search through her bag, Bertha Rider was now taking off her coat. Spotting Aidy out of the corner of her short-sighted eye, she smiled delightedly and said, 'I thought I'd missed you tonight, gel. Glad I ain't. It always does me heart good to catch sight of your pretty face. Is your Arch working late? Is that why you ain't at your own home, getting his dinner?'

While her grandmother had been chuntering away, Aidy had been staring at her blindly. Despite her own devastation, all Aidy's thoughts now centred on this old lady. Her sixty-eight-year-old gran had taken her husband's death from septicaemia several years ago very hard. Her grandparents had worshipped each other. There had been worry at the time that Gran would join him herself from a broken heart, but the love and support of her family had pulled her through. She now looked fondly back over the years spent with the love of her life and didn't burst into tears whenever he came to mind.

Jessie had been the only child out of the four she had given birth to, to survive past infancy. Mother and daughter had always been very close. Losing a husband was bad enough, but losing a a child must be the worst thing ever. Aidy dreaded to think of how her grandmother was going to react to the death of the daughter she'd doted on. And not just her gran either. Her three younger siblings, who were all obliviously out playing with their friends, would need to be told of their beloved mother's sudden death. They were all going to be devastated.

Bertha Rider suddenly sensed that she and her granddaughter were not alone. Her beady, short-sighted eyes were directed at Ty as she demanded, 'And who a' you?' She then told him in a warning tone, 'Not a salesman, I hope, 'cos we don't want anything *you're* trying to flog.'

Ty was not in the least amused by being mistaken for a salesman. He sharply introduced himself. 'I'm Doctor Strathmore. I've taken over the local surgery from Doctor McHinney.'

Squinting, Bertha scanned him closely. 'Bit young to be a doctor, ain't yer? Hardly out of short pants. I've been hearing about you. Doctor Mac'd be turning in his grave if he knew how you was changing things at the surgery. Anyway, what yer doing here? No one in this house is sick enough to need your help ... well, they weren't when I left an hour or so ago.' She then caught sight of something on the floor by the doctor's feet and squinted harder. 'What's that on the floor?' She peered at it. 'That our Jessie?' Her aged face was wreathed in bewilderment. 'What's she doing down there? Get up, our Jessie, you'll catch yer death on those cold flags. Jessie, you hear me?'

Aidy stepped over to her grandmother, placed one hand tenderly on her arm and said tremulously, 'Mam can't hear you, Gran.'

Very aware of the passing of time and the patients waiting for his return, Ty spoke up. 'I'm sorry to inform you, Mrs . . . er . . . your daughter passed away a short time ago.'

Bertha glared at him. 'Passed away?' Then she snapped harshly, 'Don't be stupid. She was as right as rain when I left here an hour ago after helping her with the dinner pots. She was going to do a bit of ironing before she settled down with her knitting. She's in the middle of a new school pullover for George that she's desperate to get finished as his other one ain't fit for the rag bag. I can't finish it off as me stiff knuckles won't let me, and Aidy can turn her hand to lots of things but knitting in't one of her talents. So Jessie is the only one that can finish George's jumper.' She gave a disdainful click of her tongue. 'Some doctor you are who doesn't know a live woman from a dead one.' She then looked over at the body on the floor and demanded, 'Come on, Jessie, get up, lovey. I don't know what yer playing at but it ain't funny.'

Aidy's grip on her arm tightened. 'Mam's not playing a joke on us, Gran.'

Bertha stared at her granddaughter for several long moments before she whispered, 'She's not?'

'Doc said her heart just stopped.'

Bertha stared back at her, desperate to find any sign that this was all a bad joke. When she couldn't, she seemed visibly to shrink inside her clothes. With pleading eyes, she uttered, 'My Jessie really gone?'

A lone tear escaped from the flood that was building behind Aidy's eyes. She swiped it away and nodded.

Bertha's aged face sagged with grief. Shrugging her arm free from her granddaughter's hold, she shuffled over to her daughter's body and slumped down beside it, tenderly lifting Jessie's head on to her lap and cradling it. The tears came then. As she rocked backwards and forwards, she softly moaned, 'Oh, Jessie love, Jessie love. How could you do this to us?'

Aidy's tears started in earnest then and both women were too consumed by their grief to notice Ty take his leave.

CHAPTER THREE

A look of annoyance filled Archibald Nelson's face at the sight that met him when he walked into the kitchen of the Greenwood household two hours later. Hungry and work-weary, he was too preoccupied with his own worries to notice the atmosphere of sadness permeating the house.

In the hard times of 1930, when any job, no matter how menial, was hard fought or even murdered for, Arch was extremely fortunate to be permanently employed at a local factory that had been in business since the middle of the last century, producing working boots and shoes, albeit his wage only just paid for basics. To earn it he worked a gruelling ten-hour shift, six days a week, operating antiquated machinery in conditions hardly improved since Victorian times. The fact that his wife Aidy worked too, however, meant the Nelsons had a marginally better standard of living than many of their kind. They were dressed a little smarter, in good-quality, second-hand clothes, and could afford a cheap cut of meat three times a week; they could also fund a night out at the pictures once a week, or cheap seats in a variety theatre, or a few drinks in the pub.

Twenty-five-year-old Arch was a good-looking man, topping six feet tall and broad shouldered, his dark brown hair neatly cut into a short back and sides and groomed into place with hair cream. During work he looked as shabby as his fellows, but outside he tried to dress as sprucely as funds would allow. The same went for his wife. Many hopes had been shattered, both male and female, the day Aidy and Arch had said their vows.

For the majority of the time their relationship was harmonious, with just the occasional spat even happily married couples have, but one subject did cause friction between them which occasionally flared into a full-scale row. After five years of marriage Aidy was more than ready to start a family whereas Arch was adamant they should wait until he'd been given his promised promotion to foreman, albeit it was anyone's guess when that would be as the present sixty-one-year-old incumbent had held the post for twenty years and didn't look like relinquishing it until forced to retire. But the eventual increase in wages would enable Arch to support his family in a lifestyle far better than the hand-to-mouth one he'd had himself as a child, and without their having to scrimp and scrape any longer. To ensure he got his way, Arch insisted they took precautions whenever they made love, which in their case was frequently.

Pushing the door shut behind him, he snapped at his wife, 'Aidy, do you know what time it is? Why are you still here and not at home, getting my dinner?'

Her face cast into shadow by the light of the flickering gas mantle, she was sitting at the rickety kitchen table, cradling her eight-year-old sister Marion on her knee.

She was so lost in her own thoughts, the unexpected sound of Arch's voice made her jump. She turned to look at him and whispered, 'Keep your voice down, Arch, I've only just got our Marion off. Could you put her to bed for me while I mash Gran a cuppa?'

He looked questioningly at her. 'But what about my dinner? I'm famished. Can't yer mam see to Marion and mashing yer gran a cuppa?'

Stroking her hand tenderly over the top of her sister's head, in a choked voice Aidy uttered, 'No, Mam can't, Arch.'

As he advanced towards her, he was disturbed to see that her face was swollen, red and blotchy. She'd been crying. Wondering what could have caused her to be so upset, he demanded, 'What's happened, love?' Automatically, because of her age, he assumed, 'Is it your gran? Has she been took sick?' He put his hand on Aidy's shoulder, giving it a reassuring squeeze. 'She'll rally round, love. Tough as old boots is your gran.'

'It's not Gran, Arch, it's me mam.' Her bottom lip trembling, Aidy told him, 'She's dead.'

He was visibly shaken by this unexpected news. He had got on well with his mother-in-law, felt a deep respect for her, had secretly wished he'd her sort as his own mother and not the type he did have. 'Oh, Lord, I'm so sorry, Aidy,' he said in all sincerity. 'Accident at one of her jobs, was it?'

She shook her head. 'It happened here in the kitchen, this evening, just before I got here. Doc said her heart just stopped. He couldn't do anything for her. She died just like that,' she said, clicking two fingers. Her face puckered then, a fresh flow of tears rolling down her cheeks, and she miserably sobbed, 'Oh, Arch, I can't bear it! She wasn't just my mother, she was my friend.'

He desperately wanted to take her in his arms and offer her what comfort he could, but the child in her arms was preventing him. Easing Marion out of her embrace as gently as he could so as not to wake her, he said, 'I won't be a minute.'

He found Aidy where he'd left her when he came back down several moments later. 'Marion never stirred,' he informed her. 'Betty is spark out too, and I poked my head around George's door and so is he.'

How Aidy wished she herself could escape into the oblivion of sleep, but that was out of the question for a while yet. Her younger siblings were not in need of her now but her grandmother would be. And, besides, first you had to fall asleep, and how did you do that when every fibre of your being was consumed by an emotional pain so strong it felt as if your heart had been ripped out?

Arch was continuing, 'I put my ear to your gran's door and couldn't hear anything, so I gather she's asleep too.'

'Gran's not in bed, Arch. She's in the parlour, laying out Mam.'

He looked astounded. 'Your gran's doing that herself!'

'She insisted. I offered to go and fetch Mrs Doubleday who sees to all that sort of thing around here, but she said no stranger was messing with her daughter. Was adamant, in fact. She shocked me, Arch. When me granddad died she fell to pieces, couldn't even go to the privy by herself for ages afterwards. She broke down when she first heard about Mam, but now it seems like a . . . well, a determination has come over her to get on with what she needs to do for Mam. Whether she'll fall apart after she's finished laying her out remains to be seen. You know how close me gran and mam were.'

Aidy paused to take a deep breath, the pain she was

suffering creasing her face, and whispered, 'I know it's me mam, but I couldn't offer to help Gran. The thought just made me feel sick. But she understood. In fact, she was relieved. She really wanted to attend to it by herself. She said her mother was the first to see to Mam when she was born, and being's she is still alive, it should be her mother who is the last to see to her too.'

The look on Arch's face betrayed the fact that, like his wife, he found the thought of what Bertha was doing totally repellent.

Getting up from her chair, Aidy said, 'I'll mash a cuppa.' As she was busying herself with her task, she told him, 'I'll be staying here tonight, Arch.'

He was sitting at the table now. Thankfully Aidy's back was to him so she didn't see the expression he pulled. Despite the circumstances, he selfishly didn't like the thought of not having his wife beside him in bed to snuggle up to tonight. This would be the first night in five years of marriage they had not slept together. He knew better than to voice his thoughts, though, as his wife would not hold back from telling him exactly what she thought of him for thinking purely of his own needs at a time when he should be thinking of others. He said, 'I suppose I'd better go and tell me mam what's happened.'

Aidy spun round to look at him, horrified. 'Can't that wait until tomorrow? I couldn't cope with her tonight, and I know Gran couldn't either.'

Arch didn't take offence at his wife's words about his mother. Pat Nelson was a big woman, in body and character. Despite Aidy herself being strong enough never to let the likes of her mother-in-law dominate her, Pat would feel duly bound to inter- fere. As soon as she learned the news of Jessie Greenwood's death, regardless of her son asking her not to, she would be round here, taking over in her bossy way, getting on her son's nerves, let alone his wife's at this extremely difficult time.

'I'll pop around tomorrow after work. What about your work, Aidy? They'll need to be told what's gone on.'

'Oh, I hadn't given work a thought. Could you call in at lunchtime and tell them for me?'

He nodded and told her that of course he would. As Aidy returned to the task of making the tea, he opened his mouth to ask if her mother's funeral arrangements had been discussed, but then thought that might not have been tackled yet. He didn't want to upset her further by bringing to mind that add- itional trauma when she was still trying to accept that her mother had actually died. Anything else he could think of to ask her, like how her day at work had gone, seemed trivial in the circumstances so a silence reigned between them, broken only by the clattering of cups as Aidy gathered them together and the sound of the water coming to boil in the kettle on the stove.

As Aidy put a cup of tea before him, a thought occurred to her and she exclaimed, 'Oh, Arch, I'm so sorry, I've completely forgotten about your dinner. I was going to heat up the remains of last night's stew and boil you some spuds. Do you think you can see to that yourself when you get back home?'

He supposed he had no choice, in the circumstances, unless he wanted to go hungry. In truth, though, he wasn't actually sure how to put the stove on. Aidy had always seen to the cooking of their meals, and his mother before her ... He once used to enjoy Pat's food, but now he had Aidy's cooking to compare it with, he could see his mother was barely an adequate cook. Oh, he knew what he'd do. He'd leave the stew for them to have the following night, when Aidy would do it, and he'd settle for fish and chips tonight. He told his wife, 'I'll leave the stew for us to have tomorrow ... save you cooking, won't it? ... and get meself a bag of chips on the way home.'

Save her cooking? What a laugh! Save him the bother of preparing a meal himself, Aidy thought. Men! What would they do without a woman in their lives, to fetch and carry for them?

Arch heard a door opening and closing. It sounded like the parlour door to him. It had a peculiar squeak to it which, despite his oiling it, would not go away. Bertha was returning. He was quite fond of the old girl and got along with her well enough, but tonight he could just about cope with comforting his wife in her grief. He didn't need her grandmother too. He was like most men: not much use around wailing women. They made him feel uncomfortable. He preferred to come to terms with his mother-in-law's death in his own way. Over a pint at the pub.

He scraped back his chair and stood up, saying, 'I'd better get to the chip shop before it shuts.'

Aidy too had heard the parlour door announce its opening and knew her grandmother had finished her task and was now on her way to join them. It was besides a lame excuse he'd used to make his escape as Hattie Cheadle who operated her fish and chip business from her front room, taking orders and handing them over through the open sash window, wouldn't close up until she was absolutely positive there were no more customers to be had that night, needing every penny as she did to support her invalid husband and ten children. But Aidy fully understood her husband's need to make an escape. Very few men were of use in emotional times like this, and all the rest merely looked on helplessly, not knowing what to say or do, and generally getting under the women's feet. Before he left she would have liked a comforting hug from him, but men like her husband did not make displays of emotion in public. The most Arch would do if others were around was give her a peck on her cheek.

He gave her a hurried one now and then shot out the back door.

Bertha looked surprised to find her granddaughter alone when she arrived a moment later. 'I thought I heard voices?'

'You did. It was Arch. I've packed him off home.'

'Best place for him. There's n'ote he can do here. I'm just glad word hasn't got around yet about Jessie. I couldn't be doing with people calling tonight. They'll be around in droves when word does get out, though. My daughter was a popular woman.' Bertha looked searchingly at her granddaughter. Aidy looked liked death. For Bertha herself losing a daughter was bad enough, but Aidy had lost her mother, and so unexpectedly, with no chance for a goodbye. Without a word, Bertha headed off into the pantry, returning moments later with a bottle in her hand. Selecting a pot cup from several that hung from hooks under a shelf on the wall, she bustled back to the table, put the cup down on it, uncorked the bottle and poured a generous measure of greenish-looking liquid into it. She forced the cork back into the bottle, then picked up the cup and thrust it at Aidy. 'Drink that,' she ordered.

Aidy looked dubiously at it. 'What is it?'

'Summat that'll do yer good.'

She took a sniff, grimacing. 'God, that smells vile.'

'How many times have I told yer? The worse it

smells, the better it is for yer. It's one of me potions
for soothing upsets. Now get it down yer.'

'Where's yours then?' Aidy challenged her.

'I had a draught earlier. Now, for God's sake, will
you do as you're told?'

Aidy knew she might as well get it over with as
her grandmother would stand over her until she did.
In truth, though, she could do with something to lift,
even a fraction, her misery for the loss of the woman
who had meant so much to her. She knocked back
the thick liquid in the cup, giving a violent shudder.
It tasted even worse than it smelled.

Handing the empty cup back to her grandmother,
she looked at Bertha hard. She was worried about
the old lady who looked as if she had aged ten years
during the past couple of hours, though that wasn't
surprising considering the shock she'd received.

'How are you bearing up, Gran?' Aidy asked.

'Well, I'm not going to go the same way I did when
yer granddad passed, so yer needn't be worriting
yerself about that. I had a good chat with yer mother
when I was seeing to her in the parlour, and I made
her a promise that I was going to stay strong for the
family on her behalf. I'm determined to.'

Aidy smiled wanly at her. 'When I was sitting in
here earlier nursing Marion, I made Mam the same
promise, Gran.'

Bertha tenderly patted her shoulder. 'Then,

between us, we'll make sure we all get through this.' But she took a deep breath, worry clouding her face. 'I'm not sure how I'm going to manage from now on without a bit of help, though, me duck. I wish I were younger and wouldn't need to burden you. It's not like your own life ain't full enough as it is.'

Aidy frowned up at her, bemused. 'Help? With what?'

'Well, the gels can help with the housework and some of the lighter jobs, but it's the heavy part that's worrying me. I ain't as strong as I used to be.'

Even more bemused, Aidy asked, 'The heavy part of what?'

'Well, while I was seeing to Jessie, I was racking me brains for how I could earn our keep, and as I can't see anyone taking me on at my age, the only option I've got is to do what she did. I'll move out of the bedroom I shared with yer mam and give that over to a lodger. I'll use a Put-u-up down here. And I'm gonna take in washing and ironing. I was wondering if yer think Arch would light the fire under the copper for me before he went to work each morning, and if you could see yer way to coming home at dinnertime and helping me with the mangling? I wish I didn't have to put this on yer, but I've no choice. I need to provide a living for the kids and meself in whatever way I can.'

Aidy gawped at her. The shock of her mother's

sudden death had been all-consuming. She hadn't given the serious matter of how life should carry on from here without Jessie a thought. Aidy's heart swelled with love for the elderly, worried-looking woman standing beside her. It took a special person at her advanced age to propose undertaking what she had just suggested doing for the sake of her family. And it wasn't just talk on her part either. But whatever the answer was to their serious problem, it was not going to involve her gran labouring over other people's dirty washing twelve hours a day, or labouring at all at her age, Aidy was adamant on that. She knew inside that there was only one answer to this situation. 'You needn't be worrying about any of that, Gran. Arch and me will be moving in here and taking care of you all.'

Bertha looked appalled by the very idea. 'Oh, but you're both young with your own lives to be getting on with and . . .'

Aidy held up a warning hand. 'You're our family, Gran. I don't want to hear another word on the matter.'

Bertha heaved a deep sigh of relief. 'Well, I can't deny that's a load off my mind, Aidy. But what about Arch? Will he be agreeable?'

'Of course he will, how can you ask? He'll see, like me, that us moving in here makes sense.'

Bertha had to agree, it did, although she still felt

it a great shame that she wasn't more bodily able, and then the burden of caring for herself and the youngsters wouldn't be down to her granddaughter and her husband. But Bertha had always pulled her weight around the house as much as she could, and would continue to do so. She said to Aidy, 'You finally got Marion to settle down then?'

Aidy sighed heavily. 'Arch took her up to bed. They're all asleep, bless them. Exhausted themselves with all their crying.'

'And with a little help from the sleeping potion I gave them in their milk before I went through to see to laying out Jessie,' Bertha informed her. Then she asked, 'Are you feeling the effects of what I've just given you yet?'

Aidy appraised herself. Considering all the pent-up anger she was experiencing at her mother being taken from them so young and without any warning, she was surprised to find she did indeed feel a kind of calm seeping through her. 'I'm not sure what it's doing, but it's doing something to me. I feel sort of relaxed . . . like you do when you've had a couple of glasses of port.'

Bertha looked happy with her response. 'That's just what my potion is supposed to do. If you want any more, just say.' As she eased herself down on a chair opposite Aidy, the young woman got up and went across to the stove, collected a cup and saucer and poured her grandmother a cup of tea. Putting it before her, she sat back down in her own chair, saying, 'I know that'll taste better than what you just made me drink.'

Bertha managed a small chuckle. Picking up the cup, she warmed her hands around it before she took a sip of the hot, sweet liquid.

Aidy asked her, 'Did you manage to do what you went through to the parlour to do, Gran?'

Bertha nodded. 'I did. Jessie always liked to look her best and she looks beautiful now, bless her. I put on her best blue dress ... the one she wore for your wedding. She loved that dress. Only one she ever had that was bought new from a shop. Took that extra job so she could save for it, she did. She so wanted to look nice for you. And she did, didn't she? I know she wasn't the religious sort, but I found the Bible the Sunday School gave her when she was a child and she's holding that. She just looks like she's asleep, Aidy love. So peaceful. I shall be sitting with her tonight. I can't bear the thought of her being left alone.'

Normally the thought of being in the vicinity of a dead body would have revolted Aidy, frightened her even, but the body was that of her beloved mother, and her grandmother would be there, so she offered, 'Would you like company, Gran?'

The old lady reached over one thin, veined hand

and gave Aidy's an affectionate pat. 'There's nothing I'd like better, if you feel you'd like to. I know your mam would appreciate it.'

They both lapsed into silence then, acutely aware this would be the last time the three of them would be together.

Taking another sip of her tea, Bertha's aged face darkened as she spat, 'I blame *him* for Jessie's death.'

Aidy looked at her knowingly. 'By *him* you mean me dad?'

'That man doesn't deserve the honour of being called yer father. He's never been one to you, or to your brother and sisters. And Arnold Greenwood was certainly no husband to yer mother after you came along. If he hadn't left Jessie high and dry, to fend single handed for her brood, she wouldn't have worn herself out trying to make ends meet, causing her heart to give out. And he didn't leave her just once, did he? *Twice* he did it.' Bertha shook her head, her face set grim. 'I took an instant dislike to the man the first time I clapped eyes on him when she brought him home to meet me and yer granddad. Yer granddad never took to him either. Don't ask me why, but there was just something about him we didn't like. It wasn't a happy day like it should have been, the day she married him, not for me and yer granddad, but Jessie had made her choice and there was n'ote we could do but grin and bear it.

'We did think we was wrong about him at first 'cos they were very happy together and he seemed to be being a good husband to her. He'd a reasonably paid job as a dyer for Corah, which gave him the means to rent this place, and he handed her a good portion of his wage for her housekeeping. But then he changed after you came along.

''Course, me and yer granddad didn't really know any of this until after he'd left. Yer mam didn't want to worry us about the way he was treating her, and she was ashamed that her marriage was going wrong. Every time we visited she'd put on an act that it was all right, so for a long time we thought it was. She told us after he'd left that not long after you were born, Arnold started going out at nights, leaving her home caring for you, and of course he needed money to fund his outings so he cut her housekeeping. And *then* he'd have the nerve to complain about the cheaper food she put in front of him, and the fact that the house wasn't as warm as he liked it because she had to be sparing with the fuel. He would give her hell too if you made a noise and disturbed his peace.'

Bertha paused long enough to finish off her tea, putting the cup back in its saucer, then pushing it towards Aidy by way of informing her she'd like a refill. Aidy already knew the story of her parents' failed marriage but her grandmother obviously felt a need to re-tell it so she patiently listened.

When Aidy got up to oblige with her refill, Bertha continued, 'Arnold left the first time without any warning whatsoever. You were three at the time. Jessie got up one morning and he'd gone, taken all his belongings with him as well as the rent money. Walked out of his job too. I'd no doubt he'd gone off with another woman and, deep down, although she never actually came out with it, I know that's what Jessie suspected too. Naturally she was very upset at the time, but there was some relief too that she hadn't to put up with his shenanigans any longer and keep thinking up excuses to cover for his absence whenever we popped in, as we frequently did. Now she'd be left in peace to raise you on her own and let you play and cause as much noise as you liked without *him* having a go at her. She was terrified, though, how she was going to manage without yer dad's wage coming in, worried about not being able to earn enough to keep this house on and having to raise you in the sort Pat Nelson lives in. Thankfully, though, she found a job the first day she started looking.

'While she went to work, I looked after you for her. Jessie loved her job. Mrs Crabtree treated her like gold, paid her a decent amount for her cooking and housework duties, and any leftover food, Jessie was allowed to bring home. Well, Jessie being Jessie she always saw to it that me and yer granddad got a share, and the neighbours too if there was enough. Mrs Crabtree was always giving Jessie her old clothes, some she'd hardly worn . . . got money to burn, she had, her husband being some bigwig for a firm in town . . . and that meant some of the clothes she was given, Jessie could use the fabric to make up things for you. Mother and daughter were at one time the best dressed around these parts, thanks to Mrs Crabtree and much to the envy of lots of the folks around here. So what with taking in a lodger too, Jessie managed just fine moneywise.'

A smile twitched at the old lady's lips. 'You remember Claudia Badger, don't you, Aidy? Who could ever forget her? I never knew quite what to make of her, meself. She dressed like a floozy in low-cut blouses and tight skirts, had her hair bleached and styled like that film star Greta Garbo . . . no, that's not the one . . . Jean . . . Jean Harlow. And she worked for Woolie's as a counter assistant, selling cheap make-up and costume jewellery, and always had some bloke in tow. At first I thought Jessie was out of her, mind, choosing her when she could have had her pick from lots at the time wanting good lodgings. I thought Claudia the type who would take advantage and abuse Jessie's hospitality, but she wouldn't listen to me 'cos she had taken to Claudia above all the others who'd wanted her room, and that was that.

'I don't mind admitting I was very wrong about Claudia. She paid her dues on time, never missing once, and sometimes even bunging Jessie a few shillings extra at Christmas and such like, and she never caused yer mam one minute of bother. She brought fun back into yer mam's life and she worshipped you, treated you like the daughter she never was to have. I'd often call in and find Claudia reading you a story or helping put you to bed, or you sitting at the table with her while she put on her make-up before she went out. And she'd give you some of her old make-up to play with, and what a mess you used to make! On her afternoon off . . . Wednesday, I'm sure it was a Wednesday she had off . . . well, she'd take you out, rain or shine. When you started school, she'd meet you at the gates and take you out then. She took you to all sorts of places. The museums, parks, rides on trains . . . During the school holidays she once took you on a trip to the country so she could show you real animals, not just pictures in books.

'Not that she begrudged Claudia any happiness, but your mam was always secretly worried that she would meet a man and marry him and then she'd lose her as her lodger. But Claudia never met anyone so special she wanted to settle down with them. She told me once that she didn't mind spending their money, but washing their dirty underpants was an entirely different matter. I always hoped yer mam would meet someone else herself, but she used to say, "once bitten, twice shy", and besides, she couldn't get married again while she still was to your dad, and Jessie wouldn't even contemplate living in sin as she had you to consider.

'Ten years Claudia lived with Jessie. It was a dreadful thing what happened to her. That run-away dray cart ploughing into her like that, killing her outright. Shame too that virtually at the same time Mrs Crabtree's husband gets moved down south with his job, so that meant yer mother lost hers. Biggest shame of all was that that was the time, out of the blue, when yer dad decided to make his return.'

Aidy's mind flashed back in time to the day her father had come home. Having been only three when he had first disappeared, she'd had no recollection of him, only knew what he looked like from the few photographs her mother possessed of him. She'd been told nothing bad about him. Only that he was a kind, loving man, but that unfortunately some men and women might love each other but could not live together, and that was why her mother and father didn't. He didn't come to visit Aidy because he'd had to move to another town far away with his job, she was told.

She was thirteen when he returned out of the blue and she discovered that he wasn't at all the kind, loving man her mother had portrayed him to be. Oh, at first he appeared to be to his daughter, in front of his wife, but behind Jessie's back he made Aidy very aware that he found her a nuisance, as he did George and Betty too when they came along. He failed to wait around long enough to meet Marion. His favourite saying to Aidy was, 'Get lost, kid.' Her home before his return had been her sanctuary, a place where she felt comfortable and welcome. It had been a happy place, full of laughter, the sight of her mother's ever-present smile, and the sound of her singing as she went about her household tasks, a delight to see and hear. Only a very short while after Aidy's father's return that was all to change as he asserted his position as head of their household again, and couldn't be bothered any longer hiding his true colours. He hadn't changed at all. But the atmosphere in the house did, and so did her mother. Tension filled the air. Jessie's smile faded, she never sang any longer, and her eyes lost their shine.

It was a happy day for Aidy when they got up one morning to find her father had disappeared again, taking all his belongings and any money he could lay his hands on besides anything saleable too. Life was harsh for the family, money so tight that sometimes a scrape of marge on their bread was looked upon as a luxury while Jessie strove to support them all on what she could earn, taking in laundry, mending, minding children . . . anything, in fact, that made her a few coppers. She worked at home until her children were of an age where she could safely leave them. But almost immediately her father departed Aidy was to see the smile return to her mother's lips, her eyes shining, and to hear her singing again.

Aidy's thoughts returned to the present and she realised her grandmother had fallen silent. 'You all right, Gran?' she asked.

Sighing, the old lady nodded. 'I was just thinking of the day Arnold Greenwood came back into Jessie's life. At the time she was grieving over the loss of Claudia and for the job she had loved so much with Mrs Crabtree. Worried too about losing the house as she was getting behind with the rent. She'd been for several interviews for jobs but for one reason or another never took or was offered one. You'd gone off to school and she was just leaving to continue with her job search when the back door opened and in he walked, bold as brass, plonked his bag on the floor and announced to her he was back. Arnold didn't even say he was sorry for leaving her high and dry. Didn't offer any explanation for where he'd been in the meantime or what he'd been doing, just expected to carry on like he'd never been away.

'When Jessie came to tell me and yer granddad of his return, I asked her what she was playing at, just letting him back in after all these years with not even a word from him. She said, "Mam, I'm in arrears with the rent, can't seem to get a job for love nor money – his return is like a Godsend to me. Don't matter whether I want him back or not, I've no choice but to have him back, 'cos you've no room to take me and my daughter in, and having him back is better than the workhouse or walking the streets."

'Whenever me and yer granddad dropped in Arnold was civil to us, and from what we saw he seemed to be being a decent husband to Jessie and a father to you. Whenever I asked her how life was, she'd just say, "Fine, Mam," and change the subject. Within a matter of months of him coming back she fell pregnant with George. Then Betty came along just over a year later, and only four months after giving birth to her, she fell for Marion. She was about seven months gone when, out of the blue, Arnold disappeared one night, again without any warning, and we've never seen nor heard anything of him since. That was when Jessie opened up to us and told us that not long after he'd returned he was back to all his old ways, but by then she was pregnant. Turned out he gave her Betty and Marion too before he finally abandoned her.'

Bertha's eyes narrowed darkly and she hissed, 'How the hell any man could abandon his pregnant wife and kids, not just once but twice, and think it right to do so ... Well, I hope he's gone to hell and rots there!

'Yer granddad had retired by then and we were struggling to make ends meet on just the bit I made from me potions ourselves, so we couldn't help Jessie moneywise. Thank God you were earning by then, and what you handed over helped enormously even though you were only training in your job. Along with the pittance she made from taking in washing and ironing and another lodger, Jessie just about scraped though, but there was nothing left over for any luxuries. If it hadn't been for the neighbours passing her hand-me-downs from their own kids, I dread to think how she'd have dressed you all.' Bertha's face puckered, the glint of tears in her aged eyes, and she uttered, 'Oh, Aidy, if only me and yer granddad had been able to help Jessie more maybe she wouldn't have put such a strain on her heart with all that hard work. Maybe she'd still be with us now.'

Aidy reminded her, 'But you *did* help her, Gran. You and Granddad both. Granddad used to come around each morning at six and light the fire under the copper while me and Mam got the kids up and dressed before I had to rush off to work and she saw to the lodger's breakfast. Then, when Granddad went off down the allotment that kept us all in veg, you would arrive and help Mam with what washing and ironing she had to do that day. And I know you wouldn't take any payment 'cos Mam told me you

67

wouldn't, even though you could have put good use to a few coppers extra. And I know you used to share your potion money with Mam when you were able to because she told me you did.' A worried expression clouded Aidy's face then. 'Maybe she'd still be alive if I hadn't got married and left home, Gran.'

Bertha sighed heavily. 'We could sit here all night worrying that something we didn't do for her contributed to her death. Anyway, I told you, if anyone's to blame it's Arnold Greenwood. And, as we both know, your Arch wanted you both to get married years before you did. It was only through yer mam overhearing you arguing with him that you wouldn't get married until all the kids were working that Jessie herself made you see reason and set a date. Of course, you being you argued the toss with her, but finally Jessie won out. Thankfully she did else you would have denied her seeing at least one of her children married and settled.' Bertha's eyes glazed over. 'I never saw her look so happy as she did that day. So proud. She kept saying to me, "Look at my girl, Mam, doesn't she look beautiful? Like a princess." And you did. Such a handsome couple you and Arch make. It's just sad for the others that they won't have their mam there on their own big days.'

They both jumped at a thump on the back door,

then it immediately burst open and a booming voice announced, 'I came as soon as I found out, to see what I could do.'

Both Aidy and Bertha looked at each other in a way that voiced 'oh, no', then both stared at the newcomer who had burst into their back room. As far as they knew no one could possibly have learned yet of Jessie's death. Arch was the only one who had, but he had promised Aidy he wouldn't say anything until tomorrow – especially to the person who had just arrived.

Aidy fixed her eyes on the huge woman before her and asked, 'How did you find out Mam had died, Mrs Nelson?'

Pat Nelson looked visibly shaken to hear this. 'Jessie's dead!' she proclaimed. In shock, she made her way over to join them at the table and sank down, the old chair she chose groaning in protest at the tremendous weight that had been placed upon it. 'I didn't know that! Mave Pollard called in to tell me she saw you hurrying in here with the new doctor so I assumed one of you was sick enough to have him called in. So Jessie's dead, eh? How'd it happen?'

Muttering under her breath, Bertha grumbled, 'Bloody busybodies around here. Yer can't go to the lavvy without someone knowing.'

Although Pat appeared not to have heard what

Bertha had muttered, Aidy did and flashed her a warning look before she informed her mother-in-law, 'Doc said her heart just stopped.'

Pat said bluntly, 'Well, I suppose that's as good a way to go as any. Right, after you've finished yer tea, you get round to Ivy Doubleday, Aidy, and tell her there's a laying out to do. Don't forget to tell her I sent yer. I suggest you use Snow's for the funeral. They did my own mother proud when she went last year. Ask for Bill Chambers and tell him I sent yer. Use Worth's for yer meat ... tell him I sent yer too.'

A thought suddenly struck her and she asked worriedly, 'Jessie did have a penny policy to pay for her funeral, I take it? Oh, yes, she did. I remember being here one night when the agent came to collect her dues. Now, we won't have trouble getting pall-bearers. There's my three lads, Gert Hoskins' two boys and Jimmy Smith. Of course, they'll expect you to bung them a couple of bob each ... except for Arch, of course, him being yer husband. My Arch will be chief pall-bearer. As for the food, we'll have ham on the bone, and tongue, sandwiches and sausage rolls. Barrel of beer for the men, sherry for the women.'

Despite the grief that had rendered her incapable of mustering the inner strength needed for a battle of wills with Arch's bossy mother, Aidy wasn't about to have her own mother's funeral railroaded. Taking a deep breath, she spoke up. 'Now look, Mrs Nelson . . .'

Bertha immediately cut in. 'I'm surprised at you, Aidy. You know it's extremely rude to butt in when someone else is speaking.' She then politely asked Pat, 'I expect you could do with a cuppa, Mrs Nelson?'

Aidy looked askance at her grandmother. Why was she encouraging this overbearing woman to stay, instead of doing the opposite?

Pat responded, 'I was beginning to think yer weren't going to offer me one. Better make it a pot, Mrs Rider. Arranging a funeral is thirsty work.'

Appearing not to notice that her granddaughter was staring daggers at her, Bertha got up and went across to the stove to put the kettle on to boil, then disappeared into the pantry.

While the kettle was boiling, she poured Pat the dregs left from the pot made earlier which she put before her, saying, 'The kettle won't be a moment. In the meantime, this'll keep yer going.'

Pat took enough time off from issuing her instructions on what route she had decided the funeral procession should take to pick up the cup of stewed tea and knock it back. After swallowing it down, she pulled a face. 'Oh, that was a bit bitter! I'll have a spoon more sugar in me next one. Now, where was I?'

Fifteen minutes later Aidy was having extreme difficulty controlling her need to tell Arch's mother to at least afford her grandmother and herself the courtesy of having some opinions on Jessie's funeral, when the woman suddenly stopped mid-flow and clutched her huge stomach, giving out a loud groan.

Looking at her worriedly, Aidy asked, 'What's wrong, Mrs Nelson?'

Her rotund face screwed up in agony, Pat bellowed, 'It's me guts. It's feels like they're dropping out. It must be that bleddy cod we had for dinner last night. I thought it looked a bit iffy when I bought it. I'll give that 'monger what for, the next time I see him.' Heaving her bulk off the chair, she announced, 'I've got to go. Don't worry, I'll be back first thing to continue where we left off.'

With that she snatched up her coat and handbag, and almost wrenched the back door off its hinges in her haste to get home.

'That'll just be us for tea then,' said Bertha matter-of-factly, getting up and bustling over to pick up the kettle that was now whistling merrily on the stove.

Her face showing her fury, Aidy hissed, 'I can't believe that woman was expecting me to *pay* Arch's brothers to pall-bear for Mam. The bloody gall of her!' Then she paused and sighed. 'Oh, Gran, as much as she irritates the life out of me, I hope her stomach ache isn't serious. It's funny, though, we had cod last night from the same 'monger she uses and Arch never complained of anything when he was here earlier. And I'm all right . . .'

'Well, it might not have been caused by summat she ate so much as summat she drank,' said Bertha dryly as she busied herself with her task.

Her tone of voice had Aidy looking at her suspiciously. Instinctively she knew her grandmother was somehow involved in Pat's sudden stomach problem. 'Gran, just what did you give Mrs Nelson?'

Bertha turned to face Aidy, a satisfied expression on her face. 'Well, I thought she looked a bit grey around the gills, and to me that's a sure sign of constipation. Out of pure kindness, I put a dose of senna in her tea.'

Aidy gawped. 'So that's why it tasted bitter to her? Gran, how big a dose did you give her?'

'Enough to clear the blockage of an elephant! Well, yer can't deny she's a big woman, so a normal dose wouldn't be of any benefit to the likes of her, now would it?' There was a twinkle of mischief in Bertha's eyes when she added, 'And with a bit of luck, lovey, we won't see her ugly mug again until after the funeral.'

Aidy couldn't help but laugh, despite the circumstances. Her grandmother deserved a medal for getting the interfering Pat out of the way, allowing them the freedom to arrange her mother's funeral the way they wanted. 'Mam would have split her sides over this one, Gran,' she spluttered.

Putting a pot of fresh tea on the table, Bertha nodded. 'She certainly would have. That woman was the bane of Jessie's life, thinking she had every right to boss us about 'cos you was married to her son. Jessie only tolerated her out of respect for you.'

Bertha began to giggle then, a moment's relief from the heartache of her daughter's sudden death.

A while later they made their way through to the parlour to begin their vigil, both to some extent dreading the ordeal, but equally determined to use this special time to talk about the good times they had shared with Jessie, their own good fortune in having the likes of her for a mother and a daughter.

CHAPTER FOUR

It didn't seem right to Aidy that the day of her mother's funeral should be so gloriously sunny. A perfect summer's day, in fact. It should have been icy cold and bleak, the way she was feeling. She knew the rest of the family agreed too.

The service had seemed never-ending to her. There had been times during it when she had had to restrain herself from shouting out to the Vicar that her mother did not need her earthly sins forgiving before God would accept her spirit back into His Kingdom. Her mother would never wittingly have done wrong against anyone. Jessie had been a good woman who had done her best to raise her children after her husband had abandoned her and left her destitute. She had been a loyal friend and neighbour, and would help even a stranger in need if it was in her power to do so. Now standing tightly packed in by neighbours around the graveside, it was unbearable to Aidy to think of her mother resting inside a box six feet under. In only a few short minutes they would be expected to say their last goodbyes then go on their way to get on with their lives. Aidy wasn't ready to say goodbye to her mother, not ready to get on with her life without Jessie in it, and she knew that neither was the rest of her family.

With sisterly protectiveness she looked in turn at her brother and two sisters. Flaxen-haired Betty was a gawky nine year old, her childish face already showing the signs of the good-looking woman she would become. She was openly crying, periodically wiping away the river of snot that was pouring from her nose, using a sodden handkerchief. Aidy's heart went out to her. She was desperate to gather the young girl in to her arms and offer her comfort, but it would have to wait until the Vicar had finished talking.

Next to her stood Marion, eight years old, chubby and mousy haired. She was clutching her favourite doll which had long since lost its hair and one of its legs. She was staring into the grave, at the coffin holding their mother. Despite having it explained to her as best they could, she couldn't quite grasp what death actually meant. That she wouldn't physically see her mother again. Marion believed that her mother was asleep inside that box, and when she wasn't tired any more she would get out and come home. How Aidy wished that was in fact the case. Since their mother's death Marion had started to wet herself, mostly during the night but occasionally throughout the day too. The fact that she now had her legs crossed made Aidy fervently hope the child could hold herself until the ceremony ended, and avoid the acute embarrassment any failure would bring.

The girls' grey school skirts and white blouses might have been cast-offs from the better off, acquired from a charitable organisation for a few coppers by her mother, but both of them looked smart and tidy, and a credit to the mother who had done her very best for them.

Aidy then cast a glance at ten-year-old George, his usually unruly brown hair parted down the middle and flattened down with help from Arch's Erasmic hair cream. The slogan on the label boasted it would keep every hair in place, but it was failing to do so as strands of George's were sticking up already on his crown, like a peacock's tail fanning out. To outsiders he came across as a hard nut who was not afraid to use his fists in defence of family, friends or himself, but to his family George was a sensitive, thoughtful and honest boy, fiercely protective of them all.

Aidy knew he felt uncomfortable wearing the borrowed suit very kindly offered to them for the day by a neighbour, Miriam Liberman, who was well aware George wouldn't possess one. The suit had been made for her son for his Bar Mitzvah last year by a kindly uncle on her husband's side, himself a tailor with a shop on Cheapside in the market place. The son was shorter than George by a couple of inches and not as broad, so the jacket was tight and the trouser legs finished above his ankles, but regardless Aidy felt his mother would have been proud of how handsome he looked. His face was mask-like, however, and Aidy knew that it was taking him all his strength not to break down in front of the rest of the congregation. Men didn't cry in public. In George's opinion he was a man, so he didn't cry either.

Next to George stood Bertha, Arch's arm hooked through hers for support. Despite the heat she was dressed in her best black woollen coat and twill dress underneath, thick black woollen stockings and sturdy black lace-up shoes. Her best black felt hat was on her head, the bunch of plastic cherries that had decorated it removed for this sober occasion.

Arch, as always, looked striking in the only suit he possessed. He'd last worn it for their own wedding five years ago, totally unaware that the next time he'd put it on it would be for such a sad event.

The sudden death of his mother-in-law had come as such a shock to Arch that he hadn't given a thought to how Aidy's grandmother and her siblings were going to continue without her. Aidy had outlined her own plan to him at her first opportunity the next day. Like herself, she knew it wouldn't be easy for Arch, abandoning the home they had worked so hard to make nice, hoping eventually to raise their own family in it when Arch finally got his promotion at work. But in the circumstances there was nothing else they could do. He had put his arms around her and assured her that he would support her as best he could in anything she undertook. Family was family. She had never loved him as much as she had done then.

Having recovered sufficiently from the 'help' Bertha had given her for her supposed bout of constipation, Pat Nelson stood next to her son, black dress pulling tightly over her huge bulk. It was not yet apparent whether she was put out by the fact that only one of the suggestions – or, in truth, instructions – she had issued for the funeral had been taken up, that of Arch being chief pall-bearer, but Aidy knew she would certainly let them know if she was displeased, at the first opportunity. She appeared to be grief stricken but Aidy knew she had been jealous of Jessie on many counts: her still youthful looks, her likeable disposition, and because Jessie lived in a bigger house in what the locals perceived to be a better part of the area. So in truth, Jessie's death was no real loss to Pat, and knowing her greediness as she did, Aidy knew her mother-in-law would be desperate for the service to end and the wake to start so she could take her fill of the food that was on offer. Arch's work-shy father hadn't come, but then Aidy had known that he wouldn't as the time of the funeral overlapped with the beginning of the lunchtime session at his local pub. He'd put in an appearance at the wake, she had no doubt of that, as there was beer on offer for the men.

At least fifty people besides themselves were present. Jessie having been as popular as she was, it was known that her funeral would be well attended, but even so none of the family had expected quite so many to take the trouble to pay their respects, not forgetting there were also those who would have liked to have attended but couldn't, due to the fact they couldn't afford to lose pay taking time off work.

Since word had got out of the death, a steady stream of people had called at the house to express their condolences. Aidy and Bertha had lost count of the number of pots of tea they had mashed between them and packets of Rich Tea biscuits they had offered. It was comforting to know that so many people were genuinely mourning the loss of Jessie, but all the family would be glad when today was over so they could begin the long process of rebuilding their own lives without her.

A short while later, as the bereft family made their way back to the house followed by the rest of the congregation, Aidy noticed Marion no longer had her doll with her. 'What happened to Janet?' she asked.

Looking up at her with large innocent eyes, Marion said, 'I didn't like the thought of Mam being down there all on her own, so when no one was looking I threw Janet in to keep her company 'til she wakes up. She'll give me Janet back when she comes back home, won't she?'

Swallowing down a lump in her throat, Aidy tenderly patted the top of her sister's head. 'That was a lovely thing to do, Marion. Mam knows how much you love Janet, and I'm sure she'll look after her for you.'

An hour later back at the house, showing no sign that she'd recently suffered a stomach upset so bad it had seen her virtually commandeering the outside privy for the last three days, Pat Nelson barged her way through the throng of mourners, packed solid in the small back room and kitchen, and advanced towards Aidy. Pat was balancing a plate piled high with food in one hand and a brimming glass of sherry in the other. Despite the fact that Aidy was already in conversation with Miriam Liberman, expressing her gratitude for the use of her son's suit which she would endeavour to return in the condition it was lent in, Pat rudely interrupted with, 'You didn't use Snow's for the funeral like I suggested.' It was very apparent she wasn't happy about this fact.

Politely excusing herself from Miriam and taking a deep breath to steel herself for the confrontation she knew was to come, Aidy turned to Pat and responded lightly, 'Gran and I liked Clatteridge's better, Mrs Nelson.'

She gave a haughty sniff. 'Jessie's death policy must have paid out well if yer've got money to throw around. I know Clatteridge's are much dearer than Snow's. The money you'd have saved using Snow's, you could have put to good use.'

The truth was all the firms had quoted around the same price but Aidy and Bertha had found the people at Clatteridge's to be the most pleasant and understanding to deal with, which was why she and her gran had settled for them. 'Mam's policy was to pay for her funeral, Mrs Nelson, and that's what we used the money for.'

Pat cocked an eyebrow in surprise and said sardonically, 'Well, as long as you're happy yer got what yer paid for. I know a bloke that works for Snow's, and as yer related to me he'd have made it his business to mek sure you did.'

Oh, so that was why Pat had wanted to insist they use Snow's. She would have got a backhander for bringing in their custom.

Aidy's mother-in-law rammed a whole sausage roll into her mouth. Not caring that she was spitting out pastry flakes, she said, 'I'm glad to see Arch was chief

82

bearer, but his brothers are really hurt you shunned them.'

Through clenched teeth Aidy responded, 'We never shunned them, Mrs Nelson. Mam was very fond of the lads we asked, had watched them grow up from babies, and they were fond of her in return. I know she would have wanted them to be given the opportunity of being her pall-bearers, and they'd have been upset if they hadn't been.'

Pat pulled a face. 'Well, to me, family comes first. And as my Arch is married to you, *we* are family.' She then prodded her fork into a piece of ham on her plate. 'I see you didn't bother with ham on the bone then? And I can't find any tongue . . .'

'It *is* ham on the bone, Mrs Nelson, only we got the butcher to slice it up for us, for convenience. Mam didn't like tongue. The food we chose was what she liked.'

'Like she's here to eat it!' Pat scoffed. Then added, 'I was looking forward to that tongue. What butcher did you use?

'The same one Mam always used. Jones.'

'Oh, him,' Pat snorted. 'Wouldn't touch his stuff meself. More gristle and fat than meat, what he serves up. It's cheap, I suppose, though. You can tell this ham's cheap, can't yer? It's not got much taste. Harry Worth would have seen you right, once you told him I'd sent yer. And it's a pity you didn't ask my Jim to get the booze for yer. One of his mates is a drayman. He could have got you three barrels of beer for less than the price you paid for one. If you paid for good sherry as well then you've been done. This stuff is barrel that's been put into bottles.'

The sherry was certainly not barrel but best Cyprus, and Pat knew that it was. Her unwarranted petty complaints were just because she was fuming she had lost out on her backhanders from the suppliers she had instructed them to use, and besides couldn't brag to the rest of the mourners that it was she who had arranged it all. It was taking all Aidy's will-power now not to snatch the plate of food back off Pat, *and* her glass of sherry, and tell her to leave, but she would not cause a scene at her own mother's wake. Evenly she said, 'Do excuse me, Mrs Nelson, but I need to thank people for coming.'

As Aidy was walking away from her she heard Pat say to another mourner: '*You off? Oh, 'course, husband's dinner to get. Well, I must be off meself as soon as I've finished me food. Packing to do. . .*'

Aidy frowned thoughtfully. Had her in-laws come into money somehow that they could afford a holiday? Pat's part-time job as a lavatory attendant didn't pay much and she was always pleading poverty, hoping to make people feel sorry for her and offer her a handout, which she always snatched before their mind was changed. Her lazy husband hadn't had a paid job for years, due to his supposedly having a bad back from a fall at work, but that didn't seem to stop him from getting to the pub and back or from operating his side line, dealing in scrap metal. Much to their wives' chagrin, the three Nelson sons each handed over a pound a week between them to their parents, even though they could not really afford to do so, but at least it ensured Pat and Jim's rent was paid, with a little left over so they didn't end up having to live with any of their offspring. Aidy wondered now if Arch or his two brothers knew of their parents' windfall.

She felt a hand grab her arm. It was Bertha's. 'I was just making my way over to rescue you since it was obvious to me that whatever Pat Nelson was saying to you, it was annoying you.'

Aidy sighed. 'Gran, the only complaint she *hasn't* got about the arrangements we made for Mam's funeral is that Arch was chief pall-bearer.' Through the crowd she spotted Arch's father knocking back a pint next to the table holding the barrel and bottles of sherry. 'I know for a fact that's Jim's fifth. I hope he's going to have the decency to leave some of the beer for the other men. Anyway, we haven't to put up with either of them much longer. They're leaving soon, to do their packing.'

Bertha frowned, bemused. 'Packing?'

Aidy shrugged. 'I overheard Pat telling Maud Gates

– I can only think to go on holiday. God knows where they got the money from. Mr Nelson must have come up trumps on a bet, that's all I can think of.'

Bertha scowled. 'I don't suppose it entered their heads that their family could use some of their good fortune, by way of repayment for what those lads have given them over the years,' she said scathingly. 'Still, look on the bright side, ducky. With them away, it gives you a rest from them coming around cadging whatever they can off you.'

Aidy smiled. 'And I'll welcome that. Have you seen the kids, Gran?'

'It's after four so school's finished. I expect they're all off playing with their friends. Best thing for 'em. Marion caught me in the kitchen a bit ago. Seems her friend Elsie has lent Marion her best doll until her mam wakes up from her sleep, comes home and gives her Janet back.'

Tears glinted in Aidy's eyes. 'Oh, Gran, I don't know how she's going to take it when she finally realises Mam is never going to wake up.'

Bertha patted Aidy's hand. 'We'll be here, lovey. Me and you together will see her through.'

Aidy flashed her a wan smile. 'That was so thoughtful of Elsie, giving Marion her doll.'

Bertha chuckled. 'The same Elsie that thumped her last week 'cos Marion wouldn't share her Sat'day penny sweets with her 'cos Elsie wouldn't share hers with her . . . or summat like that anyway. I wouldn't be surprised if the doll's back with Elsie at bedtime, the way those two fall in and out with each other on a daily basis.'

To Aidy's surprise, Bertha then stepped behind her, seeming to be using her for cover, and Aidy spun round to ask, 'What are you doing, Gran?'

'Hiding from Ivy Ibbotson. Can you believe that today of all days she's badgering me to mix her up a potion, to help draw a nasty boil she's got on her backside?'

'Oh. I wondered why she wouldn't sit down when I offered her a seat a while back.'

Bertha grinned wickedly. 'Well, now yer know why. But some people have no respect, have they? If she doesn't stop pestering me, I'll mix her up summat that'll make the boil grow twice as big! Ah, good, Nell Wright has collared her. She'll keep her ages, boring her to death about her new grandson, so I'm safe for a bit.'

Bertha bustled off. Aidy spotted Arch coming in from the kitchen then, carrying clean glasses which several benevolent neighbours had washed up and dried. He didn't see her at first but she made sure he did by catching his arm. 'Arch, can you make sure your father leaves some beer for the other men, please?' she whispered. 'He's standing guard over the barrel like a sentry. Not that I'm watching him, but he's had five glasses to my knowledge . . . and it's anyone's guess how many he's had *not* to my knowledge.'

'I'll go and have a quiet word with him.' Not that he'll take any notice of me, thought Arch. 'It's been a good turn-out, hasn't it, love?' he asked her.

'Yes, it has, but I won't be sorry to see them go.' Arch made to continue on his way, when Aidy stalled him by asking. 'Oh, have your parents had a windfall?'

He looked surprised. 'Not to my knowledge. But then, if they had, they wouldn't tell me or my brothers in case we demanded back some of the money they've fleeced us of over the years. What makes you think they have?'

'Just something your mam said about getting home soon to do the packing.'

'Oh! That's not packing for a holiday . . .'

'Packing for what then?' He seemed reluctant to tell her but it was obvious to Aidy he knew what for. 'Arch?' she urged him.

He swallowed hard. 'I haven't had a chance to tell you. I haven't found the right time, with all that's been going on.'

He looked mortally uncomfortable and she very strongly suspected that whatever he'd not had a chance to tell her, she wasn't going to like. 'Tell me what, Arch?' she demanded.

He gulped again. 'Well . . . er . . . they're packing to . . . er . . . move in here.'

Aidy's jaw dropped. Astounded, she blurted out, 'Your mother and father are *moving in with us*!' Her face then darkened thunderously as she hissed, 'They do that over my dead body! I can just about stomach your mother in small doses, but as for living with us . . . ! Same goes for Gran and the kids. I'm not sure where me and you are going to sleep yet. If your parents have been evicted for whatever reason, then they'll have to go cap in hand to one of your brothers 'cos they ain't coming *here* to sponge off us, not even for a few days, and that's final, Arch.'

'Ah, but, Aidy . . .'

'No, Arch.'

She made to walk away from him but he thrust the glasses he was holding on a mourner by him, asking him to deliver them to the drinks table, then caught Aidy's arm, pulling her back to him. 'My mother's only thinking of us. She's trying to help, so we can carry on with our own lives.'

Aidy was staring wild eyed at him. Pat Nelson didn't think of anyone else but herself. Whatever her reasons were for moving in with them, they were for her own benefit and no one else's. Grabbing Arch's arm, Aidy dragged him through the throng and outside into the backyard, hopefully out of earshot of any eavesdroppers. Letting go of his arm, she fixed him with her eyes and demanded, 'Your mother is thinking of us in what way, Arch?'

He eyed her hesitantly. 'Well, it's a huge responsibility we're taking on, looking after your gran and the kids, so that's why Mam's kindly offered to move in, so her and Dad can take care of them instead and we can go back to living our own lives.'

Aidy looked blankly at him for a moment, then the real truth behind Pat's offer struck her and she gave a scoffing laugh. 'Your mother must think I'm doo-lally not to know what her true aim is! She's always hankered after this house. She was always passing snide comments to my mam, such as it didn't seem fair she had a house like this when she'd no man supporting her, and insinuating Mam must have had something underhand going on with the landlord and *that* was how she could afford the rent. She never gave my mam any credit for hard work and determination in keeping a decent roof over our heads.

'This offer is your mother's sneaky way of getting her hands on this house. She's well aware that within weeks . . . no, I'm being generous . . . days or hours even, the kids and Gran would come running to us, begging us to take them in, not able to stand Pat's domineering ways. She'd turn them into her slaves, running after her and your dad. And that's not to mention she'd be looking to us to stump up the money for Gran and the kids' keep. She's got some nerve, Arch! Now go and tell we won't be accepting her generous offer.'

'Oh, I see Arch is breaking the good news to yer.' Pat had come out to join them. She was looking annoyed. 'But I told yer not to bother Aidy with this until after the funeral. Huh, well, it's done now.' Before either of them could get a word in, she then addressed Aidy. 'There's no need to thank me. It's the least we can do in the circumstances.' To them both she said, 'Dad's staying here, said it's not seemly we should both leave early as we're family, but I'm off to start packing.' Truth was Jim Nelson would not budge for any reason until there was not a drop of beer left in the barrel. 'Wouldn't hurt the kids to come and give me a hand, 'specially the two older ones. Find 'em, Arch, and send them round. I'll get it all done as quick as I can and then yer can help us settle in before you need to get yerselves back to yer own house. It's been a long day and you'll be wanting an early night.'

'Now look, Mrs Nelson . . .' Aidy began.

Pat put up a warning hand and interjected, 'As I said, there's no need for thanks. We're family, least we can do.' With that she heaved her bulk the short distance to the back gate and disappeared through it out into the jetty beyond.

Aidy glared in annoyance at her husband and told

him, 'You'd best go after your mother. Tell her she's wasting her time packing.'

With that she spun on her heel and marched away back into the house, leaving a worried-looking Arch staring after her.

CHAPTER FIVE

Bertha was in the kitchen drying dishes when Aidy found her. She took one look at her grand-daughter's face and knew something had greatly upset her. Discarding the pot she was drying, along with the cloth, on the draining board, she caught Aidy's arm, pulling her to a halt. Aware they were not alone in the kitchen, she whispered, 'What's up, ducky?'

Bertha would be furious herself when she learned of Pat's devious plan to get her hands on this house. But there was no need for her grandmother to know now as Aidy had put a stop to the plan. 'Nothing, Gran, I'm just tired,' she told her, which was actually true so she wasn't lying.

But Bertha knew her granddaughter well and wasn't convinced. 'You sure that's all?'

'I'm sure, Gran. Now stop fussing.'

Bertha still wasn't convinced. She wasn't that short sighted she could mistake an annoyed expression for a tired one. 'Mmm . . . well . . . have it your own way.

I'm tired too. Although I'm glad they all turned out for Jessie, I'll be glad when they go.'

Six o'clock saw the last of the mourners take their leave and the bereft family was finally on their own, to start rebuilding their lives. Well, all but one member of it. Arch was missing.

He'd had plenty of time to pay a visit to his mother. As he hadn't come back, Aidy was convinced he was feeling mortally embarrassed that he had ever allowed her to suggest her plan, and needed to get up the courage to face his wife with an apology. He'd be in the pub, gaining that courage through a couple of pints.

Arch *had* been to the pub, but it wasn't the courage to face his wife he needed. He was preparing himself for a scene with Pat. Being raised by a mother like that had made Arch a strong-minded man who could stand his ground with anyone ... except his mother, that was. Despite his no longer living under her roof, Pat still managed to keep a controlling influence on him that he just couldn't bring himself to shake off. Arch himself understood why. Although he would never admit it, his own mother terrified him. Memories of the many thrashings he'd received as a child whenever he had dared to cross her were still very vivid in his mind. Despite the fact he was now a man, Pat still treated him as she'd always done ... woe betide him if he didn't do her bidding. The thought of being on the receiving end of her wrath again and possibly suffering a battering was torture to Arch. He couldn't bear the thought of anyone knowing how he'd received his injuries. Not even Aidy.

Pat was incensed by the news her son had just hesitantly delivered. Pat herself had been born the ninth child of fourteen, to a family so poor she'd never had a pair of shoes until she was seven and only then cast-offs given to her by the kindly woman her mother cleaned for . . . before it was discovered that her mam had been thieving and was sacked from her job.

For Pat, though, the utter joy of experiencing her chilblain-riddled feet warmly encased in leather, something she'd only dreamed of before, was to be short lived. Cuddling the shoes protectively to her when she went to sleep that night on the bug-infested flock mattress she shared with four of her sisters, in a room so damp fungi grew on the walls, she awoke the next morning to find them gone. It transpired that her mother had pawned them to pay for the bread and margarine they all ate that morning for breakfast, food that Pat had to fight her siblings for in order to get her share. The loss of those precious shoes was devastating to her. It was to fuel within her an unbridled determination that, when she grew up, never would she be in such dire straits she had to pawn a pair of children's shoes in order to feed her family.

Unfortunately for Pat, though, she didn't possess the basic intelligence to realise that working her way out of poverty was the way of securing a better way of life, not marrying the first man who showed an interest in her who had a regular job, and getting herself pregnant to make sure she landed him. Jim Nelson's wage for his labouring job might have seemed a fortune to her while they were courting as, unbeknown to her, he only handed over to his weak-minded, widowed mother the smallest amount he could get away with, squandering the rest on his own enjoyment. In Pat's eyes, anyone who could afford the price of a few drinks three nights a week was rich indeed, but when it came to funding the rent and paying for life's necessities, Jim's wage went nowhere near far enough.

To her utter dismay, marriage had brought no improvement in Pat's life whatsoever. She was quick to realise there was not much hope of any change in it either. Jim Nelson rapidly proved he hadn't got it in him to provide for her any more than he was already doing, no matter how much she screamed and bullied him. Visits to the pawn with anything she could lay her hands on were as much a part of Pat's life as they always had been, as was begging for handouts from benevolent people. Now, at the age of forty-three, her determination to secure a better life for herself than her parents had had was starting to fade.

But it was to be resurrected by the death of her youngest son's mother-in-law.

This was her chance to leapfrog out of their paltry, two-bedroomed slum dwelling in the poorest street in the district, straight into Jessie's well-maintained three-bedroomed family home. That would be a triumph indeed for Pat, and she was determined to achieve her aim, no matter what.

When making her offer, she had bargained on the fact that her daughter-in-law would be so bowed down by grief and faltering at the thought of taking on her siblings and grandmother, she would eagerly accept. Pat had not considered that her offer would be turned down by Aidy. How she detested that girl! Her two other sons had married the type of women who, on first introduction to Pat, had immediately allowed her to intimidate them. Consequently both had since danced to her tune, for fear of upsetting her and the consequences. But Aidy was not the sort to allow another woman to dominate her life. From the very start, she had proved a match for Pat. Their whole relationship was one long battle of wills and, much to Pat's fury, it was Aidy who always managed to win out in the end.

But this move to Jessie's might be Pat's only chance of ever improving her lot, and she wasn't about to give it up without one hell of a fight.

Fury blazing in her eyes, she banged one fist hard on the table, bellowing at Arch, 'What d'yer mean, that wife of yours is turning down me offer?'

He took a deep breath, facing his nemesis the courage those two pints had momentarily given him rapidly vaporising. Tremulously he responded, 'Look, Mam, it's not like Aidy doesn't appreciate the sacrifice you're prepared to make for us. When I told her she was ... well ... speechless at your kindness.' Which was true, she had been speechless, but at the gall of it. 'But it's like this, you see. She'd promised her mam that if anything should happen to her, then Aidy would make sure *she* took good care of her gran and the kids.'

'And that promise means more to her than the promise she made you when she married yer, always to put you first?' his mother screeched back.

'No, 'course it doesn't. But we promised to do right by each other through good and bad, so I have stand by Aidy through this bad time of hers, don't I?'

Pat wagged one fat finger at him. 'And, like I pointed out to you when I first put me idea to you, do you really want to take on the responsibility of raising someone else's family? I'll tell you again, as it seems that thick head of yours ain't took it in ...

you go along with this and you'll never have any money to call yer own. By the time yer've forked out for keeping that lot out yer wage, you'll have n'ote left, not even a few coppers for a pint each week. Those clothes yer wearing will have to last for years. You'll never have any peace and quiet with them noisy kids, and Bertha Rider might get around all right on her pins just now, but what about when she can't and is housebound? Then yer won't even be able to speak to Aidy in private, except in yer bedroom, without *her* ear-wigging. And when she gets to that stage, Aidy will have to give up working to look after her, and then yer won't have *her* wage coming in.

'You was hoping to start a family of yer own some day. Well, yer can kiss that goodbye for the foreseeable future. By the time yer can afford to, you'll both be too old. You'll be expected to fork out for those two gels' weddings when they get married . . .' Pat stopped her tirade, having temporarily run out of obstacles to frighten her son with. Her mind whirled frantically. She had already given up the tenancy on this house, bragged to all the neighbours that the Nelsons were moving upmarket, so there was no going back. Thankfully a couple more obstacles then presented themselves 'And what about . . .'

He snapped at her, 'All right, Mam, you've made your point.' And she certainly had. Arch thought the world of his wife's family and had been fully prepared to help Aidy support them, but now, thanks to his mother, it had really hit home just what he was about to undertake and he wasn't at all sure if he really wanted to abandon his own plans for the future in favour of the bleak picture Pat had just painted.

Pat detested being interrupted when she was in full flight, and particularly in this instance when she was so very desperate to manipulate her son into doing her bidding. Before he had a chance to try to avoid her, she lunged at him and slapped him full force across his head, screaming at him, 'Don't you *dare* tell me to shut up!'

Rubbing his smarting head and fearing another slap was about to follow, Arch cried out, 'I'm sorry, Mam, I didn't mean to.'

'I should think not. Now, you get back to that fucking mouthy wife of yours . . .'

Before he could control himself, Arch interjected, 'Don't call Aidy that, Mam.'

The feared second slap came then, but much harder than the first, leaving a handprint on the side of his face. 'I'll call her what I bloody like! To me she *is* a fuckin' mouthy bitch. She's no respect for me at all as her mother-in-law, looks down her nose at me she does, and she ain't no better than I am. Now go be a man for a change. Tell her you ain't moving into her mother's house and working your guts out to keep them all, just to please her. I'm gonna get on with me packing while yer gone. I thought I told you to find the kids and send 'em round to help me . . . obviously you disobeyed me again. I'll deal with you later over that. And make sure you hurry back so you can help get our stuff round there. I wanna be moved in tonight, not termorra.'

Pat flashed a scathing glance at her hotchpotch of shabby furniture. 'New tenants can do what they like with this lot of old rubbish. I'll be glad to see the back of it.' She gave a malicious grin. 'Me new house is fully furnished with better stuff than this so I don't need none of this old crap, do I? That house is a palace in every way compared to this one. Oh, it'll be like living in heaven! Folks around here better start showing me more respect or I'll give 'em what for.'

The back door was heard to open then and seconds later the burly figure of Jim Nelson appeared in the doorway. He was visibly drunk. 'We ready for the off then?' He cast his bleary eyes over the filthy, cluttered room, and gave a loud belch. 'Space to stretch me legs out in our new place. Yer can hardly swing a cat in here.'

Pat turned on him then. 'If you'd ever got off yer fat, lazy arse and got yerself a decent job, we'd have had a house like we're moving into years ago,' she spat. Then she commanded, 'Get that old trunk out from the cellar so we can pack our clothes in it. Now, not termorra.' She addressed her son next. 'What you standing there for, like the village idiot? Order them kids to get their backsides round here to give us a hand, and tell that wife of yours what's what. And don't stand for no nonsense off her this time.'

A few streets away, cradling a cup of tea between her gnarled hands, Bertha issued a weary sigh as she sank down on a worn armchair by the range in the back room. She kicked off her shoes to reveal her misshapen feet and sighed, 'Ah, that's better.'

Marion, now changed out of her school clothes into shabbier playing-out ones, was sitting on the clippy rug by her gran's chair absently staring into the fire. Leaning over, the old lady ruffled the top of her head. 'You all right, chick?'

She shook her head. 'No, Gran, I ain't. Elsie took her doll back. She's spiteful, so she is. I'm never talking to her again.'

Bertha wasn't surprised to hear this. 'What's gone off between you both this time?'

'She was mad 'cos I never took her some cake from Mam's do. I told her there weren't any left 'cos Mrs Nelson took the last bit.' Marion turned her head and looked up at her grandmother, her own face filled with disgust. 'She took the last *three* pieces, Gran. Mrs Mullet went to get a piece and Mrs Nelson pushed her out of the way and put the three last pieces on her own plate. Arch's mam is so greedy! Anyway, Elsie didn't believe me that there weren't no cake left, said I just forgot to take her some.

'I don't care she's took her doll back, I didn't like it anyway. It hadn't got any eyes 'cos Elsie poked 'em out . . . her mam smacked her for doing that . . . and its hair was all tatty *and* its clothes, so I was gonna give it her back anyway.'

Bertha ruffled the girl's hair again. 'Oh, well, that's all right then. At least Elsie taking it back saved you doing that.'

Marion's little face puckered. 'But that means I won't get to sleep, Gran. I always slept with Janet, didn't I?'

'Yes, you did. Are you sorry you gave Janet to your mam now, to look after?'

Marion said with conviction, 'Oh, no, Gran. I'm glad I gave Janet to her, to keep her company 'til she wakes up and comes home. I'll get her back then, won't I?' She shot her grandmother a worried look. 'But I just don't know how I'm gonna sleep without a dolly to cuddle.'

'Oh, I see.' A vision of a long-limbed, threadbare rag doll, sprang to Bertha's mind. 'Oh, but what about Flossie?'

'Flossie?' Marion queried.

'You can't have forgotten about Flossie, love. Aidy

bought her for you the day you were born. You and Flossie went everywhere together until you got Janet a couple of Christmases ago.'

Her eyes lit up. 'Oh, yes, Flossie!' she cried, jumping up to clap her chubby hands in delight. Then her face fell. 'I dunno where she is, though.'

'I do.'

'You do, Gran?'

Bertha grinned mischievously at her. 'Your gran knows everything, doesn't she?'

In all seriousness Marion responded, 'That's 'cos you've got eyes in the back of yer head, ain't it, Gran?'

Keeping a straight face, Bertha answered, 'That's right. And you just keep remembering that when you're tempted to do summat yer know yer shouldn't. Your mam found Flossie, a few days after you got Janet, soaking wet in the old pram in the yard where you'd left her. What a sorry sight she looked too. Anyway, she gave her a wash, dried her off and sewed her where she needed sewing, and put her for safe-keeping in the bottom of her wardrobe, 'cos she knew one day you'd come looking for her.'

'I'll thank Mam when she comes back,' said Marion, jumping up happily to bound off and retrieve her doll.

With a tear in her eye, Bertha uttered, 'Yes, you do that, lovey.'

Aidy came through, drying her hands on a towel. 'That's the last of the pots put away.'

'Yer should have let me help yer,' her grandmother told her.

'You've done enough today, Gran. Besides, the neighbours, bless them, did most of the clearing up before they all left, so there wasn't much for me to do. Can I get you anything to eat? There's a couple of egg and cress sandwiches left. I've put a damp cloth over them to keep fresh if you fancy those. Everything else is gone, I'm afraid.' She eyed her grandmother in concern. 'You had no breakfast this morning, and I never saw you eating anything at the wake.'

Bertha hadn't. The food had all looked most appetising but she had had an emptiness in her stomach that food would not cure. It would just make her feel sick. Bertha wasn't surprised that, except for a few sandwiches, all the food had disappeared. For many of the folks around these parts, the only time they had a decent feed was at either a wedding or a funeral. Ignoring Aidy's last question so as not to lie to her, she just said, 'I might have a peck at something later.' Then she cast a querying look at the younger woman. 'Come to think on it, I never seen you eat anything. Nor did you have any breakfast.'

That was true. Aidy had had no stomach for food at all today. Just the thought of it had made her feel sick. She didn't want her grandmother worrying about her, though, so fibbed, 'I had my share. Want a fresh cuppa?'

Bertha drained the dregs in her cup and held it out to Aidy, smiling warmly. 'Never say no to a cuppa, yer know that, love. Where's Arch, by the way? I ain't seen him for ages.'

'Oh, he . . . er . . . went to the pub for a pint. He'll be home when he's home. I'll get you that cuppa,' said Aidy, going off into the kitchen.

Bertha looked after her, frowning. She had such a strong feeling that something wasn't quite right between those two. But then, it had been an awful day and none of them was their usual self.

Bertha heard the back door open and bang shut, then heard Aidy say, 'Good God, George, look at the state of you.' She heard Marion's voice too but couldn't quite make out what she was saying. George arrived in the back room then and threw himself down into the armchair opposite his grandmother's. Bertha looked over at him. He looked like he'd been dragged through a hedge backwards and thrown in a muddy puddle. Thankfully he had changed out of the borrowed suit into his old playing-out clothes of a shabby pair of short trousers and a well-worn shirt, patched at the elbows. There was a bruise forming on one cheek and a drying bloody cut on his lip. 'You been fighting, our George?' she challenged him.

It was Aidy who answered. Arriving to stand next to Bertha's chair and stare at her brother, she shot at him, 'Marion has just told me you have been, George. How could you, today of all days? I hope the lad you was fighting with ain't in the same state as you or I'll have his mam round here, playing merry hell, and that's the last thing I need right now. What was it over?' Marion, having come in to stand by her elder sister, went to speak up but Aidy silenced her with: 'I asked George, Marion. Answer me, George, or you'll have a red bum as well as a bloodied lip.'

He knew his sister's threat was no idle one. His head bent, he muttered, 'Arthur Dunn reckons now our mam is dead and we ain't got no dad, me, Betty and Marion are orphans so we'll be going to the children's home. And as Gran's old, she'll be going in the workhouse. He was making Marion cry so I thumped him.'

George jumped up from his chair then and rushed over to Aidy, throwing himself on her. There were tears in his eyes that he was fighting hard to hold back when he lifted his head to look up at her beseechingly. 'We ain't going to an orphanage, are we, Aidy? Please say we ain't?'

Crossing her legs and pressing her head to them, Marion burst into a flood of tears and wailed, 'I don't wanna go, Aidy. Please don't send us.'

Aidy could just picture the other lad goading her

siblings with his taunts. After the day they'd had, it was taking all her strength of mind not to go and seek him out herself and give him a piece of her mind for putting them through this unnecessary anguish, just for the sheer fun of it. Grabbing Marion to her and then hugging both children fiercely, Aidy told them, 'Neither of you is being put in an orphanage and nor is Betty. Gran is certainly *not* going in the workhouse. Do you think I'd ever let that happen to you? Me and Arch will be moving in here to look after you all.'

Wriggling free from her sister's hold, Marion wiped her wet face with the back of her hand. Hopping from one foot to the other, she cried out, 'Really, our Aidy?'

Looking up at her earnestly, George urged, 'Honest?'

Aidy smiled down at them 'Cross me heart and hope to die.' Then she ordered Marion, 'Get to the privy quick, before you have an accident. George, get in the scullery and clean yourself up. I'm going to make a start on your tea. In the meantime, if you're hungry there's some sandwiches left, but make sure you leave some for Betty.' Marion had shot out and George was making his way to the scullery to clean himself up. 'Where is Betty?' she asked him.

He stopped to think for a moment, then continuing on his way told her, 'Last time I saw her, she was sitting on the wall with Mary Riddle and a couple of other gels.'

'Well, when you've cleaned yourself up, you can go and fetch her in.'

A few streets away, Arch was back in the pub, downing his third pint on top of the two he'd had previously to summon up the courage to face his mother. He was now trying to summon up the courage to go and face Aidy and tell her that, despite his best endeavours, his mother wouldn't accept her refusal and Aidy was going to have to dissuade her herself.

Albeit Pat had had her own selfish reasons for picturing his future life, Arch had been in complete turmoil since his mother had made him see what lay ahead for him, should he go along with Aidy's plan and help her care for her family. He hadn't liked what he had envisioned, didn't like the idea of giving up his own home to move into his late mother-in-law's house. Wasn't happy at the thought of never having a penny of his earnings to spare for himself in the future, as it would all be needed to look after others. But he loved Aidy, couldn't bear the thought of not being with her, and if he wanted to stay married to her, it seemed he had no choice but to hide his true feelings and go along with her plan. And, in fairness to her, she had no real choice but to do what she was or she'd condemn her beloved family to lives of hell, being cared for by the authorities. And Aidy would never do that.

But then, just when he had about come to terms with his own fate, out of the blue an idea struck him. It was the perfect solution to the problem of caring for Bertha and the children, and it didn't involve either Aidy and himself or his mother and father. He was surprised Aidy hadn't thought of it herself. A surge of gladness rushed through him. His life with his wife and their own future plans were not going to be abandoned after all. Though his mother wouldn't be happy when she discovered that all her devious planning to get the Greenwood house had been in vain.

He downed the dregs in his glass and left the pub to go and break his brainwave to his wife.

Back in the Greenwood house, George had finished his ablutions. Having forgotten to fetch Betty as Aidy thought he was off doing, he was sitting in an armchair, engrossed in a tattered old copy of a *Triumph* comic he'd borrowed from his mate; Marion was playing with her Shirley Temple cut-out doll on the clippy rug in front of the range, and Bertha was dozing in her chair. Aidy was in the scullery peeling potatoes to cut into chips, pondering whether to fry enough for Arch along with the rest, but deciding to do him fresh when he arrived. As she put the chipped potatoes into the pan of hot fat, she called out, 'Betty, set the table, please.'

There was silence for a moment before George responded, 'Betty ain't here.'

The chips merrily sizzling away, Aidy popped her head around the back-room door and addressed her brother. 'You did fetch her like I asked?'

He dragged his eyes from his comic to stare blankly at her. 'Eh?'

He'd forgotten. Normally she would have given him a reprimand for this lapse but today she could overlook it. 'Go and fetch her now, please.' She heard the back door open. 'Oh, it's all right, she's here.'

Aidy turned around, fully expecting to see her sister and inform her dinner wouldn't be long. Instead she gawped at the sight of her mother-in-law, struggling to heave a heavy, battered suitcase over the threshold.

The appetising aroma of cooking chips wafted up Pat's nostrils. Licking her lips, she said, 'Oh, good, dinner's on the go, I'm starving. Get that young lad of yours to come and gimme a hand, and then he can help Mr Nelson with the trunk. He's borrowed a handcart ter bring that round. He's not far behind me.'

Aidy was staring at her, stupefied. 'But Arch went to tell you that we wouldn't be taking up your offer, Mrs Nelson. We'll be looking after Gran and the kids ourselves.'

The heavy case was half in the doorway and half out. Straightening herself up, Pat looked across at Aidy, irritated that no one was rushing to help her. 'And as I told Arch, yer in mourning, not thinking straight. No one in their right mind would lumber themselves with what you and Arch are about to. Not if they had a get out. Now, get that lad of yours to gimme a hand,' she ordered, bending over to continue with her task of shoving the suitcase into the kitchen.

Aidy felt her hackles rise at this woman's blatant refusal to give up her scheme to get her hands on the house. 'I can assure you, my thinking has never been straighter, Mrs Nelson. Now, as I've already told you, we won't be accepting your offer.'

A desperate Pat was pushing the case with all her might now, clearly of the opinion that once she'd her belongings inside the house, she had every right to remain in it. But the case had caught on the edge of a flagstone and was refusing to budge. In desperation she bellowed, 'Eh up, lad, come and give us a hand.'

Aidy snapped at her, 'You've known him long enough to remember my brother's name is George, Mrs Nelson.'

Still shoving at the obstinate suitcase, Pat snapped back, 'At the moment I don't care what the hell his name is, as long as he gets his arse in here and helps me get this bleddy case inside.'

Hearing Pat's bellowing voice in the room beyond, George and Marion, closely followed by Bertha, appeared in the doorway to find out what was going on. They all looked astonished at the sight that met them.

'Why's Mrs Nelson bringing that case in here?' George asked Aidy.

Pat's head jerked up and she told him, ''Cos me and Arch's dad are moving in to look after you lot, letting Arch and yer sister get on with their own lives, that's why. Now get yerself over here and give me a hand.'

Looks of acute horror at the very thought of the Nelsons moving in, let alone looking after them, filled the faces of Bertha, George and Marion.

'This true?' a mortified Bertha demanded of her granddaughter.

'I ain't staying here with *her*,' cried George.

'Don't make us, Aidy,' pleaded Marion.

Pat scowled across at them. 'Ungrateful lot! Well, that's what's happening so yer'd better all get used to the idea.'

Aidy hurled back at her, 'That's *not* what's happening, Mrs Nelson.' She turned to address her family then. 'You have my word that Mr and Mrs Nelson are not moving in. There's been a misunderstanding and I'm just putting Mrs Nelson right. It's me and Arch who'll be taking care of you all.'

Glaring at Aidy, Pat barked at her, 'You seem to think my son is happy to go along with flogging his guts out to keep your family, but I can tell you, he ain't.' She heard the click of the back gate and spun her head to see Arch framed in the gateway, looking mortified to find his mother here before he could warn his wife that she was still persisting in her 'offer'. He'd also been hoping to inform Aidy of his own proposed solution to their problem without his mother being present; it was his idea and he would suffer her wrath as a result.

Pat said to Aidy, 'Here he is now so yer can ask him yerself.' She then shouted to Arch, 'Get over here and tell this wife of yours you ain't prepared to take on her family. Today not termorra!' she commanded him. When Pat saw he wasn't budging, she stomped across to him, grabbed his arm and dragged him back with her to stand before his wife at the back door, urging him, 'Tell her, I said.'

Arch was very conscious of Aidy's questioning eyes boring into him. He swallowed hard, flashing a worried glance at his mother. He could see the look in her eyes, daring him to voice anything that would jeopardise her move into this house. He looked down at the ground, rocking on his feet, and chose his words carefully. 'Well, Mam did point out a few things I hadn't considered that . . . er . . .'

'That what, Arch?' Aidy urged him.

'Scared the shit out of him,' erupted Pat. 'You caught him unawares when yer first told him yer intention of looking after yer family. But now he's had time to realise just what he's taking on, he don't wanna go ahead.'

Aidy snapped at her, 'I'm sure my husband is capable of telling me himself what he feels, Mrs Nelson.'

Pat retaliated, 'Well, obviously he ain't or he would have afore now. Poor lad poured his heart out to me. Some marriage you've got when yer husband is frightened to tell yer how he really feels. So I've no choice but to.' She gave Arch a push on his back. 'Go on, tell her what I'm saying is true.' Before he could utter a word, she wagged a fat finger at Aidy and explained: 'Now listen, and listen good – my Arch don't wanna tek on someone else's family. Your duty is to your husband. What he says goes.'

'Well, that's rich, coming from the likes of you, Pat Nelson! Your husband doesn't get any say whatsoever in what goes on in his house,' piped up Bertha, unable to contain herself any longer.

Outraged, Pat completely forgot it was in her best interests to present a false picture of herself as a warm, loving woman who'd care for her daughter-in-law's family like they were the most precious people in the world to her . . . at least until she'd got her feet under the table . . . and bellowed back, 'Who asked you to stick yer interfering nose in, you wizened old crone?'

Outraged that anyone was addressing his beloved grandmother in such a way, George's temper flared and he erupted at Pat: 'Don't you dare speak to my gran like that, you fat old bag!'

Clinging to her grandmother, Marion started crying.

A stricken Arch desperately wanted to come to the defence of his wife and her family while at the same time he dreaded going against his mother and suffering the repercussions in front of them all. He was caught between the devil and the deep blue sea.

Pat was glaring furiously at George for what he'd said to her. Trying to squeeze past her case, one hand outstretched to slap him, she hissed, 'Why, you little . . .'

Aidy's own temper flared then. Shielding her brother, she told her mother-in-law, 'You lay one finger on my brother and I won't be responsible for my actions, Mrs Nelson. And I won't stand for you speaking to my grandmother like that either.'

Pat's eyes blazed at Aidy. 'You should remember who you're speaking to, lady. I'm yer mother-in-law. Now I'll speak to anyone how I bleddy well like . . .'

Aidy folded her arms and took a stance. 'Not on my doorstep, Mrs Nelson. So I'd be obliged if you'd remove yourself from it. If you thought for a minute

I would even consider you moving in here to care for my family, then you were quite wrong.' She addressed Arch. 'We obviously can't talk while your mother is present. Will you help her take her belongings back to her own house and we'll sort this out when you come back.'

The back gate opened then and Betty came tumbling through it. She looked bemused at the scene before her and worriedly yelled over to Aidy, 'What's going on, our Sis?'

Aidy called back to her, 'Get yourself in here now.'

By her tone of voice Betty knew better than to delay. Scuttling across the yard, she side-stepped Arch then squashed herself past Pat, which was no mean feat as the bulky woman practically filled the doorway. Betty clambered over the suitcase to join her gran and siblings.

Pat was livid that her plan to elevate herself had fallen foul of the obstinate madam before her. But all was not quite lost yet. She still had one ace up her sleeve. She snarled at Aidy, 'My son has said all he's gonna say to you on this subject. Get it through your thick head that he don't wanna become a father to them kids, or bankroll them and that old cow either.' There was a malicious smirk on her face when she added, 'Yer can't manage to do it yerself without Arch's wage packet, can you? You'll soon come running back to me, begging to take up my offer.' She demanded of Arch, 'Get me case.' She saw him start to speak to Aidy and, clenching one fat fist, shook it at him menacingly. 'I said, get me case!'

Arch couldn't bring himself to look at Aidy, so ashamed was he of his mother's appalling behaviour in her quest to get her own way. But, far worse than that, he was ashamed of not being man enough to stand up to Pat in front of his wife and her family. How he was ever going to regain their respect after this, he had no idea. And he still hadn't had a chance to suggest his own answer to the problem of just who was going to care for the kids and Gran to Aidy yet.

He knew his mother well enough to realise that until she'd got her way she would be keeping a watchful eye on him, to stop him acting behind her back but she couldn't watch him all the time and at the first opportunity he would attempt to sort out this mess with Aidy.

He grabbed the handle of Pat's case and heaved it off the doorstep, struggling down the yard with it and disappearing down the jetty.

Before she too went through the back gate, Pat shouted back to Aidy, 'When yer ready to accept me offer, yer know where yer can find me. I'll give yer a fortnight at the most before you realise just what yer teking on and come crawling.'

Pat and Arch met up with Jim Nelson in the jetty.

Temporarily parking the handcart laden with their heavy, battered trunk, he wiped trickles of sweat off his brow with the back of one hand and eyed them both in confusion as they arrived to join him.

Before he could enquire what was going on, his wife bellowed at him, 'Turn around, we're off back home. Only temporarily, mind. It won't tek that madam long to realise the big error she's made, trying to do it all herself.'

Jim gawped at her. 'Oh, but we can't go back home. The new tenants have already started moving in.'

'Well, they'll just have to bleddy well move out again.'

Jim looked worried. 'Even if yer got them to, Pat, I doubt the landlord would let you stay after what you said to him when yer gave him notice.'

She pulled a face. Jim had made a good point. She hadn't held back from venting her feelings to the landlord over what she perceived as his failings during the years she had been renting his hovel. Besides that she was behind with the rent, owing money which her sons had actually given her but which she'd squandered on other things rather than their accommodation. Even if the landlord did agree to their returning, he would insist they clear the arrears off first, which she'd no hope of doing. Pat said to her son, 'Looks like we'll be staying with you 'til that wife of yours comes to her senses. Hope yer've got summat tasty in fer dinner.'

Arch froze. The thought of living under the same roof as his parents, even for one night, was sheer living hell to him. One night was all he intended putting up with them. This time tomorrow night, he and Aidy would be back together under the same roof, he was determined.

CHAPTER SIX

A good twenty minutes after Arch and his parents had departed, Aidy was still standing at the back door, blindly staring down the small yard. Her mind was refusing to accept what had just happened. That her husband, the one person she had believed would stand by her through anything, was really letting her down at a time when she had never needed his support more ... Worse than that for Aidy was the fact that Arch hadn't said one word in his own defence to his mother when she had been acting like he was a mere boy, and neither had he intervened when she had been using bullying tactics while dealing with his wife and her family. Aidy had long known Arch feared upsetting his mother, bowing to her demands whether he wanted to or not. She had always put that down to his respect for her; after all, Pat was his mother. But after tonight she realised that wasn't the case at all. Arch was terrified of his own mother, to the extent of standing by and doing nothing while she unjustly abused his wife and her bereaved family.

She felt a hand on her arm and turned her head to see her gran looking worriedly at her.

'I've mashed you a cuppa, love,' Bertha told her. 'Come and sit down and drink it before it gets cold. I've fed the kids and packed 'em off upstairs for an early night.' She cupped Aidy's elbow, urging her, 'Come on in, love.'

Aidy had been so consumed by her own raging thoughts she hadn't been aware that Bertha had been busying herself, taking over in the house, or that the children had been helping her by going without a fuss off to bed. Silently she made her way into the back room and sat down in an armchair, accepting the sweetened cup of tea her grandmother handed her.

Now, settled in the armchair opposite, Bertha was looking over at her gravely. In a soft, apologetic voice, she began, 'I'm so sorry I'm such a burden to yer, lovey. As if you haven't got enough on yer hands with the kids as it is.'

Aidy's head jerked up. In no uncertain terms she told her, 'You are not a burden, Gran. Never have been, never will be. So you can stop thinking like that.'

Despite the comfort of these words, Bertha didn't feel any better about herself. She damned her own ageing body for not allowing her to fend for herself, financially and for not being able to take the burden off Aidy and Arch by caring for the children unaided. 'Look, I'm sure none of what Pat Nelson said about Arch was true, Aidy. I expect he'll be round any minute now to assure you of that himself.'

Aidy gave a heavy sigh, the sorrow she was inwardly suffering reflected in her face. As if every word was taking her a great effort to enunciate, she muttered, 'It won't make any difference to me if he does, Gran.'

Bertha's aged face screwed up in bewilderment. 'Why won't it make any difference?'

Shoulders sagging in despair, Aidy uttered, 'Oh, Gran, it hurts me so much that Arch never stood up for us when his mother was being abusive or tried to stop her when she went to chastise George. I didn't realise before just how frightened he is of his mother, but even so, he should have put her in her place when she was going on at us like that. Well, maybe I could have found a way to forgive him and carried on living with him, Gran, as his mother is ... well ... I don't need to tell you what a bully she is?'

Bertha couldn't argue with that. Over the years Pat had been a part of their lives, there had been numerous occasions when she had bullyingly manipulated her way into their family affairs and tried to take over as though she was in charge of them all.

Aidy was continuing, 'But what I *can't* cope with, Gran, is never really knowing for sure whether Mrs

Nelson was telling the truth. If perhaps Arch *did* tell her he resents the fact he's giving up everything we've built up, in order to help out here. He never tried to deny what she was saying, did he?'

'Well, in fairness to him, she wasn't allowing him to get a word in, was she?'

'Or maybe he didn't speak up because he didn't want to admit that she was telling the truth. See what I mean, Gran? I'll never be sure either way now, will I? I don't feel I can trust him any more, not knowing if he's saying one thing but thinking another.' Aidy looked up at a silver-framed, sepia head and shoulders study of her mother as a carefree young woman, before she had met her husband. It jostled for space along with other family treasures on the mantel above the range. 'Mam obviously found a way to trust Father again after he'd let her down so badly. I wish she was here to tell me how she managed to find it within herself to do that.' Aidy gave a heavy sigh. 'But anyway, it doesn't matter really, I just know I can't live with Arch while I'm uncertain of him. Marriage is a two-way partnership to me, Gran. Not one person saying or doing what the other wants, for fear of upsetting them. That's Pat Nelson's idea of marriage, not mine.'

Bertha gawped at her. Was Aidy really telling her that her marriage was over? But many married couples overcame setbacks like Arch maybe siding with his mother, and still managed to live together and make the best of what they'd got. Surely Arch could find a way to rebuild Aidy's trust in him and then they could be happy again. Bertha could only hope so.

Aidy wearily rubbed her eyes. 'I'm really tired, Gran. Been a hell of a day all round, hasn't it? Would you mind if I went to bed?'

Bertha doubted that with all that was playing on her mind she would get any restful sleep, but regardless she flashed Aidy a smile. 'No, 'course not.' She made to ease her own exhausted body out of the chair. 'I'll get the bedding for you.'

For the three nights Aidy had been staying here since her mother's death, though she knew Bertha would have welcomed her into the bed she had shared with her daughter, Aidy had opted for the sofa. It was comfortable enough for sitting on, but sleeping was a different matter. Although she had felt terribly lonely without Arch beside her, Aidy hadn't wanted to disturb her grandmother with her grieving. She doubted she'd get any actual sleep tonight, as desolate as she was at this latest turn of events and facing all the worry of looking after her helpless family entirely on her own. But knowing her beloved grandmother was beside her, someone she knew loved and cared for her no matter what, would be a real comfort to Aidy tonight.

'D'you mind company, Gran?' she asked Bertha.

Her gran smiled at her and said softly, 'You sit where you are and I'll make us both a milky drink before we go up.'

CHAPTER SEVEN

Aidy did sleep well that night. As soon as her head touched the pillow she was cast into oblivion as quick as a gas light being doused. If her mind hadn't been filled to capacity by other matters, she would have had room to realise that her restful sleep was all thanks to her grandmother secretly adding a generous measure of one of her sleeping potions into the drink she had made them both before they retired.

She woke the next morning an hour earlier than she normally would have, at five instead of six, as though her subconscious was telling her it wasn't just herself she had to get ready for the off now, but her siblings too. It wasn't fair to leave that task to her aged grandmother. The fact that she awoke in her mother's bed was an instant reminder of Jessie's death, and on top of that grief Aidy was stricken anew by the memory of what had happened with Arch.

The near-physical pain of it all made her want to do nothing more than go back to sleep, shut it all out, and pray that when she awoke it would all have been just a terrible dream. She couldn't do that, though. People she loved needed her.

Mindful of not disturbing her grandmother, Aidy carefully eased aside the bedcovers and slipped out of bed. It wasn't until she was pulling on her under-slip over her knickers and brassiere that she spotted Bertha's side of the bed was empty. A frown settled on her face. She had obviously had a restless night and Bertha had sought the refuge of the sofa so that she could sleep.

Washed and dressed now, Aidy made her way down the stairs. As she neared the bottom, she was surprised to hear sounds of life. Someone was up and about. Arriving in the back room, she saw that the range was lit, a pan of bubbling porridge sitting on one of the plates, and the person responsible for saving her all this trouble, in the process of setting the table.

On spotting Aidy, Bertha beckoned her over. 'Morning, love. Sit yerself down and I'll mash you a fresh cuppa. I wasn't expecting you up for another hour at least.'

She did as she was bidden, responding, 'I wasn't expecting to see you up and about, Gran.' Then in an apologetic tone she added, 'I'm so sorry my tossing and turning disturbed you.'

Having put dishes and cutlery down on the table,

Bertha bustled over to the range to give the thick creamy porridge a stir. 'It didn't, me duck. You slept like a log, didn't move all night.'

'So why are you up at this time? I have to be, but you don't.'

Bertha turned to face Aidy, her face set firm. 'I was up and about before, helping yer mother see the kids off to school and her off to work, and I'll do the same for you. And I'll still be doing what I can around the house, same as I did for Jessie. Porridge won't be much longer. While yer eating it, I'll rouse the kids.'

Aidy smiled warmly back at her. The worrying prospect of how she was going to manage money-wise without Arch's help was daunting, but how could she have assumed that all that went into running the house and looking after the occupants, making sure they were clean and fed, would be entirely hers to bear, too, when she had a grandmother of the special type she did? The kids would do what they were capable of also, she had no doubt of that.

'Thanks, Gran,' Aidy said softly.

On arriving down for their breakfast, the children all tentatively poked their heads around the doorway that led into the back room from the stairs. It was apparent they were checking that between the time they had gone to bed and now, there had not been a change of heart and Pat and Jim Nelson had after all moved in to take over their care. The relieved expressions on all their faces were very apparent. They were far from their normal lively selves, though, very subdued in fact, doing what was asked of them without any quibbles, obviously all still very much grieving the loss of their mother.

Mid-morning, as she was bent over her machine amongst fifty machinists, all labouring away in a large, windowless, dust-filled room, the booming voice of the department's forewoman cut into Aidy's thoughts.

'There's approaching two million unemployed in this country at the moment, Mrs Nelson, so getting a replacement for you won't be any trouble. Now, I appreciate you lost your mother only days ago, but the boss doesn't care about that. What he does care about is getting orders out, which we aren't going to do with the amount of time you are taking to sew a sleeve into one dress! Two minutes forty-five seconds is the allotted time. You've been on that one fifteen, to my certain knowledge.'

Despite fighting hard to concentrate on her work, Aidy's thoughts seemed always to be straying. She couldn't stay focused on what she was doing. Coping with her emotions was proving hard, but rising above her pain was worry about just how she was going to keep a roof over her family's heads, and them fed, clothed and warm, on only her wage and the little bit her grandmother made. Looking fearfully up at her superviser, she gulped. Somehow she had to stop her personal problems from interfering with her work. Because if she lost this job ...

She blustered to her forewoman, 'It's the material, Mrs Hardwick. It ... er ... keeps slipping. And this new batch of cotton keeps breaking, so I have to keep stopping to re-thread my machine.'

Imelda Hardwick was the no-nonsense sort of forewoman. She had to be to keep harmony and production flowing between the fifty seamstresses, ten juniors and three runabouts under her charge, all with different characters ranging from the sweet and innocent to the hard-nosed types who'd sooner lash out via verbal abuse or with their fists than calmly talk over any issues they might have with another workmate. Having started in the factory herself on first leaving school, and progressing through sheer hard work and determination to better herself, Imelda had been in her present position approaching sixteen years and meant to keep her job until she had to retire. She would not allow anyone to jeopardise that for her.

She knew every trick in the book to defend bad workmanship, had heard every excuse to justify lateness, reasons for absence, causes for finishing early or attempts to cover any manner of other misdemeanours during working hours. The excuse Aidy Nelson had just given to justify her own slackness was a well-used one that would probably appease more gullible types of forewoman, not Imelda. But despite her formidable reputation amongst her workers, that only the most brave ever dare challenge, and to their own cost, Imelda did have a compassionate streak that would surface occasionally with those she felt deserving of it.

She had been landed with numerous school leavers over the years. She'd had to keep a beady eye on them, to judge their level of ability then use her own initiative in deciding what job in the factory these individuals were best suited for. Some were not cut out for factory work at all and were dismissed to try their luck in another profession, but others displayed real promise. Aidy was one of those. From the off, she had shown she was a strong character, never allowing the older stalwarts to use or abuse or get the better of her, and Imelda had admired that quality in her. Aidy was not a natural at any job she had been given, but had been eager to learn. Imelda was to discover that drive in her continually to improve her position was fuelled by a desire to help her deserted mother and to care for her siblings. Imelda admired that quality in her too.

In all the years Aidy had worked under her, she had never before given Imelda any reason to reprimand her for trying to pass off shoddy work, a bad attitude or timekeeping. This current lapse was obviously due to grief at the death of her mother. Imelda had lost her own a couple of years back, and although mother and daughter hadn't been what could be classed as devoted, nevertheless she had been fond of her and the passing had taken her quite a while to come to terms with. Aidy had only lost her mother four days ago. Judging by the strain on her face and her subdued demeanour, she was suffering deeply. Imelda felt entitled to stretch the rigid factory rules and go gently on her this time.

Leaning over to whisper in Aidy's ear so none of the other girls could overhear ... not that it was likely over the loud buzz of fifty sewing machines plus the chattering of the workers ... she said to Aidy, 'With a headache as bad as you've got, I'm telling you to take the rest of the day off. Take tomorrow too if you need it, but I want you back in here Friday morning and I'll be expecting what I normally get from you and no less.'

Aidy stared at her for a moment, digesting what her superior was telling her. When she finally did, she blurted, 'Oh, I really appreciate that, Mrs Hardwick, you don't know how much I do, but I've already lost three days' pay from being off dealing with my mam's death. I can't afford to lose any more. I'll buck my ideas up, really I will.'

Imelda looked thoughtfully at her. Of course Aidy

needed every penny of her wage packet, like every other woman who worked in this factory, and the loss of even one penny of it could make a big difference. A penny short for the rent was a penny in arrears. A penny short of the cost of a bone for soup meant no nutritious broth for their evening meal that night. A penny short to make up a shilling for the gas meant they sat in the dark. A penny short for a bag of coal meant they went cold. She told Aidy, in a low voice, 'I'll see your pay packet isn't short, in the circumstances.'

She saw the quizzical look that Aidy gave her, knew she was wondering how her forewoman could manage to get the wages manager to sanction payment for work she hadn't done. Imelda wasn't about to divulge to her that worksheets were often lost by slipshod junior clerks en route from the factory floor, and figures were often redone from the forewoman's say so. There were always discrepancies in the output of garments too, with articles mislaid or pilfered, so if the output and hours didn't quite match, for someone in Imelda's position it was easy to write off any discrepancy.

'Go, before I change my mind,' she ordered her charge.

Bertha was busy washing and drying small brown bottles in readiness for filling with a new batch of one of the potions she was in the process of brewing. An eye-wateringly pungent smell was filling the kitchen, originating from a large blackened pan of simmering nettles and dock leaves and other peculiar-looking ingredients.

Bertha's interest in natural remedies had been sparked as a young girl by an old friend of her grandmother's. The old woman had lived in a ruin of a cottage surrounded by fields and woods a couple of miles out of town. How her grandmother had become friends with the wizened old creature in the first place would always remain a mystery to Bertha, but she would periodically pack a basket with home-made food and, taking her granddaughter along for company, set off on the two-hour journey to visit her.

The inside of that cottage was a source of wonderment to young Bertha. The low-beamed ceiling was lined with hooks from which hung bunches of wild flowers and vegetation in varying stages of drying out. Rows of shelves on the old wattle walls were crammed with bottles and jars containing ready-prepared potions and ointments. A basket of strange-looking fungi stood by the hearth. A rickety table at the back of the room was where the old crone made up her concoctions from a tattered if meticulously detailed recipe book, using a pestle and mortar and a set of weighing scales. The cooking up of her potions was done in a cauldron-like pot hanging from a hook over the fire. Bertha's grandmother always returned home from these visits with her basket filled with an assortment of potions, ointments and pastes which she'd use to help ease, or hopefully cure, the ailments suffered by herself, her family and close friends.

How the old lady went about making her potions and what went into them fascinated the young Bertha. On one visit, forgetting her manners, she bluntly asked the old lady. Delighted that a youngster was interested in her pastime, she happily answered her questions, and from then on during each visit would enlighten Bertha further on the healing and soothing properties of different plants, flowers and fruits, and how she used each one or combined it with others, with a pinch of this or that, to make up cures which covered just about every ailment. She wasn't, though, just an authority on the beneficial properties of what Mother Nature produced, but also on everyday products found in household pantries, which could also be used in the making up of healing and soothing concoctions.

It was with great sadness that on one visit Bertha and her grandmother arrived tired from their long journey to find the cottage deserted. On enquiring after the old lady's whereabouts with her nearest neighbour, they learned that she had died in her sleep a few weeks before. Much to Bertha's shock, though, the neighbour had been keeping for her a sealed box with her name scrawled on it in the old lady's spidery handwriting. Curiously opening it up, she found inside the recipe book, pestle, mortar and scales.

Even at that tender age, Bertha was very touched by the old dear's bequest to her and determined to put it to good use. The recipe book became her favourite bedtime reading and, as soon as she was allowed to go out alone, she would roam the countryside gathering her ingredients. She set up what she called her 'potion room' in her grandmother's outhouse, cooking up her ingredients in a battered old cauldron on an antiquated oil stove begged from her grandfather. It took her many failed attempts to perfect each concoction, using her long-suffering family as stooges. They all lost count of the number of rashes and sores they endured from her mistakes. But her perseverance finally paid off and soon word of her successes began to spread around the neighbourhood. People began calling in, requesting her to help ease their complaints.

When she was young, the locals labelled her 'the potion gel'. When Bertha married it was changed to 'the young wife'. Now she was reaching the end of her life, she was known as 'the old woman'.

For years her charges for these remedies had just covered her outlay in producing them, as she was content to be helping others, but on her husband's retirement and with their savings gone to help their daughter through her own difficult time, Bertha had no choice but to up her charges to make herself a little profit. These days one or more of her young grandchildren would accompany her on country expeditions, to help her gather and carry back her ingredients which were then hung to dry in the outhouse. But the preparing and cooking up was done now in the more hospitable environment of the kitchen when all the family were out, either at school or at work. Bertha could have taken the easier option and bought all her requirements from a herbalist in town, but she refused to pay what she perceived were their extortionate charges and as a result have to put up the cost of her finished products.

To her dismay, though, and despite her trying to encourage them, none of her family, including her daughter, showed the slightest interest in what she did. It was her sad conclusion that, when her time came to meet her maker, her knowledge would die with her too and the old lady's treasured recipe book lie gathering dust on a shelf.

At her unexpected return home, Bertha shot Aidy a worried look and demanded, 'What's happened? Why are you back at this time?'

Aidy explained to her.

When she had, Bertha smiled. With the likes of Pat Nelson in mind, she said, 'So there are some nice people in the world after all. Cuppa?'

On being awarded some unexpected time off by her benevolent fore woman, Aidy had decided not to waste a minute of it. The first thing she ought to do was sit down with a piece of paper and a pencil and work out the family budget from now on. She knew it was going to be tight, but it was how tight that worried her. Still, her mother had managed to keep them all on what she earned, which was less than Aidy did, so she was determined to manage.

On first walking through the back door, she had almost keeled over at the smell that met her. If it was true what her grandmother was always telling her, that the worse her remedies stank the better they were for you, then in this case whatever she was cooking up would instantly destroy the most virulent disease known to man.

Anyway, Aidy couldn't stay here while this smell was as strong as it was. She needed to pay a visit to her marital home, to collect the rest of her belongings. A surge of sorrow swamped her then. It was something she was not looking forward to. She had been so happy in that house, under the impression that she and Arch would eventually raise their children and grow old together there, and that wasn't going to be now. But she knew that to dwell on what might have been would only make her more miserable than she already was, if that were possible. She needed to get this visit over with and start looking ahead.

Hopefully, though, by the time she returned with her belongings, whatever her grandmother was cooking up would be done and the stench from it gone.

She told Bertha, 'I'll have a cuppa later, thanks, Gran. I need to go . . .' she was about to say 'home' but the house she had shared with Arch was no longer that, '. . . back to my old house and collect the rest of my stuff.'

Bertha looked at her for a moment. Going back to the home she had shared with Arch and been so happy in was going to prove very difficult for Aidy. She offered, 'My brew needs to simmer a while yet, so would you like company?'

Aidy smiled fondly at her. 'Yes, I'd like that, Gran.'

Meanwhile, hands on her wide hips, Pat was surveying the contents of Aidy's well-stocked pantry. No reason for her to be putting her hand in her own pocket to feed herself and that lazy good-for-nothing she was saddled with. He currently lay sprawled in the armchair by the fireplace, having a doze before he made a strenuous effort to get himself off down the pub for the lunchtime session while she was in that stinking hole of a public toilet, earning the money to pay their way. Never mind, at least she had all this food at her disposal. She should have been on her way to work right now. Her delay was down to the fact that she just couldn't bring herself to shift her huge body out of the comfortable bed she had slept in last night.

Compared to her own ancient mattress, her son and daughter-in-law's wooden-framed bed had been like sleeping on a cloud. Pat didn't feel any shame that after she'd insisted Arch should give up his own bed to his parents, and not yet having found the funds to buy a bed for the spare room, he'd been forced to spend an uncomfortable night on the lumpy sofa.

Having decided on a tin of stew to go with some mashed potatoes and tinned peas, she plodded back into the kitchen. The set of gleaming pans displayed on a shelf on the wall caught her eye. They weren't new when bought from a junk shop by Arch and Aidy, but were in a damned sight better condition than Pat's old battered, blackened and leaky lot that had been at least third-hand when she'd been given them on her marriage. She'd had to make do with them since, never having had the money to replace them.

She then glanced around and a surge of pure jealousy ran through her. Like they would at the Greenwood house, the better-off residents of this city would no doubt turn their noses up at this house, with its damp patches, cracked ceilings, patched up, rotting windowframes and white-washed brick walls; but compared to the almost derelict hovel she'd just moved out of, situated in a narrow alley between two factories whose chimneys constantly belched out thick clouds of black smoke, to Pat this place was a palace. Her daughter-in-law had the house and everything in it that she herself had always dreamed of having – before, that was, she had realised she was never going to get them through her own poor choice of husband. And now her spoiled daughter-in-law was throwing all her son's hard work in achieving this back in his face. She had returned to her former home to care for her family, selfishly expecting Arch to go along with it all.

A disagreeable pout disfigured Pat's already ugly face. After Aidy's reaction yesterday, Pat was well aware that her own chances of moving into the Greenwood house were very slim. She could intimidate and bully most people, but much to her chagrin Aidy had proved immune to her threats. Aidy wasn't stupid. She had known from the off what Pat's real aim was. Damn the woman! Why had Arch had to choose a woman like her and not a little mouse like her two other sons had chosen? If he had, Pat would have been well and truly established in her dream home by now.

Then suddenly an idea struck her and a gleam lit her piggy eyes. Maybe her hopes of bettering herself were not all lost. She might have lost out on the Greenwood house, but why shouldn't she have this one instead? It might be smaller, two-bedroomed against three, but like the Greenwood house it was in a better part of the area than her old place, among a much better class of people. And, as a bonus, the furniture and furnishings in this house might be second-hand or junk-shop bought, but they were definitely in better condition than anything the Greenwood house boasted. Yes, this house would do Pat nicely, and another bonus was the fact that she didn't have to put up with any other troublesome residents, like noisy kids and sharp-tongued old biddies. Whether Arch decided to stay here or move in with his wife, she didn't care any longer. So long as he didn't expect her to look after him in place of his wife if he did stay put.

Her ears pricked as she heard a key scrape in the front door. Wondering who it could be with a key to the house, as both Arch and Aidy would be at work, she plodded her way from the kitchen to the back room, throwing her snoring husband a look of disdain as she passed him by. On reaching the door leading into the parlour, she stopped short, hearing voices. Then she recognised the voices and pulled a face. It was her daughter-in-law and her grandmother! So Aidy wasn't at work today then. It was a good boss she'd obviously got who allowed her four days off for a death in the family, unlike Pat's own. She would have had to beg for just a couple of hours' leave to attend a funeral, no matter how close a relative had died.

A malicious smirk curved her lips. She was about to get her own back on her daughter-in-law for quashing her original plan to better her living conditions.

On walking into the back room, Bertha behind her, Aidy stopped short, her face displaying shock to see her father-in-law sprawled fast asleep in an armchair. The top button of his shabby trousers was undone to reveal grubby underpants, the smell of his unwashed feet wafting up to greet her, and her mother-in-law, fat arms folded under her monstrous bosom dressed in her shoddy grey work dress, staring at them stonily from the kitchen doorway.

'To what do I owe this honour?' she demanded.

Aidy gawped at her. 'Excuse me, Mrs Nelson, but this is *my* house. I should be the one asking you what *you're* doing here, by the looks of things making yourselves very much at home?'

'Well, yes, I am meking meself at home, 'cos this is my home now. My son needs looking after since his wife has put her own family above him.' Pat sneered at Aidy. 'Some wife you turned out to be! If he's any sense, he'll have n'ote more to do with yer and find someone else who'll be a proper wife to him. You can rest assured that I won't hold back from telling him that meself.'

'That's a joke, you looking after anyone. Yer can't even look after yerself,' cried an outraged Bertha.

'Who asked you to stick yer nose in?' Pat bellowed back at her.

The booming of his wife's voice woke up Jim. 'Can't a man get no peace from you women?' he asked, bleary eyed.

'And you can shurrup too, yer lazy, good-for-nothing, fat pig!' Pat yelled at him.

Jim quickly deduced that his wife was in the mood for a fight and hurriedly heaved his body out of the chair, pushing past her to get into the kitchen. Seconds later the back door was heard to slam shut.

Meanwhile Aidy was saying to her in a warning voice, 'Don't speak to my grandmother like that, Mrs Nelson.'

Pat glared back at her. 'I'll speak to anyone how I bleddy well like in my own house. Now, what was it that yer came for?'

Aidy was speechless. Was Arch mad, allowing his mother and father to stay! Knowing her mother-in-law, though, he more than likely had had no choice in the matter. But already Pat was calling it 'her' house and not Arch's. His parents had been here barely half a day and their slovenly behaviour was evident. Pat hadn't bothered to clear the breakfast dishes and it was getting on for noon. Beside the chair Jim had just vacated was a crumpled newspaper and several empty beer bottles. Aidy doubted the bed had been made, or would be before they got into it again. And she guessed that Arch had been made to give up their bed to her in-laws and it'd been one person who had used the pile of spare bedding at the side of the sofa.

It wouldn't be long before the Nelsons turned this house into the smelly, dirty pigsty they'd left behind. But Pat was right. Aidy didn't live here any longer. Who Arch invited in from now on was his choice. That didn't stop her feeling distressed to see that all the hard work and effort they had both put into making this house a lovely home was going to be destroyed if her in-laws occupied it for any length of time.

Not that she felt obliged to inform Pat why she was here, regardless Aidy told her, 'I came for the rest of my belongings.'

With visions of some of the bits and pieces she'd already earmarked for the pawn disappearing, she warned Aidy, 'Just make sure it's only yer own personal stuff and nothing my son paid for. Well, hurry up and get 'em then! Oh, and make sure yer leave yer key on yer way out.'

Aidy felt a strong desire to point out to her mother-in-law that it wasn't all down to Arch how nice this house was. If Aidy felt she wanted to take anything with her, then she was perfectly entitled to do so, but her need to get away from this odious woman was stronger. 'Come on, Gran,' she urged Bertha, heading off towards the door that led to the stairs.

Aidy might be under the impression that Bertha was following her, but she wasn't. She was incensed to see how disrespectfully Pat Nelson was treating her granddaughter and wasn't going to stand by and let her get away with it. Giving Aidy long enough to be well on her way to the bedroom, Bertha wagged a finger in Pat's direction. 'Now I don't know how you wangled yer way in here . . . and I'm pretty sure your poor son's already regretting it, but . . .'

Bertha got to say no more. Pat was upon her, grabbing her by the arm and dragging her towards the front door, yelling, 'I ain't listening to your foul gob inside me own four walls.' She had manhandled Bertha to the door by now. Wrenching it open, she pushed the old lady out, still yelling at her. 'Ever come back here uninvited and you'll get the reception yer getting now.' She slammed the door shut then, seemingly unbothered that a last hard shove had caused Bertha to lose her balance and land heavily on the hard cobbles outside.

Hearing the loud commotion, Aidy came running down to find Pat just arriving back in the back room. Seeing her grandmother nowhere in sight, she demanded, 'Where's my gran?'

Pat smirked at her. 'Well, the mouthy old bag ain't

in here, that's fer sure. Now I want you out too, whether yer've got yer stuff or not.'

And Aidy wanted to get out much more than Pat wanted her out. Her mother-in-law was dressed in her lavatory attendant's work dress so she must be going out today. Aidy decided she would return later, when Pat wasn't here, and collect her belongings and whatever else she was of a mind to take, without any interference. Spinning on her heel, she headed towards the front door.

'Oi, yer key!' Pat boomed out.

Aidy stopped short, spinning back round to find her holding out one meaty hand in readiness to accept the house key. Eyes narrowing, she said stonily, 'I'll give my keys over when I'm good and ready to, Mrs Nelson, and it will be to Arch, not you, as it's his name on the rent book.' With that she hurried on her way.

Opening the door, she froze in shock at the sight that greeted her. Sprawled on the cobbles, her old face creased in agony, lay her grandmother. A woman was bending over her.

Aidy crouched beside Bertha, crying out, 'Gran, what happened to you?'

The woman who was with Bertha answered for her. 'I seen it all, me duck. I was just passing, on me way to catch the bus into town, and I got the shock of me life when that big woman in there . . .' she nodded her head in the direction of Aidy's front door '. . . pushed this old lady out. Yelling at the poor old dear summat cruel she was. She don't look a nice woman, I have ter say. She can't be nice with a foul mouth like she's got. Anyway, before I could stop her, the old lady had toppled over and come a right cropper on the cobbles. I heard a crack. I'm awful feared she's broke summat.'

'I wish yer'd stop talking about me like I'm not here,' Bertha moaned.

Aidy's attention turned to her. 'Gran, can you tell me where you're hurt?'

'It's . . . it's me leg and arm,' she managed to mutter through waves of excruciating pain.

Just who had been the cause of her grandmother's fall and the resulting injuries flew from Aidy's mind as the need to summon urgent medical attention took over. She did not at all like the thought of leaving Bertha on her own while she fetched the doctor and asked the woman, 'I'm sorry to impose on you, but would you please stay with my gran while I fetch the Doc?'

Much to Aidy's relief, she agreed. After assuring Bertha she'd be back as quickly as she could with the doctor in tow, Aidy raced off in the direction of his surgery.

Ty had just returned from his morning calls and was busy at his desk, updating the notes of the patients he'd just called upon. He'd had very little sleep the previous night, having been called out for most of it to deal with a breach birth, and it was only thanks to his skills that the child survived. As tired as he was, he was having a job focusing on his work. He was hungry, too, having had no time for any breakfast as he'd overslept and only just made it in time for morning surgery.

He hadn't realised he'd dozed off until he was shocked awake by the door unexpectedly bursting open. A woman came rushing in, proclaiming, 'You've got to come quick, Doc! It's me gran, she's hurt really badly.'

He stared over at her, sleep dazed for a moment, as he gathered his wits, then recognition of the intruder struck. This was the woman who had rudely erupted into his surgery only days ago. Now here she was, disrespectfully interrupting once again.

'I see you haven't yet learned to knock before you invade someone's privacy. And it's *Doctor Strathmore*,' he told her.

Aidy hadn't time for what she perceived as his pettiness right now. She reiterated, 'My gran's hurt really badly, Doc. You got to come and see her *now*.'

The woman hadn't exaggerated how ill her mother was the last time she had fetched him so he had no reason to believe she was summoning him on a wild goose chase now. His first priority was to the patient.

'Name?' Ty demanded. Memory stirred within him of the last time he had asked her the same question and he added, 'The patient's name, not your own.'

Aidy's hackles rose that he hadn't given her credit for not making the same stupid mistake again. This man was so arrogant, so annoying. She inwardly fought with herself not to snap a response. After all she couldn't afford to antagonise him and risk his refusing to have anything to do with her.

'Bertha Rider. You're wasting your time looking for her record card, though. Gran is very proud of the fact she's never in her life suffered from anything bad enough to warrant seeing a doctor over. Well, until now, that is.'

Ty got up from his chair, pulled on his jacket and grabbed his bag, indicating to Aidy that she should lead the way to where her grandmother was.

CHAPTER EIGHT

It was after seven when the family all gathered round the sofa upon which Bertha was lying, a worn, patched blanket covering her.

Marion knelt on the floor beside her, looking at her grandmother earnestly. 'I don't like to see you hurt, our Gran,' she wailed.

Despite her extreme discomfort, Bertha managed to quip, 'I'm not that happy about it meself, ducky.'

'D'yer want my comic to read?' offered George from the other end of the sofa.

She flashed him a pained smile. 'Not now, love. Maybe later, eh?'

'I hate that Mrs Nelson,' piped up Betty, perched on the arm of the sofa to one side of her brother. 'I've a good mind to push her out the door meself. See how she likes it.'

'I'll come with yer and help yer do it,' offered George, his face screwed up in hatred for the woman who had caused his beloved grandmother such agony from a broken leg and wrist as well as bruising to other parts of her face and body that had hit the cobbles.

'You'll do no such thing,' Aidy told them in no uncertain terms as she arrived in the room carrying a cup of sweet tea for Bertha. Although she was having a hard job herself controlling a desire to confront her mother-in-law and repay the compliment. But all that would do would be to lower herself to Pat's level, plus show her siblings that it was all right to repay violence with violence. 'If there is any justice in this world, that woman will get her comeuppance one day. But not from us. So if I hear of any of you going anywhere near Mrs Nelson, then none of you will be able to sit down for a week. Is that clear?'

Their sister's warnings were never idle. They all vigorously nodded their heads.

'Good. Now clear out of the way and give Gran air to breathe and me room to give her a drink,' she ordered them, adding as an afterthought, 'In fact, go out and play, but be back in an hour.' When they had done as they were told she knelt beside the sofa, picked the cup up out of its saucer and held the rim to Bertha's lips so she could take a few sips.

After she had had her fill for the time being, Bertha looked gratefully at Aidy and in a weak voice said, 'Strong and sweet, just what the doctor ordered.

Thanks, me duck.' Her face then clouded over. 'Talking of doctors, there'll be a bill of his to settle. I'm hoping there's enough to cover it in me remedy tin.'

'Don't worry about that now, Gran. I told him I'd sort it out, and I will as soon as I can. I could tell he wasn't happy about that, but it's hard luck 'cos we can't give him what we haven't got, can we?' There was still an outstanding fee from his visit to her mother that Aidy hadn't settled, and he'd have to wait for that too. More important things had to be paid for out of her wage first, like the rent and food.

Bertha pulled a face. 'I don't know quite what to make of the new doctor. He seems to know his stuff, didn't take him long to work out what I was ailing from and get me sorted, but he was very brusque, made me feel like I was an inconvenience to him. He comes from money, judging by the posh voice he's got. And his clothes might be old but they're the best quality. I wonder why his sort has come to live and work round these parts?'

Aidy gave a nonchalant shrug. 'I don't know, Gran, and I don't really care. I don't like him. He spoke to me in a manner you wouldn't address a dog in when I went to fetch him for Mam and yourself. Anyway, considering the pain you must have been in at the time, still are for that matter, you noticed a lot about him?'

'Well, I had to concentrate me mind on something while he was resetting me bones.' Bertha seemed intrigued. 'There's a story behind that new doctor coming here, I'd bet my life there is. Someone with his obvious breeding doesn't voluntarily give up the high life to slum it with us.'

Aidy had no time to waste on conversation about a person she didn't care a jot for. 'Can I get you anything else?' she offered.

'You can, if you don't mind. Could you make me a bread and vinegar poultice to put on me bruises, to help bring them out and ease the throbbing? Also, from me store in the pantry, can you bring me through the bottle with "Headache Relief" on the label?'

Aidy looked at her quizzically. 'What do you want that for?'

'Help with the pain, ducky.'

'But aren't the pills the Doc gave you, to tide you over, helping at all? I'm going to the chemist for the rest tomorrow.' She was already worried whether she had enough money in her purse to cover that outlay, along with what food they'd need until she got her next pay in two days' time.

Bertha was pulling a face. 'The pills and prescription are for morphine. I've seen what that does to people. I'd sooner be in the pain I am than end up reliant on that stuff. And I'm not giving the pharmacist any of my hard-earned money when I can sort meself out.'

Aidy couldn't believe her grandmother had endured the agony of her broken bones and their resetting without any strong relief. She could, though, see Bertha's reasoning for the refusal, but regardless said, 'You will promise to take the pills the Doc gave you if your own remedy doesn't work, though?' She saw the look Bertha shot her and quickly added, 'I didn't mean your remedies aren't any good, Gran, I know they are as they've sorted my ailments out enough times over the years, but the pain you're suffering is not just a headache and your remedy might not be strong enough to ease it. So you will, won't you?

Bertha was in far more pain than ever she would let on to her granddaughter, but to be knocked into oblivion by the effects of morphine was not an option she'd choose. To appease Aidy, though, she said, 'Yes, all right.'

'Good. Now I soak the bread in hot water with a good measure of vinegar ... that's how I make the poultice, isn't it?'

Bertha nodded and quipped, 'And there's me thinking you never took any interest in what I do.'

As Aidy went off to do what she was asked, a worried expression appeared on Bertha's face. Easing the pain of her injuries was not what was really concerning her so much as the situation her injuries had left her in. Her broken leg and wrist had rendered her practically incapable while they healed. She couldn't even go to the toilet without help. It was a hard enough job looking after a family of five for a normal housewife who didn't work. Aidy did, full-time, and on top of that, she now had the problem of covering the chores Bertha herself would have been doing, plus the care of an invalid. The kids would help when they came home from school and at week-ends, but there was only so much youngsters their age could manage. Pat Nelson certainly had a lot to answer for but Bertha doubted the woman was feeling the slightest glimmer of remorse for what she'd done.

In the kitchen, as she was mashing the soggy bread and vinegar together to form the poultice, Aidy too was worrying about just how, on top of working full-time, she was going to manage all the household chores while her grandmother recovered, her only help being with the lighter tasks her siblings could perform. But somehow she would just have to. And no matter how tired she was, she must not let her grandmother know and make her feel any more guilty than she already was.

It was approaching nine o'clock and Aidy had just finished mopping the kitchen floor. Bertha's home-made pain-killing remedy certainly seemed to have done something for her. At the moment she was asleep on the sofa, although looking quite a sight with clumps of the bread poultice resembling grotesque growths covering her bruises, in the hope they'd help speed up their healing. The children had all gone to bed without so much as a murmur of protest tonight. Usually they put up some sort of lame excuse to delay bedtime for a while longer. Aidy was grateful they hadn't. They'd obviously sensed that with all she had on her mind, their sister wasn't in the mood to put up with any nonsense from them. Since their mother's death, before going up, Marion's parting words were always the same. 'Mam might be back when I get up in the morning.' All the others were always too choked to respond to her. Betty and George still cried themselves to sleep, although George would deny it. How Aidy wished she could magic away their pain, and her own, Gran's too, but she couldn't. It was only time that would help ease that.

Despite her efforts not to, she started to think about Arch then. He had been an important part of her life for the last ten years, the most important for the last five as her husband. They had been very loving and supportive of each other. She was angry with him, hurt and shocked to have witnessed a side to him she hadn't known about before and didn't like at all, but regardless she was still missing the Arch she knew and loved dreadfully. A future without him in it seemed very bleak to her.

Why couldn't she be like the majority of other women, who managed to turn a blind eye whenever their husbands were discovered to have been dishonest with them? But then a simple white lie, such as saying their wives looked nice when they looked awful or that the food was delicious when in truth it was unpalatable, was a far cry from voicing the sentiment that you were happy giving up your house and all your plans for the future, when in truth you weren't at all. And there was still the matter that Arch had stood by and done nothing when his own mother had been verbally and almost physically attacking his wife and her family.

As desperate as she was for a way to resolve matters between herself and her husband and to return to the happy couple they had been before this, Aidy didn't believe they could be reconciled.

She was just cleaning the dirty mop head in a bucket of cold water when her ears pricked as she heard the click of the latch on the yard gate, announcing the arrival of a visitor. The back door was already open to aid the drying of the floor. Propping the mop up by the pitted pot sink, she went over to look through and see who the visitor was.

It was a lovely, warm late-August evening. The voices of women gossiping on doorsteps and the laughter of children still playing out, filled the air. A keen sense of loss filled her. It was the sort of evening when she and Arch would have gone for a walk into a better-off area that had a park, or else they'd have taken chairs outside into their tiny backyard and sat there chatting about nothing in particular, just enjoying each other's company.

The man in her thoughts stood framed in the gateway, looking hesitantly over at her. For a moment all that had happened between them flew from Aidy's mind as a desperate need to rush across to him, wrap her arms around him and feel his around her, filled her. Then the reasons that had brought them to this sorry situation flooded back, along with renewed hurt at his betrayal of her. 'What do you want?' she called curtly across.

'To talk to you,' he said tentatively.

She responded, 'As far as I'm concerned, I can't think of anything we have to say to each other. You finished work three hours ago, so what kept you? You don't need to tell me ... it was your mother. Had to wait until her back was turned so you could slip out, did you?'

'No, not at all. She encouraged me to come and put things right with you. Was on at me as soon as I got in from work.' Then he added sheepishly, 'I'd have been here sooner but I needed a couple of pints for Dutch courage first.'

Aidy wasn't surprised he needed Dutch courage to face her, but she was very surprised to hear of the change of attitude in her mother-in-law, encouraging her son to make up with her, when Aidy knew that for the last ten years Pat had been doing her best to cause trouble between them, in the hope they'd part. And what about her plan to keep Arch away from her so Aidy could learn the hard way she couldn't manage to care for her family on her own and then go begging Pat to let her take up her offer? The truth slowly dawned. Of course, Pat no longer had any need to continue with that plan as she'd already succeeded in achieving a comfortable new home for herself.

Aidy wondered if Arch had twigged by now that his mother had no intention of moving out again? But, knowing lazy Pat as well as she did, it was no wonder that she was encouraging her son to mend his marriage. She herself didn't want the burden of doing his washing and cooking. But she'd still expect to receive the money she got from him each week, supposedly to pay the rent, and she'd demand that be increased from now on as the rent on his and Aidy's house was much higher than on the two-roomed hovel Pat had moved out of.

Now wasn't the time, though, to be dwelling on thoughts of her devious mother-in-law. Arch deserved to be heard, but Aidy doubted he'd anything to say to her that could resolve matters between them.

She returned back inside the kitchen to await him.

Although the distance from the gate to the back door was only short, the clatter of Arch's boots on the cobbles as he made his way over seemed to go on forever to Aidy. Finally he appeared in the doorway, looking uncertain. She was standing by the old, well-scrubbed kitchen table, both hands clutching the back of a chair for support.

'We'll talk in here as Gran's asleep on the sofa and the kids are in bed. We'll need to keep our voices down. Oh, and mind the floor, it's wet. I don't want to have to fetch the doctor again today.'

His face screwed up quizzically, he asked, 'Why have you had to fetch him? Has something happened to one of the family?'

His mother wasn't stupid. She must have known at the time that what she did to Bertha was not something an older woman would walk away from without some damage. By not even mentioning the incident to her son, she had obviously not given it a second thought. Aidy enlightened him.

'I went to our house today to collect some of my personal belongings. Gran came with me for company. While I was upstairs, Gran and your mother had words and Pat bodily threw Gran out of the house. She ended up on the cobbles with a broken wrist and leg, and covered in bruises. Your mother must have known that what she'd done would cause serious harm to my gran, but she just shut the door on her.'

Arch was staring at her, both astounded and appalled. 'Mam never said a word to me about it! Not even that you'd been round. I don't know what to say ... really I don't. I'll go and apologise to your gran.'

He made to go through to the back room but Aidy held up a warning hand to stop him. 'I told you, she's asleep. Anyway, it's not *you* who should be apologising to her. And we both know the person who should, never will.' She prompted him, 'So what did you come to speak to me about, Arch?'

'You know what, Aidy.'

Of course she did, but she wasn't going to make it easy for him. 'I'm no mind reader.'

He took a deep breath. Aidy could be exasperating at times. But then, that was one of the many things he loved about her: that she wasn't the submissive type who only did exactly what her husband dictated, whether she wanted to or not. Now, though, she was looking drained, obviously worried how she was going to manage in the future, both financially and physically, and he fought a desperate urge to go over to her and hold her, tell her he'd an answer to their every problem. But knowing she would only rebuff any advance in the frame of mind she was in now, he decided against it. But she would think better of him when she had heard him out, he was positive of that.

Speaking hesitantly, Arch said, 'Look, Aidy, after

yesterday and today, there's no point in me trying to cover up the fact any longer that my own mother terrifies the life out of me. I'd sooner face an axe-wielding lunatic than her when she's annoyed, and it don't take much to get Mam's dander up, as you well know. I promise, though . . . swear on God's honour . . . cross me heart and hope to die . . . that I'll never be such a coward in future and let her treat you and the kids and Gran the same way again. You have my word on that.

'And about what me mam told you, about me not wanting to help you look after your family . . . Well, I admit, after she pointed some things out to me, I did have a few reservations. After all, it's a big thing for a man to give up everything he's worked for and take on someone else's family, but that doesn't matter now. Looking after your brother and sisters is not our responsibility . . . not when there's someone else whose responsibility goes beyond that.'

Aidy frowned at him, bemused. 'You know it's not possible for Gran to care for them, so just who are you talking about being responsible for them? We haven't got any other family.'

He smiled at her, looking pleased with himself. 'But you have. Your father.'

Aidy gawped at him, utterly astounded and appalled by his suggestion. 'Are you serious?' she exclaimed.

He looked taken back. 'Yes. He is their father, Aidy. It's his job to look after his kids now their mother's no longer here to do it.'

She stared at Arch in shocked disbelief that he could even contemplate such a diabolical option. Her husband was well aware what type of man her father was, and what Aidy herself thought of him.

'Even supposing he would do it ... provided we could find him, that is ... do you really think that I would leave my own brother and sisters in the care of that ... that ... bastard who's already abandoned his family twice! Marion has never even met him.

'And what about Gran? Do you think he'd ever agree to look after her when she's not even related to him, except by marriage. And do you actually think she'd ever agree to live with the man she hates and blames for her own daughter's death?' Her temper kindled, Aidy cried furiously: 'I can't believe you hate the thought of helping me look after them so much you'd suggest handing them over to a devil like that. How could you, Arch? How could you?'

He looked stunned, totally shocked by her reaction to his suggestion. He really had thought she would jump at his idea, be relieved to have the burden of her family lifted from her, allowing them both to get on with their own lives. He couldn't believe he'd been so badly mistaken. Aidy was looking at him now with such shock and disillusionment that panic ran through him. He saw a gulf widening between them that was in danger of becoming unbridgeable. He saw his life without her in it and the thought was unbearable to him. He would agree to anything, suffer it all in silence, sooner than lose her.

He beseeched her, 'Aidy, please, forget what I suggested! It was only a thought. I . . . well, I don't know what I was thinking, even suggesting it. Of course I'm willing to help you. I love the kids and your gran, you know that. I'll do anything you want so long as we're together.'

She eyed him coldly. 'But you *did* suggest it, Arch, and I can't forget you did. You'd sooner the kids and Gran lived a life of misery with the likes of . . . of . . . that man, than you be lumbered with them.' She swallowed hard to stem the flood of miserable tears that threatened to choke her. 'You're not the man I thought you were.' Finding she had nothing more to say to him, she heaved a deep sigh before adding, 'I've a family to look after. If you'll excuse me, I need to get back to them.'

Arch couldn't believe it was all over between them. His thoughts raced wildly, frantically searching for a way to turn this situation around. Nothing but pitiful excuses materialised. In pure desperation, he blurted, 'Which you can't do without my help, Aidy. Without my wage packet, you'll all be on the streets in no time.'

She gasped, hurt filling her at this lack of faith in her abilities. Her eyes brimming with contempt for him, she hissed, 'Oh, can't I? Well, I'll show you that I don't need your money. And now I've seen you for what you really are, I don't need or want *you* either.'

She shot over to the door. Catching him offguard, she gave Arch a hard shove on his shoulder. He stumbled back out of the doorway into the yard, and the next thing he knew the door was slammed shut in his face and he heard the key turning in the lock.

Numb with shock, he stared blindly at the closed door. He'd come here tonight to save his marriage; instead he had managed to end it. Aidy had left him in no doubt that there was no going back for them. His broad shoulders slumped in despair, he turned and walked from the yard.

In the back room, the sound of raised voices had roused Bertha from sleep. She had recognised them immediately and hope had soared within her that her beloved granddaughter and her husband were resolving their differences and putting their marriage back on the right track again. But that hope was instantly dashed by the tone of their voices, especially Aidy's, and she knew that her wish for a reconciliation between them was not going to be granted. When she heard the slamming of the back door, and moments later the sound of Aidy weeping, her own heart broke then for the sorrow she knew her granddaughter was suffering. Bertha wept herself back to sleep.

CHAPTER NINE

Aidy pulled a length of thread from the back of the sewing machine and clipped it neatly off with scissors. She gave the collar she had sewn a smooth out and then ran a keen eye over it. It wasn't the usual perfect result, but hopefully the beady-eyed examiner would feel the very slight mistake she had made, in not tucking the pleated trim far enough into the seam, was not bad enough to fail it. To unpick and redo it would set Aidy further back with her daily quota than she was already.

She'd leaned over to pick up the completed body of a dress and begin attaching the collar to it when she realised her forewoman was standing by her, looking down at her with concern. Aidy looked back up at her worriedly, wondering what she had come to speak to her about, hoping it wasn't what she suspected it was.

Imelda Hardwick was becoming increasingly worried about Aidy. Since her mother's death, her output and the quality of her workmanship had gradually declined, despite several warnings about it. Her personal tragedy had happened over five weeks ago, long enough for Aidy outwardly to come to terms with her loss, although Imelda herself knew from experience you never actually got over the death of a loved one, just learned to live with it. Because of her own bereavement and her soft spot for Aidy, Imelda had been making allowances for her mistakes, but she couldn't afford to any longer.

She had just come out of a very tough meeting with the factory owner, the works manager, and all the rest of the departmental foremen and women. The recession was biting deeper. Thousands of jobs were being lost on a spiralling basis across local industries, with no prospect of those workers obtaining other gainful employment until the situation improved. Up to now the hosiery industry had got off lightly; people always needed clothes, and despite a huge rise in poverty amongst the working class, there were still others who did have money to spend, especially among the middle classes who bought the good-quality wares produced here. But now the recession was affecting even the moneyed classes who were also cutting back on their spending. As a result of this the factory's orders were being cut, some even cancelled. The owner had ordered that each department was to halve its workforce and warned there would be no pay rises in the foreseeable future for those who remained. Once it had been decided which workers were to lose their jobs, a general announcement would be made. Until then, management had been warned to keep tight lipped.

As she looked at Aidy, it distressed Imelda to observe how the once lively and happy young woman had changed. She seemed drained, as if her life blood were being slowly sucked from her. Imelda couldn't afford to be sentimental at a time like this when even her own job was in jeopardy, but there were many others she'd sooner get rid of than Aidy. She decided she would offer her one final warning to pull herself together or else her name would have to go on the dismissal list.

'You should have had that batch finished by now, Aidy. Your mother's been dead five weeks . . . I can't afford to carry your slacking any longer. Pull your socks up! I'm warning you, this is the last time I'm going to speak to you on this matter.'

Aidy gulped. She knew exactly what was meant. This was Imelda's way of warning her that if she didn't up her production, then it was time for her cards.

But how did you manage to summon up energy you just did not have? While still grieving terribly for the loss of her mother and her marriage . . . she wasn't sure which of them was the worst ... Aidy was working in the factory nine hours a day, five and a half days a week, plus tackling all the work involved in single-handedly looking after her family. It was all beginning to tell on her. She looked and felt exhausted. As soon as her head touched the pillow, she was swept into oblivion. But it wasn't a restful sleep, not with the constant nightmares Aidy was prey to. She suffered from vivid dreams of her family and herself knocking on the door of the work-house, that prospect being her ever-present dread. She feared it would become a reality if she didn't somehow muster the energy to up her pace and fulfil her daily work quotas.

She hadn't even the strength to make an excuse now for her underachieving. Imelda took the look on Aidy's face to mean she'd got the message, and went on her way.

'You ain't told Hardwick about yer home circumstances, have yer, Aidy? You ought to, then she'd know just why you're having a job keeping up and hopefully make allowances for you, until yer gran's back on her feet and taking some of the workload off yer.'

Aidy turned to look at her friend on the machine next to hers. Colleen Brown and she had started at the firm within a week of each other and had immediately hit it off. It wasn't long before they were spending all their free time together and had met their respective husbands within months of each other at the local youth club. The couples had often made up a foursome while they were courting. These days they didn't see each other much at all out of work as Colleen's spare time was taken up by her husband and three children, the same as Aidy's family took up her time now. Only Aidy knew that Colleen had recently missed a period and was beside herself with worry that she could be expecting her fourth child, an unaffordable addition to the family.

Colleen's widowed mother's arthritic hands were already full looking after her three boisterous under-school age kids while she was at work, let alone a baby on top of that. Colleen had no choice but to work as her husband didn't earn much from his semi-skilled job for an engineering company, and there were rumours going around already that due to the dreadful recession the order books were about empty, no new ones in the offing, and very soon it looked as if workers would be laid off there. Colleen lay awake at night praying her husband wouldn't be one of them and that she herself wasn't pregnant.

Now Aidy shook her head. 'I don't want the news about me and Arch becoming common knowledge yet, Col. I just couldn't cope with the gossip. You haven't told anyone, have you?'

'No, 'course not. You know your secrets are safe with me. Always have been, ever since we've known each other. You're lucky to have kept it quiet this long, though, Aidy. I'm surprised no one who knows you both has asked why you're living in separate houses.'

'I can't speak for Arch, of course, but in my case it's because I've fobbed off busybodies who've asked me by saying that it's just a temporary situation, while we sort out matters after my mam's death.'

Colleen looked genuinely aggrieved when she said, 'It's such a shame about you and Arch. If ever I thought a couple would last forever, it was you two. Never argued like me and my old man do, constantly, about anything. Got no kids driving yer both crazy, and the worry of ... well, you know ... what I'm worrying about might be on the way, and that yer old man might be in line for losing his job.'

Aidy sighed. 'Could you forget and forgive Bernie for wanting to hand your defenceless family over to the care of their bastard of a father, subject them to lives of purgatory, just to save himself the bother?'

'Listen here, gel. I could forgive anything from my old man sooner than him put me in the position you're in. Having the worries you're having to cope with ...'

'Well, I'd sooner have those worries, Col, and know

my family are happy. And I'll have more to worry about if I don't get back to work! Hardwick has just given me my last warning and I know she meant business.'

Try as she might, though, after the mention of him, Aidy couldn't get Arch from her mind. Their marriage was over and she had been the one to end it because she had discovered traits in his character she could not live with, but that didn't mean she was over the man she had known before that side of him had shown itself to her. It would all take time. In a way, it was a good thing she had so much else to keep her mind occupied or the loss of him would have overwhelmed her.

The time until dinner hour seemed to drag on, and by the time it came Aidy still hadn't caught up with her quota. It was a hot August day, a relentless sun blazing down from a cloudless sky, and the stuffy, airless atmosphere inside the factory had done nothing to boost her energy levels. In fact, it did the opposite, made her more tired and listless. She prayed the fresh air she'd get while she raced around completing her dinner-hour tasks would help to blow away at least some of her fatigue and she'd manage to put in a better performance this afternoon. She would try and get to bed earlier tonight, hope for once she had a good sleep, wake refreshed, and for the first time since she had returned to work after her mother died, achieve what was expected of her. She had to. Her fore-woman had left her in no doubt what would happen to her if she didn't.

Aidy had no grocery shopping to do today as Betty was under instructions to collect fresh milk from the local shop on returning home from school. For dinner that evening they were having vegetable soup and bread. The soup just needed heating. Making her own bread each evening for next day was hard work and time-consuming, but cheaper than buying shop-bought. But having no shopping to do and nothing to prepare towards the evening meal did not mean Aidy was free. She still had to go home and check on Bertha. Although neighbours and friends dropped in to see her, time permitting, her gran so looked forward to Aidy's visit home, for a quick cuppa and a chat to help break the monotony.

For Bertha the time couldn't come quick enough when the doctor pronounced her broken bones healed and removed the itchy, cumbersome plaster casts. She had always been so active, and this incar-ceration, day after day, was very testing for her although she did her best to keep her spirits up. Aidy was well aware of it too. Despite her continually assuring her grandmother that she was managing just fine, Bertha was deeply grieved by the fact that she was unable to ease her granddaughter's burden, either in the house or financially by selling her remedies. Day by day, she could see Aidy's strength and optimism dwindling.

To Aidy's surprise, Bertha was fast asleep when she arrived. As there was evidence of several visitors during the morning judging by the dirty cups they'd left, obviously she'd been tired out by them. At least Aidy knew that her grandmother hadn't been on her own all morning. She would mash herself a cuppa and drink it while she ate a quick sandwich, hoping Bertha would rouse herself before she had to return to work so that Aidy could tend to her personal needs.

Bertha was still snoring softly when, armed with her cup of tea and a plate holding a cheese sandwich, Aidy gave a blissful sigh as she sank down in the shabby armchair by the range. It felt like paradise to her to have a few minutes' peaceful relaxation before she returned to the hurly-burly of the factory. After she'd eaten her sandwich and drunk her tea Bertha still had not woken and she had ten minutes to go before she had to return to work. How vehemently she wished she hadn't to go back; that she could sit here all afternoon and rest her weary body . . .

Aidy hadn't realised she'd fallen into a deep slumber until a shrill scream jolted her awake. Sitting bolt upright, she stared around, dazed and confused, fighting to comprehend where she was. Then her eyes fell on her grandmother, in a heap on the floor nearby.

As she jumped up and ran to Bertha she cried out, 'Oh, my God, Gran! What . . .' She crouched down beside her, checking her over. She didn't need to ask if her gran was in pain. The look on her face and the fact that she couldn't speak revealed that this was serious. Aidy didn't like the fact that the plaster cast encasing Bertha's broken leg had split open and the part of it visible inside was swelling like a balloon. What on earth had caused this? She wondered. But the answer would have to wait. Bertha needed medical help, and swiftly.

Gently placing a cushion under the old woman's head and covering her with a blanket, Aidy ordered her not to move and informed her she'd be back as quickly as she could with the doctor.

She was so consumed by the need to get help for her grandmother, it never registered with Aidy that she should have been back at work, labouring away at her machine, over an hour ago.

Ty was in his kitchen, about to take a much-needed sandwich and cup of tea into the dining room, to eat sitting in one of the unyielding chairs at the table. Secretly he would have liked to have taken his meal into the lounge, sitting in the scuffed but comfortable leather wing-backed armchair. He could have done with the relaxation. But his upbringing dictated he should eat at the table, despite there being no strict parents or formidable nanny around now to make him adhere to their standards.

Ty wasn't in the best of moods, having been dragged out of bed at four-thirty that morning. He'd been summoned by the extremely anxious works manager of a local factory whose wife was expecting her first baby at the age of forty-three. The husband did not trust a midwife to see to her in case of complications due to his wife's age, and was insisting Ty himself oversee the birth.

From the symptoms the man blurted out to him, Ty knew that the patient, who had still three weeks to go before her due date, was just experiencing Braxton Hicks contractions, but the man made it plain he wasn't going to be placated by Ty's verbal diagnosis, he wanted a visit. The good thing was that Ty would be guaranteed payment for this home visit through the works remuneration scheme which covered this family. It was as he suspected, the woman had just been suffering testing pains, but by the time Ty had got back home, it hadn't been worth returning to bed so he'd used the time to catch up with some paperwork.

Morning surgery had been busy and had overrun by three quarters of an hour. He'd been late starting his morning round in the area, which then resulted in his overrunning by forty minutes. He was left with just twenty minutes to make and eat his lunch before going out again on his afternoon round. So a sudden hammering on the surgery door had him exclaiming in exasperation: 'Oh, for God's sake! Do people around here not think their doctor deserves any time to eat his lunch?'

It was on his mind to ignore the summons, pretend he wasn't at home, but the continual urgent thumping on the door had him slamming down his plate and cup of tea, slopping the contents over the table, and shouting out angrily, 'Hold on, I'm just coming.'

He glared in annoyance when he saw the intruder. What was it with this woman that each time she called upon him she was in a state of hysteria, demanding his immediate attention on a matter of life or death? He supposed in fairness the first time she had called him it had in fact been a matter of death, and the second had been a matter of some urgency. Surely, though, the odds were against her having a third emergency so soon? Before he could enquire the reason for her visit, she cried out, 'You've got to come quick, Doc, it's me gran.'

Once again he informed Aidy, 'It's Doctor Strathmore. Now, can whatever it is your grandmother needs to see me about wait until I've at least eaten my lunch?'

'No, it can't! She's had a fall. It's her leg ... The one she broke a few weeks ago ... well, I think she's damaged it again. She's in that much pain, she can't speak.' Aidy grabbed his arm, gripping it tightly. 'You've got to come *now*,' she insisted.

He wasn't amused by her manhandling of him or the tone of voice she'd used to get across her point. Wrenching himself free from her grip, he snapped, 'I'll get my bag then.'

It transpired that Bertha had re-broken her leg. Through her pain, she managed to tell Ty that she'd decided after five weeks of being driven to despair, lying on the sofa, that surely it would have healed by now ... Well, Maisie Turnbull's young son's broken leg had only taken five weeks to heal. Her leg should have been fine by now ... Only for her to discover it wasn't.

Ty had been very brusque in his response. He hadn't ordered complete bed rest for seven weeks for the fun of it, he pointed out. Old broken bones took longer to heal than younger ones. Now she would pay for not adhering to his explicit instructions by another seven weeks of complete rest and, as he'd instructed before, he would examine her to check the bone had healed before she risked putting even gentle pressure on it.

Although she hadn't been alone as yet with her

grandmother, Aidy knew that the explanation she had given the doctor for how she had come to re-break her leg was a complete lie. The truth of the matter was that she had been trying to wake Aidy up. Obviously shouting at her hadn't done the trick, so deeply had she been sleeping, and Bertha's only other option was to shake her awake.

Having shown Ty out, with a promise to settle up his mounting bill as soon as she could, Aidy returned to the back room to study her grandmother's condition. As if the last episode hadn't taken toll enough on her, this one had left her seriously depleted. Before Pat's attack on her, Bertha's age might have slowed her down a bit, she might not have been able to carry heavy loads any longer, but she'd still been very agile for a woman in her late sixties. Now she looked so old and frail . . . Aidy just hoped this was only temporary and once she'd recovered, Bertha would return to her old self.

'Can I get you anything, Gran?' she asked.

The further fracture had been so excruciating that Bertha had resorted to accepting the morphine tablet the doctor had offered her . . . but only half of it. She was therefore feeling a little dopey, as if she'd downed a couple of large schooners of good quality sherry, but the medicine had at least eradicated her pain sufficiently to let the doctor re-set and re-plaster her leg and it was still working its magic.

All she was feeling from her injury at the moment was a bearable dull throb. Once the effects of the pill wore off, though, she was adamant that her own pain-killing remedy would see her through from now on.

In a laboured voice, she responded, 'No, thanks, lovey. I just want to sleep now.'

Aidy leaned down to peck her cheek then whispered, 'This is all my fault and I'm so sorry, Gran. I know you lied to the Doc. You weren't disobeying his orders at all. You were trying to wake me up because I was late back for work, weren't you?'

Drowsily she answered, 'When I woke up and saw you fast off in the chair, then noticed the time, I was worried you'd be in trouble. I did me best to shout you awake but I just couldn't ... I didn't want to tell the doctor what really happened and make you look bad, a young woman of your age, sleeping the afternoon away ...'

Aidy wasn't listening to her. The mention of work had sent a wave of sheer panic rushing through her.

'Oh, Gran, I've got to go! I should be at work. Will you be ...'

Despite her own drug-induced state, Bertha knew why Aidy was concerned. 'Just go, love. I'll be fine. And stop worrying. Yer boss'll be understanding when you tell 'em yer old gran had an accident and you had to get the doctor to her.'

Aidy just had to pray she would be.

Having run all the way back to work, her lungs felt like they were on fire and she was gasping for breath by the time she slipped through the gates, dashed over the yard and sneaked her way round to her own department. Stopping for a moment outside the door to the workroom, she tried to compose herself then walked inside as if she had just slipped out for a moment.

As Aidy made her way to her table, her eyes darted this way and that. Thankfully there was no sign of Imelda. Hopefully she had got away with her lateness.

Colleen accosted her as soon as she slid into her seat, simultaneously pressing the button to start up her machine and grabbing the garment she had just finished making up before the dinner-time hooter had sounded.

'Where yer been, Aidy?' her friend demanded.

'It's a long story, Col. I'll fill you in later. I need to press on.'

So intent on getting on with her work was she, Aidy didn't notice Colleen was trying to tell her something. Quickly checking the cotton was threaded through her machine correctly, she placed the neckline of the dress under the needle foot, pinned a collar in place, pressed her foot down on the pedal and began to attach the collar to the dress. Over the drone of her machine and the forty-nine others, Aidy realised Colleen was shouting at her. Stopping what she was doing, she flashed an irritated look at her, snapping, 'I hope it's urgent, Colleen. You know I've a lot of catching up to do.'

'It's more than urgent, Aidy, it's critical. Hardwick wants to see you in her office. She told me to tell you you're to report there immediately you show up.'

Aidy's face paled. 'She knows I'm late back?'

'"Late back" is an understatement, Aidy. You've been missing half the afternoon. She's been here several times, asking where you were. I tried to cover up for you, told her the first time you'd gone to the privy, the second you'd had to go again 'cos you'd got a stomach upset, but the third time she wasn't wearing it. Told me to send you to see her if you did happen to show your face this afternoon. You'd better go.'

Imelda Hardwick's office was no bigger than a broom cupboard. She was sitting on an uncomfortable wooden chair at a small cluttered desk, her face wearing a pensive frown as she concentrated on the paperwork she was looking through. When a highly worried Aidy tapped on her open door, announcing her presence, Imelda looked up at her blankly for a moment before she quickly turned over the sheet she was looking at and said sardonically, 'Oh, so you have decided after all to grace us with your presence?'

Aidy blurted, 'I'm so sorry I was late back this afternoon, Mrs Hardwick, but you see . . .'

Imelda held up a warning hand to stop her. 'You've been absent without permission. That on its own is a sackable offence, but on top of your poor performance lately . . . well, I have no choice but to dismiss you.'

Aidy froze. She couldn't lose her job. How was she going to support her family? A vision of the workhouse reared up before her and she cried out, 'Oh, please, please, Mrs Hardwick, give me another chance. Once you've heard my reason for being late back . . .'

Imelda cut in, 'You're not dead, Aidy, so there's no excuse for you not being at your bench. If I am seen to let you get away with flouting company rules, the other women will be expecting the same treatment. Worse than that even, if my bosses find out I'm not doing my job properly, I could lose it.' Especially in light of what is going on, she thought. She might have a soft spot for Aidy but not at the expense of her own job. 'Your wages and cards have been made up for you, ready to collect on your way out.'

Colleen was mortified when Aidy returned to her machine to collect her personal belongings. She'd thought that her friend and work colleague was in for a good dressing down, but the sack! Not wanting to face the same situation if she was caught slacking, she hurriedly assured Aidy she would pass on her goodbyes to the rest of her colleagues, Aidy herself being too upset and humiliated due the circumstances. They promised they would get together as often as time allowed them to, but both knew that as matters stood that was a tall order.

Aidy walked off the factory floor carrying her handbag, her face stricken with worry. An uncertain future faced her and her family with no wage coming in. She was acutely conscious that many of the other workers were looking at her with understanding and pity.

She needed to find a replacement job as soon as possible, though she knew the odds were stacked against her in the current work climate. She wasn't expected home for about another hour, so decided to use that time checking shop window cards and vacancies posted outside factories in the vicinity, praying that a firm had a job she was capable of doing.

It proved to be a fruitless search. No vacancies for skilled machinists were posted on any of the factory notice boards, and the shop jobs she saw did not pay a wage anywhere near what she needed to keep a roof over her family's head and them all fed.

When Aidy arrived home she found Marion huddled under the blanket beside Bertha on the sofa. Bertha herself, although still dopey from the effects of shock and the morphine she had taken earlier, was struggling to listen to a story Marion was reading to her out of a tattered children's book. George and a friend were on the rug in front of the range, swapping cigarette cards. There was no sign of Betty. Worried about her serious predicament and what could happen to them all if she didn't resolve it, despite herself, Aidy took her frustration out on George and Marion.

'Couldn't either of you have set the table for dinner?' she barked at them. She then told George's friend, 'You'd better get off home before your mother comes looking for you.' At her tone of voice the boy grabbed his cards and scarpered out like the devil was on his tail. Then she ordered George, 'Clear those cards away and go and fill the water jug.' He didn't need another telling. She turned to address Marion next, 'Stop mithering Gran. Can't you see she's not well? Go and find something useful to do.'

Tears filled Marion's eyes. 'But I was only . . .'

'I don't care what you were *only* doing. I said, get off the sofa and leave Gran in peace! You can set the table.' She had a headache building at the thought of her siblings getting under her feet while she was trying to get the meal. 'Look, I'll collect the water and set the table, you both just go out and play, but make sure you're back in an hour and that you bring Betty with you. Go on then,' Aidy commanded them.

During this time Bertha had been staring at her fixedly. She wasn't that befuddled she did not know that something was seriously wrong with her grand-daughter.

Aidy then snapped at her, 'Do you need anything before I make a start on the dinner?'

'Yes, I do, love. I need to know what's got your goat. Summat has. You've snapped at us all like a mad dog at a bone.' She eyed her granddaughter shrewdly. 'I guess yer boss wasn't happy you were late back to work?'

Despite not wanting to tell Bertha what had tran-spired so as not to worry her, it wasn't right to lie to her. 'No, she wasn't happy, Gran. Not happy at all.' Giving a deep sigh, Aidy went over to the armchair and sank down into it, clasping her hands in her lap. Head bowed, she said tremulously, 'I got the sack.'

Bertha froze. She had suspected that whatever it was that was bothering Aidy was serious. But . . . given the sack?

Aidy could see that her grandmother was feeling guilty for the part she had played in bringing this about. 'This is not your fault, Gran. I shouldn't have fallen asleep. You were just trying to wake me. It's me who should feel guilty. You've suffered the agony of breaking your leg again and are facing another seven weeks on the sofa.'

Bertha pursed her lips, her eyes hardening. 'If anyone is to blame it's Pat Nelson for attacking me in the first place,' she snarled. She was well aware of the economic situation in the country and that jobs were getting scarcer by the day, but Aidy needed encouragement, not despondency. In an optimistic tone she said, 'Well, you'll get snapped up by another firm, with your skills.'

Aidy sighed. 'Maybe I would have a while back, Gran, but not for the foreseeable future, the way things are. I did a quick tour round several of the local factories and none was offering any vacancies for machinists. The jobs in the shop windows are all for cleaners or shop assistants, not offering a wage we could mange on.'

Still determined to offer hope, not hopelessness, Bertha said, 'There's a job somewhere with your name on it, love.'

Aidy flashed her a wan smile. 'I hope so, Gran. But what's worrying me is how long it's going to take me to find it.' She gave another deep sigh. 'Look, it's bad enough for me knowing you know about this, but I don't want the kids to get wind and them be worried too.'

Neither Aidy nor Bertha heard the back door open and someone come in to stand listening to them through the crack in the kitchen door. Or the sound of footsteps softly retreating.

'Of course I won't breathe a word to them,' Bertha assured her.

A knock sounded on the back door then. Aidy's shoulders sagged. She was in no mood for visitors tonight. 'Are you expecting anyone?' she asked Bertha. Her gran shook her head. 'Unless it's someone wanting one of me potions.' Due to her incapacity, her supply of remedies was just about depleted, so it wasn't likely she could satisfy the needs of whoever was calling.

The knock came again, more demanding this time.

Aidy sighed. 'Whoever it is isn't going to give up are they? I'll peep round the kitchen curtain, see who it is before I answer it.'

In the kitchen she secreted herself to one side of the sink, tweaked the faded curtain aside and strained her neck in an effort to see who their caller was. Whoever it was they were standing too close to the door for her to make them out but it was a man, that much she could tell. Then he stepped back and she had a full view of him. It was Arch.

She let the curtain fall back into place in case he spotted her. Why was he here? Had he come to beg her to give their marriage another go? Had he heard she'd lost her job and come to gloat? But then, did it even matter to her what he had come for? She was not yet ready for another face to face with him, still smarting from their last encounter. But was it fair of her to ignore him, not afford him even the courtesy of listening to what he had to say? She heard the clunk of his boots on the cobbles then, the back gate squeak its opening and closing. He had saved her the decision.

Returning to her seat in the armchair, she told her grandmother, 'Whoever it was had gone.' Outwardly she appeared calm and composed but inwardly her heart was breaking, her insides churning, her feelings divided. She still loved Arch, but was mourning the loss of the man she had thought her husband to be. The luxury of having time to come to terms with all this was not to be afforded her. She had people she loved beyond measure reliant on her to protect them. She had promised her dead mother she would, and had every intention of honouring that promise to the best of her ability.

Taking a deep breath, she announced to Bertha, 'When the kids are in bed I'm going to work out how much to put aside for the rent and for coal ... milk ... gas. Well, if it comes to it, we can do without light, make do with candles. And what's left ... well, we'll have to be very careful with until I get set on again. Thank goodness we don't owe anybody anything.' Then a thought struck her. 'Oh, yes, we do. I'd forgotten about the Doc's bill.'

Bertha mused, 'Time was a pie or a cake or a bit of cleaning and washing would have done that. But I suppose the new chap has to pay his bills in cash, the same as us. I've a few shillin' in me remedy money jar, which might just about cover it.'

Aidy prayed it would or they'd just have to hope they didn't have any need of his medical assistance for a long time to come.

CHAPTER TEN

'Just let me get this clear, Mrs Kilner. Starting at six-thirty every morning, you're expecting your domestic to clean out and fire up the boiler for the hot water. Then, after she's seen to the breakfast and cleared away, to clean and polish every room in the house thoroughly, even the three guest bedrooms, whether they're being used or not. Plus a weekly wash of all the windows on the inside, weekly change of all the bedding, and fresh towels in the bathrooms daily. She must tackle the washing and ironing and any mending on a daily basis, prepare lunch for yourself, then prepare and cook an evening meal for when your husband comes home. She must also provide a high tea of sandwiches and cakes for your afternoon visitors and several ladies' groups when it's your turn to entertain them, see to all the grocery and domestic supplies ordering, weekly black-lead all the grates, daily clean and polish all the boots and shoes. And in what spare time she's got, she's to help you with any other jobs you may have for her to do . . .

'She finishes in the evening when she's cleared away the meal. Oh, and she's to make herself further available on the evenings when you're having a dinner party, which you do regularly, to help prepare, cook and serve the food, and clean up afterwards. Six and a half days a week, half-day off on Wednesday.'

Marjorie Kilner was a matronly, humourless fifty-five year old, married to a bank manager. Dressed in a tweed suit, a string of pearls around her meaty neck, she sat stiffly in a high-backed chair and shot Aidy a cold look. 'Your hearing isn't impaired. I am expecting exactly that of my domestic. But you did forget the weekly polishing of the silver.'

'And the wage you're paying is fourteen shillings a week?'

'A generous amount in these hard times.'

Aidy quashed a burning desire to inform the woman that she may think herself clever for using that fact to her own advantage, but what she was actually doing was abusing those far worse off than herself. Aidy was desperate for work and didn't care how hard or how long she had to graft to earn her pay. After five days of fruitless searching, deeply worried by now that she wouldn't be able to pay the rent at the end of next week, she was getting to the stage of accepting anything. But the rent on the house was eight shillings a week, and what would be left over from the pay this woman was offering, not even a miracle worker could feed, clothe and keep a family warm on. That was, provided she even had any energy or time left over to tackle her own chores after she'd laboured for ten hours a day, and sometimes even longer, for this strict task master.

'Your last employee unexpectedly died and that's why you're looking for a replacement, is it?' Aidy asked her matter-of-factly.

The woman looked shocked, it being apparent she felt the question was impertinent. Sharply she answered, 'Not that it's any of your business why I'm interviewing for a new domestic, but Mrs Adkins retired. Why would you think she'd died?'

'I'm surprised she didn't, with all the work you expect your domestic to get through, and all for the measly wage you're offering to cover it.' Aidy got up from her chair. Quashing a strong desire to laugh at the expression of outrage on Marjorie Kilner's face, she added, 'I can see myself out.'

She'd had high hopes of that job, but, determined not to let disappointment get her down, continued with her search, revisiting places she had been to previously just in case a vacancy had cropped up meantime. She had no joy. Many places she didn't even bother enquiring when she saw the queue of people lining up to apply for the few positions being offered. There were several shops in need of staff that would have taken an experienced woman on, but the owners weren't prepared to take on someone like Aidy when there were so many trained shop assistants looking for work.

By twelve-thirty she was finding it very difficult to keep her spirits up and remain optimistic. She had been banking on landing some sort of job this week, allowing for the fact she'd have to work a week in hand. She could just about eke out her last pay for another week, provided no costly emergencies happened, but certainly no longer. The kids were getting sick of vegetable soup for their dinner, and for that matter so was she, but it was better than nothing – and nothing was what they'd be getting soon if her luck on the job front didn't take a turn for the better.

If she didn't get a job by the end of the week, though, she did have a back-up plan she would put into operation. When her father had left her mother, having no other way open to her at the time by which to provide for her family, Jessie had resorted to taking in washing and ironing and had rented out her own bedroom to a lodger. Aidy proposed to follow in her footsteps. The sleeping arrangements for the family would have to be reorganised. She and Bertha would have to move out of their room and into the girls', the girls would go into George's, and then somewhere must be found for him, though where yet she hadn't a clue. And where she was going to get the money from to buy a Put-you-up for George to sleep on, and the extra bedding, she hadn't a clue either. As matters stood, the only person she could turn to for help was her estranged husband, which would only serve to prove him right that she couldn't manage without his help. Aidy wouldn't give him the satisfaction.

Then suddenly an idea of how she could raise some further money came to her. When she had gone to collect the rest of her belongings back at the house she had shared with Arch, in her haste to get in and out, she had completely forgotten to pick up the little pot on the tallboy in her bedroom.

It contained a few pieces of silver-plated jewellery. These included a very pretty butterfly-shaped brooch with two tiny pieces of emerald depicting its eyes that Arch had bought her on their first wedding anniversary; a hat pin with a ruby inserted in the end that she'd bought herself before she'd married Arch; a charm bracelet that her mother had bought on her twenty-first birthday, one charm on it in the shape of a tiny wishbone. The intention had been to add more in time, but to date money hadn't allowed for that. Not forgetting the watch she wore on her wrist, a present from Arch last Christmas. There were besides two china ornaments, not expensive and from the second-hand shop, but nevertheless bought with love by her mother for Christmas presents, and a copper jug her grandmother had given her. If she pawned all of these, surely she'd raise enough for them from the pawnbroker to tide her over before her back-up plan started paying out.

She looked at her watch. It was gone twelve-thirty. Pat would be off to work by now and Jim down the local. Arch should be at work too. She was safe to collect what was hers. Aidy was thankful she hadn't allowed her mother-in-law to bully her into handing her keys over.

She felt like a burglar, sneaking her way into her own backyard, then creeping up to the back-room window and peeping through it to make certain the house was indeed empty. It certainly appeared to be. There was no sounds coming from inside that she could hear. Unlocking the back door, she let herself inside. The foul smell hit her first, then the sight that met her left her gasping in shock. The pot sink was heavily stained, it being obvious it hadn't been scrubbed since she'd left, and was filled with dirty crockery, spilling out on to the wooden draining board. A sack propped by the wall was filled with stinking rubbish. The saucepans that she had kept shiny were now blackened and smeared with burned food. The flag floor was filthy and sticky under her shoes. The drying towel she was positive was the same one she had been using the day her mother had died. Disgusted, she made her way into the back room. Her revulsion rose further when she saw the state of it.

The table was cluttered with the remains of breakfast and, if she wasn't mistaken, last night's meal too. Beside the armchair Jim had claimed for himself stood at least a dozen empty beer bottles and as many discarded newspapers. The arms of both easy chairs were stained with spilled tea and food. Cobwebs filled the corners of the ceiling, and the visible surfaces of the sideboard against the far wall and the mantle above the range were thick with dust. The clippy rug by the fire had very obviously not been shaken since she'd departed. The rest of the floor hadn't been swept either. Upstairs a sour smell permeated the bedroom she had shared with Arch. It was now being occupied by his parents, and the sheets on the unmade bed were, she knew, the same pair that had been on it when she had left.

In five weeks the slovenly Nelsons had turned the lovely home that she and Arch had worked so hard to make nice into a mirror imagine of the squalid hovel they had left behind. How could Arch have stood by and let this happen? Was he so frightened of his mother, he'd allowed her to wreck his own home?

Was this perhaps why he had called to see her last night? Unable to put up with living under the same roof as them again and endure their slovenly ways, had he come to beg sanctuary off her until he could either get his parents out and reclaim the house or find another place for himself? Well, hopefully her refusal to see him had done him a favour, made him face his fears and stand up to his mother. He must free himself from her selfish domination sooner rather than later.

Aidy searched high and low but there was no sign of all the items she had come to retrieve. She knew, with a sinking heart, what had happened to them. Pat would have had no qualms in claiming they were hers and selling them on to the highest bidder.

Aidy didn't know how that woman lived with herself, but then ... women like Pat had no conscience. The one good thing to have come from the ending of her marriage was that she no longer had to deal with the likes of odious, selfish, bullying Pat Nelson.

Aidy was so upset about her discovery she decided to go home for a cup of tea and to check on Bertha before continuing with her job search. Also she knew that her grandmother would be anxious for news of how she was faring, realising how increasingly despondent Aidy was becoming as the days went by. She wouldn't, however, upset Bertha by telling her of this visit to her former home and the dreadful state she had found it in.

* * *

Bertha's hopeful eyes greeted Aidy when she arrived in the back room, but as soon as she witnessed the look on her granddaughter's face she knew there was no point in asking if she'd had any success. 'Better luck this afternoon, love,' was all she said.

She didn't want to add to Aidy's worries but there was something she really ought to be aware of. 'Er . . . I had a visit this morning from the Board man. Seems our George ain't been at school all this week.'

Aidy looked bemused as she checked the kettle on the range and put it on to make them both a cup of tea. ''Course he's been at school. Where else would he be? In fact, he's been that keen this last week, he's been leaving well before he's really needed to, hasn't he? The Board man can't have his facts right.'

'That's what I said to him. He insisted he had, though, and that the school wants a good excuse for George's absence. He's coming back tomorrow at ten, to see you.'

Aidy snapped in annoyance, 'So I've got to wait in and maybe miss out on getting a job, all 'cos either the school or the Board man has made a mistake?' She gave an exasperated sigh. 'Well, I'll certainly let *them* have what for, wasting my time.' A thought suddenly occurred to her. 'Come to think of it, George has been very tired this week. Hasn't gone out at all after dinner to play with his mates, and he's gone to bed without being told.'

'Oh, that's 'cos he's been helping a mate straight from school to fix his bike up. Apparently his dad found an abandoned bike frame and George and his mate have been scavenging for parts for it from dump sites.'

'But he's supposed to come straight home from school, Gran, and see to any jobs that need doing here – him and Betty. Has he blackmailed her into doing his share?'

Bertha looked sheepish. 'Well ... er ... no, not exactly. This past week, Betty ain't been coming home straight from school either. Her best friend's mother has just had a baby, and while she's recovering in bed, her friend has fetched her younger brother and sister from the neighbour and Betty's been helping her look after them until their dad gets home from work.'

'Very commendable of her,' snapped Aidy. 'But she's got an invalid grandmother who is also in need of her help, and chores to do for me. Who has been doing both their chores while they've been skiving off then?'

'Marion.'

'Marion! Oh, bribed her into it, did they? Promise her a sweet each from their penny poke on Saturday morning? Well, they won't be able to honour that bribe as I can't afford to give them their Saturday pennies until I get set on again. But how on earth did Marion struggle to get the water and the coal in on George's behalf *and* do the bits around the house for Betty?'

'She got the lad next-door to pump it for her and fetched it in a jug at a time. She did the coal the same, a few lumps at a time. She seemed happy enough, doing what she was. Look, I did point out that it wasn't right they were defying your instructions and they should ask you if it was all right to do what they were, but they pleaded with me. George was worried that his mate would find someone else to help him look for parts and fix the bike up, and Betty the same with her friend.'

Aidy shook her head. 'Those kids wind you around their little fingers. But they still disobeyed me and, worse, roped their little sister into covering their jobs for them and you into keeping what they were up to from me. I can't turn a blind eye to that.'

She noticed Bertha was frantically searching for something under her blanket. Curious, Aidy asked her what she was looking for.

'Me knitting needle, lovey. I've an itch under me pot I need to scratch. It's been driving me mad all morning. No matter how many times I slip the needle down and give it a good rub with the end, it keeps coming back. Blasted thing.'

With a twinkle in her eye, Aidy said, 'You brag you've a potion for just about any ailment. Not got one for curing itches, I take it then?'

'Cheeky bugger! Just help me find the pin.'

As she helped, Aidy warned Bertha, 'Be careful not to damage the cast with that needle 'cos I don't fancy facing Doc's reaction if we have to call him in to re-plaster your leg again.'

At the mention of him Aidy remembered she hadn't paid his outstanding bill yet. If she didn't settle it, he could well refuse to call again on Bertha when her time was up, to check her leg had healed and pronounce her fit enough to start using it again. He'd be quite within his rights to do so. She'd pay a visit to the surgery and do the deed before carrying on with her job search that afternoon.

Meanwhile over in the surgery, eating his lunch of a hastily made cheese sandwich, the bread stale and cheese hard, Ty was searching through the patients' record boxes for the cards of those to whom he was to pay a visit that afternoon.

One of these was Freda Johnson of 19 Lemington Street. The name rang a bell with him. Hadn't he been called in to see her only last week? He felt sure he had. Yes, that's right. Her symptoms of a very inflamed throat, swollen tonsils, white-furred tongue and high fever, had led him to diagnose she was suffering from quinsy. He had written her a prescription for a mixture of prophylactic salicin and chlorate of potash in gualacum, which should help ease her discomfort until the disease had run its course. Had the woman's illness not improved or was she now suffering from something else?

He swivelled around in his chair to look with both frustration and despondency at the two huge piles of loose records he'd been stacking up beside the record boxes. Freda Johnson's card would be amongst these somewhere.

The sorting out of the record cards into a workable system had been his top priority ever since he had discovered the haphazard, unfathomable method James McHinney had used. Until he could find the time at least to make a start on that laborious and lengthy task, he had kept aside those record cards he had managed to unearth, his intention being every night after surgery finished to put those records into alphabetical order, making a start at least on a re-organised system. Unfortunately, the unrelenting demands on his time left him hardly any in which to put a proper meal together for himself or to attend to the most urgent of his personal needs, so sorting out the filing system had long since fallen by the wayside.

Ty's thoughts drifted back to his previous surgery. A far cry from this one! Leaving aside the affluent area and clientele, consultations there had been by appointment only, either at the surgery or at home. Ty had been allowed plenty of time to spend with each patient, listening in depth to their symptoms and thoroughly examining them before prescribing their treatment. All the cleaning of wounds and changing of dressings had been dealt with by a qualified nurse; an efficient clerk and receptionist had dealt with the administrative tasks. A locum doctor had dealt with all the after-hours call outs and Sunday emergencies, unless the patient in question happened to be the sort to insist on being seen only by the senior doctor.

Ty had had time then to spend as he wished, without interruption. His sleep had been unbroken and he awoke each morning feeling refreshed.

He'd not had one night of unbroken sleep since he arrived here, but prised his eyes open each morning before dragging himself from his bed, dreading what the day held for him.

Ty was very aware that if he didn't do something about easing his burden, very soon his own health would suffer. He was concerned that several times recently he had nearly misdiagnosed a serious illness because his permanent state of fatigue was affecting his concentration.

He had sworn an oath to do his best to cure people, not kill them.

There was one ray of hope that kept him going, which was that eventually he would escape this life of purgatory he had unwittingly cast himself into.

No matter how unpopular he knew it had made him, at his insistence the majority of his patients now settled his fee in cash, apart from those stalwarts who insisted on carrying on in the same way as they had in James McHinney's day. But the surgery's finances were at least much healthier than they had been when Ty had first taken over. He was now able to settle his own bills without fretting and, most important of all, he had a little left over each week to put away in a savings account towards his future.

Trouble was, the help he so desperately needed would cost him a wage, which meant his savings were going to suffer and he was stuck here even longer. But if he continued as he was, he risked not living to see his day of escape.

Affording to pay a locum or nurse was out of the question, but he could afford to pay a receptionist to take all the clerical work off his hands, and still have a little left each week to add to his savings. Better they should grow slowly than not at all. Ty felt there must be plenty of women needing a job during these desperate times and expected he would be able to have his pick. A thought struck him then. Would he be lucky enough to find a woman who wanted a receptionist's job but could also tackle some of the lighter cleaning and dressing of wounds? He sincerely hoped so.

He hurriedly glanced at his pocket watch. He

hadn't time to address this now, really should be setting off on his afternoon round, but then the way time was for him, when would he have a better opportunity? He immediately started drafting a notice of his requirements to put on the surgery door.

Aidy spotted the notice as she approached the surgery a short while after Ty had put it up.

She stared at it, her mind whirling. She liked the idea of being a doctor's receptionist. It sounded so posh! Trouble was, though, she'd no experience of office work whatsoever. Oh, but wait a minute, wasn't filling in her time sheets and logging off her completed work classed as office work? Well, by a short stretch of the imagination it could be. She'd never had cause to use a telephone, but how difficult was it to pick up a receiver and speak into it? And anyway, she doubted she'd have much cause to use one since it was unlikely any of the doctor's patients had a telephone and it cost precious money to make a call from the public box. She was reliable and trustworthy, and apart from the incident that had cost her her job, she was punctual. She might not have the best of clothes but she was at least clean and tidy. The starting time of eight-fifteen would certainly suit her better than the factory hour of seven-thirty, and that break in the afternoon from two until four-forty-five meant she could do the shopping at a more leisurely pace than the race she'd had during her one-hour dinner break from her sewing machine. On a Saturday morning the factory hours had been seven-thirty until one, whereas the doctor only needed his receptionist to work from eight-fifteen until twelve-thirty.

This job was appealing more and more to Aidy.

Then her excitement plummeted as a problem presented itself. She didn't actually like the man she'd hopefully be working for. Could she work for someone so cold and aloof? She didn't ponder too long on that problem, though. If it meant her securing a job, and especially a job that offered her all that this did, then, yes, she could put up with the man who was offering it.

Her excitement rose to fever pitch. This job certainly seemed to have her name on it. Then her high spirits sank as she read the last line of the notice. *Someone with nursing experience would be preferred.* She hadn't got any nursing experience. It didn't look like this job had her name on it after all. Then her spirits rose yet again. She certainly *did* have nursing experience. Over the years she had bathed and dressed numerous wounds suffered by her brother and sisters and Arch when they'd accidentally cut, bumped or burned themselves. None of the wounds had turned septic. And wasn't what she was doing now in respect of her grandmother nursing? It certainly felt like it to Aidy's mind.

This job *did* have her name on it. She was determined to land it.

Interviews for the position were to take place on the following Monday evening after surgery finished at seven o'clock. She'd be there prompt. She just had to hope not too many applied for it who were better qualified than herself. She was about to walk away when an idea came to her of how she could lower the odds against that happening. Flashing a hurried glance around to ascertain no one would witness what she was about to do, she snatched the notice off the door and thrust it into her pocket.

She was so excited at the prospect of getting a job she completely forgot why she had called at the doctor's surgery in the first place.

Aidy wasn't complacent enough to believe that just because she was hell-bent on getting the job as the doctor's receptionist she actually would. She knew she'd be well advised to keep on with her search meantime.

Which again turned out to be a futile. No factories, shops, yards or even scrap merchants seemed to have any vacancies for suitable jobs. It seemed at the moment the job the doctor was advertising was her only hope.

Having reluctantly called it a day, she was back at home in the scullery, peeling potatoes to make a cheese and potato pie for their dinner – although considering the small noggin of hard cheese that was left, it was more of a potato pie – when Marion burst through the door. She immediately threw herself at her sister, clasping her arms around Aidy's waist and burying her head in her midriff, wailing, 'I 'ate that Elsie Broadbent, our Sis! She's 'orrible. I ain't ever gonna be her friend again.'

Hurriedly wiping her wet hands on a towel, Aidy unhooked Marion from her person, knelt down and wiped her eyes using the bottom of her apron, saying, 'You two were as thick as thieves yesterday. You begged me to let Elsie stay for dinner as you didn't want to be parted from her during that time, only I had to say no 'cos I hadn't enough chips and bread and marge to stretch. What's happened between you two for you to hate her so much now?'

Marion blubbered, 'She . . . she told Miss Hubbard I'd wet meself! And in front of the whole class and all, so now everyone knows and they're calling me Pissy Pants.'

Aidy's heart went out to her. Running a hand tenderly down the side of the child's face, she said, 'Well, you can't help it if you have an accident. But what you could do to try and stop having them in future is keep going to the lav regularly, even if you don't feel the need to go. Will you do that, eh?'

Sniffling, Marion nodded.

'Good girl. Now, about Elsie . . . you don't think

she was trying to help you, do you?'

Marion's little face screwed up in bewilderment. 'Help me? I don't see how.'

'Maybe she didn't like the fact you were sitting there in wet clothes, and hoped that by her telling Miss Hubbard, you'd be given clean ones to borrow until your own dried. Maybe she didn't think about the rest of the class finding out when she told Miss Hubbard.'

Marion had to think about that for a moment. Finally she said, 'I suppose she could have.'

'Well, why don't you ask her before you decide you're never going to be friends with her again? If she did do it on purpose then you've every right not to talk to her, if that's what you decide, but I think she was after helping you myself.' Aidy stood up. 'You'd best get changed, and bring me those clothes you've on down so I can wash them and get them dried ready for tomorrow. But before you go and square things with Elsie, I want you to find George for me and tell him to get himself home. I want a word with him. Then find Betty and tell her the same.'

Marion was looking at her worriedly. She blustered, 'Oh, I dunno where either of them are, Aidy.'

'Don't lie, you do. You've been covering their chores while George is helping his best mate fix up his bike and Betty babysits her best friend's brother and sister.'

Marion was looking mortally uncomfortable. She blurted, 'Er . . . oh, yeah, so I have. I forgot. But I . . . er . . . don't know where their best friends live, honest I don't.'

'Well, one of their other friends is bound to, so go and ask around until you find out.'

'Can't yer wait to have a word with 'em until they come home?'

Aidy began to feel irritated with Marion now. Sharply she said to her, 'I want a word with them both *now*. The quicker you find them for me, the quicker you can sort out things with Elsie. Go and get changed then be off to do what I've asked you, or you'll end up in bed with a red bum and hungry 'cos yer've had no dinner.'

Marion spun on her heel and shot off.

Aidy sighed as she returned to her task. What did it take to get her siblings to obey her?

George finally appeared at a quarter to six. By this time Aidy had decided he had ignored Marion's summons for him to come home and her temper was at boiling point. She was in the process of setting the table. Slamming down the cutlery, hands on hips, she flew at him. 'I'll teach you to blatantly ignore my instructions to come straight home, George Greenwood. You'll stay home for a week. And then you'll stay for another week on top, for not doing as I asked which was coming home straight from school to see if Gran needed anything or if I'd left any instructions for jobs I needed you to do. And then you'll stay home for *another* week for bribing your little sister to do your chores for you while you were off enjoying yourself with your mate. That's three weeks altogether.' She noticed Betty hovering behind her brother and snapped at her, 'And the same goes for you, young lady.'

From her makeshift bed on the sofa, Bertha opened her mouth, preparing to speak up for the children, to request Aidy be a little more lenient with them as, after all, they had not long since lost their mother. But then, Aidy was their mother now, to all intents and purposes, and it wouldn't be right for Bertha to interfere with the way she decided to discipline them.

Both children's faces had paled and they were looking extremely worried.

George blurted out, 'Oh, please, don't keep me in, our Aidy, 'cos if you do I'll lose . . .' He suddenly stopped speaking, it being very obvious he'd been about to divulge something he'd sooner Aidy not know.

She eyed him suspiciously. 'You'll lose what?' she demanded.

He shuffled uncomfortably on his feet, averting his eyes from hers. 'Er . . . me friends.'

'Yeah, and me too, so please don't punish me either,' pleaded Betty.

Aidy eyed them both suspiciously. Her instincts told her they were both up to something ... especially George. He had a guilty look about him. Had the Board man not made a mistake after all? If he hadn't been to school for the last week then where had he been? She looked at him closely. At the end of the day George always looked like he'd been playing in a muck heap, but his appearance did look even more dishevelled than normal. And he did seem fit to drop. Whatever he was up to it was wearing him out.

Matter-of-factly she announced, 'Gran had a visit from the Board man today, wanting to know why you haven't been at school. 'Cause you've been at school, haven't you, George? Where else would you be, eh?'

His face was ashen now. 'The Board man's bin round?' he uttered, horrified. Then he said defiantly, 'Well, he's got me mixed up with another kid 'cos I have been at school, ain't I, Betty?'

She gulped, eyes darting everywhere but in her sister's direction, and uttered, 'Yes, he has, our Aidy. Honest he has.'

'And I know when lies are being told! You're both lying.' She wagged a finger at George. 'Shame on you, getting your sister to lie for you. Did you think I wouldn't find out you'd been truanting from school? Did you think your teacher wouldn't ask me where you were when I never sent a note in, saying why you were absent? So what *have* you been up to when you should have been in school? Larking around with your delinquent mates? Plaguing shop-keepers? Robbing old ladies? What, George?' she bellowed furiously. 'Now I'll give you one chance to tell me what you've been up to or else you're in bigger trouble than you already are, if that's even possible.'

Betty started to cry. 'Oh, please don't be cross with him, our Aidy,' she blubbered. 'He only did it to help you. I was only trying to help too. That's why I never came home straight after school, like you told me to.'

Aidy glared at her incredulously. 'How can you think that playing truant is helping me, you stupid girl?' she barked. 'I'm in trouble now with the Board man, for not making sure George was at school.' Then something Betty had said registered with her. 'What do you mean, you were only trying to help too and that's why you never came straight home from school?' She looked at them both suspiciously. 'Just what is it that you two have been up to?' They were both looking everywhere but at her so she bellowed, 'For God's sake, will you just tell me?'

Betty gave her brother a hefty nudge in his ribs. 'You do it 'cos you're the eldest, George.'

He looked up at his elder sister for several long moments before he dared to murmur: 'Working.'

'Working! What do you mean, you've been working?'

He hung his head. 'I overheard you telling Gran you'd lost yer job, so I thought if I could earn some money while you got set on in another, you wouldn't be so worried. I forgot about the Board man. When I told Betty what I was up to so she could cover for me, she wanted to help too so she's been doing it after school.'

'I've bin running errands for the neighbours,' Betty told Aidy. 'I've made one shilling and tuppence up to now. I was hoping to have two bob to give you by Friday. Not as much as George has made, but it all helps, dunnit?'

Aidy was gawping at them both, astounded. She shot a look at Bertha and saw she too was utterly astonished by this news. Returning her attention to her siblings, guilt filled her. Her emotions overspilled. With tears of gratitude rolling down her face, Aidy pulled them to her, hugging them both fiercely. Over the tops of their heads she saw their grandmother was crying too. Sensing another presence, she looked over and saw Marion had arrived back. Legs crossed, she was looking worriedly at them all, not quite knowing what was going on.

Aidy ordered her, 'You come here and get a hug too.' When Marion was encircled in her arms she said to them all, 'I really should be very angry with you. But how can I be when all you were trying to do was help?'

Aidy eventually straightened up and in a tender voice addressed them all. 'You all already do what you can to help out.' And they did, by plaguing the greengrocer on a Saturday evening as he was shutting up for any perishable vegetables he was throwing out; by following the coal cart for dropped lumps, and collecting the horse's droppings to sell on to men who had allotments; by keeping their ears open to learn where any wood was going begging; by running errands for the neighbours, and any other things they could do when opportunities presented themselves to earn extra coppers. 'What you all do helped Mam enormously, and now it does me.'

She smiled at the girls. 'You two go and finish setting the table for me. I want to speak to George.' When they had gone off to do her bidding, she asked him, 'Who employed you? You're only ten years old.'

'Nearly eleven,' he corrected her.

'Still not old enough by law to stop going to school. You have to be fourteen. You look nowhere near that. Whoever you lied to to get the job, must have known he was breaking the law.'

'I didn't need to lie about me age – I wasn't asked how old I was. I just asked if there was any work going and got set straight on, sorting out the scrap. I can't say as I enjoyed it. I'm a bit glad I got found out. It was such hard work! Some of them big bits were so heavy ... Me legs are covered in bruises. I never got to stop all day, 'cept ten minutes at lunchtime to gobble down me sandwich. When I leave school, I ain't going to work for no scrappy, that's for sure.'

Aidy was determined he wasn't going to either. She was going to make sure her brother was equipped to achieve far greater things than sorting scrap metal for a living. Fury rose within her against the unknown person who had abused her brother's need to earn a pittance by giving him back-breaking tasks to do.

'Who was it you were working for?' she insisted on knowing.

'Gibbons' scrap yard,' he told her.

She knew the place. It was not far from where her mother-in-law used to live. It was a known fact that all the firms that operated in that district were owned by swindlers and crooks. You only dealt with their like out of desperation. 'How much did Gibbons pay you?'

'He ain't paid me n'ote yet. Said he'd give me ten shilling on Friday night ... that's tomorrow ... as long as I'd proved me worth. Well, I *have* proved me worth to him. I've worked me guts out.'

And Aidy strongly suspected sly Mr Gibbons had no intention of ever paying a penny for that week of hard labour. Well, over her dead body he wouldn't!

She stepped over to the armchair and grabbed up her handbag from beside it.

'Betty, there's cheese pie ready in the oven. Dish it up and put George's and mine back in the oven to keep hot. George, you're coming with me. We won't be long,' she told them all.

Bertha didn't need to ask where she was going.

They arrived at Gibbons' scrap yard just as the owner himself was about to shut and padlock the heavy iron entrance gates for the night.

Alf Gibbons was a sixty-year-old, thick-set man with a matted greying beard and grizzled hair that resembled a bird's nest. His shabby clothes were stained with oil and dirt, a foul stench coming from them, and they obviously hadn't seen soap and water since the day he had bought them. Aidy felt there was enough dirt under his fingernails to sow potatoes in. He lived in a shambles of a shack at the back of the yard, using rainwater for drinking and washing, if indeed he ever did any of that, judging by the grime ingrained in every crease of his face.

Spotting his visitors and completely ignoring the fact one was a young boy he'd had grafting hard for him all week, he growled, 'Come back termorra. I'm shuttin' up for the night.'

Dragging George along with her, Aidy had slipped through the gate and into the yard before Gibbons could stop her. Her face set stonily, she snapped at him, 'I'll not come back tomorrow, you'll deal with me tonight! I've come to inform you that George won't be working for you any longer, and to collect the money you owe him.'

Gibbons didn't even bother to look at George. With a sly grin on his face, he responded, 'He's just a kid. I don't employ kids.'

She shot back at him, 'You employed *this* kid. You've had him slaving like a navvy for you for four days with hardly a break. Now, you'll pay him what he's due.'

Gibbons leaned towards her, a menacing glint in his eyes, a smirk on his face. 'I ain't paying him n'ote. It's my word against his. Now scarper, lady, afore I make yer sorry you came.'

A furious George bunched one fist. Shaking it at Alf, he yelled, 'Oi, don't you speak to my sister like that or you'll regret it!'

Alf Gibbons issued a nasty laugh 'Oh, I'm real scared, sonny.' He gave Aidy a shove on her shoulder. 'Now get off my land before I bodily remove yer both.'

Aidy had anticipated this reaction and was prepared for it. 'All right, I'll go, Mr Gibbons. But just to warn you, you'd better be prepared for another visit very shortly.'

'From the police?' he scoffed. 'You've no proof whatsoever that lad was working for me, so yer wasting yer time fetching them.'

'Oh, I wouldn't dream of wasting police time, Mr Gibbons. Living around these parts, I trust you know Pat Nelson?'

It amused Aidy to catch the flash of fear in his eyes at the mention of that name, just as she'd anticipated. He eyed her suspiciously. 'Yeah, I know of Pat Nelson. I've had a few dealings with her. Mostly with her old man, though, buying scrap metal off him. What's she got to do with this?'

'If you've had dealings with her then I trust you know what kind of woman she is, Mr Gibbons. It's just you might be interested to learn that George is her grandson,' she lied with no compunction. 'He's her favourite, and she isn't going to like the fact that you're trying to swindle him out of his pay.'

Gibbons stared frozen faced at Aidy for a moment before a beam split his face, revealing cigarette-stained, crooked teeth. Slapping George on the back, he said jocularly, 'Why didn't you let on you was Pat's grandkid? Just a misunderstanding, all this.' He thrust one dirty hand into his trouser pocket and pulled out a handful of change, hurriedly counting out silver and copper amounting to seven shillings and sixpence which he then held out to George. 'No point in calling by hoping for any more work, son. Things are real bad at the moment, what with this recession.'

It was Aidy who took the money from him and

quickly assessed the amount. 'Oh, I think you've made a mistake, Mr Gibbons. Obviously mistook the tanners for shillings and the shillings for half-crowns.'

'What d'yer mean?' he snapped at her.

'Seven and six in exchange for four days' hard graft? Pat ain't going to think that's fair when I tell her.'

He nearly choked. 'Well, just how much *was* you expecting? He is a kid, after all.'

'At least twice that amount. After all, you got this kid doing the work of a man, didn't you, Mr Gibbons?'

Grunting and muttering profanities under his breath, he thrust his hand once again into his trouser pocket, pulling out another handful of change along with a couple of bank notes.

As he made to count out another seven shillings and sixpence, Aidy whipped the ten-shilling note out of his hand, saying to him, 'Save you the bother of counting out change, I'll settle for this. And I'll make sure to let Pat know how good you were to her favourite grandson.' She then quickly grabbed George by the shoulder. Before Alf could detain them they had both slipped back through the gate and were hurrying off down the street.

Safely secreted around a corner, Aidy stopped and began to laugh. 'Well, dear brother, that'll teach that crook to think twice before he tries to fleece a youngster in future!' Then her face took on a serious expression. Opening her clenched hand, she held the money in it out towards George. 'Make the most of it. You won't be earning any more like that until you reach the proper age to leave school: fourteen. Now I really appreciate what you did, George, but truant again, for any reasons, and I'll make it my business to make you wish you hadn't. That clear?'

He nodded vigorously. Then said to her, 'The money's all for you, Aidy, to help keep us 'till you get another job.'

She smiled tenderly at him. 'Thank you. It'll come in very handy. But it's only fair you should have some.' She held out half a crown to him. She saw he was about to refuse it and ordered him, 'Take it, George. You deserve every penny of it. Do what you like with it. Spend it on comics, sweets, whatever you want.'

His face lit up. Accepting the money, he gazed at it in delight. Half a crown was a fortune to him, the most money he'd ever had to call his own. Just to make sure it was definitely his to spend as he wished, he reaffirmed with her, 'I can do what I like with it, really, our Aidy? Anything I want?'

Smiling, she nodded.

'Then I'm gonna buy us all fish and chips for our tea tomorrow night. And a big pickled onion for you and a gherkin for Gran.'

Aidy was far too choked to respond.

* * *

Aidy was able to placate the Board man when he called to see her the next morning by insisting that George had been off school because he had been ill with a fever. In her worry for him, she had completely forgotten she needed to inform the school as to the reason for his absence. It was very remiss of her and she felt very guilty and sorry for her failure, but hoped the Board man would see fit not to take this matter further.

She didn't think much to her chances of that, however. He looked the sort to her who took great delight in asserting his authority.

Her appraisal of Neville Hill was indeed correct. Normally he took his job very seriously and would have had her hauled before the Board for them to deal with her laxness as they saw fitting. But, luckily for Aidy, that morning, on his way to see her, he had found a ten-shilling note in the gutter as he was crossing the road. He'd beaten a woman who had also spotted it, snatching it up, to his glee and her fury. His mind was so busy deciding just how he was going to spend his windfall . . . he certainly wasn't going to tell his penny-pinching wife . . . that he couldn't wait to get this matter with the Greenwoods over with and get back to his day dreaming.

CHAPTER ELEVEN

For at least the tenth time in the last half an hour, a highly anxious Aidy asked Bertha, 'Do I look smart enough, Gran? Do I look like a receptionist should?'

She was wearing a plain navy kick-pleat skirt and white high-necked blouse. On her feet were chunky, low-heeled court shoes, a thick coating of shoe polish having been applied to hide their scuffs. Her newly washed hair was brushed to a shine and framed her pretty face. Not wanting to get off to a bad start, she had decided to play it safe and not wear any make-up, just in case the doctor deemed it unfitting for his receptionist while on duty.

Bertha very much hoped Aidy got this job because otherwise domestic service for tyrants like Majorie Kilner was all that remained, God forbid.

For the umpteenth time she responded, 'You look lovely to me, gel. Really efficient-looking. The doctor would be out of his mind not to take you on.'

'Me teacher wears a skirt and blouse like you have on, only you look prettier than she does, our Aidy,' piped up Marion, nestled beside her grandmother on the sofa.

Perched sideways on a dining chair by the table, Betty was looking over at her in awe. She thought her big sister beautiful and clever, and aspired to be just like her when she grew up. 'No one else'll stand a chance against you,' she said.

Lounging in the easy chair, one of his badly bruised and battered legs hanging over one arm, George was too engrossed in a *Dan Dare* comic he'd borrowed off a friend to be aware of anything else going on in the room.

The time showing on the old tin clock on the mantle was twenty-five minutes to seven. Aidy took one last look in the mirror that was hanging on the wall opposite the range. She gave her hair a pat, her cheeks a pinch, then smoothed her hands down her skirt. She would just have to do because she hadn't time to change now anyway.

Full of purpose, determined to prove to the doctor she was the best applicant for his job, and waved off by her family amid shouts of 'Good luck!' she set off, arriving outside the surgery at a quarter to seven. She was far too early but that was better than being late. She made to enter the waiting room but stopped short as a bout of nerves hit her. She suddenly wondered what awaited her inside. How many other applicants was she up against? Were they all far better qualified for the job than she was? What she hoped was that the doctor had failed to notice she had stolen his advertisement and hadn't replaced it with another so she'd be the only applicant. The waiting room had a small window set in the door. She would take a peek through it . . .

To her dismay, through the small glass pane she could make out at least ten women and there were possibly others sitting on the bench in an area of the room that wasn't visible to her. The women were of varying ages, from late-teens to middle aged, and looked neat and tidy. All had a look on their face showing they were as determined to make this job theirs as she was. Most of them were holding brown envelopes. For a moment she wondered what those envelopes could possibly be holding. Then it struck her. Of course, glowing references from previous employers. She hadn't got one from her last employer. It hadn't seemed worth while asking after being sacked.

A sense of deep despondency washed over Aidy. She wasn't the sort to admit defeat easily but she was also no fool. She knew that pitched against the women in that waiting room, she had no chance of landing the job. She might as well go home.

Her shoulders slumped dejectedly, she turned and

began to retrace her steps. She'd hardly gone any distance when she stopped abruptly as a sudden thought struck her like, a thunderbolt.

What if she *didn't* have any competition? If she was the only applicant, then the doctor would have no choice but to give her the job, wouldn't he?

Her mind raced as she pondered her idea. With a lot of nerve and luck on her side, it could very well work ... She had nothing to lose by having a go, everything to gain if she did succeed. What she was about to do wasn't honest, but desperate times called for desperate measures. She felt positive most of the women in the waiting room would attempt what she was about to, had they thought of her idea and were in need of this job as badly as she was.

She spun on her heel and retraced her steps, only this time she did not head for the surgery door but for one in the wall that enclosed the yard at the back of the house.

She cringed as the gate squeaked open then quickly relatched it behind her and scooted across the yard towards the back door, all the time praying she hadn't alerted the doctor to her presence. Should he look out of the window, she would be clearly visible as twilight was only just beginning to fall on this warm late-September evening.

Reaching the back door without mishap, she breathed a great sigh of relief. So far, so good. She took a tentative peek through the kitchen window. The doctor was in the house somewhere, but thankfully not in there. Deftly opening the back door, Aidy slipped inside, quickly shutting it behind her.

Now she was actually inside the house illegally, what she was in fact doing hit home and fear of discovery had her quaking. Should the doctor find her prowling uninvited around his house, she had no plausible reason to excuse her presence. With a vision of him marching her off to the police station, she shot across the black-and-white-tiled kitchen floor to the door opposite. She opened it up just far enough to steal a glance through. A long empty corridor faced her, the front door at the end along with the staircase. There were four doors leading off the corridor. Two to the left of her, two to her right. The rooms to the left were smaller than those to the right, judging by the space between the doors. She judged the first one on the left to be Doc's actual surgery, the next one to it the waiting room. The staircase rose beyond. The room to the immediate right must be his sitting room, and the room beyond the dining room. Which room was the doctor in now? Was it too much to hope he was in his bedroom, readying himself for the interviews? Anyway, hopefully she had located the waiting room, which was the one she was after. She would waste no time in getting herself inside.

She made to step out into the corridor then froze as the sound of cutlery scraping on china became audible. The sound had come from the room to the right of her she had judged to be the dining room. The doctor was in there eating his evening meal! In order to get to the waiting room she had to pass that room and he could come out of it at any second ... Plus the door was open and her getting past it unseen by him depended on whether he was sitting facing it or with his back to it. Hardly daring to breathe, her heart pounding, painfully Aidy tiptoed over and peeped through the crack between the door and the frame. She could have yelped for joy. The doctor was sitting with his back to the door! Luck was certainly on her side tonight. Dare she hope it stayed on her side a little longer ...

Creeping past the dining room and on to the waiting-room door, she paused before it just long enough to take a deep breath to calm her jangling nerves. Then, planting a smile on her face, she grabbed hold of the door knob, turned it and quickly entered, shutting the door behind her.

At her entry the fifteen occupants of the room all looked over at her expectantly.

Feeling no guilt whatsoever for the lies she was about to tell, she addressed them all breezily with, 'Doc's asked me to tell you that the job's gone.'

Before she could say anything more a disgruntled

voice piped up, 'What d'yer mean, the job's gone? None of us has had an interview for it yet.'

Aidy looked over to the person who'd protested. She hadn't noticed her when she had taken a sneaky look through the surgery window earlier. Bella Graves! A nineteen-year-old bleached blonde, her voluptuous figure encased in a shabby red tight-fitting dress, ample bosom spilling out over the low-cut top. She lived with her blowsy mother who was rumoured to be on the game . . . as quite possibly Bella herself was too . . . in a crumbling, one-roomed dwelling in a part of the area even the hardest of men thought twice about visiting. The next street to the one Aidy's in-laws had lived, in fact. Bella was a Pat Nelson in the making. It was glaringly apparent to Aidy that it wasn't the job Bella was after but the doctor himself, planning to ensnare him with her charms with a view to becoming his wife. Why any woman would want to spend any more time with that sourpuss was beyond Aidy, but was Bella mad to think a man of his obvious breeding would look twice at the likes of her, let alone contemplate marriage?

Scathingly she said, 'It's a receptionist the Doc's after, not a hostess in a cheap night club.'

Bella's painted face darkened thunderously. Clenching her fists, she jumped up, preparing to launch herself at the other girl, but stopped when Aidy commented: 'Do you really want to make yourself look a fool in front of all these respectable women?'

Bella stared murderously at Aidy for a moment, before hissing, 'You bitch,' and stomping across the room and out of the door, slamming it shut behind her.

Aidy hid a smile. One down, now for the rest, she thought.

'You said the job's gone,' said a prim-looking woman facing her. 'Are you saying that Doctor Strathmore isn't after a receptionist after all then?'

Extremely conscious that time was ticking away, Aidy hurriedly answered her, 'By "gone" I meant taken. By me. Now . . .'

'By you?' another voice cut in. 'But you haven't got what it takes to be a receptionist, Aidy Nelson. All you've ever done is factory work.'

Aidy looked across at the woman who'd spoken and recognised her as a local who lived in the next street and whose daughter she had been at school with. 'Seems the Doc thinks I have, Mrs Hatter. And I'm more qualified than you are, washing milk bottles for a dairy. Now . . .'

'Not more qualified than I am. None of you will be,' a smart-looking, very attractive woman in her thirties spoke up. 'I'm actually already a doctor's receptionist and have basic nursing qualifications too. I demand to see Doctor Strathmore and . . .'

Oh, why couldn't these women just accept the job was gone and leave? Aidy inwardly fumed. She blurted, 'You can't see Doc 'cos . . . well, he's out on an emergency . . . delivering a baby . . . won't be back for hours. Now, look, I arrived early and he decided to see me. When he saw I'd everything he was looking for, he didn't see any point in wasting his time. He asked me to lock up behind you all.' She strode across to the outer door, opening it wide and saying, 'So if you don't mind . . .'

All looking annoyed at having their time wasted and mouthing their displeasure, they trooped out. Heaving a huge sigh of relief as she shut the door after the last departee, Aidy hurriedly took a seat on the bench just as Ty appeared through the door opposite.

He looked totally confused to find only one person waiting to be interviewed. 'Where have all the other candidates disappeared to?' he asked.

She gave a shrug. 'There's only me.'

His puzzlement mounted. 'But I heard voices.'

She gave a short laugh. 'Well, I haven't resorted to talking to myself yet so you couldn't have.' She stood up then and said eagerly, 'Would you like me to come through for my interview then?'

He was thinking, I could have sworn I heard the sound of the surgery door opening and shutting on numerous occasions after I saw out the last patient.

Surely I heard it slam only moments ago? I know I heard female voices coming from in here. I know I wasn't hearing things. But all the evidence is telling me I was. Then he fixed his attention on Aidy and his heart sank. This was the last woman he would have wished his notice to attract. Judging from his previous dealings with her, they'd never be able to work together. Oh, she was dressed presentably enough, and he was gratified to note she wasn't wearing any make-up which he deemed unsuitable for a job in a medical environment. Whether she was intelligent or possessed the capacity to do the job to his exacting standards remained to be seen.

'Come through,' he sighed.

As she took a seat in the chair by the desk that Ty had indicated, Aidy stole a proper look around his surgery. On the three occasions she had visited it recently she hadn't had a chance to do so. It was very cramped in here. A fat patient, someone of Pat Nelson's build, would have to turn sideways to squeeze themself between the examination couch and a table holding medical instruments in order to reach the seat beside the doctor's desk.

Ty had by now sat down in his chair on the other side of the desk and Aidy realised he was talking to her. 'Oh, sorry, were you saying something? Only I was just having a good look around to familiarise myself with your surgery. It's a bit tight for space in here. Couldn't swing a cat, could you, not without knocking the bottles of medicine off the shelves? Wouldn't you be better off moving the surgery into a bigger room, to give yourself more space?'

His face tightened at what he saw as criticism of the way he operated his surgery, and her audacity in actually pointing it out to him. The sooner he got this interview started, the sooner he could be rid of her.

Aidy was desperate to impart the working background she had fabricated for herself, rather than answer the doctor's questions and quite possibly trip herself up. Without waiting for him to lead the interview, she launched into: 'You'll be wanting to know all about me? Since leaving school I've worked at one place, a factory, started at the bottom and worked my way up ...' She was hoping he'd assume this to mean in the office rather than on the factory floor, which was the case. What she'd said up to now was the truth, but what she was about to say was the opposite.

Without batting an eyelid she hurried on, 'My bosses must have been happy with my work or they'd have got rid of me, wouldn't they? Unfortunately the place burned down a few weeks ago ... they don't know what caused it but the shock killed the owner ... heart attack ... he was such a nice man too. Anyway, all us workers were out of a job so that's why I'm looking for one. I could get you a reference from someone who worked with me, if you need one, but of course, in the circumstances, it wouldn't be on the company paper.'

Colleen would do it for her, for old times' sake, pretending she had been Aidy's superior and professing that in her opinion Aidy had proved a faultless employee in all the years they had worked together.

She went on, 'Your notice said you were looking for someone smart. Well, as you can see, I am. I'm also conscientious and reliable. I've got all the qualifications you stated on your notice. I'll make you a very good receptionist.'

So please, please, give me the job, she inwardly begged.

She might well satisfy another doctor, but not Ty. He stared at her blankly, his mind racing. She did indeed seem to have all the qualifications he had stated he required in his receptionist, so how was he going to justify turning her down? There was, though, one remaining qualification she hadn't mentioned.

'I do also want someone with nursing experience.' He began to rise to see her out. 'Thank you for coming . . .'

'Just a minute,' she cut in. 'I have got nursing experience.'

He sank back down on his seat, hiding his inward dismay. 'But if you've only worked for that one employee, how have you gained that?'

'Through dealing with my family. My younger brother and sisters are always needing some wound tending to. You know what kids are like, forever getting into scrapes or falling over. They all had mumps and chickenpox when they were younger and I helped my mam look after them then. My husband, too, has suffered the usual cuts, scalds, you name it, and I haven't had one go septic on me yet. I'm nursing my gran through her accident and she's coming along nicely, although she did re-break her leg as you know, but that was only because she decided to try it out before it was properly healed.' Aidy flashed him a grin and jocularly concluded, 'Any more experience than that and I'd be able to do your job, wouldn't I?'

Ty stiffened. Was she really comparing his years of hard study at medical school and his term spent as a junior doctor in a hospital with her cleaning and dressing a few cuts and abrasions for her family? This woman really was infuriating. He stared at her fixedly, fighting to find some excuse to deny her the job. All he could come up with was, 'You're not really what I'm looking for.'

Aidy stared back at him, stunned. As far as she was concerned she fulfilled all the criteria he'd stipulated, so why wasn't she what he was looking for? She didn't like the cold way he was looking at her either. Then it struck her *why* she wasn't the sort he was looking for. The simple fact was, he didn't like her as a person. Well, that didn't bother her. She didn't like *him*. She'd be surprised if anyone actually did, with that abrupt, superior manner of his. But she needed the job he was offering and was determined not to leave without having secured it.

'I might not be what you're looking for, but it looks like you'll have to settle for me because no one else has applied for the job but me, have they?' she challenged him.

That was true. And he just couldn't understand why. He supposed he could advertise again, but if no one else applied and meantime this woman had got herself another job elsewhere, he'd have no one. He was desperate for someone to help him run his surgery, so as matters stood it appeared he had no choice but to suffer this applicant. She was better than nothing.

Reluctantly he told her, 'I suppose we could see how it goes.'

Aidy's face lit up.

'I can start tomorrow.' Then a thought struck her and, to show her commitment, she added, 'Unless you'd like me to do anything for you tonight?'

Perish the thought. He needed the next few hours to get used to the idea that, due to circumstances beyond his control, he would be working closely with this irritating young woman. 'No, no, tomorrow will be soon enough.'

Tomorrow would be soon enough for her too. Working with such a morose, self-important man was going to be challenging indeed, but she was up for that challenge in return for the wage it would bring her. Then it struck her she didn't know yet what wage he was offering. 'What is the pay for the job?' she bluntly asked. She prayed it was sufficient for her to keep the family on, unlike the amount Marjorie Kilner was offering.

Ty wasn't a mean man and had been fully prepared to reward the most suitable applicant with what he felt to be the fair amount. In light of the fact he didn't really want this woman working for him, he was tempted to mention an amount so low it wouldn't be worth her while, but then he reminded himself that she had been his only applicant and it would be both unethical and remiss of him not to pay her the same as anyone else. And, of course, the hours weren't the regular office ones and that had to be taken into account. He told her, 'One pound, three shillings and sixpence a week.'

Aidy wanted to clap her hands with joy. A couple of shillings short of what she'd have earned in the factory when meeting her expected targets, but with careful handling just about enough to scrape by on, helped along by the few coppers her grandmother insisted she contribute from the takings for her potions.

'It that's acceptable, I suppose I really ought to have your personal details,' Ty said to her. 'Shall we start with your name?'

Aidy was put out that she hadn't made enough of an impression on him for him to have remembered it from her visits to him recently. But she supposed that, through the course of his work, he met so many people it wasn't humanly possible for him to remember the names of all of them.

She looked at him a bit uncomfortably then. Everyone knew her as Aidy but that was not the name she had been given at birth. She was in fact called by a name she absolutely detested and had refused to use since she'd been old enough to realise she had been named at her father's insistence after his own grandmother. She'd been a mean, spiteful woman but one who, it was rumoured by the family, had had a few pounds stashed under her bed, which her father had been hoping to inherit. He'd thought the deal would be sealed by his honouring her by naming his first-born after her. The rumour had turned out to be unfounded as she died owing tradesmen and neighbours far more than the few coppers she'd had in her purse at the time.

Irritated by this delay, Ty persisted, 'You have got a name?'

'Of course I have,' she snapped back. 'I'm known as Aidy Nelson.'

He frowned at her. 'Known as? What is that supposed to mean?'

'Just what I said. I'm known as Aidy Nelson.' She noticed the suspicious look he was giving her, could see it going through his mind that she was possibly a fugitive from the law or something like that, hence the reason for her alias. She told him, 'There's nothing sinister behind it. I just don't like my name. Hate it, in fact.'

So, against the odds, he and this woman *did* have something in common after all. He couldn't abide the name his own father had bestowed on him and had been ridiculed mercilessly at school for it by his fellows and several teachers alike. In an attempt to disassociate himself from that detested name he had shortened it to Ty, refusing to answer to anything else but that, the exception being in dealings with his formidable father who would not hear of his son being addressed by anything other than the name on his birth certificate.

Ty was very curious to know what name it was that Aidy so abhorred, just to know whether it was as bad as the one he'd been given, but he knew better than to ask outright.

The last time Aidy had had what to her was the awful embarrassment of divulging her detested name had been to the vicar when she and Arch had gone to see him to book their wedding. Thankfully the kindly man had understood her plight and, when announcing it during the vows, had given a discreet cough at the appropriate time so that it wasn't audible to the congregation. She had no such saviour here with her now and, dreading the embarrassment of what she was about to suffer when the doctor insisted, was totally taken aback when insted he said to her, 'Parents can be utterly irresponsible when it comes to naming their children, not at all considering the life-long purgatory they are condemning them to. How do you spell Aidy?'

Such understanding stunned her. Was it possible that beneath that cold, humourless exterior lay a spark of humanity? Then another reason for his under-standing struck her. Was it possible the doctor too had been given a Christian name he couldn't abide? Her curiosity was roused. How she would dearly have loved to have asked him, but in all honesty didn't care about him enough to be bothered.

She spelled her name out for him, then gave him the rest of the personal details he requested.

When he had finished, so eager was Aidy to get home and break the good news to her family, she jumped up, saying, 'Well, if that's it . . .'

'No, actually, it's not. There is just one other matter we need to settle.'

She sank back down on her chair, her face wreathed in enquiry, wondering what that matter could possibly be.

He soon enlightened her. 'You have an outstanding account with me. Not really the done thing to commence employment while in debt to your employer.'

And she had been secretly hoping he would waive that now she was working for him! She supposed it was remiss of her to have expected it. He was only trying to earn his living. Thankfully she had the money with her. She delved into her handbag and retrieved it, putting four shillings on the blotting pad before him.

Meanwhile Ty had taken a book out of his desk drawer, opened it and was tracing one finger down the list of names. He stopped on finding hers. He glanced at the amount she had given him, then lifted his eyes to hers and said, 'It's actually six shillings and eightpence owed, for my three visits, plus medication and issuing a death certificate.'

Aidy hadn't known the exact amount but had suspected it was nearer six shillings than the four she had handed him, but she had been hoping he'd just accept what she'd given him as she could sorely have done with having the residue at her disposal.

Having settled the amount, she got up again, and announced, 'I'll see you tomorrow then at eight-fifteen sharp, Doc.'

She quickly hurried out, desperate to get home and impart her thrilling news to her family.

His hackles rose. As the employer it should have been himself who should have ended the proceedings not her. And she'd again disrespectfully addressed him as Doc. He heavily sighed as he leaned back in his chair and scraped a hand through his thick thatch of corn-coloured hair. Desperate for a help or not, he was already wondering if he'd just made a big mistake in employing Aidy Nelson.

CHAPTER TWELVE

The following day, mid-morning, Aidy looked dismayed and was feeling totally out of her depth before the enormous number of patients' records spread out over the dining table. And these weren't all of them by any means, only the ones Doc had dealt with to date, not returning them to their boxes as he had meant to sort them into some order himself. Now he'd hired a receptionist to do this type of work for him, only unbeknown to him Aidy had no idea how to go about it, never having done this kind of work before as she'd led him to believe she had.

She had arrived this morning to find that Doc had put a small table and chair in the middle of the waiting room for her. On the table was a ledger-type book and a pencil. In his abrupt manner, he told her that this was where she would sit during surgery hours. As people came in, she was to note their name and time of arrival. That way he hoped to avoid queue jumping and the resulting skirmishes. When the patient he was seeing left, she was to wait until she heard him call out 'Next' before she instructed whoever it was to go through. He was also entrusting her with a key to the waiting-room door. There were going to be times when she arrived to start work to find him out on a call. He made it clear that should he ever arrive back to find her anywhere in the house she should not be, then she would be instantly sacked. And should she lose the key, he would expect her to pay for a replacement.

He left her then to go into his surgery and prepare himself for the arrival of the patients. Aidy had looked thoughtfully at where he'd positioned her desk and chair for a moment, then glanced around the room. He hadn't given any thought at all to where he had put her. She'd feel as if she was in the middle of a circus arena, being looked at by the crowd. And besides, she'd have a job to hear him call out 'Next' from that far away if any of the patients who were acquainted with one another were having a gossip while they waited their turn. She really needed to be positioned by the corridor with her back to the wall. That way she could immediately see who was entering from the outer door opposite, have a complete view of the rest of the waiting area, and more importantly, would hear Doc shout any instructions to her from inside his surgery. She immediately moved the desk and chair.

Quite a few of the patients who had come in that morning she was acquainted with, and had enjoyed chatting to them during their wait. It amused her, although she was very careful not to show it, to hear the grumbling of many of the departing patients. They didn't like the new doctor's abrupt manner and seeming lack of compassion for their suffering. Aidy obviously wasn't the only one to find him a difficult man to deal with.

In fact, she had greatly enjoyed her first surgery and hoped the rest of her duties, as yet unknown to her, were this easy and enjoyable.

If she was expecting her employer to praise her for handling her first morning without any mishap, she was to be disappointed. Only minutes after the last person was out of the door, he had called through instructions for Aidy to lock the outer door and come through to his surgery. Once she was there he had immediately instructed her to make a start on sorting out the record cards. Realising she'd need space to do that, he told her to do it in the dining room. Meantime, he would eat his meals on the kitchen table. He didn't offer to help her heave the cumbersome filing boxes, still packed with records, into the dining room, or assist her on her numerous trips back and forth, taking through the records of those patients he'd already seen, which she felt he could have done before he'd gone out on his morning round.

The hope that all her duties would be easy had faded when she saw the sheer number of record cards she was expected to sort into order and file back in their boxes. Never having done this kind of work before, she didn't know where to make a start. Panic set in. If she failed to do this, she couldn't blame the doctor if he sacked her. As she stared blindly at the cards, she inwardly scolded herself, telling herself to use her brain, work out for herself what she needed to do to complete her task. She stood there for what seemed like an age, staring at them, then suddenly it was as if a fog was lifting and she saw a way to do it. There were twenty-six letters in the alphabet, weren't there? Everyone's name must begin with one of them. All she had to do was sort all the records into piles, each starting with a different letter, then put them in the appropriately labelled section of the record boxes. It really was as simple as that.

By the time Ty returned at just before one o'clock she had managed to work her way through approximately a tenth of the five thousand or so cards. It was a laborious task and her eyes hurt from having to peer so hard in her effort to decipher the names on the cards. Doctor Mac hadn't had the most legible handwriting. Her back ached too from continuously having to stretch over the table to add cards to the correct pile. And that was between answering the surgery door several times to patients who had arrived after morning surgery had finished but had persistently knocked, just to check if the doctor was in and would see them anyway.

The sudden shrilling of the telephone had her nearly jumping out of her skin. Hurrying into the hallway where it was situated by the front door, Aidy stood and stared at it for several long moments before she tentatively lifted the receiver out of its cradle and placed it to her ear, hesitantly saying, 'Hello.' A very posh-sounding woman on the other end had announced to her that she had the pharmacist who wished to speak to the doctor. When Aidy informed her he wasn't at home, she was asked to wait for a moment and then the line seemed to go dead for a while before the woman suddenly came back on again and told her the pharmacist would like to leave a message with her for the doctor, and then a male voice was speaking to her. Aidy was very careful to make sure she took the message she was being given correctly, and in her endeavours to, repeated it back three times, much to the irritation of the pharmacist. But she hadn't cared how annoyed she made him. She was more concerned with not allowing her employer to find fault with her work.

The morning round had been a particularly arduous one for Ty and consequently he was not in the best of moods on his return. The weather was atrocious, torrential rain pouring relentlessly down from a clouded sky. He was soaked to the skin. He was still trying to familiarise himself with the warren of miserable streets in the area. Several addresses had taken him an age to find, and at two he finally reached, the people who had requested a visit had not bothered to send someone to the surgery to inform him they no longer required his services on this occasion. He had known he was in fact needed, but they had obviously decided the health of the sick person he had been going to minister to was less important than his saved fee.

He didn't think he'd ever get used to the dire state of many of the dwellings his patients lived in. Sometimes as many as ten children were sleeping in one damp bedroom, with only old coats for warmth.

Aidy heard Ty return. She was very put out that he did not come to greet her but went straight into the surgery, shutting the door none too gently behind him. She wasn't sure what to do. Did she carry on with her task until he came to see her and request from her a report of what had transpired while he'd been out, or did she go and inform him in his inner sanctum? She had been working away all morning non-stop and it occurred to her that she hadn't yet had a cup of tea. She would certainly welcome one. Ty hadn't actually given her permission to go into his kitchen to make herself refreshments, but then again he hadn't told her she couldn't either, so she would. It seemed churlish of her to make one just for herself, so she decided to take him one through as well.

Having stripped off his wet overcoat and jacket, Ty was drying his dripping thatch of hair when Aidy tapped on his door and came in. He looked over at her, shocked for a moment, in his bad mood having temporarily forgotten she was there. He was too consumed by his own misery at that moment to be bothered to reprimand her for entering before he had given her permission to.

'What is it?' he asked.

Aidy took a deep breath, letting his rudeness wash over her, reminding herself that she needed this job. 'I thought you could do with a cuppa, Doc.'

'Oh! Er ... put it on my desk. And it's *Doctor Strathmore*.'

Her hackles rose that he hadn't had the grace to thank her for making him the cup of tea. If he thought she was going to apologise for calling him Doc, he could think again. She responded lightly, 'I'll try and remember that.'

Having put the cup and saucer on his desk, she told him, 'The chemist telephoned and left a message for you. You wrote out a prescription for Nancy Pointer only he can't make out whether the number of pills you want her to have is thirty or fifty.'

'Can't the man read?' snapped Ty. Flinging down the towel he was drying his hair with, he went to dig out her record card from the boxes, to check what he had written up for her, then remembered he wouldn't have it as Aidy was putting all the records in order. 'You'll have her card. Fetch it for me so I can check what I prescribed her.' Then he demanded, 'Have you finished sorting them all out yet?'

Aidy looked at him blankly. Was he really expecting her to have done this mammoth task in only a couple of hours? She might be inexperienced when it came to doing office work but even she knew that the job she was facing was not one that could be completed in so short a time.

The look on her face registered with Ty and he realised he was being unfair. He said, 'Just get it done as quickly as you can. Fetch Mrs Pointer's card first, though.'

As she hurried out to do his bidding, Aidy was inwardly fuming. No please or thank you! She only hoped she could put her hand quickly on the blessed card so as not to give him any reason to grumble at her for taking so long. Deciding to try and find it first in the large pile of Ps she had made, she was jubilant to discover it only a dozen or so cards down from the top. When she returned with it, she found the surgery empty. Hearing sounds from upstairs, she assumed Ty was up there changing his wet suit for a dry one. Leaving the card on his desk, she was about to leave his surgery and return to her task when she noticed his discarded sopping wet macintosh and trilby hat, and automatically picked them up. She took them through to the kitchen where she draped them on a clothes horse which she placed in front of the range.

Aidy was grateful their paths did not cross again before she courteously went to inform him in his surgery that she was going off for her break and would be back prompt at a quarter to five. Ty was checking his bag was fully stocked before he departed on his afternoon round and didn't even bother to stop what he was doing, but nodded his head to acknowledge what she'd told him.

When he came to depart, he was bewildered not to find his coat and hat where he had left them over the protruding arm of the weighing scales. He'd been meaning to hang them up to dry but it had slipped his memory. When he eventually found them draped on the clothes horse around the range, something he had not noticed when he had slapped together a hurried sandwich for his lunch a while earlier, he knew it was Aidy's doing. He appreciated her kind gesture but he wouldn't express that to her, not wanting her to think that their relationship was ever going to become anything other than the business arrangement it was. This woman posed no threat whatsoever to him emotionally, but he had vowed after losing his beloved wife that no woman or man would ever hurt him again. In order not to incur any risk, he would keep all other human beings at a safe distance.

Bertha was eagerly awaiting Aidy's return that afternoon.

'So how did you get on then?'

The rain was still pouring down torrentially. Having hung her saturated coat on the drying cradle in the kitchen, Aidy was already towelling off her wet hair. Sighing heavily, she answered, 'I think I'd really like the job if it wasn't for him. I'm not surprised he's not married! No woman in their right mind would put up with his ways. I don't think he's ever heard the words please or thank you. Anyway, I'm sort of getting my own back on him as he's demanding I call him Doctor Strathmore and I'm insisting on calling him just Doc.'

Well, at least, and thank God, Aidy had a job. And when she heard what Bertha had to tell her, *she* would be too. 'Have you heard what's gone off at your old place?'

Aidy looked at her gran quizzically and shook her head. 'No. What has?' Thinking there had been an accident, fire or something of the sort.

'They've laid off roughly a hundred factory-floor

workers. Mrs Fisher told me this morning when she popped in to visit me. Her neighbour works in the canteen and it was her who passed it on.'

Aidy was visibly shocked. 'Oh! I'd no idea the firm was in trouble. But then, management never told us shop-floor workers anything. Oh, God, I do hope Col wasn't one of them? The last thing she needs right now is to lose her job.'

'Last thing all those who lose a job need,' Bertha said.

Aidy whole-heartedly agreed, but with the fact her friend's husband was under threat of losing his job at any time and she with no choice but to give up hers in a few months on the birth of her fourth child ... well, the family would have no money coming in at all. The situation was more devastating for them than it would be for some. In light of this news, though, maybe it had been a blessing in disguise that Aidy had lost her job when she had. Had she not and been among those laid off now, then her job with the doctor would already have been filled by one of the woman she had got rid of, and there'd be even fewer vacancies to apply for now. She must try and find time to pay a visit to Colleen, and meanwhile pray that her friend wasn't one of those laid off.

There was a knock on the back door and it was immediately heard to open. A female voice called out, 'Cooee, Bertha, it's only me.'

She groaned. 'Oh, it's that bloody Mona Knight after a potion for her chilblains! She's popped in every day for a fortnight, asking after the same thing, and I keep telling her that I've run out until I'm back on me feet again and am able to replenish me stocks.' A mischievous glint sparked in her eyes. 'Oh, I've an idea! Tell her to come in here and then you go off and get one of me empty bottles, ducky. Put in a good measure of salt and a bit of gravy browning, then fill it up with water and give it a good shake. Won't cure her chilblains but it'll stop her badgering me for a bit while she finds out. I'll tell her it's a new potion I'm trying and she's my tester.'

After the happy woman had departed, Bertha said, 'I was so tempted to take money off her as it ain't like we couldn't use it, eh, love? But I couldn't bring myself to do it, knowing that mixture won't make a blind bit of difference to her chilblains. Oh, roll on my old bones mending! As soon as this plaster is off me leg, it's a trip to the countryside for me, and all the kids are coming to help carry back what we can between us. Then I can start making as much as possible from me potions again to help you out more.' She tapped the cast on her wrist. 'Next week this is due to come off, so at least I'll be two-armed again instead of one, able to do a bit more for meself and what I can to help you . . . peel spuds, shell peas, give meself a wash, that sort of thing.'

Any help her gran could give would be very much appreciated. Aidy was young and in good health, but working full-time as well as running a house by herself was starting to tell on her. Most mornings now she had to drag herself out of bed, and in the afternoons it took all her will-power not to curl up in the armchair for a rest before she began her chores, but resting in the afternoon, even for an hour, was a luxury she could not afford while she had no assistance at home.

Every minute of her afternoon today was accounted for. She was giving Bertha an all-over wash which her grandmother was so looking forward to; making the dough for next day's bread so it could be raising while she was back at work that evening, ready to be baked on her return; several pairs of socks needed darning, and a patch putting on George's other school shirt; the floors needed sweeping; coal needed breaking in the shed and the bucket refilled; and the evening meal needed preparing and cooking. If she had any time spare, the old gas cooker really could do with a scrub ...

But none of the patients would have realised how tired Aidy was when she arrived, smiling, for work that evening to find several people already waiting outside for the doors to open, although she wouldn't let them inside until she was instructed to by Ty not a minute before six. She went in search of him, out of courtesy, to let him know she had arrived, eventually finding him in the dining room, staring into space. Immediately she thought he had found some fault with the record cards she was in the process of sorting and tentatively asked, 'Is everything all right, Doc?'

So consumed in his thoughts he hadn't heard her come in, he looked startled for a moment before he said sharply, 'If there were, and it concerned you, I would tell you. And how many times do I need to tell you that I wish to be addressed as Doctor Strathmore?'

Aidy hid a smile. 'I will try and remember. There's a queue forming outside and it's still raining hard, so shall I let them in?'

Ty was lost in his thoughts again. Without realising, he spoke aloud. 'This room would indeed make a far better surgery.'

Aidy was delighted that he was considering the idea that she had expressed to him at her interview. 'Yes, it would, much better,' she agreed. 'I'm glad you're thinking of taking up my suggestion.'

He looked at her sharply. He did indeed have her to thank for instigating the change he was thinking of making, which would not only make his life easier but add value to the practice when it came time to sell it when he moved on. More importantly to him, it wouldn't involve any monetary outlay as he'd call upon those patients qualified to do the required tasks.

Many still had outstanding bills that they insisted on settling with their labour. He wasn't, though, about to give his receptionist any credit for her idea, in case she took his show of gratitude for more than it was.

He said curtly to her, 'I trust there's a good a reason you've disturbed me?'

Letting his brusqueness wash over her was starting to become second nature to Aidy. Breezily she responded, 'I came to let you know I'd arrived and to ask if it's all right if I open the surgery door early? Only the patients waiting outside are getting soaked and risking pneumonia.'

He reminded her, 'You are merely the receptionist, Mrs Nelson. If there are any medical diagnoses to be made, then I will be the one to make them. In the circumstances, I have however no objection to your opening the surgery door early.'

Why was he constantly doing that, reminding her of her place? Why was his manner always so cold and unyielding? And not just to her. According to the patients, he was the same with them too. He was new to these parts. He'd never make any friends if he continued to act towards people like he was now. Then a thought struck Aidy. Maybe he acted like he did on purpose. Maybe he didn't want to make any friends. Maybe he didn't care whether people liked him or not. She wondered why.

*　　*　　*

It was Aidy's opinion that it was part of her job to make people welcome when they came into the surgery, and if they wanted to chat to her while they waited she'd happily oblige. It amused her that most people who came in, especially the women, insisted on giving her all the details of the symptoms they were suffering. She'd only been employed as a receptionist for a matter of days now, but from what she had observed already it was plain to her that the number of patients demanding to see the doctor was far more than he could really cope with.

After listening to many of the patients' symptoms herself, she was of the opinion that quite a few didn't really need to see the doctor at all but could be helped by one of her grandmother's remedies instead. She decided that once Bertha was up and about again and had restocked her remedies, she would suggest to these patients that they try her gran first before they resorted to the doctor. Not only would she be helping him by lifting from him some of the demands on his time, but also saving those patients a good deal of money in not having to pay a doctor's fee and possibly the cost of a prescription from the chemist. She knew many of them would only end up as bad debtors to Doc in any case. She could save him the bother and, more importantly, put some money her grandmother's way . . .

Bertha felt very guilty when Aidy arrived home just after eight. How she wished she was able to have a hot cup of tea waiting or to put her dinner before her, which was in the oven keeping hot. She was counting the days to when she would be able to help more. 'Busy surgery, was it?' she asked as Aidy flopped down into the armchair and took off her shoes.

'Actually, no, it wasn't. Only had half a dozen in. I think the awful rain had something to do with it. I expect people thought that whatever they had wrong with them would be made worse by a good soaking. I'm glad to say it's stopped now, though. I used the remainder of my time doing a bit more sorting of the record cards.

'It's a pig of a job, Gran. It seems to me like there's millions of patients on Doc's books. It wouldn't be so bad if the surgery closed for a few days and I could sort all the cards in one go, but at the same time I'm trying to sort the back log out, patients are coming in or calling Doc out, and *their* cards are yanked out then thrown back at me ... It feels to me like I'm taking one step forward, two back. The way things are going, I'll never get it done.'

Bertha eyed her proudly and said, 'Well, you sound to me like you're doing a grand job, love. I've no doubt the doctor is very pleased with you.'

Aidy sighed. 'I wouldn't know. I can only guess

he is as he hasn't said he isn't. He's a hard man to get along with, Gran, and if I didn't need the job so badly, I'd tell him exactly what I think of him and his surly, superior attitude.' She had enough to do putting up with him during work-time; she certainly didn't want to spend the rest of her day talking about him. She changed the topic to people who did matter to her. 'Were the kids all right tonight? I hate not being here to tuck them into bed.'

'Well, that can't be helped, love, and they understand. They're all fine. Well, apart from the fact our George's got a black eye. He said he got it playing football but Marion told me he got it fighting over something one of his mates said about you.'

Aidy looked sharply at her grandmother. 'About me?'

'Seems there's a rumour going round that you bribed the doctor into giving you the receptionist's job before he'd interviewed all the other women who applied.' Bertha gave a snort. 'As if you would need to do that!'

Without batting an eyelid, Aidy enquired, 'Was it Bella Graves's brother Harry George was fighting with, by any chance?'

Bertha nodded. 'I believe that was the lad Marion mentioned.'

'Ah, that explains it. Bella applied for the job, dressed like she was applying for a job as a madame, and she's miffed 'cos she didn't stand a chance of getting it and I did. I got the job 'cos I was the best person Doc interviewed for it.' And wasn't that the truth?

'I've no doubt our George got that point across to Bella's brother and stopped him at least spreading any more of that downright lie. Going back to the kids . . . Betty was a bit off colour tonight. Came in early, complaining she didn't feel well, so I got her to make herself some hot milk and sent her to bed early. She must not have been feeling herself because she went up without a murmur. Probably got a cold coming. 'Course, then, not to be outdone, Marion announced *she* wasn't feeling well either, and so she had to have some hot milk. But then she said going to bed wouldn't make her feel better but what would was if she got in beside me for a cuddle and a story.'

Aidy smiled. 'Which you agreed to?'

Bertha grinned back. 'I was putty in her hands.'

A knock sounded on the back door and they both looked at each other as though to say, I'm not expecting anyone.

Aidy got up to answer it, hoping it was just a neighbour after something trivial. She had chores that she needed to attend to and if she didn't make a start there was a danger it wouldn't be this side of midnight she got into bed.

For a moment she stared at the stranger before her. She was just about to ask politely what they wanted when recognition struck. Her eyes blazed pure hatred then.

CHAPTER THIRTEEN

'What do you want?'

'Fine welcome, I must say.'

'If you were expecting a welcome, you came to the wrong house.'

'Then it's a good job I wasn't. Go and tell yer mam I'm back. And, on yer way, put the kettle on.'

He made to shove past her but Aidy barred his way by blocking the door with her body. 'I can't tell Mam you're back. She isn't here.'

'Then I'll tell her meself when she comes back.'

'She won't be coming back. She's dead. Shame it wasn't you instead! Now, if that's all . . .' Aidy stepped back inside the kitchen and made to shut the door, but was prevented by a booted foot placed inside the step.

'Not really going to shut the door on yer father, are yer?'

She spat back, 'Father! That's a joke, isn't it? You stopped being a father to your kids when you walked out on us for the second time, nine years ago. Not that you ever were what you could properly call a father when you were living here with us. You never stayed around even to meet Marion.'

She flashed a glance at the man who had sired her. The last time she saw him he'd been a handsome man still, dark haired, tall and broad. These last years had aged him markedly, shrinking his once muscular body to skeletal thinness. He obviously hadn't done well for himself as his clothes were as threadbare as those worn by the poorest around these parts. His face was haggard, grey hair greasy and straggly, and he looked to be in dire need of a hot bath and a shave.

Aidy snapped at him, 'Why have you come back?'

Arnold Greenwood grinned sardonically at her. 'Maybe I've missed you all.'

'Well, we haven't missed you, that's for sure.' She eyed him knowingly. 'I take it you've no job, no woman to look after you, and nowhere to live? So you've decided to come back to the people who despise you after what you did to them, sooner than sleep on the streets or beg a place in the poorhouse?'

'That's about the size of it.'

Aidy glared at him murderously. 'Over my dead body will you come back here!'

He shot her a warning look. 'Now you look here, Ad—'

Her temper erupting she flared at him, 'Don't you dare call me by that name you insisted on giving me.'

'In honour of my grandmother. You should feel privileged you were named after her.'

'What! Damned, more like! She was a nasty, mean, spiteful woman nobody went near unless they absolutely had to. You only called me after her because you hoped she'd leave you a fortune – shame she hadn't a pot to piss in, wasn't it?' Aidy paused long enough to give him a scathing glance. 'You turned out to be very like her, didn't you? Now, I'd be obliged if you'd remove yourself from my doorstep and shut the back gate behind you.'

Arnold had been fully expecting his reception to be exactly the one he'd received. After all, in view of his past behaviour towards his family, he in truth deserved nothing more. But desperate times called for desperate measures, and Arnold was a desperate man.

He'd fallen for Jessie Jackson the first moment he'd clapped eyes on her. What man wouldn't have? She had been good looking, sharp witted, strong minded. She lit up a room the instant she entered it. At that time he'd been good looking himself and earning better money than many of his peers because he'd learned a skill. He seemed to offer her a promising future. He pursued Jessie and won her.

Arnold had enjoyed being a married man until their first child had come along. That, for him, was when the rot set in. He grew resentful of having no money in his pocket to call his own; loathed their offspring disturbing his peace and disrupting their sex life; grew bored and frustrated with the monotony of life as husband and father; found himself longing for the freedom of the single life again. So he upped and left it all behind, got himself a fresh start all round in another part of town.

For a while he enjoyed his single status again, having money to call his own, going from woman to woman. Then he got one pregnant, and to escape the wrath of her family, who were insisting he marry her, hid from them back in the bosom of his own abandoned family.

Jessie did not exactly welcome him back with open arms but, thankfully for him, his return coincided with what was for her a dire period in her life. She had just lost her job and her lodger; was in danger of losing her home. A bleak existence loomed ahead for her and Aidy. For a while Arnold tolerated life as a married man again, but it wasn't long before once again he began to resent not having any spare cash. With two more young children to irritate him and disturb his peace, and another on the way, the single life beckoned him irresistibly. So he upped and left and got it back for himself.

He worked when he had to, didn't when he found a woman besotted enough by him to keep him. Those women were always the good-time sort, usually married themselves but with husbands who'd absconded or died. But even those sort sooner or later wanted some sort of commitment from him. And Arnold wasn't committing to anyone ever again. Besides, he was still married so wasn't a free man anyway, and he certainly didn't want any more children. As soon as hints about that topic began to be dropped, he was off.

The years seemed to pass like a click of his fingers and then, to his utter shock and surprise he awoke one morning to find himself a man of forty-five, with no home to call his own, hardly any possessions, his chosen lifestyle having ruined his good looks and physique; no job since he'd been laid off from his last one; no baccy for a roll-up nor money for a pint. And, to cap it all, his current woman, having realised he would never make an honest woman of her and fed up with funding him, was screaming blue murder at him to get up and get out or she'd fetch her strapping son around to bodily remove him.

Sitting on a park bench a short while later, his bag with a few belongings at his feet, Arnold had pondered his options. It seemed he had only one. To go back to his wife and family again until he found something better.

Now he hauled up the sailor's holdall at his feet, containing all his worldly belongings, slung it over his shoulder and announced to his eldest daughter,

'The only place I'm going, lady, is inside this house. There's nothing you can do to stop me moving back in and staying for as long as I like. It's *my* name on the rent book, remember.' He pushed his face into hers, a nasty twinkle in his eyes. 'I'd watch yer step, if I was you. You'd better treat me with respect or I'll have you out and those other brats of mine along with you. Don't try and test me, I mean what I say. Now, move out me way.'

Without waiting, he shoved past Aidy, knocking her back against the door. He dropped his bag on the kitchen floor and proceeded through to the back room.

Bertha gawped wide eyed, seeing who their visitor was. 'Talk about bad pennies! You've got some brass neck, showing your face here again.' She shot an accusing look at Aidy as she followed him in, as though to say, You seriously allowed this man to come in, after all he's responsible for? 'So what are you doing here?' she snarled at her detested son-in-law.

'Same mouthy old bag you always were, eh, Bertha?' he said as he plonked himself down in the nearest armchair to the range, kicking off his holed hob-nailed boots to rest smelly, dirty, sockless feet on the rail. He looked hard at her. 'You seem like yer at home, so I take it yer've moved in since I've been away?'

She curled her lip in disgust. 'It's nothing to do with you where I live.'

'It's everything to do with me. My name is on the rent book.'

Bertha scoffed, 'Might be your name on the book, but you ain't paid the rent for years.'

Arnold Greenwood grinned sardonically at her. 'Don't matter. It's my name on the book, so my decision who lives here or not. And I'll tell you what I told yer granddaughter . . . you'd better show me some respect or you'll all be finding yerselves out on the streets.'

If he could walk out on his wife and young family, leaving them destitute, then he'd have no compunction about throwing his aged mother-in-law out, thought Bertha. Regardless, the likes of that spineless creature did not scare her. She'd sooner be out on the streets than show him respect he didn't deserve. She said icily, 'I take it your current floozy's chucked you out and yer'd no one lined up to take her place? Judging by the look of yer, yer've no money either, so coming back here is a better alternative than living on the streets?'

'That's exactly it.' He smirked at her.

Bertha scowled at him darkly. 'And here was me, hoping you'd got some terrible disease and had come home to die.'

He shot her a murderous look back. 'I'll warn you

once more: show me some respect or you're out. I won't tell you again.'

Aidy shot over to her grandmother, leaned down and whispered in her ear, 'Don't push him, Gran. I've no doubt he'll do what he says. If he did throw you out, you've only one place to go. And where you go, me and the kids go with you, 'cos we're a family and stick together. All right?'

Bertha sighed in resignation. It was going to take her all her self-control to be civil to her son-in-law, but she'd have to or otherwise be responsible for Aidy, herself and the kids walking the streets until they found somewhere else to live. And she couldn't walk anywhere at the moment due to her broken leg. Tight lipped, she nodded her agreement.

Aidy straightened up and said to her father, 'I'll see what I can find to make a bed up for you in the parlour.'

He gave a snort of disgust. 'I'm sleeping on no makeshift bed in the parlour. I'll be in me own bed, in me own bedroom.'

'But that's where me and Aidy sleep! Well . . . I do when I get this cast off me leg and can get back upstairs,' Bertha told him.

'Not any more. Better get yer stuff shifted. I'm tired, so after I've had summat to eat, I'll be going up.' He demanded of Aidy then, 'What have yer got? I'm famished.'

Eyes black as thunder, she hissed at him, 'Soup. Take it or leave it.'

A stony silence descended, the hostility in the air so thick it could have been cut with a knife. Aidy, still reeling from this unexpected turn of events, busied herself getting her father something to eat. She had not remembered him as the loving, nurturing sort, and her memory was serving her well. He hadn't once asked for any information on how his family had fared since the last time he had seen them. Was not showing any grief at all to learn his wife had died during his absence. She worried how her brother and sisters were going to react to their father's return, a man they didn't know. And it was very apparent Arnold Greenwood meant to resume his position as head of the household, whether they liked it or not, due to the simple fact that it was his name on the rent book and he could use the threat of eviction against them all, should they not treat him in the manner he felt he was entitled to.

If he'd no job, it wasn't likely he proposed to make any contribution towards his keep. Their budget was tight as it was. How she was going to stretch it further to cover feeding another, Aidy had no idea. But overriding all this was her worry about how he and her grandmother were going to manage to stay even slightly civil to this man they both believed had played a huge part in Jessie's early death.

CHAPTER FOURTEEN

Aidy was torn between feeling angry and relieved the next morning when her father did not make an appearance before the children left for school and she for work. He was obviously not in any hurry to reacquaint himself with his elder children or, in Marion's case, meet her for the first time. Early in the morning, though, was not the best of times to break the sort of news Aidy had to impart. She would meet the others out of school and break the news to them on the way home, she decided.

Aidy herself was feeling wretched, her body stiff and sore, eyes gritty, the old lumpy armchair not having proved at all comfortable to spend the night in, though she'd had too much preying on her mind for the luxury of sleep anyway, she supposed. The thought of spending another night like her last was not a welcome one at all. She knew she'd have to do something about it. And for her grandmother too. Sleeping on the sofa, which was no more comfortable than the armchair, was the only option open to Bertha while she was incapacitated, but it couldn't continue after she was healed.

Doing what she'd originally proposed and taking in a lodger was one solution. Her grandmother and she could take over the girls' room, moving them into George's . . . both rooms were much smaller than they had just now and would prove a tight squeeze for all of them, but in her and her grandmother's case, would at least be big enough to hold a bed where they'd get a far more restful sleep than the sofa and armchair offered. Then a Put-u-up for George in the recess in the back room. But that meant he would have nowhere to escape his father when it wasn't possible to go out, and remembering her father from the past, and it being apparent that he hadn't changed, had in fact become worse, Aidy felt there were many times ahead when her brother would need to do that.

Turning the parlour into a bedroom for herself and her grandmother was the only other answer. But just the idea was distressing to her. That room had been her mother's pride and joy. It had taken Jessie years to furnish it with two old but quite comfortable wing-back leather chairs, given to her when an employer's father had died and Jessie had rescued them from being thrown out; a second-hand oak table just big enough to seat six was saved up for and lovingly dusted and polished ever since to a high shine every week. Several cheap but precious ornaments given her over the years by her family at Christmas and birthdays sat on the mantel over the black-leaded fireplace. It was Jessie's room, the one where she had entertained her special visitors and where she'd found peace and quiet when she felt the need.

Even to be contemplating doing what she proposed seemed to Aidy like desecrating her mother's memory. If she were alive, though, Aidy knew Jessie would be telling her there was no room for sentiment at a time like this.

She couldn't . . . wouldn't . . . get rid of any of the furniture her mother had so painstakingly acquired and treasured. Instead she'd carefully stack it up at one end of the room, and the space left would just have to do them. Finding the money for a bedstead and mattress, even second- or third-hand, was out of the question. She wondered how much the pawn-broker would want for a half-decent flock that didn't appear to be riddled with bugs and need fumigating before they could use it. It would definitely be a few shillings which at the moment she hadn't got. Would any of the neighbours have one they could borrow until she found the money? Aidy doubted it. Anything not being used by her hard-up neighbours would, she had no doubt, already have been pawned or sold.

It seemed to her that, whether she liked it or not, the armchair would stay her bed until she could come up with a way to find the money to buy a flock.

Then an idea struck her. When she had left her marital home, she had taken nothing but her clothes. She was entitled to something for all she had done towards building that home, surely? Would it be remiss of her to request the mattress off the marital bed? She didn't care, she was going to. After all, Arch was in a better position to replace it than she was. Besides, unless circumstances had changed, it wasn't Arch himself who was using it but his mother and father, Pat having told Aidy herself she'd commandeered the room on moving in. If anyone should be forking out for a replacement mattress, it was Pat. Aidy knew the other woman would not give it up without a fight, but she was prepared to stand her ground. She meant to have that mattress. She would go around tonight and tackle Arch about it. The fact she wasn't mentally prepared to face him yet didn't even enter her head. Her need for the mattress was paramount.

Having seen the children off to school and made Bertha promise to be on her best behaviour so far as her son-in-law was concerned, Aidy set off for work.

When she arrived she found a queue forming outside the waiting room. It looked like the morning surgery was going to be a busy one, which she was glad of as it would help keep her awake and her thoughts on other matters than what was happening in her personal life.

She'd let herself in when her eardrums were immediately assailed by the loud hammering and banging coming from the dining room. It seemed the doctor had wasted no time in instigating improvements. Her immediate concern was where she was going to continue with the task of sorting the record cards. Popping her head around the dining-room door, she saw the cards still spread out over the table as she had left them. It seemed she was being expected to carry on sorting them while work went on around her.

Aidy would be so glad when the improvements had been completed. Once the new shelving and cupboards to hold medical supplies and drugs was finished, and the doctor moved out of his previous tiny room into the more spacious one, the wall between the waiting room and the old surgery was to be knocked through, allowing her more room to put in a bigger desk, plus a table at the back to hold the record boxes and other items Aidy needed to do her job. There would also be a larger seating area for the patients to occupy during their wait. Formerly, when the surgery was heavily attended it had proved extremely difficult for Aidy to hear the doctor summoning her to send in the next patient over the din of their chatter, crowded around her as they were. That wouldn't be the case in the new waiting room.

Ty had intimated that he proposed to hand over more work to her when her time was freed up after she had completed reorganising the record cards. Aidy was looking forward to having a more varied workload and to feeling she was helping to ease the doctor's workload. He always looked to her as if he could do with a good night's sleep. She might not be fond of him as a person but that didn't mean she didn't feel sympathy for him, strained as he was by his unrelenting labours.

The last patient had just left and Aidy was about to lock the surgery door, then make Ty a cup of tea before he went out on his morning rounds, when the door opened and to her surprise a nun walked in. There were no convents around here that Aidy was aware of so she was surprised Doc had a nun for a patient.

Aidy studied the woman. She was of medium height. It was hard to tell what her figure was like under her habit, but her face was very pleasant with kindly eyes and she was in her late thirties or early forties. Aidy told her, 'Morning surgery's actually finished, Sister, but I'll go and tell Doc you're here. If he can fit you in before he has to go out on his round I'm sure he will, you being who you are.

Would you like to rest your legs while I go and see him?'

Just then, armed with a pile of record cards from the patients he had seen during morning surgery, Ty came in. He stopped short, taken aback for a moment to find a nun in his waiting room. Composing himself, he said to her in his usual stiff manner, 'What can I do for you, Sister?'

She smiled at him. 'It's what I can do for you, Doctor. My name is Sister Teresa. I've come from St Catherine's, Glenfield Road. Mother Superior has assigned me to your surgery. I'm ready to start as soon as you wish me to.'

Aidy stared at Ty in shock. This was the first time she had ever seen him show any emotion. Although the rest of his face was displaying his normal impassive expression, from the light kindled in his eyes it was apparent he was delighted to be gaining the services of a nun to help ease his workload.

He said to her in his usual monotone, 'Surgery generally finishes around ten in the morning, so if you arrive by ten-thirty I will have a list of patients ready for you to visit that day along with a bag of supplies. I will leave it with my receptionist, Mrs Nelson. Please express my appreciation to your Mother Superior for assigning you to my surgery. And now, do excuse me. I must get on with my rounds.'

He placed the pile of records on Aidy's reception desk and returned to his surgery.

Sister Teresa smiled at her and said, 'I'll look forward to seeing you in the morning, Mrs Nelson.'

Aidy was very pleased by this turn of events. She had been dreading the doctor asking her to undertake a dressing change on his behalf, something she had told him she was adept at during her interview when in fact she wasn't, so having the nun on board to do such things was going to save her possible embarrassment.

Despite his good fortune earlier in being awarded the invaluable help of a nun, for which he was very grateful despite the fact that her attending patients on his behalf meant a lost fee for him, Ty returned from his morning round feeling more depressed than he usually did. He had examined and decided on the best treatment for all those he had been asked to visit, ignoring as best he could the dire conditions the majority of those patients lived in. He had been bemused by a statement made by one patient, though in fact it had been said to him a couple of times previously by others visiting him at his surgery, that they were only seeing him because the old woman . . . whoever she was . . . was not available at the moment for them to get their treatments from. Then, as he'd been about to knock on the door of a patient he was treating for a nasty leg ulcer that needed redressing, the sort of chore which in future Sister Teresa could tackle on his behalf, from a house in the row opposite a woman rushed out into the street, a bundle in her arms, wailing hysterically that her baby had stopped breathing.

Automatically, Ty rushed to take the child from her, dashing with it into her house and sweeping his arm out to clear the clutter off the rickety kitchen table so that he could lay the child on it while he examined it. There was nothing he could do. The baby was already dead and long past resuscitation. It transpired that the six-month-old child had been fretful while it was teething and in her effort to quieten it, the mother had given it a dose of laudanum – or overdose as it turned out. This was not the first child who had met its end in the same or similar circumstances since Ty had taken over the practice and it reduced him to despair that some mothers around these parts would resort to using such highly addictive substances, just to stop their babies from crying. Usually he managed to keep control of his feelings and go on his way, but today he'd been unable to hold then back. Did they not realise how precious a young life was? He had vented his anger on the already distraught woman, leaving her in no doubt that she was responsible for the death of her baby.

Aidy was to find out about this incident later, and

of Ty's reaction. An idea then struck her of just how the doctor could help to avoid any repetition of the sad event in future, but putting her idea to him was a different matter. He had already made it very clear to her it wasn't her place to tell him how to run his surgery.

Due to this incident it was after two o'clock when Ty returned. Aidy had already left for her afternoon break. For a moment he stood in the hall and listened to the silence. A sudden wave of loneliness engulfed him. With a shock he realised he was actually missing his receptionist's presence; her just being here brought life to the house. He discovered he liked her welcoming him back with a hot cup of tea, asking him as she always did, 'How did the round go this morning ... this afternoon ... then, Doc?' To which he would always reply in his curt manner, 'Fine, thank you.'

It still managed to infuriate him that she insisted on addressing him as 'Doc', no matter how much he reprimanded her. He had every right to dismiss her for such patent lack of respect towards him ... but, more and more, he was beginning to realise that he actually liked her more informal way of addressing him.

So far as her work went she hadn't given him any reason to regret employing her. She seemed to be getting on with sorting the record cards, albeit it was taking her an age. Though, in fairness, it wasn't exactly a straightforward job, there being over five thousand records for her to work her way through, and many for current patients that needed to be found quickly should they call in for a consultation. He'd be glad, though, when she'd finished it and be free to take more of the mundane jobs off his shoulders, such as the resharpening of the needles and instruments on the honing block and sterilising them by boiling; ordering the drugs, doing the accounts ... how he detested that time-consuming job! He wouldn't hand that over completely to her as what he ultimately earned was a private matter, but much of the preliminary work could be done by her.

The patients seemed to like her, judging by the favourable comments he had received from several of them during their visits. She did, though, irritate him with her endless questions whenever he asked her to do something she hadn't done before, extracting every minute detail from him on just how he wanted the job doing in a way he felt an experienced clerical person like her shouldn't need to. But he passed this off as her making sure she did exactly what he was expecting of her, so that there were no mistakes on her part. And he did prefer her to do that as mistakes could cost lives in his profession.

He became aware of the deathly silence again; that overwhelming sense of loneliness reinvaded him. For a fleeting moment he wished for nothing more in the world than Aidy to appear; her presence, her zest for life, to lift his gloom. He gave himself a mental shake. Now and again he was bound to feel lonely, bound to crave the company of other human beings, but it was the price he had to pay in order not to put himself in danger again.

Very conscious that he was already late on making a start on his afternoon round, he hurried into the kitchen to put together a sandwich to wolf down while he replenished items in his medical bag. Once there he stopped short, spotting that the plate and cup he'd used for breakfast and left in the sink to see to later had been washed and put away. On the kitchen table was a plate covered by another and a cup with a saucer over it. Curiously, he stepped over to look under the plate. He found a very appetising-looking cheese and pickle sandwich. Under a saucer, in an effort to keep it hot, was a cup of tea.

As time had worn on and he had still not returned, Aidy had obviously realised his round was taking him much longer than usual. Knowing he would not have time to prepare himself lunch before he'd need to depart on his afternoon round, she had taken it upon herself to prepare something for him. It was indeed both thoughtful and efficient of her. He was very appreciative of her gesture but wouldn't express it to her, of course. For Ty, any relationship with a woman from now on would be kept strictly on a business footing.

At just after three o'clock that afternoon, basket of provisions for that day sitting at her feet, Aidy scanned her eyes over the children leaving school. They were mostly shabby and ragged-looking, a few with no shoes on their feet, spilling out of the school entrance and swarming across the playground to join their equally shabby mothers or else making their own way home with friends. There was no sign of any of her siblings. She hoped none of them had been kept back for any reason. She had been gearing herself up all day for what she had to tell them, and wanted to get it over with. After that she needed to steel herself for her visit to Arch, in the hope he would be feeling benevolent enough to agree to her taking the mattress.

Fifteen minutes later, the multitude of pupils streaming through the door and filling the playground had thinned down to a few last stragglers, and still there was no sign of Aidy's brother and sisters. It was worrying that not one of them had made an appearance yet. She was just about to go inside and make enquiries when she spotted Marion's teacher, Miss Amelia Siddings, emerging from the door dressed for home. She was a very pretty, slim woman who hardly looked old enough to have left school herself. She smiled on spotting Aidy and changed direction to join her.

'Did one of the Greenwood children forget something? The caretaker will help you find whatever it is, I'm sure. I just saw him in classroom three as I was leaving. You should still find him there. Please excuse me won't you, only I'm in a rush to get home tonight.'

Probably got a date with a handsome man, Aidy thought. She said, 'My brother and sisters certainly have forgotten something, Miss Siddings. Forgot to come out of school!'

Amelia Siddings looked taken aback for a moment before she responded, 'Oh, but aren't you aware they were all sent home mid-morning? Not only your sisters and brother but half of the school, it seems. It appears we have a measles epidemic and Marion, Betty and George have certainly succumbed to it, according to the headmistress. The children who were affected started showing the signs of being ill soon after assembly and Miss Frinton immediately recognised what was ailing them all. Thankfully I had the illness as a child so I'm immune to it. Hardly pleasant for a child to suffer, but I understand it is really nasty for adults to go through.'

Aidy was looking stunned. So Betty had been showing the first signs she'd caught this awful disease the previous night, and Aidy herself had just dismissed it as over-tiredness. And Marion wasn't just blackmailing her grandmother into a cuddle and a story, she really wasn't feeling well either. George wouldn't complain of feeling under the weather even if he was, seeing it as not the manly thing to do. Guilt swamped her for not taking more notice of her siblings. Then panic reared within her. The three of them had been sent home that morning? That meant they would have encountered their father before she'd had a chance to explain it all to them.

Much to Amelia Siddings' surprise, Aidy turned tail and ran off like the devil himself was on her tail.

She burst through the door into the back room and stopped short, taking in the scene before her. Her grandmother lay on the sofa, her face tight with suppressed anger and frustration, lips pressed together firmly. It was obviously she was fearful of saying something that could result in catastrophe for them all. Arnold lay sprawled in the armchair, his nose buried in the racing pages of a newspaper. He looked a sight cleaner than he had done when he had arrived, obviously having had a thorough wash down and a shave. Aidy just worried how much extra fuel he had used heating up all the water.

On hearing her enter, without lifting his eyes from what he was studying, he growled, 'Good, yer home. That fire needs banking up.'

She fought to stop her temper flaring. 'And couldn't you have done that?' she evenly responded.

He did lift his head then to smirk at her. 'Why should I when I have my lovely family around to wait on me hand and foot?'

She almost forgot herself then, to tell him where to go, but remembered her primary concern. She addressed Bertha. 'I understand the kids were sent home from school this morning, suffering from measles. Where are they?'

It was her father that snarled back at her. 'Where they should be. In bed. I don't wanna see their faces down here until they've been given the all clear.' Dropping the newspaper in a crumpled heap, Arnold eased his bony body out of the chair, gave a yawn and a stretch, and announced, 'I'm off to the privy. Have the fire made up and a cuppa mashed for when I get back.'

He walked out, leaving Aidy glaring after him.

His departure gave Bertha the opportunity to vent all the pent-up fury she'd had to control until now. 'That man!' she fumed. 'He'd try the patience of God Himself, let alone a saint. He wasn't the nicest of people by the time he left yer mam the second time, Aidy, but those years he's been away have turned him real nasty. Obviously the better life he thought he'd get never happened. Now he's harbouring a deep grudge over it and teking it out on all of us.'

She eyed Aidy earnestly. 'It's been hell on earth for me today, him snarling his snide sarky comments at me 'cos I can't fetch and carry for him and he had to get his own breakfast, moaning all the time 'cos there were no eggs and bread left and he had to make do with porridge. Then he was grumbling 'cos he had to boil his own water for his wash down. Mind you, at least he had one . . . a dustbin smells pleasanter than he did! Thank God you've come home. I don't think I can keep me promise to keep me mouth shut any longer, love. It took me all me strength today not to give that bastard a piece of me mind.'

Aidy reminded her, 'Well, you're just going to have to try, Gran. He will throw you out if you cross him, I've no doubt of it. And are you going to be able to live with yourself if we're all reduced to traipsing the streets?'

Bertha shook her head.

'Well, then. I know it's hard but just ignore him, Gran. Look, I promise I'll find a way to get him out.'

'I so wish you could, but I don't see how.'

'Nor do I, but I'll try and find one. Nobody wants him gone more than I do, Gran. I hate him! I hate breathing the same air as he does. I hate the thought of the kids finding out what type of man their f—.' She stopped short, her face filling with horror. 'Oh, Gran, the kids!'

Bertha's face coloured guiltily. 'I haven't been able to check on them since they came home, see if the poor little blighters need anything, 'cos I can't get off this sofa, can I? There was no point in me asking *him* if he would check on them, 'cos I knew the answer.

'Oh, Aidy, it were awful when they all trooped in, looking so sorry for themselves. It was obvious they weren't at all well. As soon as George appeared in the doorway, he told me they'd been sent home as the teacher told them they'd all got measles. On hearing the word, *he* let rip, of course. Screamed blue murder at them to get up the stairs and out of his sight, and not to come down 'til there was no danger of him catching it. I've never seen them scarper upstairs so quick in all their lives! Poor little souls have no idea who he is, let alone why he's bellowing orders at them. They must be worried witless. They haven't had a drink or anything to eat since they came home . . .'

Aidy's thoughts were in a whirl. All the time she had been shopping and waiting at the school, the children had been feeling ill and frightened. How did she explain to them that the strange man who had terrified them was their own father, and that for the foreseable future he would be living here with them?

'I'd better go and see them. Do you know what I need to do to help them? I remember having measles when I was young but I can't remember what Mam did for me. Do I need to get Doc in?' The cost of such a visit never entered Aidy's head. Her siblings were sick and, whatever it took to get them better, she would do.

Bertha shook her head. 'There's nothing either the doctor or me can give them to cure them of measles, love. How much they'll suffer depends how bad they've each got it. They'll probably have a fever, which'll need to be kept down as best yer can with cold flannels on their foreheads, and there's an awful cough that goes with it. Nothing you can give them for that either. Regular doses of honey and lemon in hot water could help ease their throats. Otherwise, make sure they drink plenty of water, and it's best not to give them too much to eat. The disease needs to run its course . . . in about a fortnight, they should be up and about again.'

Two weeks! Aidy now had four invalids to look after, her wastrel of a father to contend with, plus work full-time. She sighed. 'Well, I suppose the only good thing about this is that they'll be kept out of the way of *him*. Let's just pray that he decides to leave before they're up and about again. Or meantime, between us, we come up with a way to get rid of him.'

Aidy found the children all huddled together in Betty and Marion's bed. Not content that her children should sleep on a flock mattress on the hard floor like most children did in this area, Jessie had saved and haggled hard to obtain them proper beds to sleep in, covered with blankets. Above the bed clothes, Aidy saw that Betty had small clusters of red spots by her ears and down the sides of her neck, the other two showing signs of them beginning to erupt. All of the children looked feverish and were coughing intermittently.

Three pairs of fearful, bewildered eyes settled on Aidy as she entered the room.

In a pitiful voice George said to her, 'I feel rotten, Aidy.'

The other two agreed, just as sorrowfully, 'So do we.'

'Yes, I expect you do,' she said, looking at them all tenderly as she went over to the bed and perched on the edge of it. She put her hand on George's forehead. He felt hot to the touch. 'I'll get you a wet cloth to help cool your head for you. Gran's told me you're all to drink plenty of water, and then all that's for it is bed rest until you're over this. I'm going to make you all some hot honey and lemon to help ease your throats.'

Usually the prospect of staying in bed was viewed as a punishment, but they were all obviously feeling so poorly that they looked relieved.

Then came the question she was dreading. It was

George who asked it. 'Who's that man, our Aidy? And what's he doing in our house?'

'I don't like him. He was really nasty to us. He made me cry,' said Marion, her bottom lip quivering.

Betty blurted, 'You'll make him go, won't yer, Aidy? Yer won't let him hurt us? We've bin worried 'cos Gran's down there and we don't know what he's done to her. He ain't hurt her, has he? We had to stop George from climbing out the window, getting the coal hammer out the shed and going to tackle that man. We wouldn't let him.'

'No, we wouldn't. We sat on him 'til he promised not to,' Marion told her. ''Case that man hurt him as well as Gran.' She then eyed Aidy hopefully and said, 'If I wish hard enough, maybe Mam will wake up and come back. She'll make that man go and leave us alone.'

Aidy's heart went out to her sister. Marion still hadn't accepted the fact that her mother was never going to wake up and come back to them, no matter how hard she wished or prayed. She assured them, 'The man hasn't hurt Gran, she's fine. But she's been very worried about you all. She's sorry she couldn't manage to get up the stairs because of her broken ankle and check on you, get you anything you needed.' She looked at each of them in turn, hating herself for having to lie to them in order to explain away the appalling behaviour of their own father.

'Look, the man never meant to be nasty or to frighten you. It was him who was frightened of you. You see, measles isn't a nice illness for adults to catch. He was just worried he would, if he got too close to you all.'

'But who is he, Aidy?' Betty asked her.

She looked at them all for a moment before taking a deep breath and telling them, 'Well, he's . . . he's our father.'

They all stared at her wide eyed and opened their mouths in shock.

'But . . . but . . . he can't be,' said Betty with conviction. 'Mam told us our dad was a nice man and loved us all, but he went away 'cos some men ain't cut out to be family men and our dad was one of those.'

Their mother had loved her younger children far too much to want them to go through life knowing that their father was a thoroughly selfish man who had deserted them all because he hadn't wanted to shoulder the responsibility of a wife and children any longer. Aidy loved her siblings far too much to tell them that the only reason he'd returned was because he was destitute and had nowhere else to go.

'Mam never lied. She would never lie to you. Father wasn't cut out to be a family man and it was felt best he should leave. But he wants to try and be a family man now, and has come back to live with us and have a go. We need to show him what good children he's got and make him feel welcome. He only shouted at you earlier because it's like I said, he's frightened of catching the measles because it can make adults very, very ill. Now you all need to get better. You must stay up here until you are. I've already had it so I'm not in danger.'

She smiled at them all fondly, leaned over and tenderly ruffled George's hair. 'I don't see why you shouldn't stay in here with your sisters and be company for each other until you're all better. I'll be back up shortly with a drink for you each.'

She returned back downstairs to find her father sprawled in the armchair once more. He glared at her accusingly. 'You ain't backed up the fire nor made me a cuppa. See to it, and hurry up.'

Aidy sensed her grandmother's rage at her son-in-law's selfishness and flashed a warning look at her. She wanted to ask her father if he thought well of himself for frightening his own children witless, but knew he wouldn't give a damn if she did.

'And I want some money,' he told her then. 'A couple of bob should do me just now.'

She shot back at him, 'A couple of bob would do *me* too. Then I could have bought something better for us to have for dinner instead of days-old soup. You want money for frivolities, you'd better go out and earn some. Hopefully your conscience will see that you give me a contribution towards your keep out of it before you blow the rest on yourself.'

With that she went across to the range and snatched up the battered coal bucket sitting on the hearth, lugging it off to the coal house so she could build up the fire to boil a kettle.

CHAPTER FIFTEEN

Having fetched and carried for her sick brother and sisters and made sure they were as comfortable as she could make them, Aidy tended to her grandmother, tidied the house, made bread and left it to rise, and prepared a meal of mashed potatoes and faggots. She had to eat hers sitting opposite her despised father and being made to witness the atrocious table manners he seemed to have adopted during his absence. After his dark, brooding silence at her refusal to fund a trip to the pub for him that night, the last thing she felt like was going back to work and being pleasant to all those who came into the surgery. Listening to the petty grumbles of some of them, she had to fight the urge to inform them that if they had half of what she had on her plate to deal with, then they'd *really* have something to grouse about.

Only a handful of patients turned up to consult Ty that evening, all with minor ailments that were quickly dealt with. All that is apart from one very attractive, twenty-five-year-old woman. It was very apparent to Ty she had absolutely nothing wrong with her. The purpose of her visit was purely to seduce him. Like others before her, it didn't take her long to realise that her long, shapely legs, full breasts, puckered lips and fluttering eyelashes had no effect on him whatsoever. Like the others who had tried before her, she finally conceded defeat and stormed indignantly from his room, slamming the door shut behind her.

The sparsely attended surgery meant it was over an hour earlier than usual and Ty was extremely gratified at the prospect of some leisure time once he'd finished up his paperwork and attended to a few necessary personal chores. He had no doubt that his receptionist too would be pleased to be allowed to get home earlier than normal to her husband.

He went to join Aidy in the waiting room, finding her sharpening a pencil. Under normal circumstances she would have been equally delighted by the prospect of an early finish. But now, not only would the atmosphere in the house be anything but relaxed with her father present, she doubted he'd even allow her grandmother and her to natter away, disturbing his listening to the crystal radio set. How she wished she'd a few spare coppers to give him, so he could go off down the pub and release them from his presence. As if that weren't enough, she'd her call on Arch to make. She'd have been tempted to put it off, but the thought of continuing to sleep in the chair was a deterrent. Regardless, she expressed her gratitude to Ty and made to collect her things together to make her leave, but he forestalled her.

'Just before you go, there's something I want to ask you. I've been meaning to for a while, but whenever I've attempted to, I've been prevented in one way or another. Anyway, with you being local, do you know of someone people around here refer to as *the old woman*?'

Aidy froze. Of course she did. That was the affectionate name the locals called her grandmother by. Why was the doctor enquiring after her? A medical man wouldn't need her services surely? Cautiously she asked, 'Is it important you find out who this woman is?'

He looked at her askance. 'Not that it's your business why I want to find out who she is, Mrs Nelson, but yes, it is, as a matter of fact. On several occasions since I've been practising here, patients have mentioned that the only reason they have been reduced to consulting me was because *the old woman* was indisposed at the moment, so they couldn't get any of her remedies until she was back in business again.' A look of disdain filled his face. 'I cannot believe people are taken in by the likes of this woman. Believing her claims that her products have curative properties when I doubt they're more than coloured water. This woman is just a confidence trickster and needs to be stopped from fleecing ignorant people out of their money.' He paused for a moment, furrowing his brow. 'Not long after I came here I have a vague memory of someone going on about selling their home cures to others. But for the life of me I can't remember now either her or where I was at the time.'

Aidy cringed. She could. He'd been in their kitchen at the time, the night her mother died.

'Anyway,' he continued, 'if you are aware of who she is, I would appreciate your telling me.'

Aidy gawped at him, fighting not to show her outrage. Had dare he label her grandmother a confidence trickster? The recipes for her remedies had come down to her from a long line of individuals who had dedicated their lives to discovering the medicinal properties of plants and flowers. The lotions and potions that resulted did indeed have healing qualities. There were numerous people hereabouts whose ailments had been soothed and healed by them, including Aidy herself.

She had no idea how Doc had come to form his opinion of home remedy makers, but he obviously hadn't met a genuine one like her grandmother. She smiled inwardly to herself. Had Bertha heard Doc brand her a confidence trickster, she would not have held back from putting him right! Well, the locals wouldn't give up her grandmother to him, they all thought far too highly of her and were reliant on her cures, and Aidy herself certainly wasn't going to, so she wished him luck in discovering her for himself.

She looked him in the eye and lied. 'I've no idea who this old woman is. Never heard of her. If I do, though, I'll be sure to let you know.'

A short while later, having expected to be facing Pat and mentally preparing for a battle with her, Aidy stared in surprise at the middle-aged woman facing her, a stained wrap-around apron covering her plain working dress. Aidy decided this must be a friend of Pat's. She was surprised, though, that the likes of Pat had any!

Aidy had obviously caught the woman in the middle of doing something as she didn't look at all happy at being disturbed. 'What can I do for you?' she asked in a hurried tone.

Her indomitable mother-in-law couldn't be in. It wasn't like her to allow someone else to answer the door in what she considered to be her house. Aidy was grateful she was being spared a confrontation with her, however.

'I'd like to see Arch, please,' she told the woman.

She frowned. 'Arch? No Arch lives here.'

Aidy flashed a look at the number on the door. She'd made no mistake, this was definitely her former home. 'Archibald Nelson? He does live here because he's the tenant.'

'Oh, sorry, dear. Forgive me, my mind was else-where. I've so much to get done tonight . . . it's the previous tenant you must be after. I didn't know their name was Nelson. I know nothing about them, in fact. But I hope it's not money you've come to collect as I doubt you'll get it, judging by the disgusting state they left this place in. They didn't seem to have a penny to spare for soap. Absolutely filthy! I've had to scrub the place from top to bottom before it's fit for me and my husband to move into tomorrow.'

Aidy was gawping at her. Arch had gone?

Now the woman was saying to her, 'Maybe one of the neighbours might be able to help you. You will excuse me but I must get on or I'll still be at it when the cart arrives with my furniture in the morning.'

As she shut the door, the front door of the house next door opened and another middle-aged woman came out to put milk bottles on the doorstep. Spotting Aidy, Hilda Morris smiled broadly as recognition struck. 'Why, Aidy love, how nice to see you.' A look of genuine sadness clouded her face. 'I was so sorry to hear about yer mam. You have my condo-lences. Jessie was such a fine lady. As yer know, I used to chat to her over the yard wall when she came to visit you. I really wanted to attend the funeral to pay my last respects, but I wasn't well at all that day so couldn't manage it. I was so sorry to learn about you and Arch, too. If ever a couple was together for life, I thought it was you two.'

Aidy smiled wanly at her. 'I thought so at one time too. Er . . . I've just found out Arch has moved out of next door, Mrs Morris. Did he by any chance tell you where he was moving to before he went?'

'I can't help you there, love. He'd no idea where he was heading. Just told me what had happened to cause your marriage to end, and said that's why he'd made the decision to go away and make a fresh start.'

So he'd discussed with their neighbour the events that had led to their break up! How could he do this to Aidy? Tell others all their most personal business, for it to be gossiped and sniggered over by all and sundry. Just to confirm that she had indeed heard the woman right, Aidy asked, 'Arch called on you and told you what had gone off between us?'

'Well, no, he never actually came to see me and volunteered the information. He only told me after I found him huddled at the back of your privy, sobbing his heart out, the night it all ended between you both. I heard him . . . well, it was impossible not to . . . when I went to fill the coal bucket and popped me head over the wall to investigate. It was obvious he was deeply upset. Men like Arch don't cry openly cry like that in public without a very good reason.

It wouldn't have been very neighbourly of me not to offer my help to him, would it? I thought, you see, that it was something to do with you ... you'd had a fatal accident or something, the way he was carrying on.'

She stopped talking as a woman approached and nodded a greeting. Hilda responded then said to Aidy, 'Look, we can't talk out here – come in. Oh, and Arch left me a letter for you, which I need to give you.'

A few minutes later, a cup of stewed sweet tea cradled between her hands, Aidy was seated at Hilda's kitchen table. Her husband was asleep in the chair by the range in the back room, round horn-rimmed spectacles balancing precariously on the very end of his pug nose, the newspaper spread across his paunch.

Sitting opposite Aidy, Hilda carried on where she'd left off. 'Once Arch got started I couldn't stop him. Like a dam bursting it was. He told me how badly he'd let you down when you'd needed his full support to help you look after your grandmother and your orphaned brother and sisters. About his mother's diabolical plan to get her hands on your mother's house, too. How he'd stood by and not done anything when she was being so nasty to you and your family because he was so terrified of her turning on him in front of you all. Especially you, Aidy. He couldn't bear the thought of you witnessing just what a coward he was as far as his mother was concerned.

'He said he knew that it was over between you, and there was no going back, after he told you you wouldn't be able manage to look after your family without him. He told me he so regretted saying that to you, letting you think he had no faith in you when he knew that, if anyone could, it was you. He was desperate by then to find any way he could to get you to give him another chance. But since you'd made it very clear to him that it was over between you, he couldn't stay around here. He knew the struggle you faced, but that he would be the last person you'd turn to for help. And the thought of you maybe meeting another man ... well, he couldn't bear it. He said he had to go away.

'I tried to persuade him that he was being hasty, should just let the dust settle a bit and see how the land lay between you both then, but he said he'd let you down far too badly to hope you'd ever trust him enough again to give your marriage another go. And there was the fact that his mother and father had taken over his own home. He couldn't face the thought of having to live under the same roof as them, even for a short time until he found himself somewhere else to live ... just couldn't do it. I thought he was exaggerating how bad his mother was until I witnessed what she was like for myself. Then

I couldn't blame him for wanting to put a great distance between them.

'It was the night after Arch packed up and went that I caught Pat stealing coal out of my shed. I heard a noise in the yard and came out to investigate. Apart from the fact I hadn't a clue who she was then, when I asked her what she was doing, she told me she'd run out and didn't think I'd mind her having a few lumps as neighbours helped each other. That was when she introduced herself to me. But, as I told her then, neighbours did help each other out but usually *asked* first. And, besides, her idea of a "few lumps" of coal was to be taking all I had. Cheek of her! She didn't like it at all when I told her to put it back and that she could have just a bucketful to do her that night. I didn't mind that . . . so long as I got it back the next day. Got in a right rage then, she did. Used language I'd never heard before. Kicked a hole in my shed door in temper.

'I realised afterwards why she got so mad. She was going to sell on that coal. And how I know is because Mrs Kite, the other side of her, found all *her* coal missing the next day, and Mr Nelson was heard asking around the pub the night before if anyone was after a bit of coal on the side.

'Well, while they lived here we had a spate of things going missing from backyards hereabouts. It's stopped since they went so the finger is pointed firmly in the

Nelsons' direction. I got so fed up with her coming round asking to borrow a cup of sugar, a drop of milk, couple of spuds ... you name it ... which were never returned even though she always promised faithfully that she would. It was no good telling her I hadn't got what she was after either. Very clever was Mrs Nelson. She'd wheedle out of you in a cunning way what you'd actually got before she asked. Well, I expect you know that trick of hers better than me, you being her daughter-in-law. I don't know how you coped with her, love. I suppose there's one consolation for you in respect of your marriage breaking up. You don't have to have anything to do with Pat any more, do you?'

Before Aidy could make any response, Hilda continued. 'Anyway, I got sidetracked. I told Arch that if he was going away and, the way he was talking, might never come back to Leicester, you deserved to know. He asked me if I would tell you. I told him no, it was only fair he should tell you himself. I think he asked me because he was ashamed to face you again after the way he acted to you. Anyway, he said he'd go round and tell you what he was planning to do before he headed off for the railway station, after he'd been back home and packed his bags. I got the impression he had no intention of letting his mother in on what he was up to, just going to sneak off and let her find out after he'd gone. So didn't he come and tell you he was going away, after all?'

Yes, he had. That must have been the night he'd knocked on the door but she hadn't answered because she hadn't been ready to face him again so soon. Had she opened the door to him, would she have tried to persuade him not to go? Or would she have encouraged him to make a new life for himself, knowing there was little chance of their ever reconciling their differences? Aidy didn't know the answer, and it didn't matter anyway. She hadn't answered the door and Arch had gone off to wherever it was he was heading, to try to start a new life for himself. The letter had been left to tell her what he hadn't been able to in person. She hadn't time to analyse how she was feeling about his going off, and the fact he might never come back, as Hilda was interrupting her thoughts.

'I found an envelope addressed to you the next morning, pushed through my letter box. I should have brought it round to you straight away, but you know how time runs away with you.' She got up from her chair. 'I'll fetch it for you.' Then she went off into the back room and returned moments later, the envelope in her hand.

Retaking her seat, she said, 'Just to put your mind at rest, what Arch told me that night, Aidy ... it hasn't gone any further and it won't.'

Aidy knew she meant it. Hilda Morris listened eagerly to gossip and would keep it going by imparting it to others, but Aidy had never known her actually instigate any during all the years she had been living next door. She smiled at her gratefully. 'I appreciate that, Mrs Morris.' She'd picked up her handbag ready to leave when another question presented itself.

'Do you know what happened to Arch's parents? From what I gathered when I last saw her, Mrs Nelson had made herself well and truly at home in my old house and had no intention of leaving.' She needed to find out where they'd gone. Aidy had no doubt that Pat still had many of her possessions from the house, including the mattress. It was unlikely she was going to hand it over voluntarily but Aidy wouldn't give up on it easily, the thought of doing without it affording her the courage.

Hilda's eyes lit up and her tone of voice became excited when she responded, 'Well, didn't the Nelsons' departure have all us neighbours out in the street to watch? And weren't all of us glad to see the back of them, especially me and Mrs Kite who suffered the worst of it. I mean, we're not used to Pat's type around here, with her foul language and treating all of us like she owned the street. You could hear her shouting at her husband from halfway down the road and it weren't just the odd occasion. It were most of the time they were both at home.

'And we all do our best round here to keep the

rats down by keeping our yards clear of rubbish so it makes it difficult for them to nest. The Nelsons were only living next door a week at the most before the rubbish was piling up, and me and Mrs Kite were already remembering not to leave our back doors open.

'And the noise Mr Nelson used to make at all hours, bringing back scrap metal he'd collected and sorting through it to sell on ... Well, they might have been able to terrorise the neighbours and have them living in fear of them where they used to live, but they weren't going to get away with it here!

'I hung on a bit to make sure Arch didn't change his mind and come back, but he didn't, so last week I told Reggie Gimble, the rent collector, what was going on. That you'd both left the house and weren't coming back, and that Arch's parents had moved themselves in and of their atrocious behaviour and how they were mistreating the landlord's property. Reggie Gimble paid a call on Pat, told her he'd heard her son and his wife had moved out of the property, and that as the previous tenant's mother she was not entitled to live there without the express agreement of the landlord. Due to the state of the property and complaints from the neighbours about their behaviour, Reg Gimble told her that the landlord would never give them the official tenancy, so she and her husband had until noon the next day to quit or he

would have them forcibly removed and done for tres-
passing.

'Talk about all hell let loose! Pat was like a woman
possessed. I was in my back room at the time, she
at her front door, and I could hear it all like she was
in the same room as I was, she was bellowing at him
that loud. She threatened to have him for slander,
insinuating they were scum and not good enough to
live in this street . . . which actually was the truth of
it. She kicked Reggie Gimble on his shins, gave him
a black eye, slammed the door in his face, then
screamed at him through the letter box that this was
her house now and she wasn't leaving it. As soon as
she saw he had gone off, she came storming round
to me, banging that fat fist of hers on my front door,
yelling at the top of her voice that if she found out
it was me who had reported them to the rent collector
then I was a dead woman. Suffice to say, I never
opened the door to her.

'Then she went to Mrs Kite and threatened her the
same, but not before she threw a stone at my front
window and broke it. She did the same to Mrs Kite's
front window. Then she stood in the middle of the
road and bawled out, so loud she could be heard
from one end of the street to the other, that the
Nelsons weren't moving from their house and all of
us had better get used to that. Then she went back
inside and for the rest of the night until the early

hours of the morning all I could hear was her screaming and raving and furniture being dragged across the floors, so it wasn't much sleep me or Mr Morris got that night and neither did Mr and Mrs Kite.'

Aidy was neither shocked nor surprised to learn of Pat's despicable behaviour, knowing only too well what she was capable of. She was, though, feeling somewhat ashamed that she was associated with this woman by marriage, and hoped that people around here would not look down on her for this fact.

Hilda, though, was thoroughly enjoying herself, relating events to Aidy. 'Bang on noon the next day, Reggie Gimble turned up with six of the biggest bruisers I've ever seen. I'd only to look at them and they frightened me to death. One of them had a lump hammer with him, obviously to break the door down with should Pat not go voluntarily. They needed to use it. That furniture I'd heard being dragged across the floor the night before ... well, she'd only barricaded the front and back doors! She obviously thought she had the place as secure as Fort Knox, but she wasn't clever enough to give a thought to the windows.

'The man with the lump hammer broke through the back-room window, and him and another of the hefty blokes climbed in. While one fended off Pat from attacking them with her frying pan, the other moved the furniture away from the front door and let the rest of them in. I couldn't believe me eyes then, seeing Jim Nelson come out acting like he wasn't aware all the neighbours were watching, or that he was actually in the process of being evicted. He just went off down the road like he was taking a stroll to the pub. Probably was, come to that.

'Next thing all their belongings were being brought out and piled in a heap in the street. It had started raining an' all.' She paused for a moment to look sadly at Aidy. 'All that stuff was yours and Arch's, wasn't it? Though there didn't seem to be half what I remembered you having when you lived there. I've a mind Pat pawned most of it after Arch left and pocketed the money.

'Last thing to come out of the house was Pat Nelson herself. It took all six of those beefy men to heave her out between them and, believe me, for all their strength they were struggling under her weight. That's when all we neighbours went back inside our houses, just in case she decided to attack any of us.'

Aidy wondered where the Nelsons were now. Not back in their old place. Despite the dire condition it had been in, hardly fit for humans to live in, some desperate people would have snatched it up and be settled there now. Her in-laws wouldn't have been able to park themselves on their other two sons, as they had done with Arch. Fortunately for them both, their respective homes were only just big enough for their growing families. That left only one place the Nelsons could have gone that Aidy could think of: the Leicester Union Workhouse. She could not find it in herself to pity them after all they had done to her.

Mr Morris was heard to call out then: 'Any chance of a cuppa, love?'

Hilda called back, 'I'll put the kettle on.'

Aidy took this as her cue to leave and stood up. 'I'll let you get on, Mrs Morris.'

Hilda Morris stepped over to Aidy and, much to her surprise, took her hand and patted it, saying, 'It's a grand thing you're doing. Not many young women would abandon their own future to make sure their family has one.'

'That tea ready yet?' her husband called out, an irritated edge to his voice.

She called back good-naturedly, 'Give the kettle chance to boil.' Though she hadn't actually put it on yet.

A few minutes later, Aidy sat perched on a low factory wall. She withdrew from her pocket the envelope Hilda Morris had given her. Arch had never written a letter to her before, he'd never had cause to. For a moment she looked at it, at her name written in Arch's clumsy handwriting. Some of the letters had started to run through becoming wet. Sadness gripped her then. When Arch had been writing her name on this envelope, he'd been crying. Using a fingernail, she slit the envelope open and took out the folded piece of paper inside.

Dear Aidy,

I'm sorry I didn't stand by you when I should have. When you first told me your plan it sounded simple, but now I've had time to think about the consequences, come time, I would have ended up resenting your family for making me give up my plans for the future. I know that now.

In the circumstances, it's best I go away and make a fresh start.

I will always love you.

Arch

Aidy folded the letter back up and replaced it in the envelope. At least he was finally being honest about his own feelings now. A part of her would always love him too, and she genuinely wished him well. Hoped eventually he found love again, to take away the pain of losing her. Arch had proved to have traits in his character that she couldn't live with, but it would not be right of her to begrudge him happiness with someone else. And she did still care very much about him, always would.

He hadn't much liked his younger brother but he

was close to his elder one, Stanley, and wouldn't put him through unnecessary worry over his whereabouts and welfare. She knew Arch would let him know where he was, once he got settled, and since she'd got on well herself with Stanley, knew he would inform her how Arch was faring, to set her mind at rest.

Aidy made to put the letter safely away in her handbag. As her left hand passed through a shaft of light coming from the gas lamp there was a glint of light from the rings on her wedding finger. She held her hand out, spread her fingers and looked at them both. She knew how she could raise the money for a flock mattress . . .

It was upsetting for her that she had to resort to pawning the rings. that had been given to her with so much love, but at the moment they were the only things of any value she possessed. Arch had bought her the best he could afford at the time. The diamond on her engagement ring was only tiny, just a chip, and her wedding band was thin. But hopefully their second-hand value would cover the price of what she so desperately needed. The pawnbroker opened until nine every night except for Sunday so she had time to go tonight.

Aidy waited on tenterhooks while behind the counter Sidney Wilks took a quick glance at her engagement ring through his magnifying eye piece to assess its worth. He was an elderly little man, thin bodied and sharp featured, who always wore a red velvet smoking jacket, heavily embroidered on the collar and panels down the front. His grey hair was collar length and his short-sighted eyes peered at his customers through thick-lensed glasses. There were very few, if any, residents of the area who had not had cause to come through his doors at one time or another so he was acquainted with most of them. Although Aidy, as an adult, had never had cause to visit Sidney Wilks' establishment, he knew her from the times she had come here as a child, when Jessie had found herself short and needed to raise a shilling or two to see her through.

Aidy had always been eager to attend to her mother's business at the pawnbroker's on her behalf, when she wasn't able to go herself. This place had been a source of fascination to her. It was an Aladdin's cave ... a treasure trove. There was nothing that couldn't be got here, from a tiny silver locket to a brass-framed bedstead, an ear trumpet to a zinc bath. As a child, while she waited her turn on busy days, Aidy used to try to guess some of the uses for many of the weird, dusty objects she'd never come across before.

'Three shillings,' Sidney Wilks said gruffly to her now.

'Each?' she asked hopefully.

'For both.'

Aidy gave a disdainful tut. 'Oh, come on, Mr Wilks, my two rings are worth more than that, even second-hand.'

'I agree, they are, but I have to make a profit. I have to eat too, yer know.' He gave a deep sigh. 'Three and six, and that's my final offer.'

'And it's still too low. But it's not actual money I'm wanting to exchange them for, Mr Wilks.'

His eyebrows rose as he eyed her suspiciously. 'Just what are you after in exchange for them then?'

'A decent flock that you know comes from a good source. I was hoping for some blankets too.'

He said sardonically, 'You don't want much then. Single flock?'

'Double.'

He shook his head. 'No wonder I'm not rich when I let a pretty woman like yerself fleece me.' He looked at her for a moment before he gave a resigned sigh. 'Might be able to exchange a flock for the rings, depends what quality yer after, but as for blankets as well . . . Come through the back and I'll see what I can do.'

Fifteen minutes later Aidy returned to the front shop feeling very pleased with herself. At first Sid had tried to convince her that her choice lay between several moth-eaten, thin and stained flocks, which she had flatly refused to consider. Her two rings were worth more than those and the pawnbroker knew it. She had pointed at flocks worth well in excess of what her rings would cover. She knew it and so did the pawnbroker. This went on until finally an agreement was reached.

The flock she had settled on was the well-padded sort, covered in thick twill and according to Sid Wilks had come from a good family fallen on hard times. It had arrived only the previous day which hopefully meant bugs hadn't spread to it yet from others she knew to be infested by the looks of them stacked close by. Aidy would still give it a thorough shake and a meticulous scrub with turpentine and salt before she would sleep on it, though. That meant another night or so in the armchair while it dried, but at least she knew her discomfort was coming to an end.

Sidney Wilks had also reluctantly agreed to her having three grey army blankets, if only because Aidy had made it clear she wasn't leaving his shop until he did. Well, a flock was no good to her without blankets. Regardless, she felt she had got herself a good bargain.

Sid Wilks back behind his counter and Aidy the other side, she informed him, 'I'll take the blankets with me, then I've just got to arrange for a strapping lad to collect the flock for me. I've several neighbours whose sons I'm sure would oblige if I slip them a copper each at the end of the week. Hopefully they'll fetch it for me tonight.'

'Well, you've an hour before I close.' Sid then looked at her hopefully. 'Before you go, though, do you think you could do me a favour? Mind the shop for me while I nip out the back.' There were very few people he would entrust his shop to while he relieved himself but, although he hadn't seen Aidy for years, he knew she was the trustworthy sort.

Aidy sat herself down in the comfortable wing-back chair where Sid Wilks spent much of his time in between customers, reading books. There was one resting on the small table to one side of the chair which he had been engrossed in when she had arrived. She too enjoyed reading, losing herself in a good adventure yarn or a soppy love story, but since the death of her mother hadn't had time to enjoy such pursuits. She made to pick up the book but was stopped by the tinkle of the bell on the door, announcing the arrival of a customer.

The shop was over-full and badly lit so all Aidy was able to see was a shadowy figure approaching the counter. It was a woman, that much was evident. It wasn't until she was almost at the counter that her features could be made out. On recognising them, Aidy exclaimed, 'Col! Oh, how good to see you.'

Colleen Brown stared at Aidy, the very last person

she had expected to find behind the pawnbroker's counter. Equally as delighted to meet her, she responded, 'It's good to see you too, gel.' She then asked, puzzled, 'Are yer working here now?'

'No, just minding the shop while Mr Wilks nips out the back. He's only just gone but he shouldn't be long.' Then she told her friend proudly, 'I work for the new Doc as his receptionist.'

'I had heard that. Well, I don't know how you swung getting that receptionist's job, Aidy, being's you wouldn't have had the experience for it, but hats off to you for doing so.'

If Colleen knew the truth of just how she'd managed to land the job, would she still be so admiring? Aidy wondered.

Colleen was pulling a rum face. 'I wouldn't fancy working for that doctor meself, though. Not that I've had the pleasure of meeting him yet, and thank God I've not had to call him in as I couldn't afford his fee, but by all accounts his face would crack if he smiled, and he's rude and arrogant too . . . so it's no wonder he's not married, 'cos who'd put up with a man like him, eh? Good looking, though, so I've been told. Anyway, he can't be paying you enough if you're in here having to pawn summat.'

'Well, the wage isn't quite what I got in the factory, when I was filling my quotas, that is, but with very careful handling we can just about scrape by on it.

I'm in here for another flock and some blankets. My father unexpectedly decided to come back home.'

'Oh? I got the impression your mam was a widow, from what you told me. Well, what a relief for you. With your dad back, you're not responsible for your family now, are yer? You and Arch can sort yer differences out and carry on where yer left off.'

If only Colleen knew that her father had only come back because he was broke and had nowhere else to go. Aidy wasn't inclined to tell the whole sad truth, though, and especially not in the pawnbroker's, risking the possibility that Sid Wilks would overhear. To change the subject she said, 'I heard about the lay offs at the factory, and I was worried you was amongst them, Col.'

She flashed Aidy a wan smile. 'I was one of the lucky ones who's been kept on. For now anyway. I dread to think what the future holds, the way the country is going. Flo, Beattie, Lily and Muriel have gone. It's not so bad for the other three as their husbands are all in work, but Muriel's a widow with three kids to look after. How the hell she'll manage, I can't imagine. I fear it's the workhouse for her and her kids. I don't know what the hell I'll do if I end up losing my job. Bob got laid off two weeks ago, Aidy, and ain't had a tickle of nothing since. If he does hear of anything going, there's a queue a mile long in front of him after it too.'

Aidy was devastated to learn this. Flo, Beattie, Lily and Muriel had worked nearby and the six of them used to sit together in the canteen at tea breaks and dinner-time, chatting about the trials and tribulations of their daily lives. But Colleen was her closest friend and so it was with her that Aidy's main allegiance lay. She was relieved her job, at least for now, was safe in light of her husband losing his. But a worry did present itself to Aidy. 'I so hope Bert gets set on with something before you have to stop work yourself, with the new baby.'

'There is no baby any more, Aidy. I miscarried it the night he came home and told me he'd been laid off. It probably seems to you that I don't care I lost it, but I did. A child is precious, no matter what. But maybe it's better off than living the life we could give it. I look at my other three every night when they're in bed and wonder if me and Bert did right, bringing them into this world, with the sort of future the likes of us can offer. We're having to move to a smaller place, only one bedroom between us, all squashed together tighter than sardines in a tin. And it's at the back of a factory so all day the new place is shrouded in black sooty smoke. I'll never be able to hang any washing out . . . but needs must, eh, gel.

'I've popped in to see Mr Wilks to get an idea from him what I can hope to get for the stuff I can't take with me. Some of my bits and pieces don't bother me, but it'll break my heart having to part with the Welsh dresser me gran gave me before she died. The rooms in the new place are so tiny I can't fit it in.'

Aidy thought her own position bad enough but she couldn't compare it to what Colleen was facing. But before she could express sympathy to her friend for her dire situation, the pawnbroker returned.

A new customer meant money to be made. Nodding a quick thank you to Aidy for obliging him, he then focused all his attention on Colleen, and she in turn in her desperation tried to glean as much money as she could from him for the precious belongings she could not take with her to her new home.

Promised a penny each on Friday, a neighbour's two teenage sons eagerly shot off to collect the flock mattress for Aidy.

On her return home, before she entered by the back door, she took a deep breath to brace herself for what awaited her inside. She was surprised to find the place in complete darkness. She had to grope her way from the kitchen into the back room where the only light was coming from the dying embers of the fire.

Her grandmother's eyes were obviously accustomed to the dark because as soon as Aidy stumbled her way through the back-room door she exclaimed, 'Thank God you're home, love! The gas meter ran out not long after you left. I've been sitting in the dark since, and the kids too upstairs. It wouldn't have mattered if I could have lit some candles but with this dratted leg, I can't.'

All Aidy was conscious of was the fact her father didn't seem to be there. 'Where's *he* then?' she asked, praying vehemently the answer was that Arnold had gone to bed for the night or better still had upped and left, although she thought there was little chance of that.

'Gone out. To the pub, I guess.'

That was just the best news to Aidy but regardless a question presented itself. 'He had no money to go to the pub with to my knowledge. And if he had money, he should have put it in the meter, the selfish . . .' She stopped herself out of respect for her grandmother.

'He didn't have any money until the gas went and he went next door to borrow sixpence. I gather he got it as I haven't seen him since.'

Aidy's temper rose. Were there no depths to which that man would not sink? Leaving his family in the dark and going off down the pub with money he'd borrowed off a benevolent neighbour to replenish the meter. Money that *she'd* have to repay. Aidy was so angry she couldn't speak.

CHAPTER SIXTEEN

Aidy groaned as she looked around at the chaos in the back room. Having seen the state of the kitchen, she knew the other rooms would be just as bad – apart from her father's. Well, he wouldn't need to turn his own room over in his search for hidden money.

Much to her grief and anger, she'd found he'd already pawned the few ornaments that used to adorn the mantel in Jessie's parlour. She blamed herself for not having the sense to hide them away.

After two months of being back with his family, and many previous fruitless searches, Arnold should have realised by now that no money was left lying or hidden away in the house for him to find and dispose of as he wished. Aidy was very careful to make sure she kept securely on her person, even in bed, what money she had, every last farthing of it accounted for, as the loss of any would cause hardship to a family already struggling to cope on too little. Bertha too was as diligent over the few pennies she kept back for herself, handing over the majority to her very grateful granddaughter, to make certain they never got into her hated son-in-law's hands, now that she was back on her feet again and supplying the locals with her remedies.

Several weeks back Arnold had erupted in fury when he had finally decided to get up one day, just before Aidy was due home for her afternoon break at two, only to encounter the pungent smell of one of Bertha's potions which she was brewing up in the kitchen.

Having at long last had her casts removed, her injuries pronounced healed by the doctor, and desperate to replenish her stock, Bertha had made a trip into the countryside, having first cajoled all her young grandchildren into accompanying her since they too were fully recovered by then. She was intent on bringing back as much as they could heave between them. Autumn was just about over, winter rapidly approaching, and soon all but the hardiest of her requirements would be dying off and no use to her. But, much to her gratitude, after some foraging by them all she had amassed virtually all the different varieties of plants, leaves, fruits, bark and fungi she required, still in healthy condition. They all returned home with muscles groaning under the weight of the sacks they were lugging.

That early-afternoon Bertha had been contentedly boiling up birch leaves along with a few other ingredients which went into making a diuretic that helped with bladder problems, as well as chopping dandelion leaves in readiness for her next boil up, the juice of which was good for removing warts, when Arnold stormed in, shoved a startled Bertha aside, grabbed up the cauldron and took it to the back door where he threw the pot and its contents out into the yard, yelling at her that he wasn't putting up with any more stenches from her quack remedies so she'd better find somewhere else to make them up.

Aidy was just coming through the back gate as Arnold threw the pot and its scalding contents into the yard. Thankfully, save for a few spots on her skirt, the rest of it missed her. Her anger at his actions knew no bounds. Forgetting his threat to throw them all out should they fail to respect him, she raged at her father.

'How dare you chuck Gran's potion out 'cos you can't stand the smell? The bit of profit she makes helps me keep this house running and puts food in your mouth. We never had meat from one month to the other while Gran was indisposed with her broken bones, but now at least we can stretch to a bit of scrag end once a week. If you're going to stop her from making the bit of money she gives me, then I'll be looking to you to give it me instead.'

Before she could stop him, he'd grabbed her by her throat. He pulled her up so she was standing on tiptoes, pushed his face into hers and hissed, 'Watch yourself, girl, or I will have you all out. I'll have this place filled with lodgers before you've made it to the end of the street, so don't think I can't manage without yer.' Then he let go of her and stormed off into the back room, snarling after him, 'Make sure that old witch cooks up her poisons when I ain't home in future.'

A worried Bertha bustled out to join Aidy in the yard. 'I'll never get up to speed with all me potions if I have to wait until he goes out. Some take hours to prepare and . . .'

'Just carry on as you are, Gran,' Aidy told her firmly.

'But you heard him.'

'He's all mouth, Gran. He won't have us out and fill this house with lodgers. Lodgers don't look after themselves do they? They expect clean sheets once a week and cooked meals for their money. *He* won't do anything that involves grafting while he's got someone else cooking and cleaning for him, and he's managing to make enough money to cover his own needs, trust me.' She wasn't sure how Arnold came by that money but one thing she was sure of: it wasn't from any legitimate source.

She bent down to pick up the pot, now with a dent

in its side from where it had hit the cobbles, and handed it back to her grandmother, telling her, 'Go and get back to it, Gran. As you know, I've come up with a way to send more custom your way once you've a good stock of your remedies to sell. It's not like we couldn't do with the extra, what with having to stretch our money out to cover the extra mouth we have to feed and Christmas not far off. It'd be nice if we could find a penny or two to get the kids something each to open on Christmas morning, wouldn't it? And something a bit special for dinner.'

Now, looking around at the mess Arnold had left in his search for money, she wondered just how he managed to pay for his beer and cigarettes. It certainly wasn't from having a proper paid job. However he made it, though, it was obvious that he hadn't made enough today or he wouldn't have needed to ransack the house.

Then, suddenly, a memory surfaced and she realised how he did make his money. A few evenings ago she had come home from work to find Bertha out, visiting one of her cronies, and the children gathered around him at the table. Arnold had been showing them some tricks he knew, involving three tin cups and a dried pea. He had seemed to put the dried pea under one of the cups, then shuffled them around and told the children to guess which cup the pea was under now. Only it wasn't under any of the cups but still in his hand.

339

At the time Aidy had been most surprised by this seemingly fatherly display of entertainment when previously the children had learned, to their cost, to keep their distance from him. But now she realised this was how Arnold made his money: conning people fuddled with drink into betting on sleight-of-hand tricks they couldn't possibly win. *And* he was teaching his children how to do these tricks. Was his aim to get them skilled enough to con their friends out of their Saturday copper – those whose families could afford to give them pocket money anyway – and then hand over their ill-gotten gains to him? She certainly wouldn't put it past him, but her brother and sisters would be warned by her not to copy their father's chicanery.

It was hard to believe that the presence of one more person could change their lives so drastically, and definitely not for the better. Arnold was a constant drain on their meagre resources and ruled the house with his tyranny. No one smiled any more, no one sang. He made all their lives a misery. Despite their best efforts neither Aidy nor Bertha could think of a way to rid themselves of him, apart from murder or moving out themselves, but as it was impossible for Aidy to amass the extra week's rent to put down as security on a new place, it seemed they'd no choice but to endure him until he decided otherwise.

At least she derived pleasure from her work. Her

boss was still an extremely hard man to get along with and, at times, she had actually drawn blood from having to bite her own tongue to stop herself giving him a piece of her mind over his indifferent, sometimes rude, attitude towards her. But the majority of the patients made up for him. They treated Aidy with respect and courtesy in her role of receptionist. She had to admit, she felt more satisfaction in this job than she had in her factory position.

Now the majority of her time was no longer taken up by the laborious task of reorganising the records, besides reception duties she did all the sterilising of the instruments and the sharpening of them, ordering the drugs, checking them on delivery and putting them away, and also gave the surgery a clean after each session ended.

The arrival of Sister Teresa had also awoken in Aidy an idea of how she could better herself, and give her family a chance of a better future. If she had basic nursing skills, she could apply for jobs in such places as private nursing homes where she'd be earning more than she was now from her receptionist's job as well as hopefully working for a far more congenial employer. First, though, she had to acquire those skills. She needed to find someone who would teach them to her. The only person she knew who was equipped to do so was Sister Teresa. Aidy had always found the nun to be very pleasant and felt sure she'd readily agree to educate her in what she wanted to learn.

That morning, having packed up all she needed to carry out the visits the doctor wished her to make on his behalf, Sister Teresa was just about to take her leave when Aidy said to her, 'Is it possible to have a quick word before you go, Sister?'

Aidy was surprised to see her stiffen and felt sure there was a hint of worry in her voice when she responded, 'What about?'

'I wondered if you could see your way to helping me?'

The nun's relief to hear that was most apparent. Aidy saw her shoulders visibly relax beneath her habit. She had no time to wonder why though as Sister was pressing her, 'What sort of help are you after from me, Mrs Nelson?'

Aidy quickly told her of her desire to learn basic nursing skills, omitting to mention it was so she could apply for jobs elsewhere, not wanting to risk it getting back to the doctor's ears. She wondered if Sister Teresa would let her accompany her on some of her visits in the afternoons.

When she had finished making her request, Sister Teresa looked at her blankly for several long moments, seemingly mulling matters over in her mind before she said, 'Well, I don't think it would be appropriate for you to accompany me on any visit without my getting the patient's permission. And in any case, it would prove very distracting for me, to have you peering over my shoulder and have to answer all your questions. There's a real risk I could lose my concentration and cause harm to the patient I was treating at the time, so I'm afraid I will have to say no to your idea. I commend your ambition to better yourself, though. I'm sure if you make further enquiries you'll find someone else with nursing experience to teach you what you wish to know.' She smiled graciously at Aidy. 'Now, please excuse me, I must get on.'

A disappointed Aidy watched her glide out, the skirt of her silk habit swishing as she walked. She fully appreciated the reasons put forward to deny her request, but was determined not to let this setback stop her from earning a better life for the kids, Gran and herself. She would do what Sister suggested, ask around and keep her fingers crossed it wouldn't take too long to uncover someone willing to give up their time in this way.

'I could help you, dear.'

Aidy turned her head to see a middle-aged woman sitting close by. The surgery had been very heavily attended that morning and, in her need to speak to Sister Teresa, she had forgotten there were still several patients waiting their turn to see the doctor.

The woman smiled apologetically at her. 'I didn't mean to eavesdrop, love, it was difficult not to hear what was being said, sitting so close to you. But if it's learning some basic nursing skills yer after, then I could help you with that, if you'd like me to? I was a nurse in the last war, you see, gave it up when I got married, but I don't suppose things have changed much since I trained. I could give you an hour or two one afternoon a week, if that's all right with you?'

All right with her! Aidy didn't know how she stopped herself from jumping up and running across to give the woman a hug of gratitude. She eagerly asked, 'Can we start this afternoon?'

The woman smiled. 'I'll look out me old nursing bag as soon as I get back home.'

Now, as Aidy looked around at the mess she'd arrived home to find, she was conscious that Sadie Billson was expecting her shortly to begin her lessons so she really hadn't time to tidy the place up, but her conscience wouldn't allow her to leave it for her grandmother to come home to. Her father really was selfish. He had no consideration for his family whatsoever. If it weren't for the fact that his name was on the rent book, he'd have no right to be living here and forcing them to put up with him like this. But unless he officially gave up the tenancy himself there was nothing they could do to change this sorry state of affairs.

CHAPTER SEVENTEEN

Ty did not often make mistakes in medical matters, and when he did he admitted them, if only to himself. The mistake he had made today was not life-threatening, but it could delay the healing of Nell Crosby's ulcerated leg.

Arriving in the waiting room, he found Aidy putting on her coat to go home for her afternoon break. She had been going one afternoon a week to Sadie Billson's house for over a month, and under Sadie's patient tutelage could now properly apply a bandage to different areas of the body so that it remained in place and secure. Sadie was instructing her how to clean a wound this afternoon and Aidy was anxious to get off because, before she was due there at three, she had shopping to buy on the way. On the afternoons Aidy was with Sadie, Bertha usually did the shopping, but couldn't today as a neighbour had had a death in the family and Bertha had offered her services to prepare food for the funeral tea the next day.

Ty addressed his receptionist in his usual stiff manner. 'I do respect the fact that it's your afternoon breaktime, Mrs Nelson, but I'd appreciate it if you'd drop this in to Mrs Nell Crosby's house.' He put a small pot on her desk.

Aidy knew Nell Crosby well. She was a regular customer of her grandmother's. Aidy had been present when Nell had called on Bertha for something for her leg when it had first started causing her problems, but on inspecting the open wound that wasn't healing, Bertha had advised her she thought it to be ulcerous and to consult the doctor over it as none of her potions was strong enough heal it.

Ty was telling Aidy, 'Sister Teresa needs it to treat Mrs Crosby's leg. Mrs Crosby is her last call for today so if you go straight away you should be there before Nurse is.' He then put a small bulky brown envelope on the desk beside the pot. It was Aidy's pay packet.

With that, he turned and walked out of the room.

As she picked up the pot and her pay, Aidy realised Doc had obviously forgotten to include the pot with the other medical supplies he had handed her to put in the bag for the nun that morning. He wouldn't openly admit his oversight to her because then he wouldn't feel he could fairly chastise her should she ever err in a similar fashion. It seemed she was not even being given a choice whether or not to take the ointment in her own time but was expected to, as Ty had left without waiting for her reply.

Aware that Nell Crosby's ulcerated leg was very painful to her and inhibited her from walking, when Aidy arrived at the house she made her way around the back, tapped purposefully on the door, opened it and called out, 'Mrs Crosby, it's Aidy Nelson from the surgery.'

Nell called from the back room, 'Oh, come through, love.'

She found the old lady sitting in a shabby wooden chair by the range. Her bandaged leg was resting on a wooden stool. She was dabbing her eyes with a man's white handkerchief.

Aidy's heart went out to her. Her infected leg must be paining her something terrible for it to be making her cry.

The old lady asked, 'You've come instead of Sister to see to me leg then? Not ill is she, I hope?'

'No, she'll be with you shortly, Mrs Crosby. I've brought the ointment she needs to put on your leg when she redresses it. I forgot to put it in the supplies bag this morning. Hopefully the ointment Doc has had made up will help ease the pain for you. It must be bad to make you cry. You do have my sympathies.'

'Eh? Oh, no, lovey, the pain isn't as bad as it was now Doc's got it on the mend. I wasn't happy, yer know, when yer gran told me she couldn't be of help to me this time and advised me to see him. Well, apart from the fact I couldn't afford his fee and would have to ask one of me sons to help me out with it, I'd heard he was young and I didn't know how I felt about having a young man attending to me. I'd also heard that he was an arrogant young fella, with no niceties about him. Which turned out to be true! He's very abrupt, isn't he? Won't sit and have a bit of a chat with a cuppa, like Doctor Mac did. But I have to say, he seems to know what he's doing and I've no complaints at all about his doctoring skills. I can't imagine he's an easy man to work for, from my experience of him?'

She was looking at Aidy quizzically, waiting for her to enlighten her, but no matter how much Aidy agreed she knew it would not be right to discuss her boss in this way. She was, though, concerned to discover what had caused the old woman to be upset enough to cry, if it hadn't been her leg.

'If your leg wasn't hurting when I came in, then what was the matter, Mrs Crosby? I don't mean to pry. Just wondered if it was anything I could help you with?'

Mrs Crosby patted Aidy's hand affectionately and smiled up at her. 'Not unless you can bring my

Albert back, love. I was having a little weep 'cos it would have been his birthday today. I lost him ten year ago. Caught a cold which turned to pneumonia, he did. He was a slater by trade. Up on them roofs in all weathers. Very few slaters live to old age, what with working in wet clothes more times than dry. It weakens their chests. He was in the trenches in the war, yer know, was my Albert. Would never talk about it, though, even to me. I know he was brave. Got presented with medals to prove it. Every birthday since he died, I take them out in honour of him and give them a polish. Only I thought I'd put them back where I always do, in the top drawer of me tallboy, with me underwear, when I had them out last year. But when I went to fetch 'em out again today, they weren't there.'

Her brow creased worriedly. 'I distinctly remember putting them back in their box in the top drawer of my tallboy. My Roger was here at the time. He'd come to walk me round to his house for dinner. His wife was cooking me favourite, stuffed heart ... Roger's me eldest. He's the one who's paying the doctor's fee for me leg ... he was moaning at me to hurry up as the dinner would be spoiled and his Dorothy wouldn't be best pleased, and I told him I wasn't going anywhere until I'd put his dad's medals safely away.'

She heaved a sigh, scowling thoughtfully. 'I'm sure

I haven't moved 'em since.' She looked up at Aidy, clearly bothered. 'Maybe I've got more wrong with me than a bad leg. Maybe me brain is giving up on me.' Then she tutted and waved a hand dismissively. 'Oh, Albert's medals have got to be somewhere in here. Where else could they be? I'll have another look for 'em when I've seen Sister out.

'She's very nice, is Sister Teresa. Very gentle in her ways and most considerate. I really look forward to her coming, unlike I did the doctor before Sister started with the surgery. If I as much opened me mouth, before I'd said a word he'd be looking at me like I was about to commit a cardinal sin, being so familiar with him. Sister now ... she doesn't mind me chattering away ten to the dozen while she's tending to me. And helpful! Never fails to ask if there's anything she can do for me before she leaves as she knows how difficult it is for me to manage some chores at the moment.

'Both me daughter-in-laws do what they can for me, but they have enough to do, running after their own families. Sister very kindly changed me bed for me last time she was here. I'll be kinda sorry when me leg heals and she's no reason to come any more. I haven't got much, but I will see if I can manage to get something for Sister as a thank you for how good she's been to me. Maybe Sid Wilks has a little silver cross or something that'd be appropriate.'

'I've no doubt he will have,' said Aidy confidently, picturing the glass cabinet Sid used as his counter which was bursting with bits and pieces of second-hand jewellery. 'Well, I'd best be off, Mrs Crosby. I'm sure it won't be long before Sister is here. Oh, just a thought . . . Maybe with your son badgering you to hurry up, you put your husband's medals in another drawer and not your underwear one.'

The old lady's face lit up. 'I never thought of that. As soon as Sister's gone, I'll go up there and have a look. Thanks, love.'

Aidy managed to do her errands and make it to Sadie Billson's house just as her grandfather clock was striking three. When she left just over an hour later she wasn't sure if she'd enjoyed her session that afternoon or not. It had certainly been informative and she had learned a lot from the ex-nurse, but picking grit and slivers of glass out of a deep cut in a pig's trotter that Sadie had made was not something she'd have chosen to do. It wasn't that Aidy was squeamish or had an aversion to handling dead pig's trotters, it was just that Sadie had told her that after Aidy left, she would be boiling the trotter together with another for her own and her husband's dinner that evening. Aidy was worried that if she hadn't removed all the glass it could result in either Sadie or her husband suffering the consequences!

As she rounded a curve in the jetty and the back gate to her house came into view, she noticed that someone was loitering under the gas lamp close by. Then she realised the loiterer was in fact her grandmother. Bertha was looking very anxiously in the opposite direction from the way Aidy was coming.

She called out, 'Gran, what are you doing out here in this weather?'

She spun round to peer short-sightedly in Aidy's direction.

'Oh, love, you haven't seen George or Betty on yer travels, have yer? They should have been back by now ...'

'Back from where?' Aidy queried.

'Cobden Street.'

Aidy exclaimed, 'Cobden Street? They know they aren't allowed that far from home.'

'Arnold sent them.'

'What would he send them down there for?'

'I don't know. I only got to hear the bit I did 'cos I was stuck in the privy at the time.'

Aidy was totally confused. 'What were you doing hiding in the privy, Gran?'

'I wasn't. I was just in there doing me business. As you know, I was helping Martha prepare the funeral food for the wake tomorrow. Well, yer know what it's like, Aidy. As yer making it, yer sample a bit of it. Well, I must have sampled summat that didn't agree with me, and by the time I got home I was running to get to the lavvy before I had an accident. I was in there when I heard the kids come home from school and go in the house. I was still in there a couple of minutes later when the back door opened and shut again and I heard footsteps crossing the yard that I knew were Marion's, going into next-door to play with Elsie.

'Then I heard the door open again and Betty's voice saying, "Do we have to go? It's really cold and we ain't supposed to go that far away from home. I promised Aidy I'd have the spuds peeled for dinner." I heard Arnold say, "I'm yer bloody father and you'll both do what I tell yer to! Now go straight to the house in Cobden Street and do exactly what the man says. Hurry and get back here as quick as yer can." I heard the back gate open and looked through the crack in the privy door to see George and Betty going out. By the time I'd tidied meself and rushed after them to ask them what was going on, they'd disappeared.'

A worried frown was creasing Aidy's brow. 'What did he mean by *do exactly what the man says?* I really don't like the sound of this, Gran. Just what sort of errand has he sent the kids on? How long ago did they set off?'

'About an hour.'

'They've been gone an hour!' Aidy started to panic

then. It was nearly pitch dark and bitterly cold. The children shouldn't be out at all but indoors in the warmth, and certainly not roaming around streets they were unfamiliar with, knocking on the doors of strangers and carrying out their instructions. Just what did this mean?

She cried, 'I'm going to look for them. Cobden Street, you said? I'll head down that way, knock on every door in that street if I have to until I find them. Pray nothing has happened to them, Gran.'

Only a street away, Aidy was tearing past an abandoned factory site so fast that she didn't hear her name being called. She was vaguely aware that someone was shouting, but her mind was so filled with worry for her siblings it wasn't registering with her just what was being yelled.

She had travelled another street away before she felt a hand grab the back of her coat and yank it to bring her to a halt.

'What the hell . . .'

As her eyes fell on the person who'd accosted her, she fell to her knees, and grabbed her brother to her, hugging him fiercely and crying, 'Oh, George, you're safe. Thank God!' Then she pushed him back from her to look into his face and demanded, 'Where's Betty? Is she safe. Nothing has happened to her, has it?'

He was panting hard, gulping for breath. 'She's . . . fine . . . She's . . . she's in the old factory. We . . . Oh, just a minute, Sis, let me get me breath back.' He took several deep ones while patting his chest. Breathing more easily now, he said, 'That's better. You can't half run when you want to, our Aidy. I had hell of a job to catch you up. I was shouting your name at the top of me voice, but you never heard me. Anyway, me and Betty were both waiting in the old factory. It were bloody freezing and we ain't half hungry.' Then he realised he had blasphemed in front of his sister and exclaimed, horrified, 'Oh, I didn't mean . . .'

She ruffled his hair. 'You can swear as much as you like right this minute, George, I don't care. I'm just so happy you're safe and Betty too. But let me hear you blaspheme again after tonight and you can expect a clip around the ear and your mouth washed out with soap and water.' Then something he'd said struck her and she looked at him quizzically. 'What were you waiting in the old factory for?'

'For you to come and get us, so we could go home with you.'

She stared at him in astonishment. As far as she was aware, their father had sent them on an errand to a house in Cobden Street, so why were they in a derelict factory only a couple of streets away from where they lived, waiting for her to collect them and take them home? Her knees started to smart from the icy cold off the cobbles she was kneeling on. She stood up and vigorously rubbed them to warm them up, saying to him, 'None of this is making any sense to me, George. Let's get back to Betty. Then you can explain to me properly just what is going on.'

They found the girl where her brother had left her to give chase to Aidy. Part of the low crumbling factory wall at the front of the building had collapsed, and with the bricks someone – kids, most likely – had fashioned a three-sided, den-like structure, putting rotting planks across the top to form a roof. The bricks forming the sides of the den were piled higgledy-piggledy. The structure appeared totally unsafe, in danger of collapsing at any minute. From inside it there was a clear view through a hole in the wall out into the street.

Betty was squatting inside the makeshift den on a pile of tatty old bedding. She looked mortally relieved to see both her brother and sister step through the gap in the wall and scrambled over to greet them, flinging her arms around Aidy and hugging her tightly.

'I was so scared being left on me own after George chased after you. I'm sure I heard rats.'

'You shouldn't be in here, it's dangerous,' Aidy scolded them.

'We play here a lot, Sis. It's safe, honest, and we have loads of fun,' George told her.

It was far from safe. One of the long gabled walls was buckled and looked to be in serious danger of caving in at any minute. But Aidy had too much on her mind at the moment to waste time discussing safe and unsafe places for the children to be playing.

Moments later they were all squatting in the den. Aidy hugged the children to her for warmth and said to them, 'As far as I know from what Gran told me, Dad sent you on an errand to a house in Cobden Street, so how come you landed up in here, waiting for me to get you and take you home?'

'Well . . .' they both began together.

'Just one of you tell me,' she interrupted them sharply, by now desperate to make sense of all this. She saw they were about to argue the toss over it so made the decision for them. 'George, you tell me.'

'As soon as we got in from school, Dad told us he'd an errand we had to run for him. We was to go to a house in Cobden Street, go in the back way, and when a man opened the door, we was to tell him Arnold sent us. Dad said the man would give us a shopping bag and we was to take it where he told us to. He would give us an envelope and we . . .'

'No, that's not right,' cut in Betty. 'When we delivered the shopping bag to where the man told us to, that's where we'd get the envelope from.'

''I'm telling it,' he snapped at her.

'Well, get it right then,' Betty snapped back.

Aidy snapped at them both: 'That's enough. What were you to do with the envelope when you were given it, George?'

'Take it back to the man in Cobden Street, and then he'd give us half a crown which we'd to take straight back to Dad. He told us he'd give us a penny each, and said we'd get a penny more every time we did these errands for him. We told him we weren't allowed to go that far from the house, honest we did, Sis, but he shouted that he was our dad and we were to do as he told us.'

Aidy's face was set tight, her eyes ablaze with anger. So their father's pub tricks weren't reaping him the rewards they had any longer and he'd found himself another way to line his pockets: by farming his children out to no-good types to act as messengers, delivering their contraband to customers and collecting the payment in return. Who would ever suspect two children carrying a shopping bag of being up to no good? And how low did a man have to be, to trade his own children's involvement in a probable criminal act rather than make the effort to get himself some honest work? Well, he'd gone too far this time.

She hugged the children closer and said to them, 'We'd best get back before we freeze to death. Dad will be waiting for his money.' She noticed a look pass between brother and sister and a horrible thought struck her. 'Oh, no, you haven't lost the money, have you? Is that why you were both waiting for me, because you daren't go home and face him alone?'

'No, we ain't lost the money, Sis, but we ain't got it,' said Betty.

'I don't understand?'

'Well, we ain't got it 'cos we never went on the errand at all,' George told her. 'After you told us what you thought Dad was up to, showing us his tricks, and said that if he did anything else like that then we was to tell you, well ... we thought we ought to ask you before we went on the errand, just in case you wasn't happy about it. That's why we've been waiting here, 'cos we knew if we weren't home when you got back, you'd come looking for us. We know you don't like us out when it's so cold and dark and that you'd be worried.' His little face creased in worry. 'Did we do right, Aidy?'

She was looking at them both, stunned. So they did pay attention to her after all ... and she hadn't believed they listened to a word she said. 'You did right. You did very right,' she assured them.

'What we gonna tell Dad, though? He ain't gonna like it that we never did what he told us,' said Betty tremulously. Her father had not as yet actually hit her like she knew some of her friends' fathers did, but his nasty shouting whenever any of them had invoked his wrath was frightening enough for a little girl like her.

Aidy was thinking. No, he wasn't going to like it at all, especially as she suspected the money the kids would have made he'd been banking on getting. She smiled at the children reassuringly. 'I know, you tell Dad you knocked several times, very hard, but no one answered the door at the house. Tell him no mantles were lit inside so you didn't think anyone was in. You waited around for ages for someone to come back but they didn't, so you came home. He can't tell you off for not doing his errand for him then, can he?'

'No, he can't,' they both said together.

'And do we do the same if he sends us on another errand like this one, Sis?' asked George.

She eyed him proudly. 'That's exactly what you do.'

They spent a few minutes discussing their plan of action then set off home.

As soon as they rounded the bend in the jetty Bertha was on them, her relief to see them all safely back most apparent. Despite the bitter cold, she had not trusted herself to return inside the house and await their return, so afraid was she that she would not have been able to hold back from telling her despicable son-in-law exactly what she thought of him.

Aidy quickly outlined their plan to Bertha. They decided they would go in first, leaving the children waiting outside for a few minutes. They'd pretend they had just met up on their way home and knew nothing of where the children had been.

As soon as they walked in, Arnold appeared in the back-room doorway and looked mortally disappointed to see the new arrivals were not who he was expecting.

As she stripped off her coat, Aidy said to him, 'You look like you're expecting someone?'

He growled back at her, 'I sent the bloody kids on an errand and they should've been back by now.'

She responded lightly as she took her apron off the hook on the back of the pantry door and tied it around her, 'Well, this time of evening the shop will be busy or they could have bumped into friends and be having a quick natter. They'll be back in a minute with your baccy, I expect. Best get the dinner started or I'll be late back for work.'

An anxious Arnold returned to the back room.

Bertha was collecting potatoes out of a sack in the pantry and having a job controlling her glee. This was the first time since his return that the family had been given an opportunity to get one over on Arnold, and she was enjoying every moment.

The back door opened then. George and Betty barely had time to get a foot over the threshold before he was back in the doorway, his relief to see them very apparent. He demanded, 'Give me what yer got then.

Come on, I ain't got all day.' He was holding out his hand expectantly.

Aidy and Bertha were pretending to be taking no notice of what was going on around them but getting on with their tasks.

George and Betty stood pressed together by the back door.

It was George who nervously told him, 'We ain't got n'ote ter give yer. The bloke weren't in.'

Arnold's eyes narrowed darkly and he growled, 'Wadda yer mean, he weren't in? Why, yer lying little bleeders!' Clenching one fist, he raised his arm, shouting, 'He *was* in and you're . . .'

Seeing things were turning ugly, Aidy jumped over to stand before him, blocking his way.

'The kids don't lie. If they say the man you sent them to see wasn't in, then he wasn't. It's the bloke you made your arrangement with that's let you down, not them.'

Arnold was so fuming, Aidy felt sure she could actually see steam coming out of the top of his head. Banging one fist furiously against the back-room door, the vibrations shaking the house, he stormed back inside uttering a string of expletives that could be heard out in the street.

Aidy dashed over to the children, gathering them to her. 'Hopefully this has taught him a lesson: if he wants a job doing, he does it himself. But in future, to be on the safe side, me and Gran will do our best to make sure between us that you're never left alone with him. One of us will meet you out of school, and one of us will be here with you all the time in the house.'

'Yes, we will, kids,' confirmed Bertha.

Aidy became conscious that time was wearing on and she needed to get back to work. 'Betty, go and fetch Marion from next door. George, after you've taken your coat off, start setting the table. I've just about got time to get your dinner before I have to rush off back to work. I'll have mine when I come back.'

After they had each gone off to do her bidding, she worriedly whispered to Bertha, 'It's obvious he's no money to go out with tonight so you're going to have to put up with him. But then, hopefully, he'll go out for a bit to see the bloke he made the deal with and find out what went wrong. I should be back from work by then and you won't have to put up with his mood on your own.'

Her face set gravely. 'We've got to do something about him, Gran. There's has to be a way to get him out of our lives. I can't risk him dragging the children down with him into the world he seems to be getting himself involved in.'

As the family sat around the table in the back room eating their meal, Aidy was just about to put her coat on to take her leave for work when someone knocked purposefully on the back door. For a moment she wondered who it could be. No one called at this time of evening. Like this household, all the neighbours were busy having their dinner. Oh, all but one person . . . the rent man. With all that had happened in the last couple of hours, Aidy had temporarily forgotten it was Friday and his time to call.

She went to get the rent book from where it was kept in a drawer of the dresser in the back room, and then stopped short. A sudden thought struck her and panic rose within her. The wage packet that the doctor had given her at the end of her morning shift was in her handbag. With everything that had happened tonight, she had forgotten to take it out and hide it on her person. Her mind raced frantically. Where had she put her handbag when she had arrived in? Then she spotted it on the draining board. Dashing over, she unclipped it and pulled it wide open. Then breathed a deep sigh of relief. Tucked in by her purse was her unopened wage packet.

Aidy smiled warmly at the burly, middle-aged man facing her. He had been collecting the rent from the eighty houses his boss owned in these streets since the Greenwoods had first moved in, before Aidy was born. Leonard Trotter was dressed in a shiny brown suit, a white shirt, frayed around the collar and cuffs, and shabby brown overcoat on top. Covering his short back and sides was a black bowler hat. By his black, steel-capped boots sat a square bag, not unlike the one Doc carried, but instead of medical equipment the rent man's bag held his collections and the paperwork pertaining to his job. He also carried a cosh in a specially sewn pocket inside his coat, to fend off any potential attackers ... he had actually been robbed of his takings three times in the past. He'd a broken nose, a deep scar down one side of his face, and walked with a marked limp – all injuries received over his years spent carrying out this thankless job. People begrudged paying rent to an absentee landlord who refused to sanction all but the most basic of maintenance on his crumbling properties, not caring a jot what conditions his tenants had to endure as it was their choice if they stayed or not. There were plenty more waiting to take their places.

'Evening, Mr Trotter. You're well, I hope. And Mrs Trotter?'

Greeting her back pleasantly, he flicked through the pages of the well-used rent book Aidy handed him until he found the place where the last entry had been made the previous week. 'I need to start a new book for you. This one is full,' he said, and bent down to access his bag. Rummaging inside, he pulled out a new book, then took a fountain pen from the inside of his jacket pocket, took off the lid and opened the book on the first page so he could fill in the tenant's details.

Suddenly it felt to Aidy like a million fireworks were going off inside her brain. Her heart started to pound so hard she feared it would burst out of her chest. The only reason her father was at liberty to force his presence on his family, be a drain on their scant resources, generally make their lives a misery, was because he was the official tenant of the house they lived in. But if he weren't any longer, he would no longer have any official reason to live here and wield power over them all.

The rent man was presenting her with a miraculous opportunity to oust Arnold from their lives.

Aidy's mind raced frantically, hurriedly forming a plan of how best to achieve her aim. She was going to have to lie blatantly to this man before her. She also risked her father appearing in the kitchen while she was carrying out her plan, and showing her up for the liar she was. She must take the chance that Mr Trotter was not aware of Arnold's return. This opportunity to be rid of the man who was blighting her beloved family's lives was worth any risk to Aidy's own reputation, she decided.

Taking a deep breath, she said to the rent man, 'Pointless putting my father's name down as tenant still, Mr Trotter, since he hasn't lived here for years. Disappeared without a word nine years ago he did and we haven't heard a word from him since. He could be dead for all we know. Even if he's not, after all these years it's not likely he's going to come back, not now Mam's dead. Knowing what a selfish type he is, he's certainly not going to give up the life of Riley to look after his own kids. Good job they've got me to look after them. As it's me that's paying the rent now, Mr Trotter, it should be my name on the rent book as the official tenant, shouldn't it?'

Waiting for his response seemed to take an eternity to Aidy. In fact, he acted straight away.

Several minutes later she was clutching the new rent book to her chest as if it was the most precious thing in the world, a jubilant grin splitting her face as she watched her unsuspecting saviour depart for his next port of call. He was hoping that the tenants in that house parted with their rent as pleasantly and readily as the last one he had dealt with.

The first part of Aidy's plan successfully concluded, she had to pull off the final stage without alerting her father to what she was up to. Nothing could stop his expulsion from their lives now she had the means, but until she had physically got him and his belongings out of the house she didn't want to take any chances.

As she went into the back room, the only sound was of cutlery scraping against plates. Meal-times with Jessie had been social occasions, an opportunity for her family to share the events of the day. Upon his return however Arnold had made it clear he would not tolerate any conversation at the table. He preferred to eat his food in silence, so that's how it was now. Aidy inwardly smiled to herself. This was the last meal her family would eat under their father's selfish discipline. Mealtimes in future would return to being events to which the family looked forward and actually enjoyed, not dreaded the thought of.

Going over to the mantelpiece, she made out she was picking something up off it, then clumsily dropped whatever it was by the side of the armchair her father used. As she bent down in her pretence of retrieving it, she steadied herself by putting her hand on the arm of his chair. Making out she had picked up whatever she had supposedly dropped, she righted herself and simultaneously took her hand off the chair arm.

'I'm off then,' she said, looking at everyone around the table but her father.

Bertha smiled over at her. 'Take care, love. I'll have your dinner waiting for you when you get back.'

'I appreciate that, Gran, but I'll see to it.'

'Oh, it's no trouble . . .'

Arnold erupted, 'For God's sake, woman, be told. She doesn't want you to have her dinner ready.' A nasty glint sparked in his eye. 'Obviously don't like the thought of the muck you serve up.' Then he shot a look at George and snarled, 'You, boy! Sit up straight, shoulders back. And you . . .' he was looking at Betty '. . . stop kicking yer feet against yer chair. And you . . .' He never got to chastise Marion. She started crying, scraped back her chair and ran off up the stairs.

Aidy eyed him coldly. Considering he sat with his elbows on the table, scooping up food and shovelling it into his mouth as if he was afraid someone was going to steal it off him, he'd some gall pulling the children up for their small lapses. Bertha caught her eyes. Her expression was telling Aidy to get off to work before she was any later, and that she would see to Marion.

It seemed the one night Aidy was desperate for surgery to end so she could get home, all those who could afford the fee had turned up to see the doctor. The extended waiting room was heaving, and everyone who was sitting near enough to her insisted on engaging Aidy in conversation, which normally she delighted in but tonight found hard with her mind preoccupied with what faced her back home. Consequently surgery finished three quarters of an hour later than normal, and she still had to file all the patients' records after Ty had handed them over to her before she could leave.

When he gave her the cards, wished her good night in his usual stilted manner and then went back to finish up his own work, it didn't escape her notice that her boss looked fit to drop. Aidy wasn't surprised, though. She doubted he'd had much, if any, sleep for the last forty-eight hours. The previous day too had been busy, both during surgery and with house calls. Winter was upon them and people were falling ill with ailments related to the bitter cold. Severe chest infections, influenza, whooping cough and glandular fever were only a handful of the life-threatening diseases rampant at the moment. He would have been within his rights to insist on limiting the number of patients he could comfortably see during each session and the number of house calls every morning and afternoon, but he didn't. Just kept going until all those who needed his skills had been tended. Aidy may not much like Doc as a person, and that was his fault for making it so difficult, but as a doctor dedicated to doing his best to cure the sick under his care, she had a high regard for him.

But if the man didn't look after himself better, it was her opinion he'd be ill himself soon. There were only so many meals and nights' sleep a body could go without before it began to retaliate. Aidy wouldn't like to take a guess when he had last eaten properly, actually sat down and finished a meal, judging by the number of times she had arrived in the kitchen and found plates filled but abandoned.

Considering the constraints on his time, she

wondered why he didn't employ a woman to come in and do for him. There were many around here who would jump at the chance of the opportunity to earn themselves a few shillings a week, to cook and do the doctor's housework. She supposed he must have his reasons for not bothering although she couldn't understand what they might be. He'd lived here for months, clearly a fish out of water in such a deprived area, and still they knew next to nothing about him. Aidy herself didn't care about that. Whatever had caused him to come to this area, it had afforded her the means to support her family and for that she was grateful.

Having filed all the record cards away, she went into the kitchen to wash up her tea cup before she left and noticed a bought meat pie and a couple of potatoes on the kitchen table which the doctor had obviously taken out of the larder to make himself for dinner tonight. Her nurturing instincts rose up in her then. She felt a strong impulse to cook him his meal, stand over him while he ate it, see that he'd eaten at least one whole plateful for a change. She pictured him sitting alone at the table, eating his solitary meal, then clearing it away afterwards and sitting by himself in his armchair by the fire, no one to talk to, no one with whom to share the trials and tribulations of his daily life. No one to care for him. A great sadness filled her then. Everyone needed someone. The doctor didn't appear to have anyone or, to her observation, make any effort to do so. Aidy gave herself a mental shake. What on earth was she doing, feeling sorry for him? His lonely existence was entirely of his own making. He must be happy with his life this way or he'd do something about it. Just like she was doing something about getting rid of the cause of her family's misery.

Aidy didn't expect to find her father at home when she got back, and she didn't.

Bertha was in the kitchen, mixing ingredients into a paste in a pudding basin, to make an ointment to soothe burns. She had a dozen little brown jars lined up ready to put the ointment in when she had finished making it, along with labels to write out and fix on the jars. She smiled warmly at her granddaughter when she walked in.

'Hello, love. You really should have let me have yer dinner ready. Yer must be famished. Anyway, the kids are in bed. Marion took a bit of calming down but was fine after I'd talked to her. Oh, it breaks my heart that she still can't understand her mam isn't coming back.

'She said to me, "Gran, Mam won't let Dad shout at us like he does when she comes back, will she? Can't we go to the cemetery and make a loud noise and wake her up that way, instead of waiting for her to wake herself up?"

'What can you say to that, Aidy? We've tried to explain in every way we can think of that Jessie isn't coming back. Nothing works. And anyway, why can't Arnold leave the kids alone? Why does he always have to be picking at them? George wasn't slouching at the table tonight, or if he was then I was bent double. Arnold's got some nerve, chiding the kids for their table manners when *he's* got the manners of a pig. I deserve a medal, love, for not taking a knife to him after today. I'm very afraid it will come to that, though, if he pulls any more tricks like that.

'Anyway, seems we've had a small miracle. After he finished his dinner it was apparent he wasn't going out as he ordered me to make him a fresh cuppa and the kids all to go upstairs out of his sight. He said he wanted peace to listen to the radio but he'd only just sat down in his chair when he told me to forget the tea, he was going out after all. Must have found some money after all.' She gave a despondent sigh as she stopped her mixing long enough to scoop a spoonful of greyish powder from another bowl into the one her mixture was in and begin stirring again. 'I know we were all mourning for Jessie, and for what happened between you and Arch, but we were a happy little band before Arnold dumped himself back on us, weren't we, love?'

Aidy took the greatest of pleasure in responding

to Bertha with, 'And we will be again in a few hours, Gran.'

Bertha looked at her, confused. 'Eh?'

Aidy laughed. 'Yes, you did hear me right.' She pulled the rent book out of her coat pocket, opening the front cover to display the details of the tenant.

Putting down her wooden mixing spoon and giving her hands a wipe on the bottom of her apron, Bertha took the book off Aidy and stared at it. As her eyes scanned the words written in fresh ink, her face took on the expression of someone who could read perfectly well what the writing said but whose brain was having trouble accepting the evidence before it. 'But . . . but I don't understand? Your name is down as tenant.' She lifted her face and looked in total confusion at her granddaughter. 'But . . . but . . .' As the significance of this registered, her eyes lit up. 'But this is wonderful! It means . . . oh, God, we can get him out, Aidy.'

Her eyes were dancing merrily. 'Yes, we can, Gran.'

'But just how did you get the rent man to take Arnold's name off without his permission?'

'Lied to him. The old rent book was full so Mr Trotter needed to make us out a new one. I told him Arnold Greenwood was dead so far as we knew as we hadn't seen him for years, and you can't chase a dead man for the rent money, can you, Gran? Thankfully Arnold didn't need to come into the kitchen for anything at that moment and scupper what I was up to. And he didn't suddenly discover he'd some money to go out with tonight, I left two tanners on the arm of his chair for him to find. I did it to make sure he was out of the house when I got back tonight, so we could pack his stuff up and have his bag waiting for him in the yard when he comes back. That way we won't have the task of forcing him to leave 'cos I doubt he'd go quietly.'

Bertha started to giggle, a gleeful chuckle that filled the kitchen and set Aidy laughing too. Grabbing hold of each other, they waltzed around, both whooping with delight. It was lack of breath that finally got Bertha to stop their dance of triumph.

Having caught her own breath, Aidy told her, 'I'm off upstairs to pack his stuff.'

'I'll come and help yer, love. Be the most pleasurable job I've ever had to do.'

An hour later Arnold gave a loud belch as he arrived at the back gate and lifted the latch. He wasn't drunk. At fourpence a pint, he'd only had enough to buy three with the shilling he'd found on the arm of the chair. He still couldn't work out where the two sixpences had come from. He had realised after many fruitless searches that not even a farthing was ever left lying around the house for him to find. He knew his pockets had been empty which was why he'd been fuming about the kids returning empty handed from their errand.

And that was something else he couldn't quite work out. Who was lying to him? The bloke he'd sent the kids to do the job for or his own children? One of them was. When Arnold had sought the bloke out tonight to confront him about welching on their deal, it seemed that the bloke had been looking for *him*, to confront him over being let down. The bloke swore blind he'd been in at the appointed time. The kids swore blind he wasn't. Well, there'd be no mistake tomorrow. Arnold had badgered the bloke until he'd relented and promised to give him another chance to prove his worth. Another pick up and delivery had been arranged, same time, same place, but this time Arnold would be following the kids from a safe distance and watching their every move, to make sure they pulled it off. Then he'd make it a regular event. It would mean he'd have a supply of money coming in, not a fortune but enough to keep him in booze and fags and treat himself to a couple of changes of clothes.

Looking as shabby as he was, he wasn't attracting quite the sort of women he liked. Not the head-turners he used to attract before time started telling on him, but not so dusty either. He had his eye on the barmaid of the Stag and Pheasant. She was no spring chicken but still had plenty of life in her. There was an empty space beside him in his bed which Maisie Turnbull and her big breasts would fill nicely ... until something better came along, that was. Arnold didn't care what the rest of the household felt about him moving in a woman. It was *his* house and they'd have to lump it.

Kicking the back gate shut behind him, he sauntered his way over to the back door. A flickering light from the gas mantle in the kitchen was casting an eerie light through the window out into the yard. Halfway down it he stopped short, surprised to see a bulky bag by the back door. Then he recognised it as his holdall. It looked like it was filled with something. Anger rose up in him. Who'd been in his bedroom and taken his bag to use without his permission? Well, wouldn't they learn not to take what wasn't theirs in the future! He was curious to know what the bag was being used for, though. Reaching it, he bent down and opened the buckle securing the strap. Seemed to be clothes inside ... his clothes! And his razor and shaving brush and his few other personal possessions. What the hell was going on? Jumping up, he grabbed the knob of the back door and turned it. It would not budge. It was locked. He stood back from the door and bellowed, 'Oi! Open this fucking door!'

Two faces appeared at the kitchen window.

Glaring at them, Arnold shouted, 'What the hell's

going on? Why is the door locked? And why is my bag out here with all my stuff in it?'

Aidy shouted through the window, 'We thought you might need your belongings.'

Bewildered, he bellowed, 'Why?'

'Because you don't live here any more.'

'You stupid cow! I'm the tenant. It's me who says who lives in this house and who doesn't. If you and that old bag . . .' he shot a murderous glare at Bertha's amused face, peering at him through the window '. . . and those blasted kids want to keep living here, then open the door and let me in. I'll kick it in, and you lot out.'

Aidy couldn't remember when she'd had so much fun. 'Do that and I'll have the police on you. You aren't the tenant any longer . . . I am. It's me who says who lives here and who doesn't from now on. And you don't any longer 'cos we don't want you.' She placed the opened rent book flat against the window so he could clearly see that his name was no longer down as the tenant but his daughter's instead. 'Maybe if you'd paid some rent over to the rent man in person since you've been back, he wouldn't have believed me when I told him you hadn't lived here for years and were dead for all we knew. After that he happily handed the tenancy over to me. Now pick up your stuff and clear off!'

Arnold was left staring at her agog. He hadn't a

leg to stand on, and he knew it. His period of sponging off his family was over. He furiously snatched up his bag, which he slung over his shoulder, and stormed off down the yard disappearing through the gate to the accompaniment of loud laughter from inside the house behind him.

CHAPTER EIGHTEEN

Aidy was humming happily to herself as she entered the last patient's name into her ledger one morning. Four weeks had passed since Arnold had been driven from their lives, and from the moment the back gate had slammed shut behind him, the atmosphere in the house had returned to the happy one it had been before he'd made his unwelcome return. There was still the underlying sadness of their loss of Jessie and the breakup of Aidy's marriage, but time was helping both wounds heal.

They were all excited about Christmas and each in their own way trying their best to have a present to give every family member on Christmas morning. Aidy was certain that the children had put together their farthings and ha'pennies earned from running errands for neighbours, topped up by the odd ha'penny she or Bertha had been able to scrape together on a Saturday for them, and had bought her a box of her favourite liquorice allsorts. She knew this because Marion was terrible at keeping secrets and had dropped so many hints to Aidy that it would have been difficult for her not to guess what her siblings had done for her, although she would never spoil their surprise by letting on.

Aidy wanted to buy her family the world, but the few coppers in her purse dictated she should lower her sights. Up to now she had managed to purchase Marion a cut-out doll book; for George a second-hand Meccano set minus a couple of pieces, which was how she was able to afford it; and had fashioned a new dress for Betty from one of her mother's old frocks, hand sewing it in the evening after the children had gone to bed. And for all the family to play with, a pack of Snap cards. For Bertha she had yet to think of something as she hadn't any spare money. Should she not be able to, she knew her gran would be more than understanding, just content they were all well and happy, dry and warm under the same roof together, and more especially no longer suffering the tyranny of her detested son-in-law.

Having put the reception ledger to one side until it was needed again for evening surgery, Aidy was filling in time by sharpening pencils until she had seen the last patient out. Just then an anguished cry coming from behind the closed door of the surgery reached her ears. The cry was one of several that had been issued by the last patient she had sent through.

Aidy knew Beattie Rogers, was on chatting terms with her should they meet up in the street. She lived in the next road and the youngest of her four children was in the same class at school as Marion. She was a salt-of-the-earth sort, solid and reliable. Her husband worked for a local factory as a storeman. Like most people in these parts they hadn't much, but Beattie kept the mildew and bugs down in her home as best she could, was a good mother to her children, a good wife to her reliable husband, and a helpful neighbour. She hadn't needed to tell Aidy why she was paying a visit to the doctor as it was very apparent she'd done something to her arm. It was tightly bound by a piece of bloodied towelling and her face revealed the pain she was in.

Moments after Aidy heard Beattie's last cry, she heard the surgery door open, footsteps came across the corridor, and Ty appeared. He looked frustrated.

Seeing Aidy was alone, he said, 'Oh, Sister has already left on her visits then? I was hoping she hadn't. You'll have to do. Come through to the surgery.'

She arrived in the surgery to find Beattie Rogers seated at one side of the examination couch, her injured arm now unwrapped from the bloodied towel and laid across it. The gash on her arm was at least six inches long and half an inch deep. Ty had wrapped a rubber tourniquet tightly around her arm above her elbow, to stem the flow of blood. He was standing poised on the other side of the table, holding a suture needle threaded with thick cat gut.

He ordered Aidy, 'Restrain Mrs Rogers to stop her pulling back her arm every time I try to start stitching.' Then, to Beattie: 'Would you please stop screaming every time I make an attempt?'

She was most apologetic. 'I'm sorry, Doctor, really I am. I hate needles, you see. They terrify the life out of me. Every time I see it coming towards me, it sets me off. I know it's going to hurt when you stick it into me . . . and me arm already hurts like the devil as it is.'

He snapped at her brusquely, 'But not as much as it will should I have to amputate after septicaemia sets in – which it will if you don't allow me to close the wound and disinfect it. I keep telling you to look the other way.' He then snapped at Aidy, 'Well, hold Mrs Rogers down then.'

She was weighing up the situation. If anyone was restraining her, she would automatically fight to free herself and had no doubt that was what Beattie would do, making it impossible for Ty to work away on her arm in any case. What Aidy felt she needed to do was to distract Beattie's attention from what Ty was doing to her and on to something else. Hopefully, knowing the type of woman Beattie was, she knew just what would work. Engaging her in conversation! Rushing over to the back of Ty's desk, Aidy grabbed his chair and pulled it over to set it before Beattie Rogers, so that she had to turn her head away from the doctor to look at Aidy.

Taking Beattie's free hand in hers and squeezing it hard to get her initial attention, which thankfully she did, Aidy asked, 'Did your Avril catch the measles when we had that epidemic a few weeks ago, Mrs Rogers, or was she one of those that escaped? Marion, George and Betty all went down with it together. What a nightmare! It wasn't so bad at first when they were all too ill to do anything more than sleep, but then they started to recover and the boredom set in. How do you keep three youngsters entertained in their bedroom for a fortnight? That was the problem.'

For a moment Ty was annoyed that his receptionist seemed to be blatantly ignoring his instructions. Then, being the intelligent man he was, he realised what Aidy was attempting. She seemed to be succeeding, so without further ado he set to, hoping she would keep the patient's attention diverted long enough for him to finish his work.

Beattie was looking sympathetically at Aidy. 'Oh, I know just what you went through, ducky. Three of mine caught chicken-pox all at the same time last year. It cost me a small fortune in carbolised oil from the chemist to stop them scratching, which didn't do the job as well as the label on the bottle promised, so I did what I should have done in the first place and got some lotion from your . . .'

Aidy nearly choked, knowing what Beattie was about to divulge innocently, and interrupted to stop her, 'I've no doubt that worked. So just how did you keep your kids occupied, to stop them from driving you mental?'

'I was lucky 'cos neighbours rallied around and borrowed me some books and jigsaws, but I have to say, it was the longest three weeks of my life. I was lucky with the recent measles outbreak. My lot escaped it.

'Anyway, I haven't had chance to tell you in person but it's a grand job you're doing. Me and Mrs Fisher were only talking about you the other day. All of us around here admire you. Not many young women of your age who had their own home and husband would give it all up to care for their orphaned sisters and brother like you are. And yer've yer gran living with you as well. I know Bertha will be pulling her weight to help as much as she can, but the burden still falls mostly on you 'cos she's not as young as she used to be. Only so much she can do, and 'course a lot of her time will be taken up making her . . .'

Aidy frenziedly cut in, 'Yes, well, I couldn't manage without Gran, and the kids help out too with what they can do. I can't say it's easy, but we manage.' Desperate to change the subject, she asked Beattie,

'With all what's happening just now, Mr Rogers is still in work, I hope?'

'At the moment, thank God. Every night he comes home I have a dread on me he's going to tell me he's been laid off and be joining the groups of other desperate men gathering on street corners 'cos they've n'ote else to do. Some I've no doubt are plotting other ways to make themselves a bob or two, if yer understand me. With all the worries you must have in the circumstances, be thankful that's one you ain't got, lovey, what with you and your husband no longer being together.'

She pulled a rum face before continuing, 'Shame on him is what I say. Up and leaving you to care for your family on yer own 'cos he didn't want the responsibility. Throughout our lives, we all have to knuckle down and do things we don't want to. And, after all, family is family. I hope he's managing to live with himself, wherever it is he's gone off to. Mind you, looking at who his parents are, 'specially his mother who's all take and no give, is it surprising he did what he did, coming from her loins? Well, just thank God you had no kids of yer own, love, and he didn't leave you to look after them as well as yer sisters, brother and grandmother. Still, I bet you're glad you don't have the likes of Pat Nelson as yer mother-in-law any longer.'

Beattie's eyes suddenly brightened with curiosity.

'Actually, there is a mystery you can clear up while I've got you here. I'm positive I saw your father going about a couple of times a while back. Nelly Miller and Hattie Jones thought they saw him too. My Harry came home from the pub one night and told me he thought he'd seen Arnold. He was with a couple of those shifty-looking types that live down the bottom end and they looked like they was up to no good according to Harry. Anyway, if it was your father, he's got some brass neck, showing his face again after what he did to your mother, leaving her to struggle to raise you kids. It wasn't the first time either, was it? He did it before, when you was little. So was it him we all saw? Has he had the nerve to come back again, after all these years?'

Aidy froze. If she confirmed Beattie Roger's suspicions and it got back to the rent man that she had lied, she wasn't sure how she would stand regarding her tenancy of the house. She had in truth conned the rent man into handing it over to her. Mr Trotter was the upstanding sort and might not at all like the fact she had done so, despite her good reasons. He could even respond by taking the tenancy back and evicting them. Aidy couldn't risk that so she lied.

'That wasn't my father. We haven't heard a word from him since he left before our Marion was born. He could be dead, for all we know. Who you saw was a relative of his, his cousin. He was just stopping with us for a while as he was down on his luck, but he's gone now.'

Aidy was dying inside. Mortified that, through Beattie, her employer was learning all her sordid family history, personal secrets she had wanted to keep hidden. She vehemently hoped he was so consumed in his work he wasn't paying any attention to what was being said.

But Ty was listening. In fairness, he couldn't really not unless he was deaf, the two women being right next to him and not exactly whispering. But what he had heard had come as a shock to him. He had been under the impression that his receptionist was a happily married woman, with no other responsibilities than that. He had had no idea she was being mother to her orphaned siblings and guardian to an aged grandmother. But then, how would he? At her interview it was the abilities she possessed to do the job he required of her, not her private life, he'd been interested in, so he had only enquired of her the barest personal details about herself, like her age and place of abode. She'd announced herself to him as 'Mrs' so he'd assumed she was happily married. And since then he'd made no attempt to get to know her on a personal level.

There was far more to his receptionist that he'd thought. She hadn't led an easy life it seemed, her mother being left to raise Aidy and her siblings single handed. And neither was Aidy now just a housewife who chose to work so that she and her husband could afford a better standard of living than the majority of folks here had. No, Aidy Nelson worked because she needed the money to care for her orphaned siblings and aged grandmother, and did so on her own as her husband had left her, not wanting to share the responsibility. It took a very unselfish person to give up their own future to give their family one. He knew what he paid her, it wouldn't be easy for her to make her wage stretch all the way.

He was starting to see his receptionist in a different light. He had based his opinion of her as being rude and disrespectful on his first impression, when she had burst into his surgery and insisted he go with her to attend to her mother. He'd been angry at the time, seeing that as a blatant lack of respect for a man of his professional standing, but in truth wouldn't he have acted the same way had he found one of his parents in a similar condition?

Beattie Rogers had opened his eyes to the fact that Aidy Nelson was neither rude nor disrespectful but, when her family was in danger, a woman who would do whatever it took to get help for them. She had to be a highly principled, caring and considerate individual to have taken on the burden of her entire family after her mother's death. And she had strength of character too. Hadn't she more than proved that by putting up with him? A thought occurred to him then. She still insisted on addressing him as Doc, despite the number of times he had reprimanded her and reminded her he wished to be addressed as Doctor Strathmore. Was this her way of taking a stand against him for the arrogant way in which he treated her? If that indeed were the truth he realised he couldn't actually blame her, and even found himself admiring her way of getting her own back.

He suddenly felt guilty for his whole attitude towards her. Here was a woman still in mourning for the loss of her mother and the collapse of her marriage, struggling single handed to care for her orphaned siblings and grandmother. And as if all that wasn't enough, during work hours she had *his* uncompromising attitude to endure as well. Shame filled him suddenly and a need flooded to explain to Aidy just why he'd acted like he did, so that she did not think the worst of him. But he could not take her into his confidence. Dared not. Even platonic friendship with a woman involved an emotional attachment that held the risk of eventual hurt. He'd enough emotional scars to last him a lifetime. But, regardless, he need not be quite so curt with her in future, need he?

While Ty had been lost in his own thoughts, thankfully for Aidy she had managed to steer the conversation from her personal life and on to other matters.

They were at the moment discussing Beattie's neighbour's washing, her whites in particular, which in fact
were a dingy grey according to Beattie. Aidy was not
finding the topic at all stimulating but was trying her
best to show she was, in her effort to keep Beattie's
attention on what she was saying and not what the
doctor was doing. Out of the corner of her eye Aidy
saw Ty snip the end of the last stitch, and gratefully
exclaimed, 'That's Doc finished, Mrs Rogers.'

Beattie looked stunned. She spun her head round
to look at her arm, the gaping wound now closed by
Ty's skilful work. 'Well, bless my soul, I never felt a
thing,' she said, awestruck.

'Doc just needs to swab it with Iodoform then
dress it for you and you're all done.'

Ty eyed his receptionist, taken aback. That was
exactly what he was going to be doing next, but how
did she know? And further more, it wasn't her place
to explain medical procedures. 'You can leave us now,'
he said to Aidy tartly, then remembered he was going
to treat her with a little more kindness in future and
called after her, 'Er . . . and thank you.'

Aidy was outside in the corridor by now. She
stopped abruptly, her mouth gaping. Had Doc really
just thanked her for her help? In all the time she had
been working for him, she hadn't ever heard the
words escape his lips. Didn't think he was aware of
them. She must have misheard.

A short while later, Beattie Rogers came back out into the waiting room. Ty followed her. He handed Aidy that morning's patients' records to file away while saying, 'The list you're compiling of visits for Sister to make tomorrow ... add Mrs Rogers to it for a change of dressing. I'm off on rounds.'

With that, he left.

Beattie Rogers was looking pensive. 'That man reminds me of my Uncle Bert. He was a miserable old bugger! Give him his due, though, he did lose both legs in the war, and his wife left him 'cos she didn't want a cripple for a husband. I wonder what excuse the doctor's got for his surly manner? I don't envy you working for him, love. Can't fault him as a doctor, though. Stitched me up good and proper. I've to come back to have them removed in ten days.

'Been an expensive accident I had today with the bread knife. I've had to plunder me Christmas money to pay the doctor's fees. Thankfully I don't have ter pay for Sister's visits, only for the bandages and whatnot she uses, her services come courtesy of the convent she's with. I'm not what you could call a religious person, but at times like this I do give a thank you to whoever is up there for those who do good works as their way of serving God. What time will Sister be calling to change my bandage and check no infection has set in? Only I'll have a pot of tea ready for her.'

Without waiting for Aidy to reply she went on, 'Takes her calling very seriously does Sister. She makes it her business to find out if there's any old bodies that are on their own and drops in to see if she can do anything for them. I know this 'cos she called in on Lily Potter the other afternoon, and Lily told me when I popped in to see if she wanted any shopping the next day. Lily can't get around now, she's practically crippled by arthritis. She's no family living around here, so relies a lot on us neighbours to help her. Anyway, Sister did a few jobs for her, had a nice chat with her over a cup of tea and made Lily's day.

'Between you and me, dear, I've always wondered what it's really like inside a convent, how strict it is, and this is my chance to find out. What time will I be expecting her then so I can have the tea ready?'

Good people like Sister Teresa made up for the bad people in the world, Aidy thought, picturing the likes of her father and Pat Nelson. 'I'm sorry, Mrs Rogers, but I can't give you a time. It depends how long the visits take before yours. It'll be between ten and three, that's as much as I can say.'

Aidy had only just turned the key in the lock on the waiting-room door when an urgent thump on it from outside made her jump. Unlocking the door again, she opened it to find a woman around her mid-forties, looking extremely agitated. She seemed well-to-do with smart clothes, hair expertly coiffured, expensive leather handbag hooked over her arm. Aidy wondered what a woman of her sort was doing around these parts. As soon as she spoke, though, it was apparent that she was in fact from these parts originally, although trying to disguise the fact with her bad attempt at a posh accent. This woman had obviously escaped the life of poverty she'd been born into by snaring herself a rich husband.

Pushing past Aidy to make her way inside, she demanded, 'I need to see the doctor – now. Show me through.'

Aidy admired anyone who'd bettered themselves but that didn't give them the right to be arrogant to those they'd grown up amongst. She felt like putting this woman in her place but that might put her own job at risk if her employer heard of it. Evenly she responded, 'I'm afraid the doctor is out on his rounds, won't be back for a couple of hours or so. If it's a real emergency then I've a rough idea where he'll be and can go and fetch him for you.'

'Yes, it damn' well is an emergency. I want him to section my mother! Grace Willows, twenty-three Wheat Street. She's losing her faculties . . . accusing people of stealing. As if anyone would risk a jail sentence for stealing a few paltry trinkets worth no more than a few shillings the lot. She's put them somewhere herself and won't admit she's forgotten where. The person she's accusing is the woman I pay to keep an eye on her.

'My mother is eighty-seven and not very stable on her legs. Mrs Baker isn't at all pleased about being accused of stealing and has said she won't continue to check on Mother unless she receives an apology from her. Mother won't give her an apology as Mrs Baker is the only one who goes in to see her, and she says who else could have stolen her trinkets? I've had such a job persuading Mother to allow Mrs Baker in every day as she can be so cantankerous ... Getting someone else she will approve of could take forever, and I can't get over to see her much myself as I have a very busy schedule and we've no room at all to have her live with us.

'Anyway, all that's beside the point. It saddens me that Mother is no longer in control of her faculties but she'll only get worse, so best we get it over with now before she becomes a danger to herself. I need to have it done today because I'm going to London for a few days tomorrow, to do my Christmas shopping.'

That old lady was no more a case for the asylum than Aidy's own grandmother was. Grace Willows had had a simple lapse of memory. Upset at not being able to put her hands on her trinkets, which might be worthless junk to her daughter but were obviously precious to her, she had vented her distress by accusing her helper of stealing them. Not wanting the trouble of finding someone else to keep an eye on her, or worse still having to have her live in her own home, this selfish bitch was taking drastic measures.

Aidy certainly wasn't going to help her achieve her aim. 'Your mother isn't running amok in the street or bleeding to death, so this doesn't count as an emergency,' she said promptly. 'Evening surgery starts at six.'

The visitor snapped, 'I will be having dinner with my husband then. What time is the doctor due back from his round for his lunch? Can I see him then?'

Aidy gave a nonchalant shrug. 'Hard to say. I've known him not get back until just before evening surgery is due to start.'

Her visitor's eyes darkened thunderously. 'Oh, this is just too bad. I cannot get Mother committed without the doctor's help.' She gave a disdainful click of her tongue. 'I'll just have to deal with her when I get back from my shopping trip. With a bit of luck, she might have died meantime and I'll be free of the burden of her at long last.'

She spun on her heel and marched angrily out.

Aidy stared in disbelief after her. Someone should have *that* woman committed, for being so selfish. She doubted she would ever achieve her aim via this particular doctor. A few weeks back a patient had ranted and raved and threatened to maim him because Ty would not sign him off as unfit for work when he was clearly able. Aidy couldn't see him committing an old woman to the mental institution, just because she'd become a burden to her daughter.

Aidy caught sight of the clock ticking away on the wall above the fireplace. The last visitor and her devious plan had taken up twenty minutes of her time. She should have cleaned the surgery by now and have any medical instruments used that morning boiling in the steriliser, ready for evening surgery. She started to begin her tasks when a thought struck her. Hadn't the doctor asked her to do something just before he left? She felt sure he had but couldn't remember what. Hopefully it would come back to her as she went about her work.

CHAPTER NINETEEN

No one was prepared for the sudden change in the weather. Overnight the temperature had dropped over ten degrees and Aidy was among the thousands of people living on the east side of England, from Newcastle down to just before Northampton, who went to bed to a light drizzle pattering against their windowpanes and opened their curtains the next morning to be greeted by a thick blanket of snow, at least three inches deep, which was growing deeper from the blizzard still raging. Thankfully George had filled the water jugs the previous evening as the stand-pipe in the jetty was frozen solid now, thick, lethal-looking icicles hanging from it.

Children were about the only ones who delighted in this weather. Few adults did as it brought with it an extra strain on their already stretched resources, having to find the money to buy the additional fuel needed to combat sub-zero conditions. The thought of trudging through the biting snow-filled winds to work brought few people joy, Aidy included. At least for her, though, at journey's end her place of work would be warm. The doctor would not, for reasons Aidy couldn't work out, employ a daily to do for him, but he did pay a night watchman three shillings a week to come in at six each morning after his shift had finished, to set the fires in the downstairs rooms and bring enough fuel in to see them through the day.

Ty having already left on his morning round, before she started her other duties Aidy was going around replenishing all the fires. She pictured the doctor and the nun, trudging from house to house in the freezing cold, barely having time to warm up properly before they were off to their next port of call. She didn't envy them in the least. Most people, though, would offer them a cup of tea, unless they happened to be the desperately poor type who hadn't any to offer. She doubted, though, that Doc would have time to spare to stand and drink one as he'd a long list of patients to get round this morning, but Sister would probably snatch a minute or two as, lucky for her, her list for today was light compared to some days. Whether she had time or not, Aidy doubted Beattie Rogers would let her leave without refreshment as the woman had made it clear to Aidy yesterday that she meant Sister to have one with her, so she could satisfy her own curiosity about life inside a convent.

Then Aidy froze. *That* was what Doc had asked her to do yesterday, add Beattie Rogers' name to the list of Sister's calls today, only the visitor had annoyed her so much she had forgotten to do it.

Aidy was furious with herself. If Beattie's wound wasn't checked today but left until tomorrow and infection set in, it could be too far advanced to stem its spread, and then Beattie could end up losing her arm and it would be all Aidy's fault. There was nothing for it. She had to go and find Sister, tell her she'd another patient on her list to call on that she'd forgotten to add. Being the kind person she was, Aidy was sure Sister Teresa would be understanding, but she wasn't so sure her employer would, should he find out. Her lapse had potentially serious repercussions. He might therefore deem Aidy not fit for the responsible post of his receptionist any longer, which in turn would have very serious implications for her family and herself.

Without further ado, she abandoned the coal bucket to wrap herself up warm against the Arctic conditions, lock up the premises, and set off on her search. Half an hour later, having called on at least half a dozen of the patients, Aidy was icy cold and wet.

Hopefully Sister would be here, she thought, as she purposefully rapped on the door of the next house, so Mr Coleman would hear. Stanley

Coleman had had a tumorous growth removed from the side of his neck a week or so back by Doc, leaving a gaping hole which had not yet healed. Sister was keeping her eye on it. Aidy could hear the deaf old man slowly shuffling his way down the passage to open the door to her, and willed him to hurry before she became frozen to the spot.

When he finally did and Aidy asked her question, he slowly shook his head and shouted back, 'Sister ain't due to come for another four days. She came yesterday, ducky.'

Aidy's heart sank. She should have known that, since she'd written up the list of calls herself. 'You haven't seen her going about at all then, on your way to the shops perhaps, Mr Coleman?'

'Ain't been out, love. Don't intend to either. Got to be a damned sight warmer before I'll put me nose out of the door. Me wife's out, though. I could ask her if she saw Sister on her travels when she comes back.'

'I've seen her.'

Aidy turned to see a woman beside her, so covered in white she resembled a snow woman, just like Aidy herself in fact. She was weighed down by heavy shopping bags.

She shouted over the wind, 'Didn't mean to eavesdrop but yer can hear Stan halfway down the street, even in this blizzard. If it helps, I saw Sister about fifteen minutes ago, going in the back gate of a house in Gladstone Street, just as I was cutting through the jetty on me way to the butcher's. I remember thinking at the time that I hoped she was wearing summat warm under her habit or she'd been needing treatment herself for pneumonia.'

Aidy frowned. As far as she was aware they didn't have any patients in Gladstone Street at the moment who needed the services Sister provided. Regardless, at least thanks to this woman's hawk eyes she was closer to finding her quarry. 'You don't happen to know what number Gladstone Street she was going into, I suppose?'

The woman shook her head, which caused the build up of snow on her headscarf to dislodge and cascade over her shoulders. 'No, sorry, love. But I'd only just turned into the jetty, so at a guess I would say number four or six . . . eight at the most.'

Gladstone Street on a nice day was less than a couple of minutes' walk away, but now Aidy was battling against the blizzard it took her over ten minutes to reach.

She tried number four first but the shabby young woman who answered the door, a snotty-nosed baby in her arms and a grubby-looking toddler clinging to her skirt, told her that no nun had visited her that day. She advised Aidy that if she was making enquiries next door, she'd better go round the back as the old lady who lived there couldn't answer the door anyway. She had broken her hip a few months back in a fall and was still recovering in a makeshift bed in the back room. This information gave Aidy hope that at last she had found Sister. And she also had the answer to why the nun was in this street when it was not on her list today. Beattie Rogers had told her that Sister made it her business to find out if any old bodies were in need of her help, and would call upon them to offer her charity to them. Obviously the old lady next door was one of these cases.

After the young woman had shut the door on her Aidy stood for a moment, surrounded by the swirling snow, wondering if her trudge around the back would be worth all the trouble. Sister might have come and gone by now. But her need to find the nun was desperate. She couldn't leave any stone unturned.

When she went to open the back gate a few minutes later, it was apparent that someone had recently gone through it as it opened easily and a mound of snow was piled the other side against the wall. There was also a trail of footprints, albeit rapidly filling with snow, leading up to the back door. Aidy hoped Sister Teresa had made them and not the milkman.

There was a gap to one side of the net curtain that hung against the back window. Looking through it, Aidy saw an old lady lying in a makeshift bed in the recess at the back of the room. She appeared to be asleep. She also saw a long black garment draped across a dining chair by the ancient oak table. She was positive it was Sister Teresa's cloak. Hopefully she had found her quarry at last.

Tapping lightly on the back door so as not to frighten the old lady from her sleep, she then let herself deftly inside, hurriedly shutting the door behind her and making her way into the back room. The old lady obviously had acute hearing as she was sitting up and looking suspiciously across at Aidy when she entered.

In an apologetic tone Aidy said to her, 'I'm very sorry to come in without being asked, only I saw you were sleeping through the window and didn't want to startle you by knocking.' She thought she'd better introduce herself and added, 'I'm Aidy Nelson, from the surgery.'

The look of suspicion vanished from the old lady's prune-like face to be replaced by one of delight. In her aged voice she said, 'Oh, then welcome in, deary. I am such a blessed woman today, having all these unexpected visitors. Would you like a cuppa? Only I'm sorry to say you'll have ter mash it yerself . . . as yer can see, I'm indisposed at the moment. I am getting around a bit more now. In fact, I was out of me bed and hobbling round with the help of the walking sticks the hospital borrowed me for a good ten minutes earlier this morning. Carrie, me neighbour next door who comes in every morning to light me fire for me and regularly pops back to keep a check on it, helped me up and then back to bed afterwards, good old soul that she is. Only me little walk around tired me out and that's why yer caught me napping.'

'I appreciate your offer of tea but I'm looking for Sister Teresa. I need to speak to her urgently and I understand she could be here? That is her cloak on the back of your chair, isn't it?' Aidy wondered where Sister actually was as there was no apparent sign of her apart from her cloak.

The old lady looked disappointed for a moment that Aidy hadn't come to visit her after all but then her face brightened. 'Yes, dear, it is hers. And wasn't that a lovely surprise for me? The good Sister calling in to see if I needed anything doing as she'd heard through a patient she attends a few streets away that I'd broke me hip a few weeks back and couldn't do much for meself just now. I'm a widow, yer know, lost my Arthur a couple of years back from a heart attack.

'To be honest, dear, he wasn't that much of a loss to me. He were a good man when I married him, but over the years he grew more and more miserable, and by the time he retired he was no joy at all to be around. He'd sit in his chair all day, moaning and groaning about anything and everything he could have a grumble at, expecting me to run after him. We had three lovely daughters, though. They each come over to see me as much as they can, but they all live two bus rides away and have families of their own to see to so they can't get in as often as they'd like. I'm lucky with my neighbours though . . .'

She was rattling on and Aidy was loath to interrupt her but she really needed to tell Sister what she had to then get back to the surgery. She'd been absent for well over an hour by now and was worried she could have missed important telephone calls or visitors urgently looking for the doctor.

'I'm very sorry to interrupt you, Mrs . . . er . . . but I really do need to speak to Sister urgently. Where is she?'

'Oh, er . . . upstairs. She very kindly offered to freshen my bed up with clean bedding while she was here and give the room a sweep and dust as I'd not used it since my fall. I'm hoping to start sleeping back up there very soon. I did tell her she needn't go to all that trouble as one of me daughters would see to it, but she said it would be her pleasure. She must be doing a good job as she's been up there a good while. I expect she'll be down in a minute.'

Or she could be another five and Aidy should be getting back to work. 'Would you mind if I just went up and saw her? I really do need to get back to the surgery,' she politely asked.

The old woman looked hard at Aidy for a moment. It was apparent she wasn't happy about having a stranger in her bedroom. Obviously nuns didn't count. Finally she said, 'Well, I suppose not. You must be honest if you're the doctor's receptionist. When you get to the top of the stairs, turn right and go along the short corridor. My room is at the end, at the front of the house.'

Aidy found the door to the bedroom shut. Politely tapping on it while announcing, 'Sister, it's me, Mrs Nelson from the surgery,' she immediately opened it and went inside. Her mouth open ready to deliver her message, the words died on her lips and her jaw dropped in disbelief at the sight that met her.

Sister Teresa was kneeling on the bare floorboards by a tallboy. The bottom drawer was wide open. Items of clothing had been removed from it. In one hand she was holding an open oblong cigar-type box, and in the other a locket which she seemed to be in the process of inspecting. The skirt of her habit was spread out and on it were several pieces of jewellery – difficult to say whether it was expensive or not from where Aidy was standing – and a pocket watch. By the side of the pocket watch lay a bulky pouch. She was staring frozen faced at Aidy.

The two women looked at each other for several moments before Sister Teresa seemed to give herself a mental shake and broke the silence with, 'You startled me, Mrs Nelson. I've been giving Mrs Franks' room a freshen up, ready for her to move back into.' She nodded her head in the direction of a pile of dirty bedding at the side of the door where Aidy was standing to prove her point. 'While I was up here, Mrs Franks asked me to find a brooch that her husband had bought her. She wanted to have it close to her as a reminder of him, as she's missing him so much. That's what I'm doing . . . looking for it. I can't seem to find it, though.'

With narrowed eyes, Aidy responded matter-of-factly, 'Well, that's odd because the old dear has just told me that she *wasn't* missing her husband at all and in fact his death was a relief to her.' Her voice began to take on an accusing note. 'I know what I'm seeing, Sister, and that's *you* rifling an old lady's jewellery box! Those pieces on your skirt are what you'd already picked out for yourself before I interrupted you.' Her face darkened then. 'You're no more a nun than I am! You're a thief, using a disguise to carry out your robberies. Very clever, I must say. Whoever would suspect a nun of doing anything so ungodly? Huh! No wonder you didn't want me to go on some of your home visits with you.'

Then, suddenly, memories of past conversations came flooding back to Aidy. 'You've done this before!' she exclaimed. 'Three times, to my knowledge. To a Mrs Crosby, Mrs Potter and another old dear . . .' she paused for a moment, fighting to remember the name of the old lady presumed to be insane '. . . called Mrs Willows. And how many more I don't know about, eh? Got yourself a nice little racket going on here, haven't you, Sister? But, in all honesty, I think you could have chosen your victims a little more wisely. As you've probably realised by now, people round here ain't got what it takes to make you rich.' Aidy glared at her darkly. 'So, come on, lady, just who are you?'

While Aidy looked on, the woman kneeling on the floor bent her head as though in prayer and remained like that for several moments before she let out a deep, despondent sigh. She then slowly lifted her head and, one by one, picked up the items arranged on her skirt and put them back in the cigar box. She then put the box back in the bottom drawer of the tallboy, the clothes back on top, and shut the drawer. She picked up the pouch bag from off her skirt and rose to her feet. She put the pouch into a side pocket of her habit, clasped her hands in front of her and slowly walked over to the old lady's bed where she sank down. Then, looking across at Aidy, she fixed her eyes on hers and said with conviction, 'I am what you see, Mrs Nelson. A nun.'

Aidy sneered at her in disgust. 'A nun who's a thief?'

Clearly and precisely, she replied, 'Yes, I am.'

Her honesty shocked Aidy. She had expected her to deny it, try to convince Aidy she had not seen what she had, wriggle out of it somehow. 'But why? What good are those bits of jewellery to you? You can't wear them, can you? You're not allowed.'

'No, nuns aren't allowed anything pretty, or any frippery at all. I planned to sell the pieces when I'd got enough together, to make the amount I needed.'

Aidy was staring over at her, mystified. 'But what do you need money for? The Church provides you with all you need, doesn't it?'

'My material needs . . . food . . . a bed . . . but the Church doesn't provide for my physical needs as a woman, Mrs Nelson.' She heaved a deep sigh as her grey eyes blazed back at Aidy with a deep sorrow, the like of which she had never witnessed before. 'I have faith, I believe in God, but that doesn't mean I wanted to give up my freedom to live a bleak life serving him. I wanted to have fun like other girls, have boyfriends, get married, have children, grand-children . . . but my mother had other ideas for me.'

A look of horror filled Aidy's face. 'You mean, she forced you to become a nun?'

'That's exactly what she did. From a very early age my mother found God through her Sunday School teacher, herself a nun, who I can only think glamor-ised the life in my mother's young mind. It became her dream to become a nun, to give her life to doing the Lord's good works and securing her place beside Him when her time came. But when she informed my grandparents of her intention they were horrified, wouldn't hear of it, flatly refused to give their consent. So she calmly announced to them that she didn't need their permission when she reached the age of twenty-one. She was determined to become a nun and would let nothing stop her.

'Mother was an only child. After she was born, it wasn't possible for my grandmother to have any more children. According to my father, my grandfather was a very forceful type of man, the sort who got his way whatever it took. He was desperate for a male heir to pass on the family business to. He'd started from scratch and spent his life building it up to the success it was then. He had a factory that made ribbons and tapes. The only way he was going to get his heir was through a grandchild.

'My mother was an attractive woman, but she made herself unattractive by the plain, dull clothes she wore, had her hair cut short in the style of Joan of Arc. Everyone she came across, she would try to convert to the faith, to become the Lord's shepherds and do his good works. When she wasn't doing her Church works, she was reading the Bible. My grandfather threatened to disown her, cut off her allowance, anything to get her to stop her nonsense. But nothing he did worked. With the age of twenty-one fast approaching, when she'd be legally free to become a nun, my grandfather made it his mission to find Mother a husband.

'My father was an employee of his, a clerk in the accounts department, a very mild-mannered man, kind and gentle, who supported his widowed mother. My grandfather saw him as the ideal victim. My father was called into his office and accused of embezzling the firm's money to the tune of a thousand pounds. He was given a choice. Either he could go to jail for a very long time or he could secure himself a decent future by marrying the boss's daughter. My father really didn't have a choice. He was also told to use any means necessary to get my grandfather an heir.

'I'm not privy to how my father got my mother pregnant as he was too ashamed ever to talk of it . . . I can only assume he somehow got her intoxicated and had his way with her. My mother never knew of her own father's part in her downfall as that was part of the deal. She therefore blamed my father entirely for shattering her dream of becoming a nun, and never let him forget it. She made his life a living hell.

'The irony is that a month after my parents were married, my grandparents were both killed when the horse that was pulling their coach bolted and they were overturned. My mother was sole heir to their estate. The first thing she did was have my father dismissed from his job. She made it impossible for him to get another so that he was at her mercy day and night, because she also made sure he had no money and couldn't leave her. Besides, he adored me and couldn't bear the thought of leaving me alone with her. My mother knew this. The only social outings we went on were Church-associated. The only books in the house were religious ones. The only visitors to our house were connected to the Church.

'After seven years of misery my father could stand no more. He came to my bedroom one night, waking me up as he sat on my bed. With tears rolling down his face, he told me that he was going away and not coming back. He then told me the story I have just told you in the hope I'd understand and forgive him for what he was about to do. Before he left he hugged me so tight I couldn't breathe. I never saw him again. That night he threw himself off a bridge in front of a train.

'From as soon as I could understand, my mother made it clear what her ambition for me was. I was to live the life that had been denied her. I was going to become a nun and spend my life carrying out the Good Lord's work. Unfortunately, I had not inherited her or my grandfather's forceful nature but my father's kind and gentle one. I was no match for her. Consequently, against my will, at the age of sixteen

I joined the convent as a novice. I wasn't even allowed to keep my own name, but known as Sister Teresa Mary from that moment on.

'I had thought my life under my mother's rule was joyless enough, but inside the convent it was worse. My room was no more than a cell, big enough to take a cot bed and a small chest for my spare habit and change of underwear, the window too high up in the wall for me to see out of. The only adornment was a picture on the wall of the Holy Mother and child. My day started at four when I'd rise for prayers. As soon as they finished I helped prepare our breakfast of porridge, and spent the rest of my time on my knees, scrubbing the floors, the only breaks for prayers and lunch of bread and water. At four-thirty I would return to the kitchen to help prepare the evening meal. That was my life for two years.

'The convent had an annexe in the grounds that held two wards used to nurse the very elderly in the convent's vicinity, their way of doing good works for the local community, and Mother Superior decided I had the makings of a nurse. She assigned me to learn nursing under a strict disciplinarian of a nun who was eighty if she was a day and would punish me severely for the slightest mistake I made. She would make me kneel in the corner of the ward on a rough piece of matting that dug into my knees and recite the Lord's Prayer, over and over, until she

decided I'd had enough. I remained under her tutelage for ten years and when she died I took her place
in charge of the ward, but I can assure you that I
never punished any novice under my wing in any
other way than verbally.

'For those who freely choose their vocation it is a
very rewarding life, but I detested every minute of
it, everything about it. When all the other sisters were
saying their prayers in praise of God, I was damning
him as much as I was damning my mother for the
life I'd been forced to live. The only thing that kept
me sane was knowing that she could not live forever,
that one day she would die, and then, as her only
child, I'd be sole heir to her estate.

'I would lie in my cell at night and plan the life I
would finally have for myself. I would only take from
my inheritance enough to buy myself a little house,
and the rest I would give away to good causes. I
hoped the money that had caused such misery to
some, might bring joy to other people. To keep
myself, I would get a job using the skills I had learned
as a nurse. I hoped I might one day meet a nice man
to love me and that we'd live happily ever after.'

She gave an ironic laugh. 'I should not have under-
estimated my mother. She had decided at my birth
that she would make a present of her daughter to
God, in replacement for herself. She made sure I
couldn't have any opportunity of flouting her wishes

and leaving the sisterhood by bequeathing her entire estate to the convent. Without the means to start a new life for myself in the outside world, I was trapped. A few pounds, two or three at the most, was all I needed, but I had no way of obtaining them. There was nothing I could do but resign myself to a life that was pure purgatory to me. Accept the fact I would never know what it would feel like to be loved, kissed, hold my child in my arms, cook a meal for my family and sit around a table watching their happy faces. Then, out of the blue, a way to make my escape was presented to me. It was an opportunity I just couldn't let pass. Another might never come my way.

'A nun who had been on a missionary trip in the Congo returned. Mother Superior was busy deciding where she would prove most useful. The decision was made that she would take one of the nurse's places on the ward, and another nun would nurse where she was needed – out in the community. Mother Superior decided that this area was in most need of a nun's services at the time, and that I was to be that nun. I am sure she will never appreciate what a gift she gave to me! Getting away from the strict regime of convent life for a few hours a day was like being released into paradise for me.

'The first patient I attended was a Mrs Miller. She had had a leg amputated and I was to check the stump

417

for infection and redress it. As I finished my work on her, she asked if I would be kind enough to go up to her bedroom and fetch a shawl for her as she was feeling the cold. I would find it in the second drawer of her tallboy. I had retrieved the shawl for her, and as I was about to leave noticed a little china dish on top of the tallboy. It held several pieces of dusty, tarnished jewellery. Not elaborate by any means, just cheap pieces the old lady had obviously been given over the years. That was when the means to escape my awful life and make a new one became clear to me. How easy it would be for me to take one of those pieces! When the loss was discovered, who would ever suspect a nun of taking it? It was apparent the things in the dish hadn't been worn for years and were just lying there gathering dust. On its own, one piece might reap only a penny or two from a second-hand dealer, but if I managed to collect enough . . .

'To steal is wrong, however valid you may consider your reason for doing so, and especially from defence-less sick people. But when someone is in a desperate situation and sees a way out being given to them, then all sense and reason leave them. With today's items, I was of the opinion that I finally had enough for my needs.' She paused, looking enquiringly at Aidy. 'May I enquire how you found out what I was doing?'

Aidy had become deeply absorbed in the terrible

story she had just been told. She couldn't imagine how it must have been for this woman before her, having to live such an austere existence against her own will in order to satisfy her mother's need. She gave herself a mental shake. 'I didn't. I just came to find you. I forgot to put a patient's name on your list after Doc asked me to yesterday.'

'Oh, I see. Then it appears I will be swapping one cell for another.' With a look of sadness clouding her face, shoulders slumping in resignation, Sister Teresa unclasped her hands, stood up and asked quietly, 'Will you be accompanying me to the police station or do you trust me to present myself there, Mrs Nelson?'

Aidy stared at her blankly. This woman had been imprisoned her whole life. Would it be right to subject her to more years on top? Maybe the wrongs she had done in order to escape her purgatorial existence could be put right so that none of her victims was left to suffer from her misdeeds. And Aidy herself had the means to help her finally change her life to the one she wanted to live. She had a feeling that should she offer the chance to her, she would never come to regret it.

'Let's not be hasty, Sister. First things first, what is your real name?'

'Oh, er . . . Ruth. Mother's choice. Had to be something religious.'

'Religious or not, I wouldn't have minded being

called that instead of the name I was burdened with. Ruth is very pretty and it suits you. Well, Ruth, to make a new life for yourself, all you need is a place to sleep and some food to eat while you find yourself a job and then put some money together to get yourself somewhere to live, isn't that right?'

The nun was looking at her quizzically. 'Yes, that is all. Along with a change of clothes.'

'Not much then.'

'No, but beyond my reach.'

Aidy smiled at her. 'Not any longer. As long as you don't mind sleeping on a flock mattress squashed into one end of a tiny parlour, and putting up with three boisterous kids constantly mithering you, an old lady who never shuts up chattering and myself, then you're welcome to come home with me and stop with us until you're on your feet.'

Sister Teresa was gawping at her dumbfounded.

Aidy laughed. 'I really mean it.'

The other woman's shoulders lifted, the look of doom left her face and was replaced by one of pure joy that was a delight to witness. 'You have my promise that I will return every item I stole to its rightful owner.'

Aidy said to her, 'Can you please make Mrs Willows a priority? Her daughter is trying to have her committed as a lunatic on the basis she's gone doolally, misplacing her own jewellery and accusing others of stealing it from her. The truth is that the daughter wants rid of the burden of her so is seizing on this as an excuse.'

Ruth was visibly horrified that her actions had had such far-reaching repercussions and promised Aidy faithfully that she would return Mrs Willows' property to her today, as soon as she had finished her round.

Aidy then said to her, 'Now I wouldn't blame you for wanting to get straight back to the convent, to tell Mother Superior you're leaving the order and pack up your things . . . well, I don't suppose you've got much to pack . . . but first, could you please make a visit to the patient I forgot to put on your list? Otherwise it could end up with me getting the sack for forgetfulness, and then I wouldn't have a place to offer you to stay in.'

Ruth assured her, 'Of course. It's only fair I should finish off my list of calls. I have waited long enough for this moment, thought it would never come, so a little longer will prove no trial to me. It's only right too that I personally inform Doctor Strathmore why I will not be providing my services to him any longer. I do hope Mother Superior will find another nun to assign to the surgery to replace me.'

She gave a sigh. 'I am not looking forward to my interview with her. She is a very kindly but formidable woman. What I have to tell her will come as such a shock. I have never given her any reason to believe I was so unhappy with my life. She will do her best to persuade me not to leave the order, think I am having some sort of crisis and need time to get over it, call other nuns in to reason with me, probably suggest I go on a retreat to think carefully about what I am doing, but hopefully she will quickly realise that she is wasting her time and let me go quietly.'

Then a look of utter joy filled her face again. 'Oh, I cannot believe that after today I will no longer be living the life I've hated so much. I don't know how I will ever replay you for your charity.'

'You can do it by making sure you get that life you've always wanted, and settle for no less.'

By the time Aidy returned outside the temperature had risen enough to melt the falling snow to sleet, and the packed snow on the ground was starting to turn to slush. Slipping and sliding along as she hurried back to the surgery, she worked out that she would have been gone just over an hour and a half all told. Hopefully the doctor was still out on his rounds and would never know she had left the surgery unattended.

To her mortification, though, as soon as she unlocked the waiting-room door and let herself inside, Ty came to greet her. Disrobed of his overcoat and jacket which were hanging up to dry, he was rubbing his wet hair on a towel.

He said to her, 'I returned very briefly to the surgery over an hour ago to replenish some medicine I'd used up and found the place deserted. I returned again a few minutes ago on finishing my round and you still weren't here. Patients know to contact you here at the surgery up until two o'clock should they have an emergency and I need to be fetched, so I hope no emergency *did* arise while you were gone. I trust that whatever it was that took you away for such a length of time was a matter of great importance?'

A puddle of water forming around her, Aidy stared back at him blindly. Had he just arrived back when she returned, she had been going to tell him that she'd popped out minutes before as she'd heard a little boy crying in the street, lost in the snow, and had taken him home. It was plausible, she felt. But she could not do that now as he'd been back earlier and found her gone. All sorts of excuses to explain away her absence flashed through her mind, but none that would plausibly excuse such a long absence. She had no alternative but to tell the truth.

Fearing the worst, she said, 'I know it was wrong of me to leave the surgery but, you see, as I was making up the fires after you left this morning, I realised I'd forgotten to add Mrs Rogers to Sister's list of visits today. I knew if her wound wasn't checked and infection set in, then it could turn really nasty. It took me ages to find Sister but eventually I did.' With an invisible black cloud of doom swirling over her head, she added, 'I'll save you the trouble of telling me I'm sacked. I'll just get my handbag and be off.'

Still towelling his hair, Ty watched her thoughtfully as she made her way to the reception desk to collect her handbag where she kept it inside a drawer. Both the things she had done were serious enough to warrant instant dismissal. Her lapse of memory could have resulted in serious repercussions for the patient involved. Leaving the surgery without anyone to deal with any sudden life-or-death situations or take important telephone messages on his behalf was expressly forbidden. He was waiting for a call from the hospital about a bed he was trying to get for a patient he suspected of having a tumour in his stomach. If he had missed that call and the bed had been given to another patient, then he would be very cross. He supposed, though, that Aidy had acted immediately she'd realised her mistake about Mrs Rogers. And he couldn't deny that, up until today, she hadn't given him any reason to regret taking her on as his receptionist.

If he dismissed her, how long would it take him to find a replacement for her, considering she was the only one who'd applied the last time? But should he decide to let her go, what would become of her and her family? To his utter shock, yesterday he had learned that the money she earned from him could never in any way be classed as pin money, a bit extra to give her and her husband a marginally better stand-ard of living. Her wage, as little as it seemed to Ty, had to cover the cost of housing, keeping warm, feeding and clothing herself and four others. Jobs at the moment were proving harder and harder to come by due to the recession gripping the country. He gave a sigh. His conscience wouldn't allow him to be the cause of Aidy and her family facing a bleak future in the workhouse.

He called across to her, 'If you wish to leave my employ then that is your choice, Mrs Nelson, but I haven't asked you to leave. Another incident of this nature on your part, and I certainly will be looking for a replacement for you, however, so be warned.'

With that, he strode from the room.

Aidy had just shut the drawer after taking out her handbag. She stared after him in utter shock. Under that cold, humourless exterior, it seemed the doctor did had some humanity. She breathed a huge sigh of relief, the feeling of doom evaporating as she replaced her handbag inside the drawer, stripped off her wet coat and made to hurry and complete the tasks she should have had done hours ago.

CHAPTER TWENTY

It was just approaching two o'clock on Christmas Eve. Aidy was preparing to take her leave from the surgery for her afternoon break, planning in her head all the things she had to do during the two and three-quarter hours before she'd be back again for evening surgery. She didn't mind the surgery hours. In fact, they suited her far better than the timing at the factory. But, today of all days, she wished she hadn't to return this evening, then she could have visited the market just before closing time and found herself some last-minute bargains when the traders were practically giving what they'd left away for a few pennies, sooner than get nothing for it and leave it to rot.

Aidy so wanted this Christmas to be extra-special. Not only for her own family as this was the first Christmas they were spending without Jessie, but also for Ruth as it would be the first one she had spent in the sort of family environment she

427

had always craved. How Aidy wished she had the funds to buy her a present, something pretty and frivolous, but that was out of the question.

She tapped her fingers impatiently on the desk, willing the doctor to hurry through with her wages. Shopping at Christmas wasn't the same as it was the rest of the year. The town would be packed solid, and pushing her way through took superhuman strength. Then there were the endless queues to join, in the hope that when you finally reached the counter the item you wanted was not sold out. And she had a special present to buy. Having been extra-frugal over the past couple of weeks, Aidy now had the means to buy her gran a present. She knew what she was going to get. A woman on the market sold skeins of wool cheap – very possibly having fallen off the back of a lorry – and Aidy was going to buy one in black. For the first time that she could remember, Bertha would have some new wool, not stuff unravelled from an old garment, to knit herself a shawl with. Aidy couldn't wait to see the delight on her face when she received it. She had made a private bet with herself that before the day itself was out, the pins would be too and Bertha would have used a good measure of the wool.

She shot a frustrated glance at the clock. It was now four minutes past two. Doc had returned from his round fifteen minutes ago. How long did it take him to remove his coat, count out her wage, put it in an envelope and then bring it out to her?

Then, thankfully, she heard the surgery door opening, and his footsteps cross the corridor. He came over and handed her a bulky brown envelope, saying, 'I'll see you on Boxing Day, Mrs Nelson.'

She frowned, puzzled. 'Oh, but don't you want me to come in this evening?'

He replied matter-of-factly, 'I doubt you'll have time with all the things I suspect you have to do, considering what day it is tomorrow. The patients and I will have to do without you.'

She felt sure he flashed her just the very briefest of smiles before he turned and walked out.

Reeling in shock at this unexpected generosity, Aidy finally found her voice and called out, 'Merry Christmas to you, Doc.'

For the second time her opinion of him rose just a little.

This extra time afforded her gave Aidy the opportunity to offer Ruth an experience she suspected the other woman had never had. She wasn't sure whether Ruth would be home now or out in search for work. True to her word, as soon as she had severed her links with the Church and settled herself into her new abode, she had turned her attention to returning other people's property, and getting herself a job. The first she had successfully achieved; in fact, it had been easy to do.

She just visited each of her victims in turn, informed them why she wouldn't be calling on them under her guise of nun again, and while she was there, left behind what she had taken with her on a previous visit.

It wasn't proving so easy for her to get a job, though. She had applied for several at the General Hospital and Infirmary as well as others in nursing homes dotted around the city, and was waiting to hear the outcome by post. Aidy knew she was getting quite anxious, listening out for the postman to call every morning, not at all comfortable about taking charity off people who could ill afford to give it. She meant to start paying her way as soon as she possibly could. Ruth was a joy to have around, though, and an extra pair of hands tackling the housework was proving invaluable to Aidy.

She did, though, feel a little sorry for her lodger at the moment. The unflattering plain skirt, blouse and cardigan she was wearing when she walked away from the convent was all she possessed, so Aidy had loaned her some of her own clothes for now. Ruth was more rounded than she was so the clothes were tight, but regardless she looked presentable enough to attend interviews and was very grateful for the gesture. But it was her hair that Aidy really pitied her for. As a nun it was always kept clipped short but, worse than that, seemed to have been hacked off randomly, leaving short tufts sticking up all over. Aidy knew Ruth received some strange looks when out in public, but she didn't seem to mind. After all, her hair would grow back given time and then she could have it styled by a professional to suit her lovely face.

A while later, as she entered through the back gate, Aidy wasn't sure what she felt. On her way back home she unexpectedly bumped into Arch's eldest brother. He seemed genuinely pleased to see her, but beneath his friendly manner Aidy was sure she detected an awkwardness.

As he was telling her about his own family, and about looking forward to the festivities tomorrow, it suddenly struck her – his nervousness was to do with Arch. He must have met another woman and his brother was dreading having to pass this news on to Arch's former wife.

Seconds later she was proved right. Looking everywhere but at her, he told her that Arch had found work in Bristol in a tanning factory and had started courting one of the female workers there. He had told his brother that he could see himself settling down. At least, it seemed, Arch had learned from his mistakes, Aidy thought. A part of her was glad that he was doing well, but she couldn't help but feel sad too.

Aidy found her grandmother and the lodger seated side by side at the back-room table, Bertha's remedies book open before them. They were both so engrossed neither of them heard her come in.

'Found yourself a willing pupil at last, Gran?'

Both heads jerked up to look over at her startled.

'Oh, indeed she has,' proclaimed Ruth. 'Earlier, Bertha very kindly let me try a sample of her hand cream. It's made from lard, honey, oats and rosewater.'

'Eh, up,' Bertha chided her. 'Yer don't give recipes away or people will be making their own potions and not buying from me.'

Ruth looked mortified. 'Oh, I'm sorry. Truly I am.'

Bertha gave a chuckle. 'Well, yer safe enough this time as my granddaughter and all my grandchildren have made it perfectly clear potion-making is not for them. Anyway, you were praising my potion to Aidy, so don't let me deter yer.'

It was Ruth's turn to chuckle. 'Well, I was going to say that my hands have always felt coarse and rough after years of being scrubbed with carbolic, but after just one application of the hand lotion they're so soft and smooth. And I never knew that oil made from primroses is good for the skin, too . . . and that the water from boiled celery stalks is good for soothing chilblains, which I suffer from badly in winter.

'I've learned so much else today. That valerian can aid sleep; sage help the digestive system. I have seen several remedies Bertha has for stomach upsets that would be far kinder on the stomach that the dose of bismuth a doctor would usually prescribe for the sufferer, which can in some cases actually cause a bleed in the stomach.' She gave a thoughtful frown. 'Doctor Strathmore really should take the trouble to come and study Bertha's remedies and potions, and then he could have a wider choice in what he prescribes. I know you do well selling your non-medical remedies, Bertha, but I'm sure you'd be glad of the extra custom the doctor could send your way, and he would benefit from not spending the time it takes either to make up a medicine himself or write a prescription for the chemist.'

'Doc thinks women like Gran are nothing more than charlatans, out to fleece people of their money. He told me that himself. He's obviously had a bad experience and it's coloured his views,' Aidy explained.

'Well, life does have a way of opening our eyes to things we previously shut them to,' said Ruth, thoughtfully.

'It would have to be something of volcanic proportions to make Doc change his mind. Talking of Doc . . . I had an awful shock today. He has given me the rest of the day off! I'm beginning to think he has got a human side after all. Anyway, Ruth, this means I can go bargain hunting down the market tonight, just on closing time, and get much more for us for the money. The Christmas spirit there is wonderful.

There are usually carol singers and hot mince pies, chestnuts, roast potato sellers, and all sorts of Christmassy things going on. I wondered if you'd like to come?'

'Oh, I'd be just delighted!' she cried.

'And me, I'm coming too,' said Bertha

Aidy smiled at her. 'I took that for granted, Gran. And I expect the kids won't want to miss it, so that's all of us going.'

'You had a nice surprise today and so did I, Aidy,' Ruth told her. 'I received a letter this morning and have secured myself a job in a private nursing home. For someone who's not used to having any money, the pay sounds like a fortune but in fact it will just about allow me to keep myself if I am careful. I start on Boxing Day, the early shift from six in the morning until three in the afternoon. This means I'll be able to finance a place of my own in a couple of weeks! I know I have only been with you a matter of days but I shall so miss living with you all. You are such lovely people and have made me feel so welcome and part of your family. I was wondering if you'd have any objection if I tried to get myself a little place around here, so I could see you all often?'

'We expect no less,' Aidy told her with conviction.

'That's right,' agreed Bertha. 'Besides, for once I've found someone who's as interested in me potions as I am. I'm of the mind you might be the one to pass on all my knowledge to, so it doesn't die with me.'

'Oh, Bertha, I'd be honoured. I am definitely that someone. When I am in the nursing home owner's confidence, I shall tell her of your remedies with a view to encouraging her to buy some to try on her patients. I am sure she would definitely be interested in the lotion to help ease sores . . . I'm thinking of bed sores, you see.'

Aidy left them to it, to go into the kitchen to sort out her pay so that, after putting the weekly dues aside and accounting for Bertha's contribution, she knew what she was left with to spend on the Christmas fare. As she tipped out her wage packet on to the pine kitchen table, she immediately noticed that something wasn't right. She quickly counted the money up. Doc had given her ten shillings too much! His mistake surprised her, but it meant she'd have to make a detour by the surgery, which was out of her way, in all the slippery slush, to hand it back before she set off to town that evening to do her market shopping. Then she spotted a piece of paper sticking out of her pay packet. Curious, she pulled it out. On it was written in the doctor's handwriting: *Merry Christmas*. So he had made no mistake. He had purposely given her extra. This show of kindness on his part was very unexpected.

A warm glow filled Aidy. That ten shillings was

going to make such a difference! She could buy the
fruit and suet needed to make a pudding, get a small
chicken for them instead of rabbit, have ham on their
bread for tea instead of just margarine and a scrape
of jam, plus a bit of bacon for breakfast. Oh, what
treats! If the doctor had been there she would have
kissed him, so delighted was she. Her low opinion
of him rose for the third time.

On Christmas Day Aidy was serving up the dinner.
The chicken was cooked to perfection; the roast potatoes, sprouts and carrots all dished up ready. The
pudding was still boiling merrily away but was ready
to be eaten and its aroma mingled nicely with all the
other delicious smells filling the kitchen. In the back
room five hungry people sat waiting patiently at the
table for the food to arrive, Bertha and Ruth ready
to jump up and fetch it as soon as Aidy gave them
the go ahead. They'd already pulled the cheap crackers
she had bought and were all wearing paper hats.

The previous evening, on their return from the
market laden down with heavy bags, while Bertha
and Aidy had set to work in the kitchen preparing
the food, Ruth had set to in the back room and, along
with the children, made home-made paper chains and
hung them around the walls. Thanks to Ty's
generosity, Aidy was able to buy a tiny Christmas
tree that they had stood in an old paint pot given to

them by a neighbour and filled with cold ashes to keep the tree straight. It had been adorned with the decorations Jessie had amassed over the years, some bought, most home-made. The room looked very festive. After dinner was cleared away, they planned to play parlour games and round events off by singing carols in the firelight. Unbeknown yet to her grand-mother and Ruth, Aidy had hidden away a bottle of port for them to drink after the children had gone to bed.

'That food ready yet, I'm starving?' called out George. 'And can I have a leg all to meself, like grown-up men do?'

'I want a leg too if George is having one,' shouted Betty.

'And I want one too,' called Marion.

In the kitchen Aidy was laughing to herself, wondering how she could make a part of the chicken resemble a leg so one of the children was not disap-pointed. If it hadn't been for the doctor's generosity, she wouldn't have had that problem. Rabbits had four legs. Thinking of him, a vision of Ty rose before her. He was sitting at the table, all alone. And what would be on his plate? She knew that Doc had a regularly weekly order of food delivered to him from the local corner shop, but would he in fact go to all the trouble of cooking himself a full Christmas dinner or would he be settling for a bought meat pie and potatoes, which she knew he often did? An idea came to her then. Doc had done something special to mark Christmas for her, maybe she could do something in return. Going to the pantry, she got another plate off the shelf and put it in the oven for a while to warm up.

Minutes later, she called Bertha and Ruth to help her take the filled plates through. When they put Betty's before her, the child scanned it for her chicken leg and, not finding one but a piece of breast instead, wailed, 'How come I never got a leg but George did?' She had spotted the one on his plate.

'Because the chicken I got only had one leg. He lost his other in an accident crossing the road, and as George is the man of the house, he's the one who got the leg.' Ignoring the fact that both Bertha and Ruth were looking at her quizzically, knowing they were both wondering where the other chicken leg had gone, Aidy told them all, 'Make a start without me. My dinner is keeping hot in the oven. I have to go out on a quick errand.'

Marion piped up matter-of-factly, 'If yer going up the graveyard to wish Mam a Happy Christmas, our Aidy, then yer don't need to. Mam's not there. She died 'cos her life on earth was over and she's in . . .' she paused and looked questioningly at Ruth who prompted her, 'Spirit, dear' . . . 'Yeah, that's right, she's in spirit, up in heaven, which is just above the clouds. And she's watching over us all so she already knows we're wishing her a Happy Christmas. When our time on earth is over then we will become spirits and join Mam up in heaven. I'll get my dolly back from her then. Can I have some more gravy, Gran?'

A lump formed in Aidy's throat. Ruth had been able to do what they had failed to. In a kind and thoughtful way, she'd got Marion to accept that she would never see her mother in the flesh again. She looked at Ruth and mouthed a thank you.

Ten minutes later Aidy knocked purposefully on the front door of the doctor's residence. When it opened, for a moment she stood staring at the sight of the man before her, as if seeing him for the very first time. She was used to finding Ty dressed soberly in a three-piece suit and tie, always smart and tidy, always with a stern and formidable air about him. The man before her bore no resemblance to that. He was dressed in casual grey flannel trousers and a V-necked sleeveless pullover over a shirt worn open at the neck. He had a pair of old slippers on his feet. His usually immaculately groomed hair was tousled, as though he'd just woken from sleep, and he was sporting a day's growth of beard. But above all it was his eyes that mesmerised her. How come she had never noticed what an unusual shade of green they were, almost a pale turquoise? They seemed to be drawing her in. Then her gaze took in the rest of his face, and now that it wasn't set in its usual sternness but a sort of dreamy, kind expression, it struck her that Ty was indeed a handsome man.

A shiver ran down Aidy's spine, so strong she visibly shuddered.

The unexpected knock on his door had jolted Ty awake from a doze in the armchair. He had awoken that morning for once having had a decent night's sleep, with no nightmares having disturbed him, and no emergency call outs. In the moment before the actual reality of his life blasted back to him, in the short space of time when he was halfway between waking and sleeping, he'd experienced a momentary feeling of being glad to be alive and facing a fresh new day. But that had soon evaporated when the deafening silence of the house had stolen in on him and he was reminded of how alone he truly was. In houses all around him families were opening their presents together, preparing dinner, waiting excitedly for relatives to arrive. Even the ones who lived alone were having their neighbours dropping in to wish them good cheer, invite them to share their day perhaps. No one would be calling on him to offer any such a thing. Why would they, when he had made it very clear to all he met that he would not be receptive to any offer of friendship?

A long solitary day seemed to stretch endlessly

before him, which would only be broken should he be called out on a life-or-death emergency. Visions of past Christmases spent with people he had loved started to invade his mind. He dismissed them. Those days were gone, those people were gone, and he had moved on now into another life. But still he could not shake off his all-consuming feeling of loneliness. Best thing to help the day pass quickly was to keep himself busy. He could update his accounts. Not a job he liked doing but one that needed to be focused on so no mistakes were made, leaving little room for other thoughts.

He made his way into the surgery, sat down behind the desk and pulled open the bottom drawer where the accounts book was stored. The bottle of whisky that lay hidden beneath it met his eyes like a beacon. A drink seemed a good idea to him then. Might help lighten the melancholy mood he was in. It was Christmas Day after all and a tot of good cheer at this time of the day was acceptable. Taking the bottle out of the drawer and collecting a glass from the kitchen, he settled himself into his armchair by the blazing fire. One small draught led to another, and an hour later the bottle was half-empty. Ty, in a mellow, couldn't-care-less state of mind, drifted off into a drink-induced doze.

The loud rap on the front door had roused him from slumber. As the good-mannered man he was, he automatically rose to answer it, though he still felt dazed and his mouth was unaccountably dry.

His eyes immediately took in a very attractive face looking up at him. It belonged to a shapely woman, whose attire might be on the shabby side but still looked very becoming on her. But why she was standing on his doorstep, holding a covered plate in her hand and wearing a paper hat on her head, he couldn't understand.

Aidy meanwhile was wondering what on earth was wrong with her boss. He certainly wasn't himself. Why was he looking at her as if he'd never seen her before? And she knew a man with an admiring glint in his eyes when she saw one. Then she caught the whiff of alcohol wafting from him and realised he was looking at her through drink-glazed eyes so more than likely wasn't recognising her.

The fog in Ty's brain suddenly lifted and, to his absolute horror, he realised the woman he was looking at in a very appreciative way was in fact his receptionist. Having regained his senses, the trouble was that she was still looking rather attractive to him. This wouldn't do. It was against everything he had ever promised himself after the tragedy had struck.

His dreamy expression hardened and he spoke to her in to a businesslike fashion. 'If what is on that plate is for me, Mrs Nelson, then I appreciate your offer but I've already eaten. Excuse me, won't you, but I'm in the middle of something and must get back to it.' He stopped himself from telling her he hoped the rest of the day was a pleasant one for her and her family. He didn't want her to think for a minute he cared, even though deep down he actually did.

Ty stepped back inside the house and firmly closed the door.

Outside on the damp cobbles, Aidy was left confused and upset. She couldn't believe her boss had been so rude to her, so unappreciative of her gesture, and after her thinking he wasn't as bad as she'd first decided as well. Fury erupted inside her. To hell with him, she inwardly fumed. No wonder he wasn't married. No wonder she never witnessed any evidence of friends visiting him, or relatives either. The way he treated people, he didn't deserve them to care for him back. She had learned her lesson, though. From now on she would do the job he paid her for and no more. No making cups of tea for him or a sandwich for his lunch. No hanging his wet coat up so it was dry for when he went out next. No straightening the washing he had put on the clothes horse so it dried quicker and wasn't so rumpled. She would never, ever put herself in a position where he could humiliate her like that again.

CHAPTER TWENTY-ONE

Ty was feeling wretched. The inside of his head was pounding like a drum. His eyes felt gritty, his chest tight. He was having difficulty breathing, his skin clammy to the touch. He felt mentally and physically exhausted. He had taken a dose of quinine a while ago to help stem the building fever, but it didn't seem to have had much effect. He wanted to do nothing more than crawl back into bed. But he couldn't. He had a waiting room full of people to see and suspected the list of house calls that Aidy would be compiling was steadily mounting. It was New Year's Eve and, apart from the fact he hadn't anyone to celebrate the occasion with anyway, it looked as though he would be seeing in 1931 from under the covers of his bed.

Trying to gather strength he just didn't have, he called out as loudly as he was able, 'Next!'

In the waiting room Aidy was vaguely aware of what a new arrival was saying to her. Despite promising herself that she would take no further interest

in the doctor on a personal level after his humiliating treatment of her on Christmas Day, unfortunately she had no control of her protective instincts
which were causing her to be very concerned for
him now. Since the incident on Christmas Day they
had both been merely civil with each other, and Aidy
had made a point of having as little face-to-face
contact with Ty as she could. Regardless, she would
have to be blind not to have noticed that her
employer wasn't at all well. He looked exhausted,
in fact. She wasn't surprised. He worked long hours,
was out in all weathers, and she felt sure he didn't
eat regularly or get as much sleep as he needed. She
knew from the stilted update he had given her that
morning so she could keep the practice records
straight that he had been called out during the night
to attend to a very sick child. The result was that he
had had to perform an emergency tonsillectomy on
the kitchen table, the poor child having to be
restrained meanwhile by its frantic parents while Ty
removed the infected glands. Hopefully the patient
would make a full recovery . . . but would the doctor?
From the way he looked, it seemed he was in danger
of succumbing to illness himself. But as much as
Aidy wanted to urge him to bring a locum in to
cover for him temporarily while he had a few days'
rest, she would not risk the humiliation of being told
to mind her own business.

Pushing thoughts of her employer from her mind, she turned to the new arrival and said apologetically, 'I beg your pardon, I didn't quite catch what you were saying?'

The threadbare middle-aged woman before her gave an irritated huff and repeated, 'I want to see the doctor because . . .' She lowered her voice so that hopefully only the receptionist could hear about the embarrassing condition. 'I have terrible constipation, ducky. I ain't opened me bowels for nearly a fortnight now, and I feel like me stomach's gonna burst. I've tried everything I know of, but nothing has worked. Trouble is, I ain't seen a doctor for years so I'm not sure what the fee is. I don't even know if I can afford it. Well, if it's more than two bob, I can't.'

Inside his surgery, no patient appearing, Ty gave an irritated sigh as he rubbed his aching head. Obviously his last summons had gone unheeded as his croaky voice hadn't projected far enough to be heard in the room across the corridor. It was full of patients waiting to see him, judging from the sound of chattering voices coming from it. There was nothing else for it, he would have to go and fetch the next patient in himself.

Back in the waiting room, Aidy was thinking that this woman was one for her grandmother. 'You don't really need to trouble Doc,' she told her. 'It's my grandmother you want to go and see, and a visit to her won't cost you as much as Doc's fee would.'

The woman looked knowingly at her. 'Oh, is your grandmother *the old woman*?'

Aidy nodded. 'She's got a potion that'd shift a constipated elephant so she'll fix you up no trouble.'

'I've heard good things about her but never had any need to go to her before. If I've got any ailments, I usually manage to sort meself out. I swear by Epsom Salts and Friar's Balsam, but neither has worked its magic on me this time. So where can I find yer grandmother then, lovey? I'll mek me way straight round there now.'

Aidy heard someone clear their throat beside her and automatically turned her head. Her employer! Sheer panic filled her. She could tell by the look on his face that he had been privy to her conversation with the woman.

Ty said to the patient, 'Would you excuse my receptionist for a moment? I need to speak to her in private.' To Aidy he ordered, 'Come through to the surgery.'

He was holding the door open for her, and as she passed through shut it firmly behind her. Before she had a chance to turn and look at him he was saying in an accusing tone, 'You lied to me when I asked you if you knew who the locals referred to as *the old woman*. You said you didn't have a clue who she was. When all the time you knew damned well who she was and where she lived ... she's your *grand-mother*. And now I find that you're actually poaching my patients so they will buy her useless potions off her.'

Aidy erupted, 'If you would just let me ...'

He held up a warning hand. 'I don't want to hear any excuses for your behaviour. Nothing could excuse it. I'm just wondering, over the months you've worked for me, how many patients you have stolen from me in this way? Not to mention putting their health at risk, sending them to a fraudster making false claims for her filthy mixtures.'

Beads of perspiration were forming on Ty's brow from the fever that was building inside him. His headache was so bad it hit him like a gong. Discovering his receptionist had been acting behind his back for her own benefit had wounded him deeply. He might have been curt in his manner towards her, but otherwise felt he had been a very fair employer. She had taken advantage of that to double cross him. To think he had actually started to look upon her as ... Thank goodness he had had the sense to put a stop to that before it had gone any further.

In no uncertain terms, he told her now, 'Your employment at this surgery is terminated with immediate effect. Please collect your belongings and leave. What pay you are due can be collected on your behalf on Friday, along with your cards. I'd prefer you didn't come here again, unless of course you have need of my medical services. Leave your door key in the top drawer of the desk.'

She had to make him listen to her, hear her explain that she had not been defrauding him but *helping* him by what she had been doing. Aidy implored him, 'But, please, will you just ...'

His look was enough to stop her cold.

At just before four o'clock that afternoon, Ruth was humming happily as she let herself into the kitchen, stamped her booted feet to rid them of rainwater and took off her coat which she hung on the back of the door. Picking up her handbag, she made her way into the back room and stopped short, a worried expression clouding her face to see Aidy and Bertha sitting at the table. Bertha seemed deeply troubled. Aidy was cradling her head in despair.

'Is it one of the children?' Ruth exclaimed.

Bertha looked shocked for a moment, so consumed by worry she hadn't heard Ruth come in. 'Oh, hello, love. No, the kids are fine. We sent them all out to play soon as they got home from school. We didn't want them getting wind of this and worrying their little heads over it.'

Ruth was getting extremely worried herself now. She stepped over to the table and pulled a chair out. 'If it's none of my business, please tell me to go away but has someone died or . . .'

Bertha shook her head. 'Aidy's been sacked.'

Ruth was stunned. 'Sacked? The doctor's sacked her! What good reason would he have to do that?'

Aidy's head jerked up. 'He thinks I've betrayed him. If only he had let me explain, I'm sure he'd have seen I wasn't doing any such thing but actually trying to help him. And yes, okay, Gran too with the extra money she earned from what I did . . .'

'Just what did you do, Aidy?' Ruth asked her, bemused.

'Well, as you know, Doc's always really busy. He can hardly handle the number of patients he gets through his door and has to visit in their homes. Most days he never ever has time to stop and have his lunch. And, of course, now he's lost you, Ruth, and there's no sign of a replacement for you, he's even more pushed.

'You see, many of the patients who come in insist on telling me what they need to see the doctor for, even though really it isn't my business. But sometimes patients come in with minor ailments that I know Gran would have a potion or ointment for that would be just as good as anything he could prescribe. I can also tell when they haven't got the money to pay him his fee anyway, or only in dribs and drabs over God knows how long. The ones I sent Gran's way were that sort, I swear. Where's the harm in that?

'Anyway, there's no point in going over it now. Doc has sacked me, and that's that. The good thing is that at least I don't have to put up with his coldness any longer. Apart from that, though, I really loved the job.' Aidy gave a wan smile. 'I'm worried 'cos there's not much work going, is there? But then, I'm in a better position than I was when I got dismissed from the factory. I now have office skills to my credit and basic nursing, thanks to Sadie Billson. I know at least enough to apply for a ward orderly's job or such like.'

Ruth leaned over and patted her hand. 'And you'll be snapped up. I can give you the names of the nursing homes I tried. They weren't needing qualified nurses but they might want an orderly. And while you're looking we have my money coming in, and the bit that Bertha makes, so we aren't quite destitute.'

Aidy smiled warmly at her. It seemed her lapse of memory was turning out to have been a blessing in disguise.

Later that evening, they were just finishing their dinner of soup and slices of thick, homemade crusty bread scraped with margarine, when the back door was hammered upon.

Aidy had had her fill so she rose to respond to it. It would more than likely be someone wanting a remedy from her grandmother.

Opening the door, she found Elsie Stringer on the doorstep. She was a neighbour from the end of the street and an occasional customer of Bertha's. Aidy was just going to ask her to step in and tell her that Bertha would be with her in a minute, when she had finished her meal, when the other woman blurted out, 'I volunteered to fetch you. Yer late! It's nearly half-past six. We're all getting frozen, standing outside that surgery waiting fer you to come and open up.'

'But, I don't work at the surgery any longer, Mrs Stringer.'

'Oh! Who's yer replacement then, 'cos she's late?'

'I shouldn't think Doc's had time to take anyone else on yet. I only left this morning. He's probably out on an emergency. Has no one informed you when to expect him back?'

'I was there waiting for the door to open at ten to six and no one's been near with a message from the doctor.'

'Oh, well, maybe it hasn't been possible. You'll just have to wait until Doc gets back himself and lets you all in.'

Elsie didn't look too pleased at the thought of having to wait outside in the cold until the doctor showed up. However long that would be. 'Well, shame on you for walking out and leaving him high and dry like that. I thought you had more about yer, Aidy Nelson.'

She stalked off, abruptly.

Despite having plenty to keep her occupied that evening, Aidy couldn't quite get the reason for Elsie Stringer's visit off her mind. It was really unusual for Doc to be late for evening surgery. He'd only ever been so once while she had been working for him, and then had got a message delivered to inform her of his delay and a rough estimate of the time he'd be back. But what was really concerning her was that the doctor himself had not been at all well that morning, and she wondered if his absence was in fact due to that. But if that were the case, would he not have put a notice on the surgery door? Despite the fact that anything to do with Doc was no longer her business, she could not quell the niggle of worry inside her.

When George came in at seven-thirty from playing out, she asked him, 'Could you pop to Elsie Stringer's for me and ask her if the doctor eventually turned up for surgery?'

He pulled a face and wailed, 'Ah, Sis, it's cold out there! Do I have to?'

'It didn't seem to be cold when you were playing football out there for the past two hours!'

'Weren't playing football . . . we been playing cops and robbers in the old factory.'

'I've told you not to play there, it's dangerous,' she scolded him.

'No, you didn't, Sis, honest.'

'Well, I'm sure I did. Look, I've no time for this. Go on that errand like I asked you or . . .'

George was gone.

He returned ten minutes later and plonked himself down in an easy chair, hanging one leg casually over its arm. 'Mrs Stringer said the doctor hadn't shown by the time she gave up and came home at seventhirty. Can I have some hot cocoa?'

'Me too, please,' said Marion who was sitting at the table with Ruth, cutting out clothes for the paper doll she had got for Christmas.

'And me,' said Betty, who was standing behind Ruth and playing hairdressers with what hair she had, painstakingly twirling sections into kiss curls and securing them with grips.

'I'm just making you all one,' Bertha shouted in from the kitchen.

Ruth carefully turned her head so as not to disturb her hairdresser too much. 'You're worried about the doctor, aren't you, Aidy?'

Busy with a pile of rumpled clothes, she spat on the iron to check its heat and replied: 'I couldn't give a damn about the bloody man.' Then she sighed. 'All right, yes, I am, though he really doesn't warrant me bothering. Only it isn't like him not to turn up for surgery or at least send a message. He wasn't well this morning . . .'

'Well then, he's probably recovering in bed,' Ruth suggested.

'He wouldn't have just gone to bed and not informed the patients surgery was cancelled tonight.'

'Mmm, from what I know of Doctor Strathmore as a man, I agree with you there – he wouldn't have. Well, I was actually thinking of taking a walk. I could go by the surgery and check for any signs of life.'

'I think I'll come with you. I could do with a walk myself.'

Ruth smiled to herself. Aidy might have every reason to be angry with her ex-employer for the way he had treated her while she worked there and for not hearing her out before he had sacked her. But, regardless, she certainly had a soft spot for him, whether she realised it or not.

A short while later they both stood staring over at the doctor's house. It appeared to be in complete darkness, no light shining through any window.

'That doesn't mean to say Doctor Strathmore isn't home and tucked safely up in bed, nursing his cold or whatever it is he's suffering from,' Ruth told Aidy.

She looked pensive. 'No, it doesn't. But you know when you have a feeling that something isn't right? I'm going to go around the back . . . see if I can see anything through the windows.'

'And what if the doctor looks back at you from the other side?'

'Then I'll shout "Boo!" and scarper off quick and hope he thinks it's kids larking about.'

CHAPTER TWENTY-TWO

Ty had had the strangest dream. He seemed to have been floating in a mist and had either felt so swelteringly hot he was on fire or so shiveringly cold he was embedded in ice. But the strangest thing of all was that for some of the time he'd been hearing voices somewhere above him, ghost-like, whispering voices, but no matter how hard he had strained, he couldn't hear what they were saying.

He fought to open his eyes, wondering why his body felt so stiff, his head as if his brain was too big for it and pushing against his skull. Finally he prised his eyes open and instantly snapped them shut as a bright light blinded him. He tried again, slowly, and as his vision began to focus, nearly shrieked in shock as the ghostly face hovering above him began to materialise.

Then he heard a quiet voice say, 'You're finally back with us, Doctor Strathmore. Obviously the light is bothering you. Keep your eyes shut for a moment and I will draw the curtains again.'

With eyes tight shut he lay still, listening to the sound of light footsteps. His mind was racing. What was this? He was in his own bed, that much he did know from the familiar feel of the lumpy mattress beneath him. But who was in the room with him? The voice that had spoken to him had belonged to a female. What was a woman doing in his bedroom?

As soon as he heard the sound of the curtains being pulled to he fully opened his eyes and fought to focus his vision. He saw a woman coming towards him. As she came into focus he noted she was in her late thirties and had a kind face though her haircut did not do her justice. He felt she was familiar to him but there was something different about her . . . he couldn't place her. He made to ask who she was and why she was here, but found his throat was so dry he couldn't speak.

The woman obviously realised his dilemma. A spoon was being placed next to his lips with water in it. As he sipped the water slowly he couldn't understand why he felt he had done this same thing several times recently.

Finally his throat felt easy enough for him to pose some questions. 'Who are you?' he asked the woman.

There was a surprised tone to her voice when she answered, 'Ruth Whelham, Doctor Strathmore.'

He looked puzzled as he tried to ease himself up

a little higher on his pillows. 'I don't recall the name, yet I feel I should know you.'

Ruth automatically slipped her arm around his back and gently helped him sit up, then settled the pillows comfortably around him, saying, 'Maybe you remember me better as Sister Teresa.'

'Oh, yes, of course. Yes, it's coming back to me now. You've left the order. How are you coping back in the outside world?'

As she spooned more water into his mouth, she told him, 'With the help of my new family, I'm adapting extremely well. I have much to be grateful to them for.'

He was looking at her quizzically. 'So why are you here, Sis . . . Miss Whelham? How did you come to be with me?'

She sat down on the chair to one side of his bed. 'You've been very poorly, Doctor Strathmore. Needed constant attention in case you should take a turn for the worse. You gave real cause for concern on a couple of occasions when your temperature suddenly shot up. It took a lot of cold sponging to get it down again. Anyway, the fever finally broke this morning, I'm glad to say, but you're still very weak and will need to stay in bed a little longer to regain your strength.'

'How long have I been ill?'

'Three days, all told.'

'I've been unconscious in a fever for three days? Well, I owe you a real debt of gratitude, nursing me for all this time, Miss Whelham. I will, of course, reimburse you.'

'Oh, I haven't been nursing you, Doctor, or sitting with you to keep an eye on you. Not all this time. I had to go to work, you see. Mrs Nelson did it mostly, and her grandmother helped out too for an hour or so, here and there. I'm only here now to give Aidy a break.'

His eyes blazed with sudden anger. 'Mrs Nelson! After what she did, I told her never to darken my door again.'

Evenly Ruth responded, 'Well, if I were you, Doctor Strathmore, I'd be grateful she *did* or you might not be alive now. Aidy . . . Mrs Nelson . . . had an uncomfortable feeling that all was not right with you when she heard you hadn't attended evening surgery the day you dismissed her. She was aware you weren't at all well earlier that day and was very concerned something wasn't right. She decided to quell her worry by paying a visit to your house, to check for signs that you were not in distress. I accompanied her. We found the house in darkness. After checking through the windows and seeing no sign of life at all, we assumed you must have retired to bed, having dosed yourself with medicine, hoping to sleep off what was ailing you.

'Thankfully, though, Aidy decided to take a peek through the letter box as a final check before we went home, and that's when she spotted you. The hall was dark but she could just make you out, lying at the bottom of the stairs. She called through the letter box to you several times but received no response. We immediately went round the back and broke the glass in the door so we could let ourselves in. Please don't worry, we have had it fixed since.'

A memory stirred in Ty. 'I remember now ... I was about to go upstairs and ready myself for evening surgery when suddenly I felt myself go very hot and then start to feel faint ... and that's it.'

'It was very apparent the moment we set eyes on you that you had a raging fever. We fetched a strapping young man from a few doors down and he put you over his shoulder and carried you up here. When I first checked you over, I was worried you could have typhus or scarlet fever but there were no spots or other symptoms. Bertha ... Mrs Rider ... agreed with me. She thought the same as I did, that you were suffering from complete exhaustion and had caught a very bad chill.'

'Mrs Rider?' Ty queried, the name not being familiar to him. 'Who is Mrs Rider?'

'Aidy ... Mrs Nelson's grandmother.'

'*That woman* has been in my house? *She* made a diagnosis of my illness! She's no more qualified to do that than my milkman is. I'm surprised at you, a trained nurse, being in cahoots with a charlatan like her and actually seeming to believe in her. People like that should be jailed for making fraudulent claims. Oh, I expect she's going to try and make me believe that my life was miraculously saved by one of her potions and then I'll change my mind about her being a con merchant?'

Ruth had spent her life being subservient to others, doing as she was told by strong-minded people who forced her do their bidding. But this man before her had just spoken out very unfairly against people she knew were not at all the type he was denouncing them as. They weren't here to defend themselves, but Ruth was.

Taking a deep breath she said, 'No, your life wasn't saved by one of Bertha's potions. It was she who suggested, in fact, that quinine was the only medicine which would help get your fever down. I agreed with her, so regular doses of quinine is what you were given. Only, as a matter of interest, Doctor, isn't quinine obtained from the bark of a tree?

'And I can assure you, Mrs Rider is no charlatan. She is in fact an expert in what she does. For your information, she learned her craft at a very young age from a woman who had learned from her own mother. They both spent their lives studying the medicinal properties of what Mother Nature provides for us, making detailed records of their findings along with beautiful drawings of each individual plant, flower and fungus.' Ruth paused and looked at the doctor meaningfully. 'Is that not how you learned your own profession, Doctor Strathmore, by listening to someone who had spent their own life studying it? But whereas you learned medicine in a recognised educational establishment, Bertha learned her craft in a cottage kitchen.'

She paused slightly to let the doctor digest what she had just said before she continued. 'Bertha too has spent her life refining her remedies and using her expertise to concoct a few new ones. She has great faith in her medicines but would never claim that they will cure every ailment. Should someone approach her for help that she feels she cannot provide, she will tell them that it is a stronger medicine from the doctor that is called for on that occasion.

'I was quite sceptical when I first learned what she did. Couldn't imagine for one minute that the juice from the dandelion weed is actually good for helping anaemia, or that a geranium leaf placed on a cut will stop it bleeding almost immediately. Of course, as with all medicines, whether made from natural ingredients or chemical compounds, they work better on some patients than with others. I have been spending quite a lot of time with Bertha, getting an overview of her work, and it has certainly captured my interest enough for me to want to learn more. May I ask how you came to the conclusion that women who make home remedies are all fraudsters out to cheat people of their money, Doctor Strathmore?'

'I have very good reason, I can assure you, Miss Whelham. As part of my training, I worked as a registrar in a hospital. An hysterical woman came running in with a child in her arms one day. On examination, from the profusion of yellow ulcers in the child's mouth and other symptoms, it was clear that it was at an advanced stage of diphtheria, which the woman had been treating with a bottle of medicine her neighbour had made up for her, charging her a penny and claiming it was a cure-all. The child died the next day. Had the mother not believed this woman's fraudulent claim and taken her offspring to the doctor when it first showed signs of being ill, there's a good chance it would still be alive today. I tested the medicine afterwards and found it to be no more than water with a few drops of laudanum and arrowroot, to thicken it a little and turn it white.'

'A dreadful tale, Doctor Strathmore, but I'm surprised a man of your intelligence has based his opinion entirely on one incident. Maybe if you took the trouble to spend just a little time with Bertha, she would make you see that your decision to brand all home remedy makers as fraudsters was a bit hasty. You might even feel that some of her potions merit being prescribed by yourself, for certain patients.

'And while I have your ear, Doctor, you would not allow Mrs Nelson the courtesy of explaining to you her motives for sending some of your patients her grandmother's way. She saw for herself how over-worked you are, how little time you have for your-self, and it was apparent to her that some patients' ailments could very easily be remedied by one of her grandmother's potions. She also knew those patients didn't, in fact, have the means to settle your account. So, you see, she wasn't stealing patients from you and their fees along with them, but was in fact trying to ease your burden a little. And, yes, the bonus was that a little more money came the family's way, which they make very good use of, I can assure you.'

Ruth rose to her feet. 'There is some soup down-stairs waiting for you. Bertha made it herself, but I promise you all the ingredients came from the green-grocer's apart from the bone for the stock. It's very nourishing and should help to start building your strength up. Do you feel you could manage a little? The sooner you start eating, the quicker you'll be back on your feet.'

He snapped at her, 'I am well aware of that, Miss Whelham. I *am* a doctor.'

Ty was feeling wretched. This time, though, it

wasn't through illness. The ex-nun, in her quiet, calm way, had made him feel totally ashamed of himself. She was right. an intelligent man, he should not have based his opinion of remedy makers on only one fraudster. And he should have allowed Aidy to explain her reasons for why she had acted as she did before he sacked her out of hand. But he had, and now he was the worse for it. She had proved him wrong from the onset, turning out to be an excellent receptionist, and filling her place wasn't going to be easy.

And now he'd listened to Ruth enthusing over the home-made remedies he had proclaimed worthless in the past, he really would have liked the opportunity to have learned more about them. But how could he expect that family to show any forbearance towards him after the shoddy way he had treated them? What was concerning him most, though, was that he suspected from what Ruth had told him that very shortly Aidy herself would be making an appearance to take over his care. Now his eyes had been opened as they had, he couldn't bear the embarrassment of coming face to face with her and having to admit his mistakes. He suddenly realised that he was actually frightened of doing so in case he started to see her again the way he had on Christmas Day . . .

He said to Ruth stiltedly, 'Please tell Mrs Nelson I can manage for myself. I won't need her or you to call on me again. And I shan't be needing the soup so please take it away with you. I am perfectly capable of making food for myself that will build up my strength. Would you pull the door to behind you as you leave, Miss Whelham?'

But as she saw herself out, Ruth was not seeing the rude and arrogant man most people remembered after an encounter with Ty. She was instead seeing someone who was afraid to let people get close to him. That could only mean that he had been so terribly hurt in the past, he couldn't bear to be hurt again. And the only way to avoid being hurt was never to allow yourself to become emotionally attached to other human beings. She suspected that he had based his behaviour on one devastating incident that had cut him deep.

Aidy was very vocal when Ruth told her that the doctor had said in no uncertain terms they were no longer required.

'Bloody ungrateful sod!' she snapped. 'We should have left him at the bottom of those stairs, where we found him. Better still, should never have taken the trouble to go and check if he was all right in the first place. I promised myself after the last time he humiliated me I would never put myself in that position again, and I damned well have!'

They were alone in the kitchen at the time. Ruth placed her hand on Aidy's arm and said very quietly to her, 'Are you angry with the doctor for humiliating you again or angry with yourself, Aidy?'

She looked taken aback. 'Angry with myself? Why would I be angry with myself?'

'For falling in love with a man who is clearly frightened of letting anyone get close to him.'

'What! Oh, don't be ridiculous. I can't stand that . . .' Aidy stopped mid-sentence. She had been about to deny flatly that she could ever fall for a man like the doctor, when she realised it was true, she had.

As she had sat by his bed in the small hours of the night, watching him closely for any signs that his fever was climbing again, or as she was sponging him to get his fever down when it had shot up, she had found herself forgetting the man she knew him to be while at work, and seeing him instead as the man she had met on Christmas Day when he first opened the door to her. The man who had temporarily forgotten to show the austere side of himself he usually displayed to the world. Just a glimpse she had had of that other man, but she had liked what she saw.

She sighed heavily and said, 'Yes, I have fallen for him, Ruth. Not the man he pretends he is to the world, but the man I know he is behind that cold, indifferent mask. It's ironic, really. I fell in love with Arch when he pretended to be one thing, and fell out of love with him when I found out the side of himself he was hiding from me. Something terrible must have happened to Doc to make him like he is. I wonder what it was that was so bad?

'Anyway, I would be a fool to think a man of his standing would ever look in my direction. It's a good job I'm no longer working for him. It would be awful seeing him day after day, knowing my feelings for him were completely wasted.'

CHAPTER TWENTY-THREE

'It's a job, Gran, and that's what matters.'

'Yes, love, it is, and not to be sneezed at. But the hospital laundry! You're worth more that.'

'Gran, the couple of ward orderly jobs had a queue of people going for them. Someone who's been an orderly before will get set on over me. And I can't hang around another week, waiting to hear if I've been successful or not, and then find out I haven't and lose another week's pay. If it hadn't been for Ruth stumping up all her wage packet to help us last week, I dread to think . . .

'Anyway, it doesn't mean to say I can't still be on the look out for something else while I'm working at the laundry, does it? I start tomorrow morning at seven. The pay is ten shillings a week less than what I was getting at the surgery, so things are going to be tighter than usual.'

Aidy was in fact very worried about their future finances. That ten shillings a week less was the difference between having a pint of milk a day or eking it out over two days, making half a bag of coal last a week instead of three bags, turning the gas mantles down to their lowest and, after the kids went to bed, turning them off altogether and using only one candle. Meat in any guise would be a distant memory. Having to beg from the parish for clothes and shoes was a possibility.

Ruth had been sitting very quietly, listening to what was being said. She knew Aidy was worried about her cut in pay and how she was going to make what she did get go around, and Ruth's own recent contribution wasn't being taken into consideration since they thought that at any time she could announce she had found a place of her own and was moving out. Little did Aidy and Bertha know that Ruth herself felt so comfortable being a part of this family, she wasn't even looking for a place, and until it was made clear to her that she had outstayed her welcome, she had no plans to. But she had had an idea for how the family's income could be improved. It had come to her a few days ago and, after thinking about it to make sure it was workable, she was ready to impart it.

'Could I just have a word before you go through to make a start on the dinner, Aidy dear? You see, I might have an idea for how you can improve your finances.' That statement had Aidy sitting back down again, and she and Bertha were both looking at Ruth enquiringly. 'Of course, a shop would be ideal though that is out of the question at the moment for obvious reasons, but we could turn the front room into one . . . I really have no objection to sleeping on the flock in the recess in here for this to go ahead. I've noticed several people around here have turned their parlours into shops. There's a lady in Denton Street who cuts hair in hers. A lady in the street behind sells sweets; another wools and haberdashery. All we would need is some shelves put up, and the dining table could be used as a sort of counter and for displaying the goods on as well.' She eyed them both eagerly. 'So what do you both think of the idea?'

'Sounds a grand idea to me,' Aidy said enthusiastically.

'And me too,' said Bertha.

'Just one question, though,' said Aidy.

'The same one I'm going to ask, I expect,' said Bertha.

'Oh, and what's that?' asked Ruth.

'What are you proposing we sell?' Bertha queried.

Ruth smiled. 'Oh, didn't I make that clear? Your remedies, Bertha dear.'

They both stared at her agog.

'Do I take it you think my idea a good one then?' she asked them.

She did not get an answer. A loud and very urgent

hammering began on the back door and shouts of: 'Aidy! Bertha! Come quick!'

Aidy reached the door first, and yanked it open to be greeted by a frenzied Ava Charman, mother of one of George's friends, who lived in the street behind them.

Before Aidy, Bertha or Ruth could ask what the urgency was, Ava blurted, 'It's the old factory! Apparently a wall's collapsed. One of the boys that was in there got out, and according to the lad, your George and my boy were amongst the kids still inside that ain't come out. I'm on me way now but I didn't know whether you'd heard ...'

Aidy's coat was already off the back of the door and she was pulling it on. Ruth had run off to get her nurse's bag from her makeshift bedroom in the parlour.

Aidy ordered Bertha, 'Gran, you stay here. Marion is next door so she's safe.' Then, with fear in her eyes, she demanded, 'Where did Betty go off to when she went out earlier, do you know?'

Face ashen, Bertha helplessly shrugged. 'Sometimes she goes to a friend's house. Sometimes she plays with other gels, skipping and hopscotch and whatnot, in the jetty. But sometimes ... well, they all play together, girls and boys, so she could ... Oh, Aidy, she could be with George, trapped inside the factory!'

Ruth, her coat on and carrying her bag, had

returned by now. Aidy grabbed her arm and pulled her outside to join Ava Charman. Without a word passed between them they ran off in the direction of the disused factory.

As they rounded a corner and the factory came into sight, they all stopped abruptly to stare at it in shock. The evening was a dark one, the only light coming from two flickering gas lamps to the front of the building and from a three-quarter moon in a cloudless sky. The rest of the dilapidated building was still standing but one of the gabled walls was gone, the bricks now lying in a huge mound on the ground and scattered round about. A section of the roof had come down too, taking part of the second floor with it.

Aidy gasped, horror-stricken. Her brother was possibly under that mound of bricks, her sister too. She just had to hope and pray, with every ounce of her being, that they had been playing on the other side of the factory when the collapse had happened.

She noticed no one was standing beside her and looked down to see that Ava had collapsed in shock in a dead faint. Ruth was kneeling over, administering first aid.

A lone policeman was standing guard in front of the building. Plenty of people seemed to be milling around, talking amongst themselves, but no one seemed to be doing anything by way of searching for survivors. Aidy dashed up to a group of people, demanding, 'Is anyone in the building yet, searching for the kids who might have been playing there when the wall went down? Has anyone fetched the doctor in case ... in case?' She could not bring herself to say in case he was needed to deal with the injured.

She was told, 'Copper said he'd been instructed not to let anyone in the building until the others arrive and decide what's to be done. They shouldn't be long. I thought I saw the doctor arrive a few minutes ago but I can't see him around now ...

'I was the one who first raised the alarm. I was just about to pass by the factory on me way home from work when, without warning, the far wall suddenly came down. Just like someone had stuck a stick of dynamite under it and blown it up. I ain't never seen so much dust. Look at me, I'm covered in it. And then part of the roof and second floor came down almost straight after. Bloody place has been a death trap for years. It should have been bulldozed to the ground long ago. Anyway, it ain't safe in there, that's why no one's gone inside yet until the police set up a search party. Someone else said there could possibly be some kids in there. Well, if they were still able they'd have come out by now, so if there are any in there, it don't look good for 'em, does it?'

Aidy was barely listening. She couldn't stand here, knowing her brother or sister or some other poor children were trapped and frightened and needing help. She rushed back to Ruth, still trying to revive the unconscious Ava, and snatched up her nursing bag.

Ruth caught sight of this out of the corner of her eye and demanded, 'What are you up to with my bag, Aidy?'

'I might need it, Ruth. I can't wait around for the Cavalry to arrive when my brother and sister could be in there needing help. I'm going inside to look for them.'

In the far-off distance the clamour of a police siren could be heard.

Ruth cried, 'No, wait, Aidy! That's the police on their . . .'

Her words fell on deaf ears. Aidy was already running off towards the ruined building, her mind racing as she weighed up the best way to get inside.

She mustn't let the policeman on guard see her or he'd stop her. To make her way inside by clambering over the mound of bricks could prove counter-productive as they were loose and, should anyone be trapped under them, she could cause further hurt. The double door at the front was chained and padlocked shut, so that was out. The glass in the windows at the front was all broken and jagged. She'd cut herself to ribbons getting in that way . . . besides, she couldn't do it without the policeman on guard seeing her. Then she realised that the children had to have been able to get in somehow. Hopefully their access point was through a door or window in the gabled wall still standing and not the one that had collapsed.

Making her way to the left side of the building, when the policeman was looking the other way, Aidy kicked up her heels and darted down the path that ran the length of the building on this side. It was choked with weeds and muddy underfoot. In no time her only pair of shoes was clogged with mud and sharp brambles were ripping her stockings to shreds and scratching her legs, but she didn't care, too set on finding a way inside and safely locating her brother and sister.

Surely the building couldn't extend much further back, she thought. She seemed to have gone miles down this path, but in fact it was a dozen or so yards. The only light she had to guide her was the moon's eerie glow and it was very difficult for her to see anything ahead. Then suddenly she came across it. A door in the wall, hanging open. This must be where the children got in.

Aidy gingerly walked through it. Once inside she stopped to take stock of her surroundings. It was almost pitch black as she had no moonlight in here to help her. Across a wide expanse of floor she could make out the dark sky, some stars twinkling where the wall used to be. All around her objects of different shapes and sizes loomed eerily. If she had been expecting a huge bare room and the children to be sitting safely in the middle, waiting patiently for her to arrive, then she was disappointed.

Where did she begin her search? Then the obvious struck her. Why not call out and see if she got any response? Taking a deep breath, she hollered at the top of her voice: 'George! Betty! Anyone else here?' And she repeated her call again. Then she listened.

Her heart raced. She felt sure she heard a muffled, 'Over here.'

She hollered again, 'Did someone shout out?'

A muffled voice came back. 'Yes. Over here. And hurry!'

The voice seemed to have come from somewhere towards the middle of the room but below her, which didn't make sense to Aidy. She was worried, though, as although the voice had been muffled, she could tell it had belonged to an adult male, not a child.

Outside the sound of a police siren nearing the factory could be heard. Better late than never, she thought.

Tentatively, with eyes now accustomed to the dark, she picked her way around and over objects like old discarded tin drums, work trolleys, beams from the ceiling . . . and what was this? . . . an old rusting mangle minus its rollers. Obviously people had been dumping their rubbish in here. Along with the objects, she began to come across scattered bricks from the fallen wall. She stopped short at the sound of a loud groan and a cracking sound coming from nearby. It was apparent to Aidy that the rest of the building wouldn't be standing for much longer.

A few yards further on she stopped and hollered again, 'Am I near you yet?'

The muffled voice, a bit clearer to her now, called back, 'A bit further in! Be careful to look for a hole in the floor.'

'Are you near the hole in the floor?' she hollered.

'We're down it,' came the answer.

Whoever it was, they were down in the basement of the building!

'Keep calling to me and I'll head towards your voice,' Aidy shouted out.

To the continued call of ... *this way* ... *this way* ... *this way* ... she headed in the direction of the voice, being careful to avoid any obstacles and look out for the hole in the floor.

Then she came upon it. She had expected a perfectly round hole, for some reason, but this had jagged edges and was about the size of the kitchen table. She got on her knees, inched her way gingerly to the side and peered down. She hadn't expected to see anything so was shocked to find a candle lighting the space below, which looked like it had once been a small store room as in the corner were stacked several old tea chests and a couple of discarded office items. Four faces were visible, ghost-like in the flickering candle-light bouncing off them. Two faces in particular caused her a sigh of relief. 'George . . . Betty! You're alive. Oh, thank God.'

George shouted back, 'I told the doctor yer'd come looking for us soon as you heard what's happened, and I was right.'

Doc! Her eyes met those of her previous employer. So that was where the candle had come from. Doctors always carried them in case they needed light in an emergency.

Before she had a chance to ask how come he was in there with the children or why in fact the children had come to be in the basement, Ty shouted up to her in a commanding tone, 'We need to get these children out of here quickly before any more of the building comes down. This is a small room we're in and the door is jammed solid. We can't get out that way. There's no other way out of here except back through the ceiling – the way we fell in.'

The sound of the police siren was much louder. Their arrival could be only moments away.

'I'll go and fetch help,' Aidy told him.

There was a loud groaning noise from above, and nearby a crash resounded. Another part of the roof had come down nearby.

'There's no time for that,' Ty cried back. 'One of the boys has broken his leg and is in danger of going into shock. We need to get him out first. I've given him a dose of laudanum so he can't feel much at the moment and he's pretty dopey.'

That was when Aidy fully took in the scene below, or as much as the flickering candlelight would allow. She could make out that George, a gash on his cheek caked in drying blood, was sitting on the floor with Ava's son Brian's head in his lap. A battered-looking Betty crouched to one side, holding the boy's hand. The boy himself was limp and still, his eyes shut. Ty had fashioned a very crude splint on his right leg from two bits of discarded wood and a bandage from his black bag, which lay open to one side of him. Blood was seeping through the bandage.

While she had been taking in the scene, Ty had already dragged three of the empty chests from the corner of the room and put them under the hole, two side by side and the other on top. While she watched, he clambered up on the top box and tested it for strength. Seeming satisfied it would hold his weight, he jumped down to gather the half-comatose child in his arms, then lifted him high enough to gently place him on the top tea chest.

Aidy knew what Ty was expecting her to do. Dropping the nurse's bag she was holding to one side of the hole, she lay down then swung her top half so that it projected over the void beneath. She just hoped the edge didn't give way under her.

Meanwhile Ty had clambered back up on the tea chest, balanced himself on it, bent down and tentatively lifted the boy up in his arms. The action caused the tea chest to wobble and she could hear the wood crack.

Aidy gasped, fearing the chest, or one of the two below it, was about to give way under the weight it was supporting. It seemed to be holding. Taking a deep breath, Ty heaved the limp child up in his arms as far as he could above his head, crying to Aidy, 'Grab him, quickly. I can't hold him up for long . . .'

Aidy reached down as far as she could, her aim being to grab hold of the waistband of the boy's trousers and haul him up. But it was just out of her grasp. Hurriedly she inched her way a little further over the hole, mindful that if she wasn't careful she could topple over into it, and mindful too that Ty's strength must be giving out. She reached down again. This time she did manage to grab hold of the boy's waistband, and with a strength she didn't realise she had, heaved him up with all her might.

As she pulled him through the hole, a jagged piece of wood pierced the boy's thigh and broke off as she pulled him clear, to virtually throw him down on the solid floor beside her, leaving a piece at least two inches long protruding from his leg. Thankfully the dose of laudanum the doctor had given him had rendered him unable to feel the pain of his new injury or from his broken leg.

Aidy looked back down the hole to see that Ty now had Betty in his arms. Once he saw she was ready to receive another child, he heaved her up to stand on his shoulders. With Ty's arms clamped around her legs, Betty stretched up her arms to her sister. Reaching down, Aidy grabbed hold of her hands and heaved her up so the child could grab her shoulders then pull herself up from there.

Next came George. With him being the heaviest of the three, it took her every ounce of her strength to heave him up through the hole. Aidy pretended not to notice as he was coming through that the edge of the floor she was lying on was moving beneath her and she heard the sound of breaking wood.

As George cleared the hole enough to scramble the rest of the way out himself, she ordered him and Betty to drag Brian further away from the hole.

Then, coming from across the other side of the building where she had come in, she heard a shout. 'Anyone there?'

'Over here!' she hollered.

As they were dragging Brian away from the hole, George and Betty both bellowed over to the rescue party in unison, 'Over here!'

A loud rumbling sound came from above. Aidy's

heart was hammering. The whole building was going to come down any minute . . . She looked back down into the hole and cried urgently to Ty, who had now clambered off the chests and back on to firm ground: 'You next, Doc, come on.' To stress her point, she reached down her arms to him.

He called back up, 'I'm too much for you to lift. You'll never manage. I'll have to wait for the men to arrive and pull me out.'

The rumbling from above resounded again.

Aidy flashed a look to where the children were and, to her relief, saw that three policemen had reached them. Each had one of the children in his arms and was hurrying off.

There was a rending sound above her.

She looked back down the hole and cried, 'There's no time to wait, Doc. I'm sure the main roof is about to come down. Come on, we've got to give it a . . .'

Her voice trailed off as, with a shriek of timber, a roof beam fell in. At the same time, the weakened floor beneath her gave way and Aidy felt herself falling, letting out a scream of shock as she plummeted down the hole.

CHAPTER TWENTY-FOUR

Aidy was lying on something soft. The air was thick with dust and she was coughing and spluttering. She tried to open her eyes so she could see something then realised they were open, it was just that it was pitch black. She heard a soft groan and felt movement beneath her, realising with horror the something soft she was lying on, that had in fact broken her fall, was the body of Doc.

Her immediate thought was, Of all the people to be trapped in a room with, it had to be him! But she had worse things than her unreciprocated feelings to worry about at the moment.

Easing herself off him, Aidy cried urgently: 'Doc . . . Doc, are you all right? Answer me!'

Finally he groaned and told her haltingly: 'I . . . think . . . my shoulder . . . is either . . . dislocated or broken. And I can't . . . move my right leg.' He seemed to lapse into silence then and she feared he had passed out.

At least they were both alive, she thought. Her mind was racing. She needed to get some light in here so she could assess the situation. There had been a candle ... Oh, it could be anywhere now. Did the doctor carry only one candle with him or more? If she could find his bag, she could check.

On her knees, hands outstretched, she began tentatively feeling around her. She remembered she hadn't seen much in the room when she had looked down into it from above, except for the tea chests, several old chairs and a few other long-discarded items stacked against the far wall. Now the floor was littered with chunks of plaster and wood from the part of the ceiling that had broken off beneath her. Inch by inch, shuffling forward on her knees as she did so, the sharp debris on the floor stabbing painfully at her, she felt her way around, but the doctor's bag seemed to be eluding her. Then, finally, her fingertips hit something made of leather.

She let out a small cry of triumph. It was the doctor's bag! It was covered in rubble and Aidy swiped her hands over it to clear off as much as she could. Oh, but wait a minute, it couldn't be the doctor's bag as she remembered seeing that was open while looking down on it from above. This one was shut ... it was Ruth's nurse's bag. Aidy's heart dropped. Would a nurse carry candles? She could only hope.

Opening the bag, she plunged in her hand and carefully felt around. Right at the bottom, underneath several bandages and other things wrapped in waxy paper, her hand clasped around two long cylinders. Candles! She pulled them out, then realised they'd be no good without matches. But if Ruth carried candles, she must carry matches to light them with. Aidy put her hand back in the bag and found the box near where the candles had been stored.

Once the candles were lit, holding them in her hands, she took a good look around her. The room they were in was about twelve foot by twelve. There was a door to her right that Doc had told her was jammed shut. Apart from the discarded packing cases and several office items, the space was empty. The doctor's body was lying a few feet away. He was groaning softly in agony. Pinning down his right leg was part of a thick beam that must have broken off when the floor above fell in. There was a dark stain on his trouser leg which was obviously blood. It was all right, though, because the police would be appearing at any minute to rescue them. Automatically Aidy looked up towards the hole she had fallen through, hoping to see faces peering back at her. She gawped in horror. The hole was there no longer! Something was completely blocking it. The rest of the building could now be piled on top of them, for all she knew.

Ty gave a loud, pitiful groan and she lowered her gaze to look him over. Sadie Billson had instilled in her that a nurse should be calm and clear minded at all times, concentrating only on her patient. That advice came in useful now. Putting all thoughts of their dire situation to the back of her mind, Aidy concentrated on the doctor and seeing what she could do for him until hopefully help eventually reached them. It was extremely cold down here. Before she did anything else, she took off her coat and put it over Ty so he didn't go into shock from the cold.

Shivering herself now, she cleared a space on the floor beside her, then tipped one of the candles up so that melted wax trickled on to the ground. She quickly secured the candle upon it. Then she stood up and stepped over the rubble to the other side of the doctor and did the same with the other candle. Now an area around them was illuminated well enough for her to see reasonably well. Quickly glancing him over, Aidy felt the first thing she should do was remove the heavy length of beam from his leg. If she had just heaved three children through a hole, this beam would be like a matchstick in comparison. Stooping by his feet, she clasped both her hands around the beam and, taking a huge breath, heaved at it with all her might. It was heavier than she'd thought but slowly it hovered an inch or so above his leg. Then, grunting and groaning, she heaved it sideways until Ty was free.

She let go of it and it fell to the floor with a dull thud, scattering some of the chunks of debris beneath. One piece caught her cheek and she felt the trickle of blood which she hurriedly wiped away.

Aidy then set about ripping open Ty's trouser leg and examining the wound the beam had made. It wasn't deep, thankfully. From Ruth's bag she took out antiseptic and cloths for cleaning and dressing. Five minutes later she surveyed her own handiwork. Not bad if she said so herself. It would pass Matron's inspection.

Ty seemed to be waking up. He was groaning softly, clutching his shoulder, then he tried to move and as he did so let out a painful cry. 'Anthea ... get ... the ... laudanum ... from my bag. Anthea, darling ... please.'

Who was Anthea? There wasn't time for Aidy to wonder, though. She scrambled over to where she could see his open bag, now part filled with rubble. She scrabbled enough out to unearth a clear, cork-topped bottle with a label on it reading *Laudanum*. But to her dismay it was broken, all the precious liquid that had been inside drained away.

'Anthea, darling, did ... you ... find the laudanum?'

Like any woman who harboured unreciprocated feelings for a man, even though she was trying hard to quash those feelings, Aidy was annoyed to hear him calling her by another woman's name.

'I'm just looking for it,' she snapped back.

Her abrupt response seemed to snap him out of his pain-fuddled state. 'Mrs Nelson, is that you?'

Aidy was too busy looking through his bag for other means of pain relief to answer him. She unearthed a small pill box and pulled it out to inspect it. The label on it spelled out *Morphine*. Well, *this* should be strong enough to take away his pain. She eased off the lid, finding a white grainy substance inside. She wasn't sure how much to give him. She supposed she ought to try one grain first to see how well that worked, but he did look to be in so much pain . . . Oh, what the hell? She'd give him two.

Ten minutes later Ty was feeling very light headed and mellowing more by the second. The pain in his shoulder had eased sufficiently for him actually to sit up and support his back against a wall. Aidy had tucked her coat around him. He couldn't remember how he'd come to damage his shoulder. Something heavy falling on it when the ceiling came down, he presumed. He noticed the dressing on his leg. He couldn't remember tending to himself and applying that, but it looked to be professionally done.

Aidy was watching him and knew what he was thinking. 'Yes, I did it,' she told him. 'I've been learning basic nursing from an old wartime nurse in my spare time. I'm not bad, if I say so myself.'

His eyes drifted lazily across to look at her, now

perched on top of one of the tea chests. His speech was very sluggish, almost drunkenly slurred, when he said, 'Not bad at all, Mrs Nelson. Not bad at all. Pity you no longer work for me or I could have sent you out sometimes on nursing duties.'

She looked terribly cold to him. In fact, she was shivering. 'Haven't you a coat? You really ought to put it on, you're shivering.'

'I'm fine,' she said. 'How's your shoulder now?'

'Bearable, thank you. But you really are shivering.' He suddenly found he had a great need to protect this woman from the cold. It was overwhelming, in fact. With his good arm, almost in slow motion, he lifted Aidy's coat from around him and held it out to her. 'Please borrow my coat. I'd really hate you to catch a chill.'

It was he who was most at risk from the cold, since he was badly injured. 'I'm fine, honest. Please put it back over you. You really do need to keep warm. Please, Doc,' she urged him.

He gave a laugh, a silly sort of chuckle, as he laid the coat back across himself.

'What's so funny?' she snapped at him, considering their situation was anything but.

'You addressing me as Doc. It's funny because you know it infuriates me, you addressing me disrespect-fully.' He chuckled again and flashed her a boyish grin. 'To be honest, though, at the moment I really don't care what you call me.' Then, like a naughty schoolboy, he said in a sing-song voice, 'You tell me your name and I'll tell you mine ... I mean, Aidy isn't your real name, is it? You told me that at your interview. Well, Ty isn't my full name, just the name I call myself. So we do seem to have at least something in common, Mrs Nelson.'

She said tartly, 'I had no idea what your Christian name was because you didn't think me good enough to call you by it.'

He said aghast, 'Oh, no, it wasn't because I didn't think you good enough to be on first-name terms with me. No, that's not it at all. I do have a good reason for being so standoffish with you. It's the way it's had to be.' He then chuckled again and said in a boyish manner, 'So what is your name then? Come on, out with it?'

Aidy sighed. She never divulged it to anyone unless she was absolutely forced to, she hated it so much. But she supposed it wouldn't hurt her to humour Ty, considering the way he was acting. It was apparent to her by now that she had given him far more morphine than she had needed to; it was making him act as if he'd consumed a good quantity of alcohol. It was doubtful he'd remember any of this once the effects wore off so her secret was safe. She took a breath and said: 'Adafonsia.'

She could see he was doing his best not to laugh

out loud. 'Well, yes, that is ... er ... But I have an even worse name.'

'That's not possible,' she said.

'Oh, it is.'

'Well, go on then. If you don't tell me, I can't judge.'

He announced it as if he was divulging a state secret. 'Titus.'

She gawped first then started to giggle. 'Oh, yes, that *is* awful, but still not as bad as mine.'

He started to chuckle then. 'Oh, it is.'

They both laughed together.

'Both our fathers have a lot to answer for,' said Aidy.

The laughter suddenly died on Ty's face and he uttered, 'Oh, mine certainly has. Much more than giving me an awful name to put up with. You see, he killed my wife and baby.'

Aidy stared at him in utter shock. 'What!'

Unable to stop himself due to the tongue-loosening effect the morphine was having on him, he poured out his sorry tale. His words came out soft and slurred.

'My father did not set out to murder my wife and child, but when it came down to it, that is what he did because he knew what he was doing. He was an eminent physician. Had a thriving practice where only the very wealthy could afford his fees. He was a well-respected man in his field. I admired him, loved him, all I wanted to do was emulate him.'

He paused for a moment, seeming to drift off into his own little world, then suddenly returned from wherever he had been in his mind and continued where he'd left off. 'As soon as I qualified, I joined him in his practice and he made me joint partner. It was with great shock and sadness that at the age of fifty-five it was discovered my father was suffering from Parkinson's Disease. Of course, it was the end of his career. He took it very hard.

'I had met and married my wife Anthea by this time. She was beautiful and sweet, the love of my life. She was expecting our first baby.'

Ty paused and drifted off again for a moment before saying, 'My mother had died ten years previously, so at Anthea's insistence we moved out of our own home and into my father's house, to help care for him. Anthea was getting near her time and we were very excited about the imminent birth. She had three weeks to go and it was about twelve o'clock one morning when a telephone call was put through to me. It was my father's housekeeper. She was frantic. She'd been out to do the shopping and came home to find a terrible thing had happened. Would I please come back straight away? She put the telephone down abruptly. I thought something dreadful had happened to my father. He'd had one of his bouts and fallen over and hurt himself badly . . . something like that. I wasn't at all prepared for what I was to find.

'Anthea was dead and so was our baby. She was lying on our bed with her stomach cut open, her womb exposed and that half cut open too. I could see part of the baby inside. There was blood everywhere. My father was sitting in the chair by our bed with his head in his hands. I was frozen, paralysed by shock, and at first hardly taking in what my father was telling me, begging me to forgive him.

'The housekeeper had not long gone out when Anthea suddenly began to suffer from horrendous pains in her stomach. She was screaming out in agony. It was apparent to my father that something was dreadfully wrong and the baby needed delivering as soon as possible. The surgery was only a short drive away. I'd have been there in a matter of minutes. He knew he should have gone straight to telephone me to come home. He didn't, though, because he said he'd felt fine, no sign of the shakes at all. And he was being given a chance, he said, for one last time to experience surgery again. Actually given the opportunity of delivering his own grandchild by Caesarian section. He couldn't let that opportunity go. It was a simple procedure for him. He had performed it many times before. He helped Anthea on to our bed and fetched his bag.

'I can only assume that my wife was in such pain

and so frightened of what was happening to her, she wasn't really aware of what my father's intentions were. I know she would not willingly have allowed him to operate on her. He gave her a whiff of chloroform to send her to sleep and immediately set about cutting her open to take out the baby. He got as far as he did when the spasms started. By the time the spasm stopped he was powerless to stop Anthea from bleeding to death or save the baby. He knew he was wrong to attempt what he did. Was well aware how suddenly an episode could take him. He had selfishly seized his last chance to practise his skills, and this was the result. He begged my forgiveness, hoped that as a physician like himself I would understand why he'd done what he had. Then he went into his room, got his duck gun out of its case, put the barrel in his mouth and pulled the trigger.

'I have never felt pain like it. I almost went out of my mind. I was mad with grief. I thought I'd never come to terms with it. Eventually you do, though. The pain never goes but you learn to live with it. I am so frightened of going through anything like that again, I avoid the risk altogether. It's a very lonely life. If I could only be sure that I could trust someone enough to open my heart to them ... but I'm too afraid to take the chance.'

He paused and went silent for a moment before picking up, 'I wouldn't go to my own father's funeral.

It would have been hypocritical of me, pretending I was sorry for his death when I wasn't. As soon as Anthea and our baby's funeral was over, I took off. I left everything behind, just abandoned it and lived for two years on what I had in my bank account. When that ran out I had to get a job. I didn't want to work in the medical profession again, couldn't bear people whispering behind my back when they discovered who I was because it was front-page news at the time, but doctoring is the only thing I know I'm good at. So I landed up here.' He heaved a sigh. 'The ironic thing is that my wife loved life and lost hers through no fault of her own. Now here I am, working all hours, killing myself really, trying to keep people alive who don't take the most elementary care of themselves. Their ignorance is their own undoing.'

His sad tale had touched Aidy deeply. She now understood completely why he acted as he did, pushing people away, being rude to them so they wouldn't want to get close to him, but she wasn't going to put up with his last statement, whether it had been voiced through a loose tongue from morphine or not. Hands on her hips she blurted out, 'Well, have you ever thought that instead of looking down on those so-called ignorant people, if you took the time and trouble to teach them better, you wouldn't be flogging your guts out, having to treat the diseases they wouldn't then be catching, would you? People can't put into practice what they don't know, can they? For instance, there's a couple of women in our street who wouldn't think to wash a baby's teat after it accidentally fell in a full potty 'cos their mothers knew no better and so neither do they. They wouldn't take kindly to the likes of me telling them they're risking their babies' lives with their dirty habits, but they would listen to the likes of you putting them right.'

She took a deep breath and said, 'And think about this, Doc. You're never going to know if you've met someone you can trust if you don't at least give them the opportunity to prove it to you. And you won't do that if you don't allow them even to get close to you a little or take the trouble to get to know them.'

She realised Ty wasn't listening to her as his eyes were closed and his head had slumped to one side. He was asleep. Aidy slipped off the tea chest and went over to him, kneeled down and pulled her coat further around him for warmth. She then gently ran her hand over his forehead and said softly, 'I wish you'd take a chance on me, to see if we could be happy together. I could be happy with you, I know I could. Not the man I saw at work, though, he's not a nice man at all, but the man I saw on Christmas Day who had forgotten to put a front on. And the man I've seen just now, laughing. I like that man, he's just my type.' She heaved a sad sigh. 'Oh, but

I wouldn't presume a man like you would ever look twice at a woman who comes from these parts.'

She caught sight of the candle to one side of him. It was rapidly diminishing. So was the other one. If rescue didn't arrive soon, they'd be plunged into pitch darkness. And it was so very cold down here.

Suddenly she thought she heard a scraping noise from above. Her eyes darted upwards. The noise was getting louder. She heard a faint cry: 'You all right down there? You both all right?'

'Yes,' she screamed back. 'Doc's badly injured, though, and needs urgent attention . . .'

'Hold tight. We've a bit more rubble to clear away then we'll be with you.'

CHAPTER TWENTY-FIVE

'So here lieth the local hero. Well, national really. Your heroics made front-page news, dear boy.'

Inwardly groaning, Ty opened his eyes to settle them on the well-made man in his early thirties who was unbuttoning a mohair top coat and making himself comfortable in the chair by the bed. He was expensively dressed in hand-tailored clothes, hand-made leather shoes on his feet, and his girth portrayed the fact that he liked his food: the sort cooked by top chefs in classy restaurants, or by his own cook in a lavish home that he drove to and from in a Rolls-Royce.

'I was hardly the hero,' growled Ty. 'I read the reports too and they missed out the real heroine. She hardly got a mention.'

'Well, dear boy, stands to reason. A working woman, people don't care a fig about. But a prominent doctor who's had a great tragedy in his past ... Riveting reading.'

Ty groaned again. 'They had no right to drag all that up. Damned reporters are just out for a good story, don't care at all who they could be hurting in the process. Anyway, Cuthbert, what brings you to these lowly parts?'

Dr Cuthbert Gosforth looked shocked that Ty would even be asking. 'Why you, dear boy. You went off without a word and we've all been very worried about you. When you first went off, we all thought you just wanted some time on your own, which was very understandable. It's not every day one's own father kills one's wife and child and then himself, is it? But as time passed, we didn't know whether you were alive or dead.

'Mind you, having seen for myself where you have been burying yourself, you could hardly class *that* as living! God, what a hell-hole. Couldn't understand a word the creatures were saying when I was making enquiries about your whereabouts. I of course made other enquiries before I set out and was told you were no longer a patient here so I assumed you'd discharged yourself home . . . only to find you were in fact still here, having told the staff not to reveal you were in residence because you were so fed up with the local dignitaries dropping in to pay homage.

'I can't imagine what state of mind you've been in, dear boy, to have taken on a practice where you